MW01125459

THE LOST MASTERPIECE

ALSO BY THE AUTHOR

Metropolis

The Collector's Apprentice

The Muralist

The Art Forger

The Safe Room

Blind Spot

See No Evil

Blameless

Shattered Echoes

The Big Squeeze

THE LOST MASTERPIECE

A NOVEL BY

B. A. SHAPIRO

ALGONQUIN BOOKS OF CHAPEL HILL
LITTLE, BROWN AND COMPANY

Algonquin Books of Chapel Hill / Little, Brown and Company
Hachette Book Group
1290 Avenue of the Americas, New York, NY 10104
algonquinbooks.com

First Edition: June 2025

Algonquin Books of Chapel Hill is an imprint of Little, Brown and Company, a division of Hachette Book Group, Inc. The Algonquin Books name and logo are trademarks of Hachette Book Group, Inc.

Design by Steve Godwin

ISBN 978-1-64375-637-0 (hardcover) / 978-1-64375-637-0-639-4 (ebook)
LCCN 2025933703

Printing 1, 2025
LSC-C
Printed in the United States of America

To Snuggle Candy,
the ones I love best

Here are six lunatics, one of which is a woman, a group of unfortunates deranged by ambition. These Impressionists take some canvas, paint and brushes, throw a few colors at random, and then sign the lot. Like inmates of a madhouse who pluck up stones in the road and believe they have found diamonds.

—Albert Wolff, *Le Figaro*, in reference to the second Impressionist show in Paris, 1876

PART ONE

Tamara, the present

ONE

I hate spam. Well, obviously everyone hates spam, but I hate it with an admittedly unwarranted ferocity. When I see it, my blood pressure rises, my fingers curl inward, and my jaw throbs. A bit excessive, I know. But this response is mild compared to my reaction when spam is audible. Unwanted emails and phishing texts are bad enough, but when spam hits my voicemail, my nerves migrate to the outside of my skin and I'm ready to scream.

I block and I block and I block. I report and report and report. I unsubscribe and unsubscribe and unsubscribe. I get free trials to Clean Spam, Robokiller, and Barracuda. I register my number with the National Do Not Call database. And still the spam arrives. My head and my chest verge on explosion. Hello, heart attack.

And now there's a superspammer who just won't quit. He's purportedly from something called the Boston office of the Conference on Jewish Material Claims Against Germany. Really? Granted, I'm Jewish, although not in any religious way, but both sides of my family have been in the United States since well before World War II. My father's at the turn of the twentieth century, and my mother's in the 1930s, I think.

"Jonathan Stein" says he's a lawyer representing this so-called Claims Conference—why does a conference need a lawyer?—and has something very important to discuss with me. Which we can only do in person. Right, like I'm an idiot who's going to run off to meet some fake guy because he says it's "very important." I wonder how many people he has to contact before he gets a hit. Got to be thousands. What a way to make a living.

A tiny part of me wants to hear what he has to say, but most of me wants to wrap my hands around his neck and squeeze. It's important to note that I'm no killer—I have friends who claim to love me and have stuck around for decades—I'm just suffering from millennial outrage, trying to weather the stormy twenty-first century. And after a harried day at work, this outraged millennial loses it. In a way I don't think I have ever before. When

Stein leaves another voicemail as I'm walking home, I hit return call and start in on him as soon as he answers.

"What exactly is it you want?" I demand loud enough that a few people on the sidewalk turn to look at me.

"You're Tamara Rubin, I take it," Jonathan Stein says with what sounds like a smile in his voice.

This is even more infuriating. "If you contact me one more time, I'm taking out a restraining order against you and your so-called conference." I have no idea if I can do this, but it sounds good.

"Okay, I get it. Feeling like you're being harassed is—"

"I don't *feel* like I'm being harassed. I am being harassed."

"Please just check me out, check us out. We're legit. What I need to tell you is legit—and it could be a life changer."

I bark a laugh. "That's what all you scammers say." I end the call with a punch of my thumb, ridiculously pleased with myself. But by the time I arrive home, I'm not so pleased. Rudeness isn't my thing. Or it wasn't my thing. Deep breaths.

Curiosity wins over my natural cynicism, and I plop down in front of my computer, put on my glasses, then hesitate. Could searching his name be part of the plan? A way to steal my identity or whatever else these scammers do? But, lo and behold, Jonathan Stein is an attorney at the Boston office of the Claims Conference, a nonprofit that, as stated on its website, "secures material compensation for Holocaust survivors." Since no one in my family is a Holocaust survivor, I'm still not buying it. Whoever called me could easily have found this website, and using an actual lawyer's identity, contacted me because my last name sounds Jewish.

I close the site and pull up the incomplete regulatory dossier I have to submit to the FDA tomorrow. In my previous job as senior VP of regulatory affairs at EVTX, a multinational biotech firm, I had an operations team of five to do this kind of thing—as well as support from regulatory affairs specialists and groups dedicated to pharmacovigilance, compliance, and intelligence.

But as senior VP of regulatory affairs at Calliope, a biotech start-up with about fifty employees, I have a dedicated staff of two, along with an assistant I share with the senior VP of quality assurance. So in conjunction with my management responsibilities, I'm also personally responsible for tasks I used to happily delegate. This is both incredibly frustrating—particularly because it reminds me of the misogyny that necessitated my job change in the first place—and leads to sixty-hour work weeks. Which could be why I lost it with Jonathan Stein.

I'M UP UNTIL two finishing the damn dossier, and getting out of bed at six isn't easy. I make a double-strength cup of coffee and stare out my window overlooking Tremont Street, barely able to focus through my exhaustion, ruminating on the unfairness of my lot. I know, I know—this is despicable, given my privilege and all the horror and heartbreak in the world. But in addition to being outraged, I'm also still resentful because of the EVTX hoodwink. Or am I outraged because I'm resentful? Hard to figure.

It's just that Nick Winspear turned out to be a bad bet—following my bad bet on Simon, my ex-husband. You know how it is at the beginning of a relationship. You're not at your most discriminating, dismissing the red flags as unimportant, biking without a helmet for the pure exhilaration of the ride. Wind in your hair and all that crap. And then you smash right into a tree.

It's Nick's fault I'm currently underemployed, overworked, and taking home tens of thousands of dollars less than I was previously paid. Well, to be perfectly fair, the blame also rests with the inbred men on the EVTX board. It was ostensibly my choice to leave, but it wasn't a choice at all. One positive is that Calliope is much closer to where I live than EVTX was, walking distance instead of a maddening commute. So there's that.

Despite my orneriness, when I get outside, I've got to acknowledge it's a beautiful October morning, although all the tourists who are currently swarming the city in search of fall foliage are going to be disappointed. The leaves don't change until November in Boston, no matter what the brochures tell you. Which is fine with me. The longer the green lasts, the better. I'm less than a mile from the office, and I always walk unless it's storming or freezing. One of the many pleasures of my small big city. Or big small city.

As usual, the excursion cheers me. From the bustle of Tremont to the brick sidewalks and fine nineteenth-century town houses of West Canton Street to the Southwest Corridor Park, blooming with so many flowers you'd think it was June, not October. Puffy pink-and-white sedum, purple

Jim Crocketts, tons of bright chrysanthemums, and all those colorful tiny pansy faces that remind me of Sagan, the beloved dog I lost a year ago.

And then there's the wildlife. Parents with strollers, kids on scooters, squirrels scrambling up trees, dogs of every type and size walked by owners of every type and size. Men and women carrying backpacks and briefcases, some dressed for success, others who look as if they're still in their pajamas. Runners. Walkers. Sitters. Teenagers smoking pot, adults doing the same. There are also the homeless people, usually two or three talking quietly—or not so quietly—sometimes sleeping alone on a bench, wrapped in a blanket. My sadly and gloriously diversified city. Black, white, brown, Asian, combos of all the above. Old, young, in the middle. Rich, poor, in the middle. Some folks are exhilarated by nature, the quiet and serenity of mountains and fields. For me, it's the bustle, the hustle.

WHEN MY HALF ASSISTANT sticks his head in the door, it's already getting dark. This is how you know it's October, not June, as it's not yet five o'clock. "There's a Jonathan Stein downstairs, who says he needs to see you," Alexander informs me. "Wouldn't tell me what he wanted, but figured I'd check with you before I told him to take a hike."

This is exactly what I'd like Jonathan Stein to do, but I decide to check the guy out, maybe even to hear his pitch, so I say, "Buzz him in, please."

I don't know what I was expecting, but Jonathan Stein isn't it. Would it be awful stereotyping to admit I was imagining him as some nebbishy short guy with glasses? Instead, he's close to six feet, no glasses, wearing nice jeans, a collared shirt, and white Hoka running shoes. His skin is golden, his eyes dark brown. Quite handsome, actually. He looks me directly in the eye and smiles with no unease or shiftiness. "Had to give it one more try," he says.

But just because he doesn't look like I thought he would on the outside, that doesn't mean he isn't who I thought he was on the inside. I don't invite him to sit. I let him stand there. "Why don't you tell me what it is you want, Mr. Stein."

He glances at the open door, at Alexander watching us from his desk, then back at me.

I push my glasses up on my nose and say nothing.

He takes a couple of steps closer. "Are you aware you have relatives whose property was stolen by the Nazis?"

"All of my family was here before the war, so that isn't possible."

"I see." He takes a seat in the chair in front of me. "Do the names Colette and Samuel Bernheim mean anything to you?" he asks. "They lived in Paris, and after the Germans occupied France, they escaped and immigrated here."

I tell him I've never heard of either of them.

"This isn't the way we usually work—most of the time it's the family who contacts us to investigate their lost art, not the other way around. But in this case, the Conference on Jewish Material Claims Against Germany started with the painting."

"And this has to do with me because . . . ?"

"The Conference has established that the Bernheims were your great-great-grandparents," he explains. "That you're their only living heir, and as such, you're now the owner of what appears to be a masterwork by Édouard Manet, *Party on the Seine*, which was part of their confiscated art collection."

I'm not an art connoisseur by any stretch, but I'm knowledgeable enough to know that Édouard Manet is one of the most famous French Impressionists—and that his work has to sell for six or seven, if not eight, figures. Stein seems sure of himself and his information, and even to my overly skeptical mind, he appears pretty straightforward. Trustworthy, even.

"We don't want anything from you." He stands and places his card on my desk. "Our job is to return stolen goods to their rightful owners. And in this case, we believe the rightful owner is you. Please do your due diligence and contact me so we can get this moving."

I SEARCH ONLINE for "Édouard Manet, *Party on the Seine*," and then to do a deeper dive into the Claims Conference and Jonathan Stein. I find a photo confirming that the man who came to my office is actually Stein, and discover the Claims Conference has been in operation since 1951, doing what he said they do: disbursing many millions of dollars of the German government's money to Holocaust survivors and their families, along with returning—or providing reparations for—Jewish property stolen before and during the war.

Édouard Manet is even more of a superstar than I thought, but I was right about the value of his work. *Party on the Seine* is apparently both large and critically acclaimed—and likely worth a lot. Especially because it was—I guess up until now—mourned as a lost masterpiece, either destroyed or hanging in the home of some SS officer's descendant. I can't imagine a scenario in which it might belong to me.

There's nothing online about Colette or Samuel Bernheim. My dad died when I was ten, and my mom's dementia took her down four years ago, so I can't ask them. They were both only children, and I have no siblings either, which means I'm shit out of luck on family confirmation either way.

Although I must admit that my lack of relatives does lend an odd credence to the whole only-heir business. As does the fact that *Party on the Seine* disappeared sometime in the late 1930s. There's no mention anywhere about its rediscovery, which could be because Jonathan Stein is making it all up—an option that's looking more and more unlikely—or because he's telling the truth, and it's such a new discovery that almost no one is aware of it yet.

TWO

Jonathan Stein sent an email late last night with a short history of the life of *Party on the Seine* between the Nazi era and now, along with an attachment that contains information about my lineage, which I didn't get a chance to look at because of an early-morning meeting. Now, back in my office, I pause before opening it, left hand hovering over the touchpad. Even I have to acknowledge that it would be an excessively elaborate hoax for him to hide some kind of software bomb inside the attachment. It's not like I'm famous or rich or have anything to hide. And if he wanted to steal my identity, there have to be easier ways.

I double-click. Bingo. A family tree with Tamara Rubin as the lone name on the lowest level. No multiplying boxes above me. I sit back in my chair. The genealogical chart I dangle from drops straight down like the tail of a kite. A direct and narrow dive. Six singleton daughters of six singleton daughters. For over 150 years. Other branches did sprout, but they apparently all failed to thrive. Dead young or childless. Who knew? I certainly didn't. I never had any extended family, and suddenly here they are, even if they're a trunk with no leaves.

Without reading further, I get up and close my office door, lean against it for a moment, and stare out at the Charles River—or the sliver of it that I can see between the obstructing buildings. A few bobbing white sailboats scurry across. This view, narrow as it is, usually calms me, but not today. My stomach is jumpy, and someone-walking-over-your-grave goose bumps ripple up my arms.

All my meetings go on too long, and as always, I'm cramped for time. I need to review the revised marketing plan for our latest drug, Zymidline, but instead I pull up Jonathan's attachment and scrutinize the diagram. Working upward, there's me, then my mother, my grandmother Josephine, my great-grandmother Genevieve, my great-great-grandmother Colette, and my great-great-great-grandmother Aimée, with my great-great-great-great-grandmother Berthe at the top.

I have a vivid memory of the first time I realized all the other kids had grandparents and aunts and uncles and cousins, family dinners and vacations and big holiday celebrations. I was standing on the playground in second grade, waiting for my ups in kickball, and all around me everyone was jabbering about what they'd done over Christmas break. With their grandparents and aunts and uncles and cousins. So much fun. So much excitement. Parties, tons of presents, skiing, beaches, a cruise through the Panama Canal. While I, with the exception of a couple of movies and a smattering of random Hanukkah gifts, had done a whole bunch of nothing.

I was as disconsolate as a seven-year-old faced with serious FOMO can be. Heartbroken and oh so alone, I'd struggled to keep myself from bursting into tears. How could my parents have done this to me? Not even a sibling? And then, in a future that wasn't all that distant, they went off and died young to boot. Even then, I knew it wasn't their fault, but I was lonely for kin, and I suppose I still am. But now, wonder of wonders, right in front me on the screen are relatives. As I said, not that many, and all of them, obviously, dead. Yet none of this matters, because they're mine.

IT'S DAYS BEFORE I can get back to my family tree. First, there was a trip to Washington, DC, to meet with regulators who wanted clarity on our request for an orphan-disease designation for clostridial myonecrosis. Calliope specializes in drugs that treat rare diseases that affect only a small number of people, which clostridial myonecrosis, a life-threatening bacterial infection, is. The first step in this process is for the Food and Drug Administration to add clostridial myonecrosis to its orphan list. After that's done, we can request government assistance to finance the research and development of a drug to cure or treat it, a so-called orphan drug.

As much as I miss the money and staff at my previous job, I do appreciate that what I'm doing at Calliope helps people, which wasn't the case at EVTX, a company mostly dedicated to corporate greed. As I was quite convincing in Washington—if I do say so myself—I think the official okay will be coming down soon, and then we can jump on the challenging work of figuring out how to alleviate a devastating disease. See, I'm not always cranky and cynical.

Then there was a leak in my kitchen ceiling, because the lamebrain above me didn't turn off his faucet, and my friend Holly's knee surgery, which necessitated a number of trips to and from the hospital and baking two batches of lasagna. What single buddies do for each other.

Finally, I have a little time to get to know my family—even if it is a family of ghosts. I'm familiar with my parents' lives and the little bit my mother told me about her mother's life, but unfortunately, Grandma Josephine had some kind of a falling-out with her own mother, and anything before that is a complete mystery. There's nothing online about Genevieve, Colette, or Aimée, whose lives were probably just as ordinary as those of my more recent ancestors.

Then I hit pay dirt with Great-Great-Great-Great-Grandma Berthe Manet, who painted under her maiden name, Berthe Morisot. I've never heard of her, but she was an artist, an Impressionist like Édouard Manet, and she exhibited her paintings along with Monet, Renoir, Degas, and lots of other famous people. Even better, it turns out good ol' Grandpa Times Four was Édouard's brother, Gène Manet, lending more weight to a possible *Party on the Seine* connection. Okay, Mr. Stein, I've got to give you some points here.

I call him. "So you're thinking Édouard Manet gave the painting to his brother Gène, who passed it down to his daughter Aimée?" I ask without preamble.

"I have no idea—nor does the Conference—but I suppose it's a possibility."

"How can you not know when you just gave me my family tree from the nineteenth century?"

"We only have that because an intern got interested and created it on her own. We hardly ever go back to anything before Hitler's rise, so we only know for sure that the Nazis stole *Party on the Seine* from the Bernheims. We traced and verified your connection to them, but—despite the intern's attempts—have no way of knowing how they came to possess it."

"Okay," I say, slightly disappointed, and check the tree again. "So it must have been that Colette, Aimée's daughter, inherited it from her mother, and the Nazis stole it from her."

"Could have been."

"But it doesn't say anything about the Manets being Jewish."

"As far as I know, they weren't."

"So were they resisters or Roma or any of the other folks the Nazis wanted to get rid of?"

"Samuel Bernheim was Jewish. Colette's husband."

I close my eyes and imagine I'm at my desk at home instead of at the office. The French doors of my study open into the living room, where there's a triptych of mixed-media pieces between the two windows. From the photographs I've seen of *Party on the Seine*, it seems likely the painting would fit there. Roughly four feet tall and five feet wide, if I remember correctly. Large, but, yes—the space is well over five feet.

I open my eyes and turn my chair around to try to catch a sailboat on my tiny piece of river. Are there any people on a boat having a party? Am I really picturing a painting by Édouard Manet, worth millions of dollars, hanging in my apartment?

"Tamara?" Jonathan asks into my silence.

"It's so off-the-wall."

"These cases often are."

"But you and your Claims Conference and all those experts who investigated this are sure that it's mine?"

"As sure as we can be."

This is huge. An Impressionist masterpiece, believed lost to the world, now risen from the dead. But along with ownership will come a slew of unknown consequences. Good and bad. Am I rich? "What the hell am I supposed to do with it?" I blurt.

Jonathan chuckles. "I wondered when you were going to get to that."

My suspicions flare. "And I suppose you have an answer for me? Like your conference buying it? Or brokering it to get your cut?"

"Has anyone ever told you that you're a cynical woman?"

I'm not about to tell him they have, and I ask instead, "Do I have reason to be?"

Now his laugh is full-throated. "You finally accept the fact that one of the greatest pieces of art ever created belongs to you, and your first thought is that I'm cheating you?"

"I've been thinking that from the first time you contacted me," I grumble, thawing.

"Good point."

I sigh. "So do you have any answers?"

"I'm in no position to tell you what to do, but it seems to me you have a few options. One is to give it to a museum and get a big tax write-off. Or you could sell it to one, but you'll only get a fraction of what it's worth on the open market. You could lend it to a museum, retaining ownership and maybe, although not likely, getting them to pay you a fee. The other alternative is to have an auction house sell it for you. They take a pretty hefty cut, but given what they can probably get for it, you'll still end up with a nice windfall. A very nice one."

"What if I want to keep it?"

"I'd strongly suggest that you don't take physical custody of it now. Or probably ever."

"Why not?" I think again about the multimedia triptych, which I've never particularly liked. I could move that to the empty wall in the guest room, over the futon. *Party on the Seine* needs to hang between the windows, where I'll be able to see it from both my desk and the living room couch. A family heirloom, an inheritance from ancestors I never knew I had. A gift that will bring me closer to them, remind me of my roots, of who I am. A comforting presence.

"It's your choice," he says. "But the painting is worth tens of millions of dollars, and you'd need insurance that would run you at least fifty grand a year, if not more. It also needs a controlled environment. Temperature, humidity, things like that. Old paintings are fragile, easily damaged, so you'd have to figure out a way to provide these kinds of conditions."

"You told me that the Nazis stashed it in a salt mine in some mountain in Austria during the war," I argue. "That it's been in a crate in the basement of a museum in Brazil ever since then."

"The other thing is that you're not in a secure location. Again, I'm not going to tell you what to do, but if the media discovers you have an original Manet—which they inevitably will—the lure for thieves would be overwhelming, endangering both your safety and the painting's. Not to mention that you live in a building with apartments, not condos. More turnovers, less scrutiny of residents, unknown people who sublease."

I don't know what's more annoying, that he knows what kind of building I live in or that he keeps telling me that it's my choice, that he's not going to tell me what to do, and then does exactly that. The latter being something I've been averse to since I was a child. I also don't appreciate being spied on.

Before I can respond, he adds, "There's a small museum outside of Philadelphia, the Columbia, that has a wing devoted to recovered Holocaust artwork, and you could send it there on a temporary basis—until you make your final decision."

"Condos or no condos, Tremont245 is extremely safe," I tell him testily. "Twenty-four-hour security, long-term employees, cameras everywhere. And discretion is paramount. A senator and a star Red Sox pitcher live there—and it's safe enough for them."

"Do either of them have a multimillion-dollar painting?"

"It's quite possible," I counter. "I'll check with the building and my insurance agent and see what I can arrange."

I'M GOING TO keep the painting here until I figure out my next best steps, just for a short time, a few weeks maybe. Definitely not long enough to warrant buying insurance or sending it to that museum. And, really, if it withstood decades inside a mountain and in a basement, how much destruction could a modest sojourn to my apartment do?

A week later, an unmarked truck pulls into the service bay behind Tremont245. Alyce, the building manager, texts me, and I go down to meet her. Two guards, guns perceptible under their uniforms, lift a green crate from the back of the truck. It has to be at least four times the size of *Party*, far larger than I imagined, vaguely reminiscent of a giant's coffin.

Under the harsh gaze of the truck driver, who I assume is also armed, the guards carefully position the crate on a dolly and roll it into the service elevator. The four of us ride silently up to my apartment. Alyce bows out as the men place it on the floor between the two windows. Then they proceed to put on gloves and remove it from its coffin, which takes no time at all. The top is easily unhinged, and inside, the painting is fastened in place, encased within layers of what looks like hard plastic. The guards carefully twist the bolts securing it, and *Party on the Seine* is free. They lean it gently against the wall.

"Is this where you want it?" the taller of the two asks.

I can't take my eyes off the painting—my painting—can barely speak. "Y-yeah, yes, perfect."

"Centered on the wall?"

"You're going to hang it too?"

For the first time, he smiles. Then the other one pulls out a drawer in the side of the crate and removes a drill and a half dozen hooks so heavy-duty I don't think I would have recognized them as hooks under different circumstances. "Please, yes," I stutter. "And, and, yes, centered. Please. Thank you. Thanks."

This goes as quickly as the unpacking did, and soon it's just me and *Party on the Seine*. I sit on the couch, try to take it in, my head and my body and my mind buzzing. No focus, no frame of reference. I flash hot. I flash cold. When I belatedly realize that this was created by my very own uncle times five, all I can do is grin. Unforeseen consequences be damned.

WHILE IT'S TRUE that I don't know much about art, I do recognize that *Party on the Seine* is extraordinary. Even a small child could see that, and I find myself spending more time than I should sitting on the living room couch, just looking. Instead of working at my desk, I stare through the open French doors, lost inside the painting, losing time in its swirl of life, communing with my kite tail of ancestors—my family—many of whom probably sat as rapt as I am before this masterpiece.

It's so vibrant, sunshine jumping from a necklace, to a cheek, to an eye, to the rippling river, illuminating a moment of spontaneous fun. I want to plumb its depths. There are fourteen discernible faces behind a lone woman looking out over the river to an unseen bank, her back to the others. The partyers closest to her are more detailed, while the farther away the people get, the more indistinct they become, although somehow still radiating their personalities despite the soft edges. I need to know what they're talking about, what they're thinking, how they happen to be on this boat together. Who they are.

While I've read a little about the painting, so far I haven't come across any specifics on the people in it—whether they were actual friends or models or just figments of Manet's imagination—so I'm kind of at a loss here. Why is that dark-haired woman at the railing so melancholy? Is the pretty blonde in a red-striped dress and a straw hat flirting with the guy sitting across from her or the one leaning in from behind? And that man in the top hat with the pointing finger and flashing eyes, is he arguing with his girlfriend or his wife, or maybe, given the deep V at the neckline of her dress, with a prostitute? I have no idea why these questions are suddenly important to me.

Maybe it's the bright colors or the way the people are positioned so intimately. I stand less than a foot from the canvas, close enough to see individual brushstrokes. Some appear to have been painted with a wide brush, loose and kind of messy, while others, particularly around facial features and the women's clothing, have clearly been put there with a much smaller and finer tool, graceful and refined. I presume this was done with intent, but I wonder why.

So now I want to understand more about brushstrokes? I've never considered a brushstroke in my life. It's almost as if I've fallen in love, greedily lapping up all the stories, all the minutiae, needing to know, to bond, to intertwine. Riding a bike without a helmet. Wind in my hair.

PART TWO

Berthe, 1868–1869

THREE

1868

Berthe sits next to Edma in the Galerie Médicis in the Louvre. Her sister is completely engrossed in copying Rubens's *The Exchange of the Two Princesses*, but Berthe is distracted. The gallery is suffocatingly hot, the stiff crinolines under her dress gouge at her legs, and the stays dig into her ribs. As part of their artistic training, she and Edma have been enrolled as copyists at the museum for the past five years. And although Berthe has learned much, she's losing interest in transferring some other artist's work onto her canvas. She prefers to create her own paintings outside, plein air, where she can invent rather than imitate. Where she can breathe.

She returns to duplicating the shimmering detail of the taller princess's dress, which Rubens rendered as if it were molten silver. Even though she's exploring the techniques of one of the great masters of luminosity, this isn't the type of luminosity that interests her. Rubens's light showcases the representational aspects of his painting, while Berthe's fascination lies in how light reflects and bounces off objects, emphasizing a single branch or the edge of a leaf while leaving the rest in shadow, details blurred, as they are in life.

Berthe wants someone to look at her painting and feel as if they are standing in front of the real tree, experiencing it. No one looking at *The Exchange of the Two Princesses* feels as if they are actually on a barge between France and Spain, a part of the strategic trade of one young woman for another.

"Is something wrong, dear?" Edma asks, as always attuned to her sister's changeable tempers. She's only two years older than Berthe, but she often acts as if the distance between them is larger. And in some ways, particularly levelheadedness and equanimity, it is. Yet they adore each other, inseparable since they were small children.

"No, I was just thinking about what Monsieur Corot taught us about light," Berthe replies. "How it jumps, rather than shines in a straight line."

"That may be, but the jury at the Salon prefers its light to shine evenly."

Berthe is keenly aware of the truth of this. She just wishes it could be otherwise. Change is anathema to the Salon de Paris, the official art exhibition of the Académie des Beaux-Arts, the irrefutable arbiter of the finest of French painting, heralded, at least by the French, as the greatest in the world. Held each year during the first two weeks of May, it's the social event of the season. But for most artists, the selection process is grueling and often humiliating, and the show itself even more so.

The Salon accepted two of Berthe's landscapes for each of its shows in 1864, 1865, and 1866, but not last year. And she hasn't yet heard about the three she submitted for 1868. She doubts the Salon judges will consent to exhibit her meager offerings and often wonders why they included her paintings in their earlier shows. Despite a few somewhat-positive comments from critics, and even a sale, she knows her work isn't what it should be, what it can be. Hopefully, what it will be.

She wishes she hadn't submitted those paintings, had never allowed them to be seen, as she's unsatisfied with their quality. But recognition by the Salon de Paris is the only way to be considered a legitimate artist, the only avenue to sales, and, especially for a woman, the only way to be taken seriously. And she's impatient.

Still, she says, "Degas was telling me about his discussion with Pissarro, who thinks classic compositions are finished."

"Why do you continue to do this to yourself?"

Berthe doesn't know how to respond in a way that Edma will understand. It's not that her sister isn't smart or a talented painter, it's just that she's serene by nature. She doesn't experience Berthe's rumblings of frustration and anger, the desire for what seems to be beyond reach. Edma is at ease with the world and her place within it. "Because I don't know how to be happy?" she asks with a smile to soften her words, to imply that she's joking.

Edma isn't fooled. "And that, my dearest sister, might be the saddest thing of all."

There are footfalls behind them, and while Edma returns her attention to her painting, Berthe turns to see who it might be. It's their friend and painter Henri Fantin-Latour, who she's aware is interested in more than a friendship with her, although she's quite content with the relationship they have.

With Fantin-Latour is the artist Édouard Manet. Berthe and Edma have never been properly introduced to Monsieur Manet, but they know of him, as seemingly everyone in Paris does. Whether for his wit, charm, and good looks, or for his infamous painting *Luncheon on the Grass*, the man is admired and reviled in equal measure, the talk of the city. Berthe is intrigued.

The two men bow, but Manet bows more deeply, his top hat pressed to his chest. He's dressed at the height of fashion, from his narrow pants to the intricately carved cane he holds with such nonchalance, more than a bit of a dandy. When he raises his head, he looks straight into Berthe's eyes. This is highly improper, and the correct response would be for her to lower hers. She does not.

"Please introduce me to these two beautiful ladies," he says to Fantin-Latour, but his eyes cling to Berthe. "The talented Morisot sisters, I presume."

Highly, highly improper. Berthe is relieved that her mother's sour stomach kept her from chaperoning her daughters' museum visit today, as she usually does. Berthe ignores him, adds a dab of a watery silver to her painting, scrutinizes it, nods, and then slowly puts her brush down on the ledge of the easel. When she glances over, Manet's expression is mischievous, the slight smile curling his lips indicating he has seen through her feigned indifference.

Fantin-Latour does as Manet asks, but Berthe surprises herself and, clearly, her sister, when instead of remaining demurely seated, she stands and holds out her hand. Not to be kissed, but to be shaken. An uncommon gesture for a woman, but Manet is a married man, so her boldness isn't as unbecoming as it would be if he didn't have a wife. Again, she's glad her mother has remained at home.

Manet shakes her hand and then shakes his head in amusement, his long reddish curls swinging behind him, as if they, too, are tickled. "It is my deepest pleasure to finally make your acquaintance, Mademoiselle," he says with another bow, slighter this time. "I was very much impressed with the paintings you displayed at the Salon two years ago. Particularly the riverscape, so full of translucent mist and light."

Berthe tries to hide her pleasure at his compliments. "Not as much as I was by your *Luncheon on the Grass*."

He rocks on his heels, taken aback, and she can tell that for all his swagger, he's as unsure of his work as she is of hers. "In a good or bad way?" he asks stiffly, as if bracing himself for an unfavorable reply.

Luncheon depicts two men and two women enjoying a picnic in the woods, a classical subject traditionally composed, inspired by Titian and Raphael. It was rejected by the Salon de Paris, so Manet exhibited it at the Salon des Refusés, along with the work of other artists whom the Salon snubbed.

It did indeed create the uproar the Salon feared, as the two women are naked and the two men are impeccably clothed in decidedly fashionable outfits. It's more two-dimensional than three, and the lighting is harsh. Immoral and shocking was the verdict of most of the critics and the public, but not of the many artists who expressed appreciation of his daring and style. The latter group includes Berthe.

She sits down and folds her hands loosely in her lap. "It's a bold and unique statement on the establishment's narrow-mindedness. It is also a remarkable painting."

Joy lights up Manet's face, and his eyes crease with pleasure. "Thank you, Mademoiselle Morisot. It's indeed an honor to hear such a response from an artist of your skill and intuition. I only hope that we may have many future opportunities to share and discuss each other's work."

Berthe smiles politely and picks up her brush. She will ensure these future opportunities come to fruition.

Fantin-Latour and Edma both watch this exchange with discomfort, if for different reasons.

AS THE CHURCH bells chime five times, Rémy, their coachman, arrives to bring Berthe and Edma home. A cheerful man who has had a sweet spot for Berthe since she was a little girl, he carries their canvases and supplies to their father's horse-drawn carriage, then puts down the stepstool and helps them up. Edma is careful her ankles don't show as she climbs, but Berthe is fond of the curve of the heels of her soulier pompadours, and she lifts her skirt a little higher than necessary to avoid the mud and refuse running along the cobblestones. Small rebellions. Small pleasures.

The barouche has a folding hood, which Rémy raises to protect them from the curious eyes of those on the streets, as befits women of their class and unmarried status. Edma, as always, is unaware these are restrictions, completely unperturbed by, and accepting of, the rules Berthe chafes under.

The horses quickly take them from the dirty streets and shanties that surround the Louvre to the airy expanse of the Boulevard des Italiens. As they pass Café de Bade, Berthe cranes her neck to catch a glimpse of the restaurant. Manet reserves two tables at five o'clock most afternoons, and there he and many of the other artists struggling with the limitations of the Salon gather.

Her fellow artists and friends, Edgar Degas, Claude Monet, Camille Pissarro, Pierre-Auguste Renoir, and Alfred Sisley, are surely ensconced at his table at this moment. Berthe has painted with them many times, always under her mother's watchful eye, which is unnecessary, as Berthe isn't taken with any of them in that way.

They have all told her of their café conversations, critiques of Delacroix, heated debates about the power of the Salon, as well as discussions of their work and possible new directions for French painting. But she cannot join them, as much as she and they would welcome her inclusion. For entering a café unchaperoned to take a seat at a table of men to whom she is not related would bring down the wrath of all those who purport to know what correct behavior is. And she cannot turn her back to these close-minded people any more than she can pay no heed to the power of the Salon.

Edma puts a hand on her arm. "You know he's a married man." Her voice contains more concern than consternation.

Berthe is startled by her sister's misreading of her thoughts, which is rare. She covers Edma's hand with her own. "It's not him I'm longing for. It's the chance to be like him." But as she says this, she wonders if Edma might not be right.

FOUR

1868

A few days after Berthe and Edma met Édouard Manet at the Louvre, the Morisots receive an invitation to his mother's Thursday evening musical soiree. The families travel in the same social circles, both wealthy and cultured, and Madame Manet's salons are frequented by the most prominent musicians, artists, and writers in Paris. Berthe's good friend, Edgar Degas, declares Mme Manet's gatherings to be hot and cramped, with lukewarm drinks and inedible food. Nonetheless, he's a frequent visitor.

And indeed, Degas is correct. Although the house is sizable by any standard, pieces of massive furniture overwhelm the space, which is undeniably hot, overcrowded, and visually burdened by far too many artworks and knickknacks. Still, Berthe's mother, Cornélie, is delighted to once again be asked here.

Cornélie also holds weekly soirees, on Tuesday evenings in season, often with similar attendees, although leaning more toward art than music. She and Édouard's mother, Antoinette, are congenial acquaintances, a relationship Cornélie is keen to expand into an intimate friendship.

Berthe is also pleased to be at the Manets', free to mingle with her fellow artists and friends, but she has to admit a touch of disappointment that Édouard Manet isn't present, which unfortunately has been the case the few times she has been invited before.

His absences are even more strange as he and his wife live here and many of his paintings hang on the walls: *Music in the Tuileries Garden*, *The Absinthe Drinker*, and a relatively new one she hasn't seen before, *The Guitar Player*. When she walks over to it, she recognizes the model, the notorious Victorine Meurent. She's the woman Édouard depicted in *Luncheon* to scandalous response, for in that painting Victorine is nude and staring boldly at the viewer while sitting comfortably among the fully clothed men. There are rumors the two are lovers, as so many of Manet's models are said to be, and Berthe is surprised to find herself annoyed by this. It's not as if Monet, Renoir, and so many other painters don't do the same.

But this doesn't interfere with her admiration for the new painting, which is elegant in its simplicity. It's large, and Victorine wears a flowing white dress, in stark contrast to the flat, dark background. Berthe takes a step closer, scrutinizes the strokes, tighter than her own. His rich deep colors breathe life into the inert wooden instrument, imbuing it with depth and texture. How does he do such a thing? It is far beyond her meager talents. There's no doubt this man is a master, with perhaps more to teach her than even the great Reubens.

"Ah, my lovely," Degas says, taking her arm in his. "You are even more ravishing tonight than usual. Although I do wish you would wear a color other than black."

She pats his hand. "And how are you this evening, Edgar?" They have known each other for years, as Degas is also of their social circle. This is not true of many of their struggling compatriots, such as the more impoverished painters Monet and Renoir, who are standing together uneasily in a far corner, humbled by the grandeur.

"I fear from the odor of overcooked meat that yet another disastrous dinner will be served soon," Degas grouses in his usual dry tone.

"You don't come for the food."

"No, I come to partake in your dazzling beauty. Those voluptuous black curls, those dark, intense eyes against your pale skin . . ."

Berthe shakes her head. Degas is a shameless flirt, eloquent and manipulative in equal measure, rendered harmless to an unmarried woman by his confirmed bachelorhood and seeming lack of romantic interest in the opposite sex. "You didn't know I would be here."

"And now that you are, I beg you to stay by my side all evening," he continues. "Especially when that dreadful, fat Suzanne begins to play her piano."

"Must you be so unkind?" Berthe detaches her arm from his and adds primly, "She's an excellent musician and is also one of our hostesses." But she can't suppress a smile. Suzanne, Édouard Manet's wife, is large and not particularly attractive, quiet and meek. His sudden marriage to her continues to be a matter of extensive and unflattering gossip five years after the wedding.

Degas's eyes sparkle. "I had no idea you were so fond of her."

"It has nothing to do with fondness. Everyone acknowledges Suzanne is a talented pianist, and you can't deny she and Édouard live here," Berthe insists. "Everything I said is true."

"That may be so, my dear, but it's the spirt behind your words I question."

"I think I'll go join Edma," she says before Degas can provoke her to continue in this vein. "You go find someone else to be the object of your sweet talk. Perhaps you'll have better luck with her than you're having with me."

He bows deeply. "As you wish." When he stands, he grins at her.

As she moves toward her sister, her mother intercepts her. "As fond as I am of Monsieur Degas, he is not to whom you should be speaking. You remember Pierre St. Gelais, I'm sure. We met him last summer in Cherbourg? The very day Edma was first introduced to Monsieur Adolphe Pontillon. Let's go talk with Monsieur St. Gelais instead."

Before Cornélie can draw her across the room to that tiresome man who can barely raise his eyes from the floor, let alone converse, Berthe says, "I see dinner is being served. I'll collect Edma, and you find Papa so we can eat together." Then she turns and slips into the crowd, frowning at the thought of Adolphe Pontillon. She's concerned Maman is going to talk Edma into marrying him, something neither sister wants.

ÉDOUARD MANET DOESN'T arrive until after dessert has been served. He sweeps into the room, flings off his handsome cape, and kisses his mother on both cheeks. "I am so sorry, Maman," he declares loudly. "Work has yet again kept me from one of your wonderful evenings." His eyes take in the assemblage, and he bows. "My regrets to all of you also. I'll now have to catch up on the titillating conversation I've surely missed."

It is as if the entire house has been rekindled by a roaring fire. Shouts of welcome, glasses raised, broad smiles, flushed cheeks. Berthe notices there is no paint under Manet's fingernails nor any on his elegant clothes. Has he been with Victorine? Or has he thrown her over for another, as she's heard is often his way? Berthe glances at Suzanne, who appears pleased by her husband's appearance, even though he hasn't acknowledged her.

As he more closely surveys the gathering, his eyes find Berthe's. Emile Zola once told her that Manet's eyes were the blue of the Mediterranean in full sunlight, which is an apt description. Now, as when they first met, she holds his gaze, unsmiling, chin tilted upward. Her father has just left to smoke a cigar, and the seat beside her is empty. Manet gestures toward it. "May I join you, Madame Morisot?" he asks Cornélie.

Cornélie has no choice but to acquiesce, and Berthe can tell from her pursed lips that she would rather he did not. Her mother is both sharp-eyed and sharp-tongued, so Berthe has no doubt she caught the look that passed between herself and Manet.

"Madame Morisot," he says as soon as he sits, ignoring Berthe. "It is a pleasure to meet you again." He nods to Edma. "As it is to once again be in the company of your very lovely and talented daughters."

Cornélie frowns at him. "I was not aware you had met my daughters." She shoots Berthe her well-known evil eye.

"While we were copying at the Louvre," Edma interjects quickly. "Just last week. We were introduced by Henri Fantin-Latour."

Although Edma says this to placate their mother, it has the opposite effect, and Cornélie's jaw clenches. Cornélie would much prefer for Berthe to be using her time to woo Fantin-Latour, who does not have a wife.

Manet easily relieves the tension by asking Cornélie about Tiburce, who is in America investigating business opportunities. Cornélie loves her three daughters, Yves, Edma, and Berthe, but Tiburce, five years Berthe's junior, the son and heir she'd feared she would never be able to give her husband, is her heart. After ten minutes of answering Manet's questions with more detail than necessary, due to his unwavering and possibly contrived interest, she's smiling at him. At one point, she even touches his sleeve affectionately.

"I compliment you on Tiburce's many successes," he says, tactfully turning the subject. "But I would be remiss if I didn't also note your daughters' many gifts and accomplishments. You must be very proud, Madame Morisot, with the acceptance of so many of their paintings at the Salon."

Cornélie beams at Edma and Berthe. "I am very proud indeed." And this is true. Cornélie encouraged both girls to paint at a young age, procuring excellent tutors, most recently Camille Corot, who has been teaching them as seriously as he would any man. While other mothers might have feared their daughter's growing talent, Cornélie celebrates it.

"If not for Maman, there would be no Morisot paintings at the Salon," Berthe says. "She is, and always has been, our champion."

Manet remains focused on Cornélie. "Well, Madame, your efforts have been realized. I was so awed by Mademoiselle Berthe's *The Seine Below the Pont d'Iena* that I've decided to take up the same position on the riverbank and try to capture the wondrous light, as in her sky, the magic of its reflection off the plants at the river's edge. I've always painted in my studio, never plein air, and I believed I never would. But now, I find myself intrigued by the process and would like to try it." He finally turns to Berthe. "I hope this is acceptable to you."

Berthe studies him for signs of disingenuousness, but there don't appear to be any. She's stunned, tongue-tied. "Why, why, Monsieur, this is a high compliment, very high indeed." Could Édouard Manet actually try a new style of painting because of the influence of one of her works? Impossible.

"Then may I be so presumptuous as to invite both you and Edma, and, of course, Madame Morisot, to paint alongside me Tuesday afternoon, if the weather is agreeable? I would appreciate any help you can give me in my virgin attempt."

This is an even more dumbfounding proposition. He's seeking her instruction? Both girls turn to their mother, and Berthe worries she won't allow such an adventure. But Cornélie says she'd be thrilled to accompany her daughters, and that it will be a special delight to watch him work. Not only is Édouard a master painter, but he's a master charmer as well.

THE WEATHER ON Tuesday is lovely, with a soft breeze pushing the buoyant clouds. Rémy helps the three women alight at the top of a grassy rise overlooking the Seine. He sets up their painting materials and a chair for Cornélie, then returns to the carriage until he's needed for the trip home.

Manet is already there, staring fiercely out over the river, his canvas untouched and no sketchbook in sight. He greets them, smiling widely. Cornélie is captivated, Edma is wary, and Berthe isn't sure how to describe the current of emotions coursing through her.

She's immensely excited at the prospect of painting with, and maybe even being helpful to, Manet, but there's more to it than just this. Being near him fills her with a tingling. It's not unpleasant, but not particularly pleasant either. Maybe more of a stinging than a tingling. She busies herself with her easel and her paints.

Cornélie ensures that Edma's easel is next to Manet's, with Berthe on Edma's other side. As usual, her mother's interference is an annoyance, but there is little Berthe can do to stop this. Manet watches in silence and then, without a word, picks up his easel and settles it down next to Berthe. "I need to watch your brushstrokes. So much looser than mine," he says. "How you capture the light in a real setting. And I'd like you to watch me and tell me what I'm doing wrong."

Berthe can't help but smile at how he has delivered her mother this small defeat. "Have you made any sketches?" she asks.

"I thought I would just go at the canvas."

Edma and Berthe glance at each other. Neither of them would ever attempt a painting without preliminary sketches and many revisions. "You're a brave man," Edma says.

"Or a fool too willing to waste time and paint." His self-deprecating laugh is full and rich, inviting them to join in.

Even Cornélie titters, although Berthe can tell she's out of sorts due to Manet's easel maneuver. She's not a woman used to being bested, and Berthe assumes her mother will find a way to retaliate.

Manet does just as he promised he would. He mixes an unlikely number of colors on his palette, throws Berthe a boyish look of glee, and then practically attacks the canvas with a wide brush spitting green. He grabs a thinner one, immerses it in blue, and bends toward his canvas. Now his strokes are structured and deliberate, but no less confident. Berthe and Edma watch in amazement.

"I'm thinking that plein air painting demands abandon," he declares. "What's in front of me transferred onto the canvas with as little as possible in between!"

Berthe wonders why he asked for her advice when he plans to do whatever he wants. He couldn't be trying to pursue her, given his married state and the company of her sister and her mother, but if not that, why did he invite her to paint with him?

She has many pencil and pastel drawings of this particular spot and flips through her sketchbook to find them. In *The Seine Below the Pont d'Iena*, she chose a full riverscape, only nature, but now a boy is fishing on the other bank. She'll include him in this next painting, off-center and tiny, his figure drawing the viewer into the painting. While Manet continues his exuberant brushstrokes, she reaches for a muted pastel stick and lightly roughs in her initial attempt at the composition in the book. Then she walks back and forth behind the easels, steps closer to the river, and walks some more, her eyes tethered to the expanse she wants to re-create.

Edma is used to her sister's pacing and pays her no mind, but Manet stops and watches her, the brush in his hand raised. Berthe feels his eyes on her, but she's more focused on what she's going to paint. When she stops moving and glances over at him, she realizes that he's looking at her the same way she was looking at the fisherman. It's not that he wants her advice or to pay court to her. It's that he wants to paint her. This would be highly inappropriate given her social status, but she finds herself wishing it were not so.

FIVE

1869

As Berthe feared, Edma surrenders to their mother's entreaties and weds Adolphe Pontillon in a small ceremony at which both the bride and Berthe struggle to hold back tears. At thirty, Edma has come to the age when a woman must face the decision to either acquiesce to tradition or live in pitiable spinsterhood. Berthe has always known Edma's tendency to yield would make this moment inevitable, yet this does nothing to relieve her sorrow. Nor does it diminish her dread that now she, at twenty-eight, will become the sole focus of Cornélie's zeal to find suitable husbands for her daughters. Yves, the oldest of the three sisters, is already married and settled.

A week later, Edma leaves Paris to live in Lorient with her new husband. After years of being together almost continuously, sharing a studio, a bedroom, and the most intimate of confidences, the sisters are separated for the first time. Spring is arriving, which usually turns Berthe's temperament toward the sunny, but this year there's no brightening her mood. As the only Morisot sibling left in the house with a meddlesome mother and a busy father, she spends her days sitting at her desk crying and writing letters to Edma. Then crying even more when she receives one in return.

"It is time to take yourself in hand," Cornélie orders one evening as Berthe wordlessly pushes food around her plate. "These attacks of melancholy are tiresome." She looks over to her husband for support, but as usual he's not listening, consumed with his many responsibilities as prefect of the department of Cher, so she turns back to her daughter. "And if you don't start eating you will waste away into nothing, and no man will find you fit to marry."

Berthe is unmoved by her mother's scolding, impassive to everything but her missing sister. She can't paint, she can't eat, and she barely sleeps, sliding between fits of irritability and bedridden silence. It is as if the blood is slowly draining from her body, leaving her without the will to do anything beyond wandering aimlessly through the house, fatigue her sole companion.

She's experienced these bouts of despair since early childhood, along with frequent episodes of ill health, diagnosed by Dr. Aguillard as neurasthenia. But this is the deepest well she's ever fallen into, so profound and dark that light barely penetrates. The good doctor comes almost daily, counseling iron salts, stinging nettles, and raw liver, all of which she refuses. Although her state is disagreeable, it's impossible to contemplate leaving it. There's nowhere else to go.

Cornélie tries a different tack. "Dear Bijou, your poor little face is so sad, and this breaks my heart. Please come back to me. Please come back to you."

"This is my life now," Berthe tells her.

Desperate with concern, Cornélie contacts Degas, who suggests she and Berthe come with him to Manet's new studio. "Monet, Renoir, and I often work there with Manet, other artist friends of Berthe's too," Degas says. "It's possible the camaraderie, conversation, and the smell of paint will pull her from this lethargy."

Berthe claims she can't do anything of the sort, so Cornélie asks Degas to come to the house for a visit, but Berthe turns him away. Edma sends letters daily, worried about Berthe's failing health, urging her sister to return to the living.

My dearest Berthe,

The days here are dreadfully dull and lonely. If only you could visit me, or I you. But I am to immerse myself in my happy life as a married woman, responsible to a husband, not to a sister or mother.

It will do my heart good to know you are once again painting and talking with M. Degas, laughing and philosophizing with M. Manet, and standing before your easel as you create your next masterpiece. I so wish for you to partake in the enviable life open to you, both for your sake and mine, vicarious as the latter may be.

Although Berthe detects Maman's prodding between Edma's lines, she's moved, and the plaintiveness of her sister's words cuts through her self-absorption. Edma is far more alone than she, with a husband she barely knows, no family or friends or other artists to meet with, and a mother-in-law who is barely tolerable.

Berthe begins to dress in the morning and walk in the garden, sometimes stopping by her studio, although she's not ready to paint. As spring turns to summer, she begins to eat again.

MANET'S STUDIO IS located in Batignolles, a bohemian area of the city. When Berthe steps inside, accompanied by Cornélie, she's taken by the high ceilings and the spacious rooms filled with light. Numerous large fireplaces are scattered throughout, and there's even a curtained-off area, private and empty except for a rocking chair and a long humpbacked sofa where a weary artist might rest.

The place is a messy hive of color and frenzied activity, finished and unfinished canvases strewn everywhere, at least a dozen easels, some holding paintings, others standing at the ready. Drop cloths crawl the room like fungus, unnecessary, as the floors are more splattered with paint than the sheets meant to protect them. She breathes in the thick aroma of turpentine, paint, and canvas, which fills her with both nostalgia and hope. Degas and Renoir are there, along with Manet, and the three immediately put down their brushes.

"My dear Berthe," Degas says, rushing forward to take her hands in his. "You look so much better than I feared from your mother's description. I daresay the paleness of your skin becomes you. Ethereal. More beautiful than ever." He bows to Cornélie.

"And very paintable," Manet adds as he comes to Berthe's side, a little too familiarly for Cornélie, who steps between them with a steely gaze at her daughter.

"Thank you so much for your kind invitation, Monsieur Manet," Cornélie says with a sharpness that belies her words. "It is an honor for both me and my daughter." She turns to Renoir. "And it is lovely to see you once again, Monsieur Renoir. I have much enjoyed our conversations at Madame Manet's gatherings."

Renoir, who Berthe doubts has had many conversations with her mother, bows. "Yes, Madame, I agree."

Berthe smiles at each of her friends and takes a full breath of the delicious air. "I can't tell you how happy I am to be here," she says, "but please, go back to your paints. My mother and I are here to observe, not interfere."

"You would never be considered an interference, Mademoiselle Morisot." Manet's eyes lock on to hers, the limpid blue reaching out to her.

Cornélie grabs Berthe's arm, turns her quickly away from Manet, and leads her to a set of chairs. "Sit," she says. "You are just recovering, and there is no need to exhaust yourself." Then she takes a seat in the other.

Once again outmaneuvered by her mother, Berthe says, "I heard talking before we came in. Please go on with both your painting and your discussion."

"It's the Salon, of course," Degas explains to her. "What else would it be? The rejections we keep getting. Their rigid criteria of what is 'good' and what is 'bad' art."

"Historical images. Grand landscapes. Portraits of the wealthy and powerful!" Renoir turns to her and throws his hands up in disgust. "Stray from these and there's no recognition, no sales, possibly the end of a career."

"I refuse to be stuck in the Renaissance!" Degas cries.

Berthe already knows everything they're telling her, and although they're aware of this also, men always feel the need to educate women, even if this edification is unnecessary. She patiently waits out their explanations, and then responds with what she knows they already know, although she's aware this irony will be lost on them. "And when they do accept a painting that's unusual," she says, "they position it poorly and no one notices it's there." At the Salon, artwork is displayed fifteen or twenty or more pieces to a wall, stretching from floor to ceiling, rendering those at the top and the bottom virtually invisible to the thousands of people pouring through the rooms.

"So you agree with us that this must change?" Degas asks.

"I do," she says. "But the Salon jury is made up of men who don't want anything to change."

"We can organize our own exhibition," Degas declares. "Like the Salon des Refusés."

"We're not emperors," Manet reminds him, a harsh cut to his voice. It was Napoleon III who established the alternative exhibition. "And that show was also neither critically nor financially successful." As his *Luncheon on the Grass* was exhibited at the Salon des Refusés to prodigious derision, he is still indignant.

"So we have to keep our mouths shut and accept their censorship, Édouard?" Degas demands. "We are the future of French art, and if we allow them to crush us, there will only be the past. Moribund art."

"Why only one or the other?" Berthe asks. "Why not pursue our new notions while also submitting to the Salon? Maybe we'll find cracks in their rigidity, push our ideas forward that way. If this fails, then we can consider our own show."

"Not enough!" Degas cries. "We must race forward, not take baby steps. Otherwise, we'll all be dead before any changes are made."

Manet nods to Berthe in appreciation. "The Salon has power over our exposure and success, not to mention sales, and we can't pretend it doesn't. As Berthe says, at some future date we'll be able to hold our own exhibition, but that time is not now."

"This will not—"

"Think about it, Edgar," Manet interrupts. "We've already begun developing our own style. The three of us, along with some of the others, have been working together, sharing ideas, and have become quite a like-minded coterie." He turns to Berthe. "A painter of your skill and vision, not to mention diplomacy, would be a brilliant addition to our group. You will make us better, and we will endeavor to do the same for you. Would you consider joining our bande? Becoming one of us?"

A burst of pure pleasure shoots through her, an emotion she hasn't experienced since the announcement of Edma's engagement. "If this request includes my mother," she says to quell the alarm on Cornélie's face, "I would very much like to accept your kind offer."

"WHAT HAS BECOME of your manners?" Cornélie demands as soon as they climb into the carriage. "You may not make a commitment, especially to a married man, without my approval."

Berthe is so elated by the afternoon, by the thrill of being in the company of artists and being included in a group whose ambitions parallel her own, that it takes a moment for her to understand what her mother is saying. A commitment to a married man? She made no such thing. When she realizes Cornélie's concern, her elation deflates.

"There is your reputation to consider. And that of the entire Morisot family!"

"But, Maman, I didn't do anything improper," she says, and is further distressed when she sees from Cornélie's expression that her mother completely disagrees. How can she become a true artist if the strictures of society will not allow her to flourish? Seeing the flush rising on Cornélie's cheeks, she adds, "But I'm sorry if I made you uncomfortable."

"Uncomfortable? I am not uncomfortable. I am outraged and humiliated! What will people think? Édouard's mother, Antoinette, and I have become close over the months of your illness, even speaking of our families spending next summer in the countryside together, and now, if she catches word of your behavior, I see no future for our friendship." She dabs her eyes with a handkerchief, although there are no signs of tears. "She is the goddaughter of the king of Sweden, after all."

"I'm sorry I didn't ask your permission, but I did include you as a condition for my consent. And I don't see why there would be a reason for any of them to repeat such a banal exchange to others."

"As they live in the same house, Édouard will surely tell his mother you agreed to come to his studio, and she will just as surely inquire about my reaction. Open your eyes, Berthe. You aren't a child, and I despair that you behave as if you still are."

Berthe wonders how she can be expected to act as an adult when she's treated like a child, but knows better than to ask. Although Cornélie may be concerned about her own relationship with Manet's mother, Berthe knows her true worry is that if her daughter works in Manet's studio it will tarnish her chances of finding a proper husband. Between Manet's infamous paintings and his unrepentant philandering, he's viewed by many in Paris as a disreputable sort, and she would be, by association, considered the same. She also fears her hawk-eyed mother is aware of her growing interest in him. "I need to paint," she says.

"I understand this, and I'm pleased that your recovery is far enough along for you to have the stamina to return to your canvases," Cornélie says in a more conciliatory tone. "You know I've always nurtured your painting.

But you have a studio right in your own home. Why would you need to go elsewhere, especially to Manet's?"

"Because it's best for my work," Berthe retorts, knowing her mother might take her response as impertinence. But now that she's experienced Manet's studio, all that it could mean, she's unable to control herself. "And it isn't as if I'll be alone with him. Degas, Renoir, and possibly Monet or Sisley will be there also. Pissarro too. And you will be with me at all times."

Cornélie's eyes flash. "That is irrelevant to the issue at hand, which is your standing in society. As your mother, I will not allow you to destroy your reputation. You are not to go to his studio, with or without me."

Berthe stares out the window, takes a few shallow breaths, tries to tamp down her growing fury. She should have been more appeasing, as Edma would have been. If her sister were here, she would have put her hand on Berthe's, silently reminding her to think before she speaks. Yet another reason to mourn her absence.

"Bijou," Cornélie pleads. "You must think of your future."

"I am," she says stubbornly, foolishly.

"This is my fault. I was the one who ignored the warnings, who allowed you to pursue this folly."

"Which I'm very appreciative of."

"But now I see that you have misinterpreted my enthusiasm. Painting is not a future for you, or for any woman. It's a pastime. You will never paint as well as a man."

Berthe turns and glares at her mother. This tactless comment is inflaming, and not without precedent. "Well, Manet obviously disagrees with you, and so do I," she snaps. "He wouldn't have asked me to join them if he didn't believe I was as good as the other artists in the group, including himself."

"I saw the look that passed between you and Édouard Manet. That man is a danger to you."

"Not painting is a danger to me."

WHEN THEY ARRIVE home, a letter from Edma is waiting.

The beautiful weather has improved my spirits, and I unpacked my paints for the first time since I arrived in Lorient. The day's work was very bad, but I was outside and pleased to be painting again. Then, to my despair, Adolphe returned and found me in the meadow. He was as angry as I have ever seen him, and I was both astonished and frightened by his wrath.

He said it was not proper for a woman to sit alone in a field, and now that I am Madame Pontillon, I am not to paint; I am to be the mistress of his estate. My dearest sister, I despair of my choices. In my thoughts, I follow you about in the studio and wish that I could escape and breathe in the air in which we lived for many long years.

Berthe takes to her bed, refusing dinner, as well as the ox-blood broth Cornélie brings to her room, another of Dr. Aguillard's vile remedies. She can't allow her mother to do to her what she did to Edma, but right now she's too shattered to fathom how to prevent such a thing.

SIX

1869

In the most unlikely of circumstances, it's Manet's mother, Antoinette, who comes to Berthe's rescue. Cornélie expected her friend to react negatively to Berthe joining Manet's "bande," but Antoinette embraces the idea, suggesting she and Cornélie chaperone together, drinking tea, eating pastries, and gossiping to their hearts' delight while neglecting the management of their households to ensure Berthe's honor.

Even before dates can be arranged, Berthe returns to her studio, which is in a small, sun-filled edifice across from their house's private garden. A studio she used to share with Edma, but now is, sadly, hers alone. Their father had it built for them, finally bending to his wife's entreaties to keep the girls at home and away from the possibility of coming in contact with undesirable men.

Berthe finds herself doing little more than shuffling through finished and half-finished canvases, rearranging paints and pastels, cleaning brushes, all the while missing Edma. Manet's proposition initially gave her confidence in her abilities and talent, but now as she contemplates her next piece, she's overwhelmed by familiar insecurities. How could she have boasted to her mother that she was as good an artist as Manet? As Degas and Renoir? What madness.

Manet is a notorious womanizer, and she has little doubt he harbors an interest in her that has nothing to do with her painting skills. Could his invitation be an attempt at seduction, rather than an appreciation of the contribution she might bring to the group? Heat rises to her cheeks at the thought of being seduced by a man as exciting and brilliant as he, so different from the bland suitors her mother is always thrusting upon her. She allows herself a few seconds to contemplate the softness of his full lips on hers, their life together after he leaves Suzanne. Then she rips herself from this flight of fancy. She is, indeed, mad.

She grabs a blank canvas and props it on an empty easel. She has to prepare a number of paintings she won't be ashamed to share with the bande. But her imagination fails her, and she scours the room for inspiration. Through the mullioned window, a riot of peonies raise their heads to the sky. A rather mundane and undistinguished subject, but she'll make it her own. Or at least try.

After fetching a vase from the dining room, Berthe cuts a half dozen flowers and plays with them in the glass vessel half filled with water. A single peony or many? Three, she decides, and places the vase under plentiful sunlight. A few petals fall on the table, and she brushes them to the floor. She begins a series of pencil drawings in a sketchbook, lightly drafting the outlines of the composition she envisions. The table slightly tilted, the vase a bit off-center. She likes asymmetry, values the way it creates a sense of movement where there is none.

The peonies are a muted pink and need a contrasting background. She takes a blue pastel stick, then a purple, making a series of drawings on many pages. Using the long side of the sticks, she sweeps strokes of color that jaggedly outline the pencil drawing, loose and unfinished. Too dark around the edges of the leaves. A paler purple, a touch of yellow. She uses her fingers to blend the pastels, careful not to allow the blue and yellow to bleed into a green too similar to the flowers' stems. The vase is left white for now, the table a deep brown.

Berthe walks across the room a number of times, returns to stare intensely at the flowers and vase, then just as intensely at the sketches. She stands at her easel and begins. But transferred to canvas, the painting is too quiet, tiresome. She snatches up a brown pastel and zigzags it along the front edge of the table, tapering off before the table does, injecting a disconcerting element into the picture. Her hair falls to her forehead, and she pushes the curls back, too absorbed to notice she's streaking her face with yellow and purple.

It's not until the sunlight on the peonies fades that she realizes the day is easing into evening. She hasn't worked this hard or for this long in months, and she starts to call out to Edma to come see what's she done. She needs her sister to advise her, to suggest ways to make the painting better, as they have always done for each other. But then she remembers that Edma is not there and all she can do is sit in a chair, rub her shoulders and lower back, try to imagine what Edma would have said.

It's bad, lifeless. M. Corot taught her that light is the heart and soul of painting, that she must witness it closely, immerse herself in it, play with it, tame it to her purpose. He was much impressed with her skills, lightheartedly warning Maman that his teaching would make Berthe a painter, not an amateur copyist. While another type of mother might have seen this as a possible catastrophe for her daughter, Cornélie had encouraged him to do that very thing. A decision Maman now obviously regrets, although Berthe is forever indebted to her for it. Corot taught her to see.

He instructed her to study how light falls, how it skips and reflects, how it defines every surface in a singular way, each petal and leaf, each aspect of each petal and leaf. And she's failed to do any of this here. She should destroy the painting, as she has done with so many of her other inadequate attempts, but she's too exhausted to make the effort. She leaves it where it is and returns to the house.

THE FOLLOWING WEEK, Degas comes to Cornélie's soiree and corners Berthe. "I understand from your mother that you've started painting again. You must let me to see what you've accomplished."

"What I've accomplished is not worthy of being seen."

"My dear Berthe, this is what you always say about your work, and it's never true."

"And that isn't true. You have seen many of my failures, labeled a number of my attempts as 'rehearsals,' if I remember correctly."

Degas laughs delightedly. "But that was long ago, and now you've moved far beyond rehearsals. I demand you take me into your studio and show me what you have done!"

"Some other time, Edgar. I assure you I'm making the correct assessment in this case."

"I do not accept that." He points to the door that opens into the garden. "Lead the way!"

Antoinette Manet overhears their conversation, and, like her friend Cornélie, she must speak to the subject, even if it does not involve her. "Oh, do go with him, Berthe. Once you are part of Édouard's bande and are painting in his studio, we will all be seeing your works in progress." She waves both her hands at them. "Shoo, shoo. I will keep a watch on you. Just leave the doors to the garden and the studio open, and let Monsieur Degas feast his eyes on the wondrous paintings I am sure you have created."

Berthe has no choice but to do as commanded. Antoinette, also like Maman, is not one to be refused. Yet Berthe bristles at the indignity of once again being treated like a child, especially by a woman who is not a relative.

Degas follows her out the door with a smirk on his face. "She is a bossy old sort, even if this time it suits my purposes."

"Why don't we sit for a moment in the garden?" Berthe proposes, hoping to stall and possibly dissuade him. "I want to hear your latest thinking about the Salon."

Degas's smirk transforms into a grin. "Directness is one of your qualities I'm most fond of, and your attempts at misdirection don't serve you well, as you do not know how to be anything but transparent. I daresay you need to take note of the more coquettish in our circle and learn how to get a man to do your bidding."

"And you are all too pleased with yourself, Monsieur, which does not serve you well," she counters. "In addition, you sound like my mother. And Madame Manet."

"Anything but that." He raises his hands in mock horror. "Please, anything but that."

"You must admit you are a bit of a busybody."

"And that is one of my many charms." He pulls open the door of her studio, bows, and ushers her inside, leaving it open as Antoinette ordered. Then he strides toward the canvas of the peonies.

Berthe shifts uneasily as he silently scrutinizes the painting. It's not ready to be looked at this carefully. It's a dull subject painted dully, the main flower falling awkwardly forward. A woman's painting, and a poor one at that. She was going to destroy it, but she had a dream Edma told her not to, so she reworked the original pastel in oil. But this hasn't achieved the luminosity she was hoping the oil would create. It remains flat and conventional. She's humiliated, and she wishes that Antoinette Manet had minded her own business.

"You've done a remarkable job with the translucence of the vase," Degas finally says. "And its reflection on the table. As for the central flower, well, all I can say is that it's exquisite." He steps closer. "The rough brush strokes, the pink and white tones, so imprecise and yet instantly recognizable. The light leaping from one petal to another, yet no individual petals in sight."

Berthe is astonished by his words. "What about the lack of depth and detail? I thought about adding dimension, but somehow this is how it felt to me."

"And you were correct. The flatness is one of the painting's strongest virtues. The flower is muscularly three-dimensional, while its surroundings are not. This, as well as the peony's instability, throws the composition off-kilter, gives a sense of movement, of power."

She drops into a chair, unmoored by his praise. Could he be saying these things just to lift her spirits? Had Cornélie warned him not to be negative? "I worry it's too traditional, too conventional." She purses her lips. "Too feminine."

Degas takes another chair. "It is those things, and I agree that it lacks the boldness of some of your other paintings, but that doesn't necessarily make it a lesser work."

"But it is. And I fear it and I won't be taken seriously."

He considers this, picks up a handful of the browning petals from the floor, drops them to one side of the vase. "What if you slightly altered the bottom left here? A few petals scattered and dying on the table? This would contrast with the large peony in full bloom, add tension, a larger story. Life and death."

She sees it as he describes it, as she will make it. "You're brilliant, Edgar. Thank you. That's exactly what it needs." She reaches over and lightly touches his knee. "And you are a generous and thoughtful friend."

Degas shifts uneasily under her compliments. "I'm struggling with my latest too."

"Tell me."

He describes his painting of a racetrack in Saint-Cloud, a western suburb of Paris. An oversized canvas depicting a furious competition, jockeys and horses straining toward victory, the stands filled with men and women urging them on.

"I want to explore the movement and motion, the long strides of the horses," he explains. "The jockeys hunched and hurtling forward, the crowd standing and cheering. But my efforts are too feverish. The picture is overfull and lacks focus." He frowns. "But it's exactly this teeming frenzy, the crowd's and the horses' intense desire to win, that I'm trying to express."

"So there's too much going on in the actual scene, maybe too much going on in your painting?"

"Exactly."

"Could you narrow the composition?" she suggests. "Maybe include just a few of the horses, put only a slice of the crowd off to one side of the canvas?"

"That will diminish the dynamism."

"Maybe, but a tighter view might allow you to pinpoint the detail of the jockeys' expressions, catch the fierceness of their determination." She's excited by her advice, by the idea of painting a bustling scene on a large canvas. "The same could be done with the horses. The power of their bodies, their sweat, the thrust of their muscles driving forward."

Now it's Degas who touches Berthe's knee. "You have as good an eye for dramatic scenes as you do for your more delicate domestic ones."

"If only I could paint them." Berthe sighs. "How can it be a disgrace for me to even think of such a thing, let alone do it? Men and horses and public scenes. Why would this bring shame on me and my family, while there is nothing shameful if a man does the same? What is there to be ashamed of?"

Degas studies her, his eyes troubled. "I don't know, Berthe. I wish I could tell you, and even more, I wish it weren't so." He bows his head.

"I fear that without the ability to expand and choose my own subjects, to push boundaries, I'll never become a real artist."

"Nonsense," he declares, clearly astounded by her comment. "You are a real artist. One of the best of us, with so much more to offer, so much more greatness to achieve."

She points to the peonies. "How can I do that when I'm consigned to the small space of a woman's life on canvases as small as my subjects? Portraits, mothers and children, gardens. Nothing beyond."

"You paint landscapes, and they can be very dramatic, as many of yours are."

It's amazing to her how blind her good friend and fellow painter is to her boundaries, both in her life and in her art. "Yes," she responds, aware that nothing she can say will help him see what's invisible to him. "Maybe I should do more of those."

ONCE BERTHE BEGINS painting at Manet's studio, her anxiety about the quality of her work ebbs. The other artists are full of compliments and thoughtful critiques, and working with them to move beyond classical representation into the immediacy of the captured moment is invigorating. Although watching them paint racetracks and backstages and parties, where men and women enjoy themselves, chafes.

She's working on a domestic scene, a young woman reading by a window opening onto a garden. Berthe's rebellion is in her use of bold, swirling brushstrokes to suggest the tumultuous wind throwing the flowers and leaves outside into motion. As well as the tumult within the girl. No acquiescent female here. She's trying to create tension between her subject's posture and her facial expression, indicating that, along with the furious movement of the garden, she isn't as demure as she may appear to be. The other artists, especially Manet, praise her for turning what might have been an unremarkable portrait into a moody drama. She still misses Edma, but not as desperately.

Cornélie has become so comfortable in the studio that sometimes she and Antoinette take a walk outside, leaving Berthe alone with the men. They're never gone long, but Berthe treasures every second of freedom from their watchful gazes. And Manet takes advantage of their absences to stand by her, bending in toward her easel, often touching his shoulder to hers.

Today, when the mothers go out for a stroll, Manet steps up and points the back of his brush at the light blues and sweeping greens that give dimension to the receding garden. "How you capture the play of light and shadow here is inspired, how it prances from one plane to another." He edges closer and whispers, "You must show me how to do this, my melancholy beauty."

Manet's lips are close to her ear, his breath warm on her neck. She closes her eyes and takes in the intoxicating scent of him. When he steps away and she opens her eyes, Degas is watching her with his signature smirk.

SEVEN

1869

Cornélie's Tuesday soiree is in full swing, and conversation explodes throughout the drawing room. How to respond to Emperor Napoleon III's refusal to consider the republican demands for more democracy? Are Emile Zola's novels, portraying the harsh social conditions of the poor, appropriate to be read and discussed in polite society? What to do about the increasing crime in Paris? And then, as always, the Salon. Everyone has an opinion on everything. From the noise level, it appears to Berthe that most of these views are in opposition to each other.

Manet crosses the room to her. "I have a proposition for you," he says without prelude.

Berthe, as always, is startled at the power of his presence, by the way the heat of his body heats her own. A proposition? "This sounds dangerous." She strains to keep her voice even.

"Only a little." His smile is wide, irresistible. "I have an idea for a painting. A balcony with three people standing and one sitting in the sunshine, a dim, recessed background behind them. A genre painting, like Goya's *Majas on a Balcony* or Whistler's *Symphony in White*, but this one will be mine, of our time, of our style, the present moment. Two men, two women, the seated women deep and wistful, mysterious. What do you think?"

This can't be categorized as a proposition, or not the sort Berthe imagined, and she's first disappointed and then reassured. "It's all in the execution, as you well know."

"I saw the balcony scene on holiday and immediately envisaged the completed painting."

Berthe touches his shoulder, her fingers lingering on the sleeve of his jacket. "This has happened to me too. Not often, but when it does, isn't it magical?"

Their eyes connect for longer than her mother would consider appropriate, and he says, "We have much in common. As we spend more time together, which I truly hope we will do, I suspect we'll discover these commonalities will only expand."

An inexplicable but pleasurable warmth spreads outward from the center of her body. She moves a tad away from him, smooths her skirt.

"I'm planning to ask the painter Antoine Guillemet to be one of the male figures, and my godson Léon to be the other," he tells her.

Berthe nods. Guillemet has a distinguished bearing, and Léon is one of Édouard's regular models. "Who are the women?"

"I believe you have met Fanny Claus, the violinist at the Saint Cecilia Quartet. The young woman with the extremely round face?" His eyes twinkle mischievously. "A striking contrast to your own."

Confused, Berthe asks, "To mine?" But as soon as the words leave her lips, she understands where this conversation has been heading all along. Since the afternoon they were painting on the riverbank.

Manet bows. "Would you do me the honor of posing for me? It was you I saw sitting at the front of the composition, leaning against the edge of the balcony and pensively observing the street below."

As nice as it would be to watch him work, to be with him for the many sittings necessary, she must refuse. For unless it were for a privately commissioned portrait, it is unacceptable for her to be an artist's model. "You know as well as I do that my mother will never allow it."

"Because of Victorine? *Luncheon on the Grass*? All of that is in the past, and, of course, you would be fully clothed. And I daresay your mother seems quite comfortable, even happy, in her role as chaperone."

"This is an entirely different situation. I wouldn't be in your studio as a painter or as part of a group of artists working together." Almost all Parisian models are of lower social standing, many toiling as washerwomen or prostitutes, and the supposition that they are also the artists' mistresses would raise questions of her virtue. Something with which Cornélie is acutely concerned, and she supposes she is too.

"Perhaps I can approach my mother, who, if she's willing, can approach your mother . . ."

Berthe is frustrated by his obliviousness, his inability to see the world from eyes other than his own. Just like his friend Degas. "I very much doubt this will be successful."

"You may be correct, but I am going to try anyway."

A WEEK LATER, Berthe stands in Manet's studio along with Guillemet, Fanny, and Léon, ready to pose for *The Balcony*. The two mothers are perched in their customary seats. Berthe isn't privy to the details surrounding this feat, but charming men do have a way of getting what they desire. Which, if she's wise, she will remember in her future dealings with Édouard Manet.

He mutters to himself while fussing with their arrangement, a pencil behind his ear, then positions a chair in front of one of the few darkened areas of the room and orders Berthe to sit. "Not like that," he says. "Turn to your right." When she does, he frowns at her as if she's an exasperating child. "Your upper body to the right, not the rest of you!"

Berthe throws a glance at the older women, hoping Cornélie or Antoinette will tell him to mind his manners. But they are engrossed in their conversation, and neither is aware of anything else. There will be no help coming from that quarter. Berthe had hoped modeling for Manet would be an opportunity for them to get to know each other better, but if he's going to be this high and mighty, concerned with nothing beyond himself and his painting, she wonders if this whole adventure is a mistake.

He starts barking at Fanny. "Stand to her left, arms down at your sides." He grabs an umbrella from a corner and thrusts it at her. "Hold this. No, not that way, like you would hold a baby. Arms crossed over your chest." Fanny doesn't appear any happier with Édouard's behavior than Berthe is.

He treats Guillemet just as poorly, commanding him to one side of Fanny, then to the other, closer to Berthe, then farther away. Manet positions Léon behind all of them, almost completely obscured. Then he glares at the tableau, rearranges them, puts them back the way they were. "Where's the damn dog?" he bellows to no one.

Antoinette snaps her head around. "Édouard!" she cries. "There are ladies present, including your mother. Your language is disgraceful. You bring shame to me and your family."

His shoulders droop under his mother's rebuke. "Sorry, Maman," he says sheepishly.

Berthe is amused by this show of filial contrition, and sees that Cornélie is also. Her mother, who has clearly sensed Berthe's interest in Manet, is more aware of what's happening in the studio than she appears to be. Another thing Berthe would be wise to remember.

Manet glances at the others, bows slightly. "Apologies, Madame Morisot, Berthe, Fanny. I meant no disrespect." He picks up the dog, who was sleeping under a table to his left, and places her at Berthe's feet.

He drops a blank canvas on his easel and resettles the group a few more times but speaks in a more modulated voice. At one point, he places an empty easel facing backward in front of Berthe. "This will stand in for the balcony's upper railing," he explains. "Rest your right arm on the canvas ledge here, as if it were the horizontal bar on the top." Still an order, but in a less insufferable tone. Then he leans down and whispers in her ear, "Mothers. Damned if you do, damned if you don't."

She's amazed he would curse in front of her again, which is highly provocative, even disrespectful. And yet she feels included in his joke, a joke he would normally only share with another man, a confession of his feigned act of repentance.

Two hours later, Manet is growing more and more unhappy and marches them all out of the studio and over to his mother's house to attempt a more realistic composition on her balcony. After more hours of posing them in the spitting rain and chilly air, he returns from the street soaked through but seemingly satisfied with his efforts. No one else is, though. He's reverted to his earlier high-handedness, and Berthe grumbles about this with the others when he allows them back into the house at last.

Guillemet is particularly irate. "I am a painter, and I would never treat my models in this manner. I will speak to him about this, and if he's not willing to listen, he will have to find someone to replace me."

Léon is less strident, but also annoyed. "This is his way when he's painting, but I don't think he means to be insulting. I would speak to Suzanne, but my sister has little sway with him. Perhaps after you talk to him, Monsieur Guillemet, I can add a word of my own."

"I will tell him my mind," Berthe adds. "This is reprehensible behavior, and I will not stand for it either. If he isn't willing to change his ways, I suggest we all mutiny."

Fanny says nothing, not even goodbye. She just puts on her coat and slips out the door. The three of them stare after her.

THE NEXT TIME Manet gathers them at his studio, he's in one of his expansive moods, exuberantly circling the large rooms, throwing his arms in the air and singing his favorite song from the operetta *La Belle Hélène*, "Au Mont Ida," in his off-key baritone. He stops at his canvas and cries, "This painting is going to be a masterpiece! I know it. I can feel it!"

Berthe clears her throat, struggling not to succumb to his infectious enthusiasm. "We have something to discuss with you," she says, as they had agreed she would, based on Guillemet's certainty that she's the one who has the best chance of influencing him.

"Of course, my dark-haired beauty." He bows deeply, oblivious to the coldness emanating from the models. "Discuss away."

"This is serious," she continues. "If you don't hear us out, your masterpiece will never come to fruition."

He scans the four somber faces. "Why would that be?"

"Because none of us is willing to pose for this painting unless you treat us with more respect."

"We are not your usual models," Guillemet declares. "We are fellow artists, and each of us is doing this as a favor to you, as your friend, not as a hired worker."

Manet looks to Léon, who is his wife's younger brother. The boy lives with the Manets and has since their marriage. "I agree," Léon says simply.

For once, Fanny opens her mouth. "As do I."

To Manet's credit, he listens carefully, acknowledges their complaints as legitimate, apologizes, and promises to do better. Everyone is gratified, although Berthe, remembering his sham remorse for his bad language, is skeptical.

But Manet is good to his word. He is not just civil. He's polite and courteous, encouraging them to take breaks, asking about their comfort during the tedious sittings. As is the case when Cornélie and Antoinette chaperone Berthe when she works in his studio, the mothers come and go throughout the sessions, growing laxer as time passes. Although it's difficult to hold a pose for hours on end, Berthe is enthralled by watching him paint, and this, at least for her, makes it more bearable.

She's painted alongside him before, but she's never had the opportunity to observe him this closely. His energy, his passion, and his powers of concentration defy comparison. As a student, as a copyist at the Louvre, and as a painter, Berthe has been in the company of many artists while they work, and she has never seen anyone attack a canvas as Manet does. At times, his expression is wild, bordering on madness. His eyes blaze with an intensity that seems capable of igniting his canvas into flames.

She begins to notice that these eyes are on her far more than on the others. She is the main figure in the composition, but it's more than that. He's not just painting what she looks like from the outside, but unpeeling her soul. Which is disconcerting and, admittedly, exhilarating, as if she's teetering on the edge of an abyss. She writes about this to Edma, who warns her that men like Manet are not to be trusted, that Berthe is naïve about their motivations and doings.

After a series of sessions, Manet begins to focus on each individual sitter and asks them to come to the studio separately. The process is taking forever, and Berthe wonders if Manet's spontaneity is acting against him, if he's reworking images that with more care, he would have already finished. Even the mothers are fidgety, and there have been a number of days when Antoinette doesn't appear at all, increasing Cornélie's boredom and impatience with the process. Which is how Berthe ends up alone with Édouard one afternoon.

She's seated in her usual place, wearing the silk organza gown he's chosen and holding a fan, one arm resting on the ledge of the easel. The Manets' dog, Tama, runs excitedly in circles around the bottom of her billowing white dress. Her mother is home overseeing the preparations for her soiree that evening, and Antoinette had a luncheon to attend. Berthe feels his eyes burning through her and tries to maintain her position, gazing down at the street scene below her. But this is impossible, and she looks up.

Édouard puts down his brush, wipes his hands with a rag, and comes to her. "Berthe," he says, taking her hand and pressing it between both of his own. "You cannot imagine the power you hold over me." He pulls her to a stand. "You are in need of a break. Come sit with me on the sofa."

In a daze, she looks into his handsome face, at his full lips, and although she has never kissed a man before, a true kiss, that is all she now wants to do. But this is wrong, dangerous, the end of everything her mother hopes for her. Still, she allows him to lead her behind the curtain to the red sofa in the alcove.

He releases her hand when they sit. "What are we to do, my dearest one?"

She shakes her head, unable to think or even breathe.

He runs a finger along her collarbone. "My impossible love."

It's as if every part of her is liquefying under his touch. She's flowing toward him, unable to resist him, unwilling to resist him. She raises her chin. He wraps her in his arms and kisses her. It is unlike anything she has experienced before, falling into the wetness, the sweetness. Into a velvety chasm and never wanting to climb out.

Then he pulls away abruptly and stands. "I want you more than I have ever wanted any woman," he says, his voice catching. "But I cannot have you now. I need to think about what may happen, how it might affect you. We both need to think."

Berthe stands too. "I, I, yes," she stutters, her breath coming quickly. "You are right. I must think too." She grabs her cloak and rushes out into the cold afternoon, where Rémy is waiting to take her home.

That evening, she writes to Edma: *I do not know who I am. I do not know what I do. I believe I am drowning.*

PART THREE

Tamara, the present

EIGHT

My love affair with *Party* is becoming more consuming. Calliope sucks up most of my daylight hours, and the only time I can find to be with the object of my affection is when I'm usually in bed. To push the analogy further than it should be pushed, it's similar to the way you're always exhausted during the early days of a relationship because you're having lots of sex instead of sleeping.

Obviously, I'm not actually fantasizing about having sex with a painting—particularly one that represents my family to me, which, I suppose, would be incest—but the desire to be near it feels comparable. I don't get it, but I'm learning to live with it, to embrace it, even. Again, I'm not hugging the painting, but I do admit to lightly touching some of the thicker brushstrokes, feeling the sensual rise and fall of the oil ridges. I'm sure this is yet another thing that Jonathan Stein would suggest I not do.

It's the middle of a workday, and I shouldn't take a break, but I pull up the Museum of Fine Arts' website anyway. The museum is less than a mile down Huntington Ave from the office, and I search for Édouard Manet. They have eight of his paintings, and I need to see them. If I'm having a love affair, will this be like cheating on *Party*?

Okay, I'll stop.

When I tell Alexander I'll be back in an hour, he gives me a surprised look—I hardly ever leave the office except for appointments on my calendar, which he has access to. Then he nods, no questions asked. I slip on my sneakers and head to the museum. I'm embarrassed to say that in all the years I've lived in Boston, I've only been to the MFA a smattering of times. Mostly for fancy benefit dinners or for impressing a visiting scientist or regulator, not for appreciating the artwork.

I pause when I reach the edge of the semicircular drive in front of the main entrance. The building is made of white granite, grand and imposing, intimidating—or at least it is to me. A portico five stories tall, lined with Ionic columns, flanks a wide set of steps. Wings flare off both sides, each with dozens of towering, mullioned windows two or three times the size of a person, topped by carved lintels. I think the style is called neoclassical.

I pay my admission and go to the information desk. "Can you please tell me where I can find these paintings by Édouard Manet?" I hand the young man with dreadlocks a list of the eight titles.

He checks his computer. "We do have all of these paintings in the collection, but only four of them are on display today."

"But they're by Édouard Manet," I say, put off that the museum would keep my famous uncle's works out of view. "Why wouldn't all of them be on display?"

"I know," he says. "It would seem that way, wouldn't it? But the museum has so many major pieces that we need to rotate them. Not enough wall space." He takes a map from the top of the pile next to him, circles the galleries where I can find the four.

I thank him and, far more disappointed than I should be, walk to the closest one, *Execution of the Emperor Maximilian*. My disappointment intensifies when I see it. It doesn't look like *Party* at all. It's dark, kind of horrific, most of the faces and bodies obscured by gun smoke. I'd taken a quick look at the renditions on the website but not that closely. This is realistic and detailed, not what I expected.

I glance at my watch and hurry to *Monk in Prayer*. It's creepy, also starkly real, with none of the freshness of my painting's dappled light. The monk is wearing a dark-brown robe against a dark-green background, and the little light there is falls partially on his homely face and outstretched hands, but mostly on a gruesome skull on the ground in front of him. I'm amazed that the man who created *Party on the Seine* also created this. But an artist as talented and skilled as Édouard Manet must have dabbled in all sorts of styles over his lifetime, and these are most likely early works. When I check my phone, I see I'm right.

The next two canvases are more reminiscent of *Party*, and I find myself strangely relieved. *The Guitar Player* depicts a handsome woman in a billowing white dress, the skirt almost alive as it streams from her body. Can a dress stream? Under Manet's hand it does. The model is holding a guitar that's dark against the dress's whiteness, but its colors are so rich and deep and sensuous that it seems alive too. *Street Singer* is another portrait of a woman, a hand covering her mouth as she looks steadily out on the world. Both are more detailed and realistic than *Party*, but I can see the connections.

The two portraits are compelling, the women unique and strongly rendered, but somehow the paintings don't pull me in like *Party* does. Nor do they draw my intense curiosity over the brushstrokes or the subjects' personalities. *Party* should be relieved that, fickle as I sometimes can be, my ardor is not about to wander off to any of these four.

Sorry. Now I really will cut it out.

ON MY WAY home from work, on impulse I stop at a store that sells art materials and buy a drawing pad and a package of colored pencils. I played around with art in high school, and I've always been able to draw a reasonable facsimile of what's in front of me, but I'm certainly not an artist. Even though a number of my art teachers were encouraging, math and all that STEM stuff was more to my liking, along with a lot of partying. But now that my interest has been piqued—not to mention that I'm related to the great Manet, even if far removed—it seems like I should give it another try.

Then I duck into the pot shop on Columbus and grab a container of Wana mango sativa gummies, my favorites. What better way to incentivize my DNA than by adding some cannabis into the mix? And what better way to get to know *Party* then to get stoned and sketch it?

It's after ten when I'm able to clear my desk and settle on the couch with my pad and pencils. I open the box, inspect the colorful array neatly nestled within, then flip to the first page. *Party* is across from me, its complexity overwhelming. The blank sheet on my lap taunts me. I can't draw this. What was I thinking? Pure hubris. Blasphemy, even. And yet I want the connection, to the painting, to my family. I'll start with a small piece of it. Maybe just one person.

While most of the people in the painting are interacting with others—it is a party, after all—there are a few standing alone. The woman leaning against the railing catches my eye again. Although she's gazing moodily at the unseen bank on the other side of the river, she's also looking right at me, like in Manet's other portraits. She's beautiful, much more so than the models for *The Guitar Player* and *Street Singer.* Curling tendrils of black hair frame her face and brow. Her equally dark eyes are large and penetrating. *Go ahead,* she seems to be telling me. *What the hell do you have to lose?* Although I'm pretty sure no woman of her day would phrase her encouragement in that way.

My first attempt isn't good, but it's better than I thought it would be—admittedly, a low bar. Her facial features are all wrong, not even close, but I did an adequate job capturing the slope of her shoulders and the curve of her arms resting on the rail. I try to replicate the flow of her skirt. A complete failure, but I'm thinking I can do better.

I check my phone. It's almost three in the morning. I put my pencil down and realize I forgot to take the gummy. Which gives me even more hope for my next attempt.

But when I climb into bed, I can't fall asleep. I keep seeing the woman, the way her eyes locked onto mine, the sense of familiarity hovering around her, my desire to know more about her. This appears to be *Party*'s superpower, a scene filled with people who are complex individuals rather than mannequins holding a position in the composition. Full of light and questions.

As I start to drift off, I have a shadowy recollection, a fleeting certainty that I've seen the black-haired woman before. I try to push this away, to fall into sleep, but it nags at me, pushes back. Defeated, I stare at the ceiling, try to catch the memory, and then I remember. Or think I remember. Her face. It was on a computer screen. Was she a model for another of Manet's paintings? Or did I see her during my initial searches about my family? But there weren't any faces in that search. My relatives were all unknowns. Except for Great-Great-Great-Great-Grandmother Berthe. It might have been on her Wikipedia page.

I need to sleep, but I take my cellphone off the night table, aware its light will be yet another impediment. I search "Berthe Morisot." There she is, the woman at the railing, my grandmother times four. I'm going to be a zombie at the office tomorrow.

I MANAGE TO get through the day without any major errors, extricate myself at seven, and race home to be with *Party*. To hang with my grandmother times four. As soon as I walk in the door, our eyes engage, a connection I feel in my stomach. Not only was this painted by my own great-great-great-great-great-uncle, but it includes the figure of my own great-great-great-great-grandmother. Wow. Not a particularly sophisticated response to an artistic masterpiece, but there it is.

All these prefixes are growing cumbersome and unwieldy, so I'm going to drop all the greats and just think of them as Édouard and Berthe. I see now that although there are many others on the boat, Berthe is the central figure. Not necessarily larger, but she's the only one whose gaze is focused unswervingly on the viewer. Subtle but commanding. I get out my pencils and turn to a new sheet on the pad. I'm going to try to capture those eyes.

I have to keep removing and then putting my glasses back on, which is a pain. I need them to clearly see the painting, but they're too strong for the close work of drawing. After almost a dozen attempts scattered over the page, I have to admit defeat—and I can't blame my poor vision. Drawing eyes is too advanced for someone with my limited skills. I have a little better luck with the skirt, improving on what I did yesterday, but not much.

Many of his strokes are unfinished, suggesting rather than specifying, bringing the observer, me, into the painting as I mentally fill in the gaps. And somehow, what's left out makes it all that much richer, more real, more like the way it would be if I were actually standing on the boat instead of looking in from the outside. If that makes any sense, which I'm not sure it does.

I pop one of my mango gummies, make a quick omelet, scarf it down, and return to the couch. I punch a pillow behind my back, pull the wool coverlet over my shoulders, and settle in. The sketch pad and pencils are next to me, but instead of picking them up, my mind wanders through the painting. I see myself raising a glass from the cluttered table, eating a grape, eavesdropping on the conversations.

It seems the woman with the two suitors prefers the one leaning in, and the two men with their heads pressed together are brothers. Could they be Édouard and Gène, my great-great-great-great-grandfather? There's a young girl with a big red bow in her hair. Aimée? I can almost taste the colors, smell the breeze off the river, and I drop into it.

When I come back to myself, Berthe is looking at me strangely. I know that sounds bizarre, but that's what it seems like. She's still staring out of the frame as she was before, but now her eyes, which held such a confusing mix of melancholy and defiance, are almost smiling. At me. Maybe in a loving, grandmotherly way? I shake my head, take my glasses off, wipe them on my shirt, and then return them to my nose.

Her head is now cocked to the left, where before I could have sworn it sat tall on her long neck. And then she winks at me. Okay, right. She didn't wink at me. The THC content in gummies can fluctuate from batch to batch, and clearly this is a hell of a potent one. It's only ten o'clock, but I leave my materials in the living room and, for once, go to bed early. Even more than I need the rest, I want sleep to wash me free of the fright intertwined with exhilaration.

THE NEXT MORNING, I feel much better. Both well rested and convinced that whatever I thought I saw last night, I hadn't. As if a woman on a canvas painted almost 150 years ago could have winked at me. I check the strength of the gummies. The label claims each contains five milligrams of THC, the usual dose. Still, it's not an exact science.

In the late afternoon, Alexander comes into my office and hands me a certified letter. My first thought is that it's from the FDA and, from its slimness, not good. But the letter has nothing to do with Calliope. The return address is the Édouard Manet Foundation in Paris.

It's from Damien Manet, the director of the foundation, presumably a distant cousin of mine, which electrifies me—until I read his words. He informs me that his duties include compiling and overseeing Manet's catalogue raisonné, the official listing of the artist's work. This involves not only obtaining the description and authentication of each piece, but also ascertaining its current location.

He was notified that the Claims Conference had determined I was the owner of *Party on the Seine*, and he's writing to apprise me that this is an error. That as a direct descendant of Édouard, he's the rightful heir. That I'm only from a side branch of the family—which I guess is true—and that all of Édouard's works were left to his son, Léon, Damien's great-great-great-grandfather. He demands that *Party* be sent to him immediately and offers, oh so graciously, to arrange for the foundation to pack up the painting and transport it to Paris at its own expense. Shit.

NINE

I immediately phone Jonathan Stein. "What do you think this guy is up to?" I ask after reading him Damien Manet's letter.

"Hard to tell," he says cautiously. "*Party on the Seine* was traced back to the Bernheims through Nazi documents—and we all know how good they were at recordkeeping, so we can count on that connection. But like I told you before, our mission has nothing to do with how the Bernheims might have acquired it—or even whether it's an authentic Manet. We go from point A to point B: finding who it was stolen from and then returning it to the heirs. But if you want, I'll take a look at our archives to see if there's anything there. Which is probably unlikely."

"*Party* might not be mine?" Tears sting the backs of my eyes. Am I going to cry? I never cry. No crying in biotech.

"Do you always jump to the worst possible conclusion?"

This seems to me to be an overly familiar question to ask a virtual stranger, even if it is spot-on. "No," I respond. "I consider myself to be a generally optimistic person."

He laughs. "Okay, if you say so."

"Please let me know as soon as you find anything." I'm still riled at his question, although I suppose I don't have any right to be. He's offered to do me a favor, which he didn't have to do, and I'm giving him grief for it. "I appreciate this," I add. "Thanks."

HE CALLS BACK a few hours later. "I've got good news and bad news. Normally, I'd ask which one a person wants to hear first, but as I'm talking to you, I'll go straight to the bad."

"I want the good news first."

"Of course you do," he says with a poorly restrained chuckle.

I'm self-aware enough to laugh at my mulishness. "You've made your point. Now tell me."

"Good or bad?"

"Jonathan . . ."

"All good on our end. The evidence the Conference used to establish the Bernheims owned *Party* is fully documented."

"And my connection to the Bernheims?"

"Also well-documented. Let me pull up the paperwork." A pause. "Colette, Samuel, and Genevieve's immigration papers. American birth certificates for your grandmother Josephine, your mother, Nicole, not to mention your own."

"And now I can tell good ol' long-lost cousin Damien—along with the whole Édouard Manet Foundation—to shove it?" So there, Jonathan Stein, see how positive I can be? Although I suppose a true optimist wouldn't have posed this as a question.

"Maybe, maybe not."

"I'm not going to ask you for the bad news."

"It's the other side of the equation. The painting's provenance between Manet and the Bernheims."

I take this in. "So while there's proof the Nazis stole *Party* from the Bernheims and that I'm their heir, there isn't anything establishing how it came to belong to them?"

"That about sums it up. But it doesn't necessarily mean the painting wasn't theirs. It's just that you're going to have to verify that yourself."

Terrific. I have no time to do any such thing—and even less expertise. I stare through the window, at the dusky shadows snuffing out the last of the day's sunlight. "Would you, or someone at the Conference, be willing to send verification of what you discovered to Damien and the foundation? Maybe that would be enough to get them to back off?" Yet another question mark that points to my cynicism. Now that I think about it, another thing Jonathan accused me of.

"We can do that. No problem. I'll make sure it gets written up—full of official-sounding legalese—and send it over to you sometime tomorrow."

"Thank you," I say, this time with genuine gratitude. "Above and beyond. Really, really good of you to help."

"You're welcome. Let me know if it works—or if you need anything else."

From: Tamara Rubin
To: Damien Manet, Director of the Edouard Manet Foundation
Cc: Jonathan Stein, Counsel to the Conference on Jewish Claims Against Germany
Re: Party on the Seine
Date: 10/29

Please find attached an affidavit provided by the Conference on Jewish Claims Against Germany attesting to my ownership of Edouard Manet's *Party on the Seine.* As you can see, it verifies that the painting was stolen during World War II from my great-great-grandparents, Samuel and Colette Bernheim, and that I am their only heir. Therefore I'm going to have to turn down your kind offer to pack and transport *Party* to Paris.

From: Damien Manet, Director of the Édouard Manet Foundation
To: Tamara Rubin
Cc: Jonathan Stein, Counsel to the Conference on Jewish Claims Against Germany
Re: Party on the Seine
Date: 30 October

We regret to inform you that although *Party on the Seine* may have indeed been stolen from the Bernheims, this does not verify that they were the lawful owners of the painting. As discussed earlier, according to Édouard Manet's will, he left his entire oeuvre to his son, Léon Manet, my great-great-great-grandfather, and there is no codicil indicating an exception to this bequest. Therefore, our transporters will arrive at 245 Tremont Street, #9C, Boston, Massachusetts, on 8 November at 10:00 a.m. to retrieve our property. If you persist in your claim of ownership, the Édouard Manet Foundation will be forced to litigate for its return.

From: Tamara Rubin
To: Damien Manet, Director of the Edouard Manet Foundation
Cc: Jonathan Stein, Counsel to the Conference on Jewish Claims Against Germany

Re: Party on the Seine
Date: 10/30

And I regret to inform you that your transporters will not be allowed access to the building on that day or any other.

From: Damien Manet, Director of the Édouard Manet Foundation
To: Tamara Rubin
Cc: Jonathan Stein, Counsel to the Conference on Jewish Claims Against Germany
Re: Party on the Seine
Date: 5 November

The New York office of the Édouard Manet Foundation, 37 Gansevoort Street, Suite 708, New York, NY, has filed a plaintiff complaint against Tamara Rubin, 245 Tremont Street, #9C, Boston, MA, in the US District Court for the Southern District of New York, for illegal possession of property owned by the Manet Foundation, *Party on the Seine* by Édouard Manet. A copy of the complaint will be served within the next forty-eight hours detailing the specifics of the lawsuit. We request contact information for your attorney.

WRONG, COUSIN DAMIEN. It isn't your property. It's mine. And there's nothing illegal about it. I'm not about to give up *Party* without a battle—a big, bad brawling one if necessary, one I intend to win. I check my family tree. Great-Great-Grandmother Colette must have inherited the painting from her mother, Great-Great-Great-Grandmother Aimée, Berthe and Gène Manet's daughter. And there are lots of ways it could be legally hers.

For example, off the top of my head, Édouard might have given *Party on the Seine* to his brother Gène, as a gift—or even to his sister-in-law Berthe, as she's the central figure in the composition. If this was the case, it would have been passed down to Aimée, whose parents both died young, and therefore wouldn't have belonged to Édouard when he died. Hence, it wasn't inherited by Léon. Or Damien. And that's only one of the many possibilities I haven't had a chance to think up yet.

True or false, I need an attorney. My friend Holly is a lawyer, and I send her the email thread. "Interesting," she says when I talk to her later. "Too bad they didn't bring the suit in France. That would have held it up for years, and you could've kept the painting during that time—which I suppose is why they filed from their New York office."

"Do you think they have a case?"

"It depends how strong your proof is."

"What I've got only goes halfway back."

"Halfway back to where?"

I explain the situation in detail, the major holes in the verification of my ownership. Then I offer her my gave-it-to-his-brother theory.

"It sounds like you don't just need a lawyer. You also need a private investigator."

"Are there people who do both?"

"No one in my firm does anything like that, but there are some that hire PI agencies—even a few that have someone in-house. The ones that handle mostly defense work."

"Can you recommend someone who's local?"

"Let me think . . ." I hear the sound of a clicking keyboard. "Yeah, here he is. I met him at a party a couple of months ago, and the host told me he's one to watch—smart, ambitious, a drive to win. And I've got to tell you, he's got these Hollywood good looks, but he's way too young for either of us. Which is unfortunate."

"Is this going to cost me big bucks?"

"Probably. He's at Beacon, Exeter."

"Ouch. What's his name?"

"Wyatt Butler."

I hang up with Holly and set up an initial consultation with Wyatt Butler for next week, even though I can't afford to hire him. But if he can help me prove *Party* is mine, then I'll have more than enough to pay his bill. Maybe finally buy my own place. I've never mentioned that my life has had many ups and downs—and that I've managed to surf the crests and dips while remaining vertical, if, every now and then, shakily. So I've got seasoned legs to carry me through this. Sort of.

I won't bother to go into all the gory details, so this list will have to suffice. Early death of my father. Multiple colleges. Multiple gap years. Successful marketing/development career. Unsuccessful marketing/development career.

Harvard Business School. Happy marriage. Death of my mother. Unhappy divorce and financial disaster. Burgeoning biotech career. Downgraded biotech career. The mind-blowing gift of a Manet masterpiece.

Not smooth riding by any means, but despite a few bruises here and there, I'm still standing. And I'll remain vertical this time too. Damien Manet clearly underestimates me, and that's going to be my most powerful weapon.

WHEN I GET home, I'm hit by one of my ocular migraines. It's not a typical migraine, because I don't get a headache, and I've been having them since I was a kid. Apparently, they ran in my father's family. I sit on the living room couch and close my eyes as flickering lights and colorful zigzagging lines play against my lids. When I open them, I can barely see *Party*, which is obscured by the same lights and lines, along with a wavelike morphing that makes the river appear to be moving. I'm less concerned than I am annoyed. I stagger into the kitchen and take two Tylenol, which I know will eradicate the aura—but will take at least an hour to do.

As my vision clears, I am, as always, exhausted, and I once again abandon the texts and emails and piles of paperwork calling to me from my study and remain on the couch to hang out with *Party*. I put on my glasses, open my sketch pad, and, taking my glasses off again, start with the bunting that edges the roof of the partially enclosed boat. Blue, white, and red fabric fluttering in the breeze, the colors of the French flag. Because this is much less complicated than drawing people, I quickly lose interest and turn my attention to Berthe.

That stunning and unfathomable face, her startling white skin in contrast to the burning black eyes staring directly into mine, so expressive, but mysteriously so. There seems to be sadness hovering, a longing, but also a sense of defiance, maybe even of triumph. Perhaps coupled with a veneer of fear? She's thin, almost waiflike, while exuding a strength incongruous with her small frame. I rough out the strong chin, slightly raised, move on to her high cheekbones, but I struggle with the lustrous milkiness of her face. The chin isn't bad, but the skin is all off.

This is clearly far above my pay grade. But then I remember one of my art teachers saying that in order to render white, you need to search for the surprising tints that radiate from it, including the reflections of the neighboring colors falling on it. There's pink, a touch of yellow, and maybe even some green from the passing trees hiding within Édouard's brushstrokes. I try to emulate this. No such luck.

Disgusted with my attempts, I glance back up at Berthe, and the pencil falls from my grasp. I look again, put on my glasses, take them off, put them back on, look once more. Berthe's left arm, instead of resting on the railing where it's always been, is reaching down toward the water.

Did I take a gummy and forget about it?

No gummy. It must have been a shift in the light. Maybe a flash of headlights or the blue strobe of a police car.

I grab my phone and take a photo, and when I check it, my panic begins to subside. Berthe is standing as she always was, just as Édouard painted her. I murmur, "Thank you"—to whom I have no idea. But when I raise my eyes to *Party*, Berthe's forefinger is still pointing emphatically to the small waves on the bottom right of the painting.

PART FOUR

Berthe, 1869–1874

TEN

1869

Berthe stretches luxuriously across her bed and presses her right palm over her heart, her left to the spot below her navel. She can't sleep, doesn't want to sleep. She only wants to relive the kiss. Again and again. The give of Édouard's lips, of her own. Drowning in the taste of him, the smell of him, the rightness of the moment, their moment. Her willing surrender into pure sensation. This must be the love the poets write about, the unimaginable perfect thing she never quite believed existed. But now that it has happened to her, she has no more doubts.

And the gallant way Édouard stopped her from falling farther. His concern for what is best for her, for both her feelings and her position in society. He may be a well-known flirt and philanderer, but his consideration for her was that of a gentleman keenly aware that she is not an off-the-street model he seeks to take as a mistress, but a woman to be treated with respect.

My dearest one. My impossible love. Whether by fate or destiny or God's hand, they are meant to be together. He doesn't love Suzanne, never touches her, barely even acknowledges her presence. How could he have said those things to her, Berthe, if he did? How could he have kissed her like that?

As Degas is always pointing out, Suzanne has no flare, is submissive and ungainly, no match for Édouard's charm and good looks, his slim waist and broad shoulders. There have always been questions about his unlikely choice of Suzanne, who was the Manet brothers' piano teacher, including Édouard's, hired by their parents to instill some musical culture in their sons, and seven years Édouard's senior. Decidedly odd. In addition, they have no children, further suggesting a loveless marriage.

Berthe finally drifts off, but when she wakes, the rapture of yesterday has turned on itself. She's filled with doubts, her mood as cloudy as the sky beyond her bedroom window. Zola once described Édouard to her as an elegant cavalier, a promiscuous adventurer, always with an eye toward his own self-interest. Could she have misinterpreted his chivalry entirely? Had Édouard ended the kiss as the first phase of a planned seduction rather than as an act of deference? Had he assumed an inexperienced woman such as herself needed a slower touch? Was this a strategic act, one he'd performed before? Perhaps many times?

But no. She saw the concern in his eyes, felt the reluctance with which he pulled away from her. Certainly, the wonder and desire on his face had been real. He experienced exactly what she experienced, felt exactly what she felt. He wanted to be with her as much as she wanted to be with him. He will divorce Suzanne, and then they will marry.

To be a wife is a circumstance Berthe has always viewed skeptically, fearing a husband would disapprove of her desire to be a professional artist, perhaps even forbid it. But her marriage to Édouard would be nothing like that. Not just their love for one another, but their shared passion for art, their respect for each other's work and ambitions. He would never do what Adolphe Pontillon has done to Edma. They will paint side by side in the same studio, helping each other grow, applauding successes and ministering sympathy when difficulties inevitably arise.

She brightens at this image, but as she unscrolls her fantasy marriage, she's confronted by the myriad difficulties standing in the way. Divorce is infrequent and highly frowned upon in their circle, and both the Morisots and Manets are Catholic, although neither family is particularly religious. There is no doubt this would create a huge scandal, the talk of every soiree and dinner party, in the seats of every theater and opera house for months, probably longer. All made worse by the false rumors the gossips would take such delight in creating and spreading.

Could the shame cause their families to disown them, to turn them out? This doesn't seem likely, given Maman and Antoinette's love for their children, but both women are overly concerned with their social status, so it is not outside the realm of possibility. But even if their families stood by them, would she and Édouard be rejected by society? Perhaps even by their fellow artists?

Not Degas and their bande, but there are many others who might not be as loyal. As a parade of disapproving artists fills her mind, she has an even more distressing thought: *The Salon.* Those old men, with their pomposity and unwavering defense of tradition, would not respond well when she and Édouard submitted their next paintings.

Berthe stares at the shifting light reflecting on the ceiling. It would be devastating for Édouard to be spurned by the Salon a second time. This would be discouraging for her also, but she's not as enamored of it as he, going as far as recently discussing with Degas and Renoir the possibility of putting on their own show. An idea Édouard ridiculed as infantile and career-ending. He might decide a divorce isn't worth the price of losing his chances at the Salon.

Above all else, Édouard yearns to be awarded the Legion of Honor medal, France's highest commendation, a distinction bestowed by the emperor for a lifetime of contributions to French society, a prize his father received. Without the Salon's backing, this will never come to be. Does he want the medal more than he wants her? He is nothing if not ambitious.

She must go to him, discover his true feelings, his intentions. But that would be presumptuous, unladylike. Berthe smiles to herself. As if her behavior yesterday was ladylike. Perhaps he will send her a note today, and if so, she will be able to respond and suggest a time to meet, with Cornélie unfortunately in attendance. If there is no word, she will find another avenue to him.

No letter arrives, but Berthe swallows her disappointment and decides to use this interval to move forward with her new painting, which will make the time pass quickly and provide an acceptable path back to Édouard's studio. The painting is of Edma and Yves, *Two Sisters on a Couch*, she's calling it, and she's found that working on it sometimes makes her less lonely for them. But just as often, as she fleshes out her sisters on the canvas, grows them into themselves, she misses them even more. She's depicted them as younger than they are now, and she wishes they all still were.

She completed the preliminary drawings at Édouard's, and the other artists were quite complimentary, but she knows it needs to be so much more. She'll spend a few days finishing the watercolor rendition and then layer on the oils. When this is complete, she'll bring it to the bande. And to Édouard.

She puts on her paint-splattered smock, walks past the dining room where her parents are having breakfast, and steps into the garden.

"Berthe, your breakfast!" Cornélie calls.

She pops her head back through the door. "I have an idea, Maman. I'll be back for lunch."

"You need sustenance, my child. Come join us."

"Lunch." Berthe waves merrily, crosses the garden, and goes into her studio. She's far from a child, her mother's or anyone else's, as she's blossomed into a full woman overnight. And doesn't it feel wonderful.

Berthe has taken advantage of the many sketches she did of her sisters in the days before Edma and Yves married and moved away, when the three of them painted and prowled the house and garden together, amusing themselves with gibes at Maman's overbearing ways and climbing trees they were not allowed to climb. If only she could talk to Edma now, confide what transpired with Édouard, share her rioting emotions and deep quandaries. But she dare not put this on paper. It is quite possible Adolphe reads Edma's letters.

In the painting, Yves and Edma are sitting together, Edma looking out, Yves glancing off to the side. But they are only inches apart, and there's a hint they're holding hands behind Yves's fan. Their dresses are elegant and fashionable, as is the hair piled atop their heads. Pretty sisters enjoying each other's company.

Berthe applies her brushstrokes loosely but carefully, striving for the pastel colors of the afternoon sun to illuminate the tenderness between them. She falls short of breathing life into them, and they sit flat and uninteresting on the canvas. She puts down her brush and palette, paces the room in frustration. How to fix this? She stands before the painting, wrestling it with her eyes, searching for the missing key.

Then she grabs the brush she dropped to the table and studies it even more deeply. Real painters only understand with a brush in their hands. It needs more atmosphere, more nuance, subtle allusions to what the girls are feeling beyond what their gestures and facial expressions portray. A lighter touch, softer edges blending their dresses into the couch, the couch into the wallpaper. She begins again.

A LITTLE OVER a week later, Rémy follows Berthe, Cornélie, and Antoinette into Édouard's studio, carrying *Two Sisters* along with Berthe's painting materials. Degas, Renoir, and Édouard are there. Berthe greets the men without making eye contact with any of them, particularly Édouard.

She tries to smooth her breathing, the slight tremble in her fingers, hopes her reddened face will be taken as the result of the heat of the fire after the cold of the outdoors. She busies herself, showing Rémy the easel where she wants the painting to rest, ensuring the mothers are comfortably seated. She's been longing for this moment and dreading it in equal measure.

Degas's eyes narrow. "Are you not well, Berthe? You seem unsteady, not your usual contained self."

"I'm perfectly fine, Edgar." She turns to him with as much of a smile as she can muster. "Thank you for inquiring."

This further arouses his suspicions. "Then why are you all aflutter? Flushed? Those fiery eyes darting everywhere and nowhere?"

Berthe looks at Renoir. "Am I all aflutter, Auguste? Or is Monsieur Degas once again making a fuss over nothing?"

"I would not take his words very seriously." Renoir grins at Degas. "The man's only pleasure is to be cantankerous."

Degas jumps to his feet and throws his arms wide. "Renoir, that is not so!" he roars. "I am a genial bear of a man, loved by many, if not all."

Everyone laughs, including the mothers, and Berthe dares a glance at Édouard. His eyes shift from Degas to her. He nods slightly, then turns back to his easel.

The day is frigid with bits of blowing snow, so Cornélie and Antoinette don't take their usual stroll. Instead, they huddle together close to the fire, drinking tea and chattering while the artists work. Berthe had feared this, given the horrid cold that has overtaken Paris, and is frustrated because Édouard has not spoken a word or moved from his spot since her arrival, apparently consumed by his painting.

Two Sisters is getting somewhat better. With the oil paint, she's loosened the girls' poses, leaning Yves slightly toward Edma. A little thing, but strangely effective in emphasizing the tenderness of their relationship. And she's made the illumination more indirect, homier, which she believes adds a sense of intimacy. Teasing the light, as M. Corot taught her, taming it to her own needs. But she worries it's too superficial, saying little about the world beyond domestic harmony. The curse of womanhood.

After working for over an hour, she stands, wraps her shawl over her shoulders, and walks around the studio, rubbing her hands together, further smearing them with paint. Antoinette's maid stopped by earlier, bringing tea and pastries, and Cornélie pours Berthe a cup and forces a piece of coconut cake on her. She eats the cake to avoid her mother's reprimands, although her stomach is jumpy with Édouard so near and reticent. Teacup in hand, she wanders over to a corner with two large windows, which Degas has permanently appropriated as his own.

He's working from a number of sketches of ballet dancers rehearsing for a performance. Even this early, she can see it will be extraordinary. Instead of a broad and majestic display of costume and choreography, each dancer's face is individually highlighted, many with expressions of fatigue and boredom. The interior reality of the ballet rather than the outward splendor the audience experiences. No superficiality here.

She stands behind Renoir, who's putting the finishing touches on a painting that also depicts the life of Parisians as it is lived. The subject is the Frog Pond, a resort on the banks of the Seine. Flecks of sun glitter on the river, flinging pinpricks of brightness across the canvas. Ordinary men and women in everyday dress cluster tightly together on a dock amidst the boats passing in the background, delighting in each other's company.

Berthe is impressed with his flowing brushwork and envious of his freedom to paint such a carefree and spontaneous scene. It isn't proper for a woman of her class to paint a man she's not related to, nor anyone outside her social circle. And therefore painting the boisterous joy of a party that includes men, and possibly women of lesser repute, is beyond her cloistered reach.

She nonchalantly makes her way to Édouard. He's completely engrossed, palette gripped in one hand, a brush in the other, a thinner brush clamped in his teeth, oblivious to her presence. She knows this state well, the complete subjugation of the outside world to the work, and she tries not to take offense. But she's close enough to feel the torridness of his frenzy, to inhale the odor of his skin mixed with oil and turpentine, and cannot help but wonder if he is as unaware of her as he appears.

Her eyes turn to his easel, and she freezes. It's a painting of Suzanne sitting at the piano in Antoinette's parlor, fingers resting on the keys, head slightly tilted as she gazes rapturously at the sheet music before her. She's elegantly dressed in a glowing black gown, her hair tied back in a chignon, a ribbon at her neck. The painting is decidedly representational, except that it does not represent Suzanne as she actually is.

Although she does play the piano, it is an idealization of her, a false rendition. In the picture, she is at least fifty pounds lighter and her features have been molded into an attractive face, which she does not possess. Could this be how Édouard sees his wife? And if this is so, then she, Berthe, has been taken for a fool.

When he finally turns toward her, she's on her way back to her easel.

"I FEAR EDGAR may have been right yesterday," Berthe tells Cornélie when she comes into her room to inquire as to why she's still in bed this late in the morning. "Maybe I have come down with something." Which she has not. She wants to hide away with her shame.

Cornélie gently sweeps falling curls from Berthe's forehead and presses her lips there. When she stands, she studies her daughter's face. "There is no fever I can sense, but you don't look well. Perhaps the long day at Édouard's studio has taken a toll on your health. I will have Marie bring you some ox-blood broth."

Berthe closes her eyes. "Thank you, Maman," she says, although she has no intention of eating that vile soup, which tastes like metal. "I think I'll rest for the remainder of the day."

"I have invited Degas for luncheon, and I do so hope you will be able to join us. I'm sure he accepted so readily because he expected to spend the time with you, not me."

Berthe reconsiders. Degas is an astute observer of human behavior, as well as a lover of gossip, and he might have insight into Édouard's painting. At the least, he'll be eager to discuss the absurdity of the depiction of Suzanne as thin and attractive. His witty take on this will hopefully prove to be a salve.

"It's possible I'll feel stronger after the broth," she says. "And if not, perhaps you will allow him upstairs to sit with me for a little while." As her mother views Degas as no threat to Berthe's virtue, due to his years as a flamboyantly single man, she assumes Cornélie will acquiesce.

Cornélie leans back over Berthe, this time to kiss her on the cheek. "I'll return to see how you are in a little while, my darling."

Berthe feels a touch of guilt for worrying her mother, who frets endlessly over her health, but the thought of Degas has perked her up. Going down for lunch will not do, given her pretend illness just two hours before it's to be served. But after disposing of the soup in the chamber pot, it might be believable that she feels well enough to dress and meet with him in the upstairs sitting room.

When Degas climbs the stairs after a quick lunch with her mother, he kisses her hand. "So you are ill, my dear Berthe," he says. Then he adds with a mischievous sparkle in his eyes, "I cannot tell you how sorry I am to hear this."

She pulls the blanket resting on the back of the chair over her shoulders. "As you so rightly noted yesterday."

"Ah, I did, did I not? Most astute of me." He sits in the chair next to hers and considers her closely. "Although I must admit I see nothing of the trembling and flushness I observed then. And your eyes are quite calm and focused."

"Oh, Edgar, please spare me your idle banter."

"It isn't idle banter, Berthe. You are swimming in dangerous waters."

It is impossible to elude his keen eye. "I have no idea what you are talking about."

He raises an eyebrow. "I don't believe that any more than I believe you are sick. As I have noted before, you are rather transparent with your emotions."

"What am I to do with you, you wicked man?"

"Listen to me. Heed my advice."

"What do you think of Édouard's painting of his lovely wife?"

"So be it," he says to make it clear that he's on to her, then bursts into an impish grin. "Can you believe? It's completely preposterous, ludicrous. I daresay even Suzanne will not be pleased, as it could be taken as an insult to be so misrepresented as a slender beauty when she's aware she is neither."

"Do you think this could be how Édouard perceives her? Not as she is, but as a slender beauty?"

Degas's eyes soften with rare compassion, and he shakes his head. "My dear Berthe, that is not the derivation of this painting."

"What do you mean?"

"As you are not privy to our more explicit conversations at Café de Bade, you have not heard of my quarrel with Édouard."

"I have seen no indication of this at the studio."

"That's because we have reconciled, but this painting of Suzanne is his parting jab at me."

Berthe throws the blanket off and leans toward him. "Parting jab?"

He stretches out in his chair. "Édouard asked me to do a portrait of the two of them, which I did, and named it, very cleverly I think, *Monsieur and Madame Édouard Manet*."

She clenches her jaw when she hears the title. If only it were a picture of Édouard and her, not Édouard and Suzanne. Fortunately, Degas is too captivated by his own story to notice her reaction.

"I thought it was a rather good composition and likeness, but when Édouard saw it, he did not agree. He accused me of making a mockery of his wife. He was so livid he took a knife and slashed Suzanne out of the canvas."

"He destroyed your painting?" she asks, astounded. It is beyond belief for one artist to deface another's work, nearly equivalent to defacing the artist himself.

"He did just that. He thought the figure of Madame Manet detracted from the effect. But I don't, and I'm going to try to paint her back in again."

"You have the pieces in your possession?"

"I had a fearful shock when I saw it like that. I picked it up and walked off, without even saying goodbye."

"Oh, Edgar, of course you did."

"I suppose I shouldn't have portrayed her that way," he says with startling candor, not one to be self-reflective, particularly in a negative way. "Manet knows Suzanne is derided for her girth and unsightliness, and although there is no love lost there, she is still his wife. Perhaps in his shoes, I might have done the same."

"You are certain there is no love lost?"

Degas takes both of her hands. "I wish I could tell you otherwise, my innocent Berthe. It would be far better for you if their marriage were a happy one. But it is not, and I fear this will be your downfall."

Rather than scaring her, which was no doubt Degas's intention, she's elated.

ELEVEN

1870

Rémy has become Berthe's abettor, driving her places Cornélie would not approve of, speaking nothing of it to anyone, not even to his daughter Marie, the Morisots' maid. Berthe tells Maman she's shopping or visiting with female friends, and Rémy whisks her wherever she wants to go, which is almost always Édouard's studio.

Rémy has been with the family since her father was a young man, and he's always doted on Berthe, slipping her candies as a child, taking her out for aimless carriage rides when she was older and didn't want to go home to her mother's intrusive meddling. He makes no judgments, just wants her to have some freedom from Cornélie. He says she needs to breathe the fresh air.

For the past two months, Édouard's moods have been akin to the tides of the ocean, swelling toward her with verve, then retreating cautiously, although without the predictable rhythm of the sea. Whether she's at his studio to pose for him or to paint with the other artists, she never knows what to expect when she walks through his door. He's fickle and thoughtless, flinging her into flights of joy or plunging her into despondency. Yet she cannot stay away from him.

Today, she has no reason to go there, as it is not a bande day, but the freezing rain and constant clouds of the past week have imprisoned her inside the house, suffocated by Cornélie. It is impossible to remain at home any longer, no matter the weather.

It's cold and gusty, but there are a few slices of sun, so Berthe bundles herself in her warmest fur coat, hat, and muff. Rémy leaves her at Édouard's, promising to return in two hours. Even with the hot water bottle Marie gave her, after riding in the frigid coach and walking from street to building with the wind searing her exposed skin, she's shivering when she gets inside.

Édouard strides forward, his arms open wide, then abruptly stops before he reaches her. His arms drop, and his eyes grow glazed, fixed on her face. "Sit down right there." He points to a worn chair that has to be one of Antoinette's castoffs. "Leave your coat on," he orders.

Berthe sits, his intense gaze warming her more rapidly than she would have thought possible a minute ago. "And what shall I do next, Your Majesty?" she asks. Édouard usually appreciates a touch of the acerbic.

But he remains frozen in place, most likely unhearing. "I must paint you just as you are."

"Now? Here?"

"Don't move." He rushes into the main studio, grabs an easel along with a blank canvas. "Keep your collar up," he says as he dashes back for his palette and paints. "Don't take off the muff."

She holds the pose. Édouard's fixated attention fills her with hope that she is as special to him as he is to her. As do his fanatical brushstrokes and the look of wonder as he begins to paint her.

"Turn your head slightly toward me."

She does as he asks.

"No, that is too much!" he cries. "Slightly, I said! Didn't you hear me? I need a partial profile. Two eyes looking directly at me. Chin a tad sideways. Just a tad! Do you not understand this?"

Berthe pulls her hands from the muff, presses her collar down, and turns her full face toward him. She says nothing.

He's perplexed for a moment, and then he begins to laugh. "Yes, my dearest, you are correct. I should not speak to you in this manner. I am truly sorry. It's just that you're so stunning today." He bows slightly. "I'm afraid I gave in to my desire to make love to you with my brush."

Make love to you with my brush. He wants to make love to her in the only way open to them for now. "And this is what I wish you to do also," she whispers.

He kneels by her chair, touches the top button of her coat. "May I?"

She nods.

He gently drops the coat from her shoulders, and it falls to the chair with a soft whoosh. Without a word, he stands and pulls her up with him.

Once again, they are kissing, but this time Berthe presses her body into his, and he pulls her even tighter, closer. His whole self against her whole self, her softness against his taut muscles. Her knees begin to wobble, and she fears her legs will collapse.

Édouard sets her against the wall to steady her. "Oh, my love," he murmurs with a soft groan. "My exquisite love."

This is what she wants. To be with him like this, to fuse with him, their two souls entwined. A hardness pushes against her dress, aligns with her lower belly, the top of her legs. And a warmth, deep and almost liquid within her, strains toward him.

Sudden terror consumes her. She knows little of lovemaking, even less about this manner of passion, but if what's happening between them is what she believes it to be, she must stop it. She pushes him away, her breath coming short and ragged, and staggers back to the chair.

He drops down next to her again, but this time he puts his head in her lap, wraps his arms around her waist. "I know, my precious one. I know."

The warmth of his cheek against her skirt makes her yearn to kiss him again, to forget all that is proper and virtuous. To allow him to take her, for her to take him. But she is her mother's daughter, raised to be a lady, and it is not possible. Slowly, she lifts his head. "I must go."

That night, she composes a letter to Edma.

My dearest sister,

I have behaved in a ruinous way. Done what I should not have done. More than once. And I tell you in the strictest confidence that I long to do it again. Please do not think badly of me, although this is what I deserve, but I must share my anguish with you. As well as my joy.

I will write to you of what has occurred, but I beg your assurance that my letter will not fall into your husband's hands. This communication must remain only between us and is to be destroyed after reading. Please send a reply posthaste.

AFTER THAT, BERTHE goes to Édouard's studio only if Cornélie is with her. This is not what she desires, nor what she supposes Édouard desires, but it's the only course open to her until they find an opportunity to discuss what must come next. The difficulty is that this conversation can only take place in a crowded spot, allowing them to speak quietly but privately amidst a noisy throng. For until he agrees to marry her, they cannot be alone. As much as she longs to be in his arms, she will not bring shame upon herself or her family.

She invites him to her mother's Tuesday soirees, but he hasn't come thus far, and although she's been attending his mother's Thursday events religiously, he hasn't been there either. She fears he's with another woman, and she's suspicious of his new protégée, Eva Gonzalez.

A few weeks ago, Maman went to Édouard's to return a book and found him there with Eva, who he introduced as his student. Cornélie was surprised, as he had never taken on a student before and always claimed he never would. When she returned home, she went directly to Berthe's studio, rushing, breathless, through the door, oblivious to the fact that she was interfering with her daughter's work.

She reported the events to Berthe in detail, describing Eva as a stunningly beautiful young woman with high spirits and impressive talent, noting that she is also the daughter of Emmanuel Gonzalez, the acclaimed novelist. "Manet seemed quite enamored of the young thing," her mother continued. "I daresay she must be at least six or seven years your junior. As I was leaving, Édouard did finally after ask after you and Edma, but he seemed more polite than interested." Then she added almost gleefully, "I fear he has all but forgotten you now that he has fallen under the blazing light of Mademoiselle Gonzalez."

Cornélie had watched her daughter carefully as she imparted this news, hoping, Berthe knew, to put a wedge between herself and Édouard. Berthe had picked up her brush, affecting disinterest, although she was seething with a jealousy so green it matched the tone she was using to depict the leaves of a tree. Who was this woman? This girl? And how had she cajoled Édouard into becoming her teacher? Berthe was not fond of the most likely answers.

At the next Tuesday soiree, Degas tells her that Édouard has begun a portrait of Eva, who he, Degas, is not particularly fond of. Unlike Cornélie, he takes no joy in this news, even though he also prefers a wedge to be solidly entrenched. "She's not as good a painter as either of them seems to believe," he says with a twitch of his nose. "In addition, she's a poor model, like a child. Unable to restrain herself from squirming and complaining, which, as you are well aware, Manet has no patience for. And from what I've seen, the work is not coming well."

This is small consolation to Berthe, who has been sulking for days. She hasn't been to Édouard's studio since hearing about Eva, fearing he will be working on the painting or, worse, that Eva might be present. Everyone there is busy with preparations for the Salon, but Berthe has decided not to enter this year. Nothing she's created in the past months is worthy of submission, and she's tired of her staid domestic scenes. The bande isn't happy with her decision, especially Édouard and Degas, who are hounding her to submit *Two Sisters on a Couch*, but she refuses. That evening, she receives a letter from Edma that further lowers her spirits.

Alas, my dearest sister, I beg you not to write to me of your concerns, as it is not safe to do so. I am not certain my mail is being read, but I fear from things Adolphe has said to me that he is privy to knowledge I have not shared with him.

And you must know there is nothing you could ever do to make me think badly of you. I reach out to you with all my sympathy and love. My greatest wish is to be your confidante, as we always have been to each other, to soothe your worries and cares. I shall do everything I can to arrange a trip to Paris, but Adolphe is not fond of travel and will surely not allow me to travel alone. Still, I am coming to you as soon as I am able.

Édouard's *The Balcony* is accepted by the Salon, three months hence, along with a number of paintings by Degas, Renoir, and Monet. Berthe is pleased for them, but she's concerned about the critics' reaction to *The Balcony*, fearing the slightly less representational style and flattened perspective will be derided as unfinished and an indication of shoddiness.

Shoddy and unfinished it decidedly is not, as she and the other models who sat for endless days know all too well. And with the exception of her own portrayal, Berthe finds it quite fine. Excellent, even. Édouard's use of color, the scattering of deep greens in the shutters, in the railing, in Fanny's umbrella, and in the ribbon around her own neck, is masterful. As is his subtle repetition of triangles, from the composition of the three front-facing figures to the angle created by the slant of the umbrella with the closed fan Berthe holds in her hands.

Cornélie's concerns are different. She's worried that, as this is the first work Manet has shown since the scandalous naked paintings of Victorine, that Berthe, the central female, will be presumed either a prostitute or his mistress, as Victorine was. Berthe has not been identified as the model, but she is a familiar figure in Paris and will surely be recognized by many. She tells her mother that few will conclude there is anything between them, especially those who know her, but she keeps to herself the fear that he has "made love to her with his brush," and that this might be discernible to an observant viewer.

Over time, she returns to Édouard's studio, finding herself unable to work without the company of others. She's begun two paintings, one a commission of a friend's son who is two years old, and although she recognizes that a child of that age cannot be expected to sit still, it's taking longer than she'd hoped to complete it. The second is a pot of colorful dahlias riotously bursting from a delicately painted porcelain vase, set against a neutral background. She's proud of the way the bright petals are accentuated by the pale wall behind them, but frets once again that her work is too simple, too "pretty," without meaning or symbolism.

Degas is adamant that this is not true. "You are very wrong. Look how nature glows under your brush. Here, the purple to green to yellow to red and blue. Astounding. I can almost smell them."

Even Édouard has kind words, which is surprising, as lately he's been praising the infernal Mlle Gonzalez for her perseverance and growing skills, while criticizing Berthe for not submitting to the Salon. "It's almost as if the leaves are waving," he says after leaning in to study the painting, his cheek inches from her own. "Your use of light to create movement where there is none is dazzling. Well beyond the efforts of those of us who struggle here."

She's thrilled with both his words and the softness in his eyes as he smiles at her. She meets them and feels her face flushing. Fighting back her feelings, she says stiffly, "Thank you very much, Édouard. I do not believe you for a moment, but I do appreciate the encouragement."

Noting the falseness in her daughter's voice and how close Édouard is to her, Cornélie throws Berthe a warning glance. "I, too, think it is coming well," she calls across the room. "Portraying nature is as important as portraying people. Maybe more so, as it is more picturesque and brings more pleasure to the heart."

THE SALON OPENS on a sunny day in May, and as masses of people ascend the staircase of the Palais de l'Industrie, it seems to Berthe as if every Parisian is in attendance, including, she has been told, the emperor himself. All the patrons are in their high finery. Men with their newly fashionable tall collars, wearing either top or bowler hats, gold watches swinging across their waists. Women in brightly colored bell-shaped spring gowns, parasols or painted fans in hand.

But Berthe, who usually has a keen eye for fashion, is more interested in finding *The Balcony* and, of course, Édouard. There are over four thousand works of art on display, with paintings filling the entirety of the walls, so tightly aligned their frames press against one another. The pieces are ordered alphabetically by artist across thirty rooms.

"Should we first find room M?" she asks Cornélie as they enter the magnificent lobby.

"Yes. That is where we shall go."

This is not an easy task. The crowds are thick, the rooms stifling and poorly lit. In addition she and Maman must greet their many friends and acquaintances, the artists, writers, poets, musicians, and the others of their circle, which makes forward motion difficult. These encounters are part of the festival atmosphere Berthe usually enjoys, but today she's impatient with the interruptions.

Finally, they make their way to room M, and to her delight Édouard is there. However, he is not himself, or, more correctly, he is himself, but even more so.

"Berthe, Berthe," he cries, taking her hands despite Cornélie's presence. "You must come see the picture. Tell me how it is. I cannot go in there. A gentleman who I don't know has made an inquiry into its price, but I have also heard many unflattering responses from others." His palms are sweaty, his eyes glazed. He drops her hands. "I think people are avoiding me. No one wants to face me in my disgrace."

"No one is avoiding you," Berthe assures him, although she suspects this might be true. "And of course I will go see it. That's why we've come."

"There's no reason to be this dismayed, my boy," Cornélie says. "I know this painting very well, and I believe it will be a huge success." Berthe is startled by her mother's comment, aware of her many apprehensions about both *The Balcony* and Édouard. But Cornélie, for all her sharpness, has a soft spot for those she believes have been mistreated.

Apropos of nothing Berthe can detect, Édouard bursts into loud laughter. "Yes, yes, Madame Morisot, you are correct. Thank you. Thank you. I have nothing to fear! It's good. More than good. Especially with your most magnificent daughter at its heart!"

At this Cornélie frowns. "I daresay."

His face falls at her comment. "It is dreadful. I know it is. I'm certain the only reason that man requested a price was to make fun of me and my painting." Then, just as unexpectedly, he swings back to optimism. "The problem is that I am before my time. Our entire bande is. We are looking forward into the future and being savaged for our impertinence. If our time is not now, it will come!"

Berthe is stirred by his turmoil, his fears of being snubbed by the critics, his desire to cover this up with boasts and false cheer, his need to be respected. Poor man. She wants to comfort him, to hold him, to tell him it all will be well. Instead, she says, "You stay here, and my mother and I will go to the painting. When we return, we'll give you our honest appraisal. Which, as we've both told you before, and despite what some of the unschooled might say, is that it is a triumph."

Seeing the clamor of emotions roiling his face, Berthe can't stop herself, and touches his upper arm. "The only thing that would make it better is if you had chosen a more attractive model."

"There is no other model more attractive than the one I chose."

Cornélie loops her arm through Berthe's and gives it a tug. "Let us go. There are many more pictures to be seen and we cannot dawdle here."

Berthe slowly approaches *The Balcony*. It's the first time she's seen it finished and framed, and she's assaulted by conflicting impressions: awe, envy, pride, and fear. Awe at the majesty of Édouard's skill, envy at the preciseness with which he captured the scene, pride that the man she loves created such a thing, and fear that the critics will be merciless to both him and to her.

"Why didn't he finish it?" someone asks behind her.

"Maybe he got tired or he's just lazy," is the response. "The better question is why the Salon accepted it."

Berthe wants to turn around and tell them they are wrong, that they are fools to say and think such things, but she does not. She remains where she is, looking up at the strange woman she knows is herself yet isn't herself. She has to admit that in contrast with Fanny, whose vacant, round face and oversized white flower of a hat make her appear more lapdog than woman, she, Berthe, is by far the more interesting. At least her expression contains some mystery, indicating some depth of character. But her face is too pale, her hair too dark, and her nose too thin.

"I am more strange than ugly," she says to Cornélie.

"Oh, dear Bijou, you are more strange than ugly if that is what you believe. Édouard has painted you as a beautiful young woman." Then she adds, "As I fear is how he views you."

Berthe swallows a sigh. Couldn't her mother have just said something nice? Or at least neutral? Why did she have to imply that Berthe isn't beautiful while also making a point of expressing her distrust of Édouard, and, by implication, of Berthe.

"The dark-haired woman is quite arresting," a man on their left declares.

"Arresting?" his companion says. "I'd call her a femme fatale. From what I've heard of these artists, most likely his mistress."

When the men turn to another picture, Berthe looks at her mother in invented distress. "Oh, Maman, how horrible," she says. But she's secretly pleased. This is how Édouard sees her. As a femme fatale.

"I fear I have a headache coming on." Cornélie points to a sofa at the end of the room, far from the painting and beyond hearing distance of the spectators. "I think I shall sit. You find someone to accompany you and wander for a while. When you're finished, come get me."

Berthe walks back to Édouard, who is now with Suzanne and Antoinette. "Tell me!" he demands of Berthe, cutting off Suzanne, who is speaking to him.

"If there is any criticism of that painting," she tells him, "it will come from those with small minds, no imagination, and a foolish attachment to the past."

Even with his wife and mother standing next to him, Édouard grabs her, lifts her off her feet, and twirls her around. "The gentleman returned and has agreed to buy it. You are my good luck charm, Berthe Morisot!" He puts her down with a flourish. "Do come with us to look at the other pictures. We were just about to go next door."

Berthe steadies herself and attempts to appear annoyed at his presumptuousness, although she's too thrilled by his abandon and the pressure of his hands on her waist to do a credible job. He must love her, or at least care about her deeply, to do such a thing in front of Suzanne. Perhaps if she strolls with them, she and Édouard will have the chance to talk amidst the commotion. It is time.

The four of them go to many rooms and view many paintings, along with statues in the glassed sculpture garden, which is full of men with cigars gawking at nude women made of stone. Berthe and Édouard chuckle over their prurient attentions, while Suzanne pretends not to notice her husband's preoccupation with Berthe. Antoinette watches them closely, although with far less displeasure than Cornélie would have in her shoes.

Hoping the two women will move on and she and Édouard can speak, she maneuvers him to a small painting of Degas's, which, despite the fact that its subject is a rather homely woman in black, is surprisingly pretty. She steps to one side and then the other, pondering how he managed such a thing. Perhaps it's the corner of the mantelpiece in half tones behind the woman or maybe the gentle swell of the cashmere shawl falling off one shoulder. Either way, it's delightful. When she turns to ask Édouard for his thoughts, he's disappeared, along with Suzanne and Antoinette.

She must have taken longer studying the painting than she thought. This is something she does often, sinking into another artist's work as she sinks into her own. They can't have gone far. She goes into the next room, but there is no sign of them there either.

It isn't acceptable for her to walk without being escorted, and she sees no one who would be suitable for this task. How could Édouard, possibly her future husband, have abandoned her this way? He, so seemingly interested in her virtue, is obviously not. She's aware he can be heedless, but this is far beyond that.

Mortified, she begins to wend her way back to Maman, smiling slightly and nodding to acquaintances as if she's unbothered by being alone. Unfortunately, she strayed far into the Palais, and her mother is on the other side of the building. Halfway there, she finds Édouard in front of one of Antoine Guillemet's entries and walks quickly to him. "You should not have left me alone in this crowd," she says in a voice louder and bolder than intended. A few people turn and look at them, their expressions full of curiosity.

Antoinette, who is across the room, marches over. "Berthe is correct," she reproaches her son. "I raised you to be a gentleman, and I'm disappointed that you weren't aware of her predicament. I assumed you had left her with a proper companion."

Édouard bows to Berthe, but his face is as stony as those of the statues in the sculpture garden. "Please accept my deepest apologies, Mademoiselle Morisot. You can count on my timeless devotion, but I nonetheless will not play the role of a child's nurse."

Berthe raises a hand to her cheek, his words like a slap in the face.

"Édouard!" Antoinette cries. "That is not a proper apology."

But before he can say anything more, Berthe has already started toward the room where her mother waits.

TWELVE

1870

Berthe's displeasure with Édouard's behavior at the Salon is overshadowed by the news that Edma will soon be arriving from Lorient, and the even better news that her sister is with child and plans to stay with them in Paris until late June or early July, when she must return home for her confinement.

Cornélie throws herself into a frenzy of activity, planning elaborate meals and excursions. She makes lengthy guest lists for Edma's homecoming party that are filled with cross-outs and new additions, some of which are later excised and then reinserted. Berthe only cares about having Edma return to her, her closest friend and confidante, her most beloved sister.

When Edma finally alights from the carriage in front of the house, she and Berthe throw themselves at each other and sob as if grieving a lost family member. "Silly you," Berthe says into Edma's hair, which smells just like Edma. Her sister is here, really here, back with her again. As it should be.

"And silly you, dearest dearest," is her sister's reply.

Maman wraps her arms around both of them. "My babies, my babies, you are still such babies. Still crying all the time." Her eyes well with tears as she says this. Then she quickly takes herself in hand and adds briskly, "Enough, enough. Let us go inside. There is no reason for everyone in the city to see your foolishness." But a smile cracks through her stern facade. "Come now." She tries to pull her daughters apart, which they reluctantly allow. But as they follow her into the house, their arms once again join, their skirts overlapping as they run up the steps.

Lunch is a boisterous and happy affair, and although they are only four, there is more food than ten people could eat, and just as much wine. Papa, who never leaves work midday, is home, his color high as he raises his glass to toast his grandchild-to-be and beams at Edma. "Santé!" he cries. It's as if the moribund house has come alive again. As if Berthe has come alive again.

The sisters aren't alone until late that evening, when they settle into the room they shared for so many years. After they slip into their nightgowns, Edma presses her hand to her barely rounded belly. "Such a peculiar thing."

"What does it feel like?"

"Not much, actually. Except for my breasts, which are sore all the time." Edma places her hands under her breasts and lifts them. "And so big!" She starts to giggle. "Remember when we put handkerchiefs into the top of our dresses to pretend we were grown women?"

They fall into their oh-so-familiar laughter, tickled by the memory, elated to be together again. "Do you think Maman will come in and tell us to be quiet and go to bed, like she used to?" Berthe asks when they calm.

"I wouldn't doubt it," Edma says dryly. "Maman is nothing if not reliably Maman."

The door bursts open, and Cornélie stands there, also in her nightclothes, arms crossed over her chest. But before she can utter a word, her daughters hoot so loud she backs up. "I do not care how old you are. You still need your sleep," she mutters irritably. "You, especially, Edma. The baby's health must be foremost in your mind at all times."

Which, of course, sends them back into gales of hilarity. Edma manages to gain control of herself first. "Yes, Maman, we will do that." But Berthe giggles, and Edma dissolves back into uncontrollable mirth.

"Tut-tut," Cornélie grumbles and closes the door.

"She said 'Tut-tut'!" Berthe slides from her bed to the floor, tears running down her cheeks. "I can't believe she actually said 'Tut-tut.'"

Exhausted from laughing, Edma drops down next to her sister and takes her hands. "I've missed you every day, and now I know I will miss you even more when I have to leave."

Berthe presses her forehead to Edma's, as they used to do when they were girls. "I have been so alone."

"Tell me what you couldn't put in a letter."

Berthe sighs and leans against the bed. "It, it is not a pretty tale."

"I did not think it would be."

"Well . . ." Now that the moment has arrived, Berthe finds that she doesn't want to talk about it. What if Edma turns against her when she hears? Even her loyal sister might be offended by what she's done. It would have been so much easier to share this confidence in writing.

"We've never had secrets from each another," Edma says. "And I believe you will be unburdened by telling me this one."

"The burden will still be there."

"But now I'll be able to help you carry it."

Berthe tells Edma everything. From Édouard's flirtations, to the modeling sessions, to the kisses and loving words, to his erratic and then rude behavior at the Salon. Of her growing attraction to him.

Edma touches Berthe's knee sympathetically at the most difficult admissions, but makes no comment during the recitation. When her sister finishes, she says, "There is nothing here that you should be ashamed of. You are unfamiliar with the ways of men, and Édouard is all too familiar with the ways of women."

Berthe takes a deep breath. Although Edma has remained empathetic so far, what Berthe has to tell her next could very well change her sister's mind. "This may be so, but my feelings for him remain. And, and I fear what I may do if we are alone together again."

Rather than looking shocked, as Berthe expected, Edma looks sad, almost brooding. "It's not worth it. And I don't just mean your reputation or, God forbid, you become with child. I am speaking of the act."

Berthe is caught off guard, as much by her sister's odd reaction as by her words. "The act?"

"I would not tell you this under other circumstances, but now that you have described your situation to me, I feel it's important for you to know the truth." Edma looks down at her hands, up at Berthe, then back at her hands. Her cheeks flush, and she clears her throat, but no words are forthcoming.

"What truth do you need to tell me?"

"It, I mean the act, it's humiliating, even degrading. And painful, very much so. There is no pleasure or joy, or even love." Edma meets Berthe's eyes. "I think George Sand said something about it being 'a furious breaking ground for male dominance.' And this is so. As a wife, I must succumb, but there is no reason for you to suffer this indignity. It does not matter how you felt when you kissed him. You will not like this. I promise you that."

Berthe listens to Edma, nodding her head as if she's in agreement. But she's not at all convinced by her sister's account, as heartfelt as it may be. In truth, she feels sympathy for Edma, who hasn't experienced what she, Berthe, has experienced and, as Adolphe's wife, most likely never will.

BERTHE DECIDES TO paint a double portrait of Edma and Maman now that they are all together. A quite salacious idea, as it's considered improper to portray a woman when she's in Edma's delicate condition. But who decided this is salacious? Berthe supposes the same people who deemed she cannot paint a man to whom she is not related or enjoy the company of her fellow artists at Café de Bade. And while she isn't comfortable breaching the last two conventions, she is willing to disregard the first. Particularly as Edma's pregnancy isn't apparent under her dresses, and it's a secret not known to anyone but the family.

Cornélie claims she's overwhelmed by preparations for the homecoming party, but Edma convinces her to sit for an hour each day, which she grudgingly does. Berthe dresses her mother in a black gown with lace at the neck and sleeves, her sister in white, with a blue bow holding back her hair. They sit close on the couch in the parlor, Cornélie reading to Edma, who's bathed in light and looking downward. There are purple flowers on the table to her right, and although the rendition of Edma is accurate, it isn't obvious to the viewer that she's with child.

Berthe is in heaven to be painting her sister again, to have her in the house every day. Maman isn't a good model, too anxious and fidgety, so Berthe sketches her quickly and allows her to go. Edma is a far more patient sitter, and without Cornélie present, they have plenty of time to chat, although Berthe doesn't mention Édouard again. It isn't that she doesn't wish to speak of him, which she would dearly love to do, but because her sister knows her too well. She fears Edma will recognize that she, Berthe, is in deeper than is wise and that she's unlikely to follow any sisterly advice. Even worse, it's possible Edma might go to Maman, believing she will be sparing Berthe terrible heartbreak and folly. And then she will never be permitted to be in Édouard's company again.

TO BERTHE AND Edma's relief, the day of the party is finally upon them. Cornélie is bustling everywhere, too busy with last-minute details to direct her nervous energy toward her daughters, but Marie, their maid, suffers greatly. Papa left early for his office and doesn't plan to return until the party is well underway. The sisters hide in the studio until it's time for them to dress.

The party is a great success. It's a lovely June evening, and the windows and doors are thrown wide, the house filled with the best people in their finery. Lively conversation and laughter ricochet off the walls, despite the undercurrent of a possible looming war with Germany. Food and drinks flow freely, and people keep arriving in what seems an endless stream. Berthe wonders if Maman ultimately decided to invite everyone on her list.

Degas and Renoir, along with many other artists, writers, and musicians are here. As are Édouard's mother, Suzanne, and Léon, and Édouard's brother Gène, a pale and nervous man whom, much to Berthe's horror, Maman has offered up as a suitable husband. As usual, Édouard is absent. Berthe keeps searching the crowd, but now that Edma knows her secrets, she almost wishes he won't come. Still, she searches.

Degas links his arm through hers. "I hear you are in the midst of creating a scandalous painting. How brave and modern of you."

At first, Berthe has no idea what he's talking about and shakes her head in confusion. But she quickly realizes to what he's referring. "You are always awash in rumors, Edgar. And you should not be spreading whatever nonsense you are alluding to."

"I don't mean to be telling false tales, but I believed you were working on a double portrait of your mother and Edma." His expression is uniquely Degas, a sneer with humor encircling it. "This is not so?"

"It is, but there's nothing at all scandalous about it."

"Now it is you who are telling false tales, my dear Berthe. Do you believe a picture of a woman in Edma's condition will be considered proper?"

"She's not in any condition."

"Why are you maintaining this fiction when the truth is widely known?"

"There is no truth for anyone to know," Berthe counters. Maman has been adamant that they remain mum about Edma's pregnancy until she returns home for her confinement, and both Berthe and Edma have done as she asked.

Degas bursts into laughter. "Did you honestly believe your mother would tell no one this news? Or that the woman in whom she confided would not tell another? How can you be so naïve about the world while standing up to it so courageously?"

"You are being most unkind, and I bid you to find someone else to insult. I have duties to perform here. I must converse with the other guests to ensure they have whatever they may need."

Still laughing, Degas bows. "As you command."

After he walks away, there's a touch on her shoulder, and Berthe turns, a polite hostess smile on her face. It's Édouard, and his expression is sober, which is surprising, as he's usually his most jovial at a party, when he deigns to attend. "I've been thinking about what I said to you at the Salon," he tells her as he maneuvers her into a far corner. "And there's no excuse whatsoever for my rudeness."

As pleased as she is to see him, she appraises him coolly. "No, there is not."

"I'm so sorry, but I wasn't myself. The pressure of the moment, the possible sale, the ridicule of my work . . . I was up. I was down. I was not in my right senses."

"It sounds to me as if you are making excuses."

He grabs her hands. "Oh, my Berthe, my Berthe. There are so many things I love about you, but your frankness has to be my favorite."

She should shake his hands off, especially in a public place, but she doesn't. "You are insufferable."

"But lovable, no?" he asks playfully.

"Too much for your own good." She attempts to keep an edge of sharpness in her voice but is unsuccessful.

"Meet me in your studio in ten minutes," he whispers.

"We cannot do that," she says, despite her desire to do exactly as he suggests. "I will not do that."

"We must," he pleads. "We have to talk."

Berthe hesitates, then pulls her hands from his and walks to where her mother is sitting. She settles on the arm of Cornélie's chair. "What a fabulous evening you've created, Maman! Surely a triumph."

Cornélie beams at her. "Thank you, my darling." She stands. "I met the most charming young man. Monsieur Faucheux, a banker, new to our city. Come, let me introduce you."

Berthe allows herself to be led, but turns to see if Édouard is watching her. He is, and he pulls out his pocket watch, holding it up with an irresistible glint in his eyes. She continues to follow her mother. When she meets the "charming" M. Faucheux, he is anything but, and after an awkward and inane conversation about the economics of war, she moves on, wondering if ten minutes have passed. The guests have been imbibing for hours, full of themselves and their conversations, and are unlikely to notice her absence.

She edges her way to the door that leads to her studio, lightheaded with trepidation and eagerness, her breath coming quickly. When she enters the studio, closing the door behind her, he's looking at the unfinished painting of Edma and Cornélie.

She comes up alongside him, but he doesn't take his eyes from the canvas. "It's as if they're actually here, so natural and comfortable in their togetherness," he says softly, almost reverently. "You've captured their bond, their moment, and although they might be Edma and Cornélie, they're also all mothers and daughters. Or at least how we prefer to believe all mothers and daughters to be."

Berthe is elated, not only by what he's saying, but by his understanding of her work. "Édouard, I, I—"

He takes her in his arms gently, adoringly, as if she were a Russian jeweled egg. He doesn't kiss her, just holds her. "Your perfume, your light powdery scent, so fresh, so elegant," he breathes. "Almost as intoxicating as you are."

"Guerlain's Violette de Paine," she murmurs, pressing her cheek into his chest, taking him in with all her senses.

"I love you," he whispers into her ear. "Truly."

"And I love you too." She raises her face to his, and when they kiss, all she feels is happiness. No more fear or trepidation. He's hers now. And forever. He loves her.

There's a knock on the door, and they jump apart. "Come in," she calls, her voice hoarse and a little shaky. It's Edma.

Édouard bows. "I was just complimenting your sister on the masterful job she's doing with this painting."

"I agree," Edma says. "It is already a magnificent work and will grow only more so when it's complete."

Berthe looks from one to the other, and the silence grows awkward. "Thank you both," she says, just to say something.

"Maman is looking for you." Edma's tone is casual, but her eyes are darkly serious, locked on her sister's. "I thought it would be best for me to come find you before she does."

EDMA RETURNS HOME to Lorient at the end of June, and it's difficult to know which of the sisters is more upset by their separation. Cornélie is sympathetic to Berthe's unhappiness for a day or two, then begins berating her for moping around the house and not eating enough. "Your sister has a life and will soon have a family, and it is high time you do the same," she says more than once.

It's not only the loss of her sister that Berthe is mourning. Since Edma's interruption the night of the party, she and Édouard have had no chance to discuss their future. Only a few days later, the Manets left Paris for a rented estate in the Loire Valley and will not be back in the city until the end of August. Usually the Morisots would be on summer holiday also, but Papa must remain in Paris, for he is now the minister of the interior and deeply involved in the government's negotiations to avert a war with Germany.

The city is hot and dirty, and the stench is horrible. All Berthe's friends and fellow artists have fled to either the coast or the countryside, but she, as the only unmarried daughter, must remain to look after her parents, although they need no looking after.

She tries to work in her studio, but there is little breeze, and after less than an hour, she's often faint from the heat. The house is little better, although there are more windows to open. She spends miserable day after miserable day lying in her sweltering bedroom with cold compresses on her forehead that turn warm within minutes and drip water down her neck into the pillows.

In July, when the talks with Germany fail and war is declared, everyone floods back into the city to pack up their homes and retreat to England or Portugal or the Mediterranean, some even to America. The Manets decide to stay in France but are going to the Basses-Pyrénées. Just before they go, Édouard and his brother Gène come to the Morisots home to try to convince them that they, too, must leave the city. Although their concern is for the whole family, and they claim they came on Antoinette's urging, Berthe knows it's Édouard's fear for her safety that's the real cause of the visit.

She is, of course, elated to see him, but once again, they have no opportunity to be alone. The brothers are in a great rush, and Papa and Maman are dogged about staying, impervious to their arguments. Her father cannot leave his post, especially now with war raging, and her mother will not abandon him or her own aging parents. Papa tried to convince Cornélie and Berthe to go, but Cornélie refused.

After much back-and-forth, Gène says, "If that is your decision, Madame Morisot, we will respect it." This is his first utterance since he arrived, and Berthe is surprised he's spoken at all, as he has always appeared to be a silent spectator of life rather than an active participant. It occurs to her that it's Gène whom Suzanne should have married, comfortably bonded in their blandness.

"But there's no reason that Berthe cannot go to Yves in Mirande," Édouard argues. "There will certainly be no action there, as it's so distant, and just as certainly there will be action in Paris. It is completely reckless for her to remain in the city. And isn't Mirande where Edma is, now that Adolphe has been recalled? I understand why you must remain," he says to Papa. "But the only safe place for Berthe is with her sisters."

Berthe wants to stand and step into his arms, to thank him for caring for her so, but all she can do is sit where she is. "My place is with my parents, Édouard," she says as firmly as she can. "My grandparents aren't well, and it would be remiss of me to leave all the caretaking to my mother."

"But you need to get out while you can!" Édouard's eyes are beseeching. "What good will you do if you are wounded or disfigured? How will you be able to help anyone then?"

"I wish it could be otherwise, as with so much that is happening these days," she says, looking at her lap. "But I must stay."

Édouard's face is an iron mask as he and Gène take their leave, and Berthe has no doubt he's furious with her. But if she were to abandon her family and something happened to any of them, she would never forgive herself. She can only hope Édouard will be able to find it in his heart to forgive her.

THIRTEEN

1870–1871

The Franco-Prussian War is a devastating blow to the country, but it's even more so for the city of Paris, which by September is completely surrounded by the German army. Smoke fills the streets, along with bursts of heavy cannon fire, but the French refuse to surrender. In retaliation, the enemy initiates a complete embargo of goods to starve the capitol into submission.

Unfortunately, this is a success, and the siege ends with a capitulation in late January, just weeks after Berthe's thirtieth birthday. The terms imposed are a humiliation to the proud country, barely endurable. France must pay an exorbitant war fee, turn over Alsace and Lorraine, and recognize the new expanded German empire, which is particularly galling, as stopping Germany's consolidation of power was the reason the French went to war in the first place,

As food slowly returns to the stores, everyone is grateful to eat something other than moldy bread. But as is true of the rest of her compatriots, Berthe is infuriated by the government's inability to protect its people. It's well-known that casualties are high, yet the family has received no news of those who have been in battle. Berthe's brother, Tiburce, is somewhere at sea, as is Edma's husband, Adolphe. Édouard is in the National Guard's artillery, Degas in the infantry, Renoir in a regiment of the cuirassiers. The list goes on.

Any hope the Morisots had that now that the fighting had stopped things might improve is quickly destroyed. It is announced that France must submit to German occupation until a treaty is fully ratified by both sides, with the German army to quarter in Paris immediately. The soldiers not only billet in the Morisots' house but also in Berthe's studio, and she frets endlessly about her men at war.

With the exception of her brother and brother-in-law, who have served before, most of her friends are artists, not soldiers, with neither the skills nor the temperament to be fighters. During the siege, the Germans closed post offices and train stations, along with severing telegraph connections, so she hasn't heard from Edma since Christmas. At last, a letter from her sister gets through by carrier pigeon, heralding the arrival of a healthy baby girl named Jeanne and giving assurances that both mother and child are doing well.

Berthe is also still recovering from a return of her neurasthenia, the usual combination of lack of energy, lack of interest in food, lack of interest in life. This has perpetuated a considerable weight loss that has thrown her mother into fits of anxiety. Berthe also suffers from an ongoing despondency, brought on by her isolation and fears. This last is being called "siege fever," as many in the city are experiencing the same condition, but she, Cornélie, and Dr. Aguillard know it is not only the result of the political situation. It's in Berthe's nature to fall into recurring blue periods.

After nine months of war, siege, and occupation, the Germans return home in May and France is free of occupiers. But now the country is beset by internal strife, with a battle brewing between the left-wing Paris Commune and the right-wing French government. Fighting once again erupts in Paris, which quickly turns brutal and bloody, and the Morisots finally flee the city. They take up residence in a small house in Saint-Germain-en-Laye, and everyone's health and spirits improve in the countryside.

The family's morale rises further when they learn all their men have survived and are safe, far from the battles underway in the capital. Berthe's brother, as well as Yves's husband and Edma's husband, should be home within a month. Édouard sends a telegram informing the Morisots that he, Degas, and Renoir will soon be relieved of their duties and hope to return to Paris in the fall. Although Berthe is delighted with this news, she wishes Édouard had sent along a more personal note, something just for her. Three days later, a letter arrives.

My dearest, dearest,

I am much relieved to hear that you have left Paris and can only hope you are safe and happily painting in Saint-Germain. My mother tells me she has been assured of your safety, but I will only believe this when I hear it from your lips and see it upon your face. Until this is possible, a letter by your hand will have to be my comfort.

I have received a promotion to lieutenant, and am currently under the command of our friend and fellow artist, Ernest Meissonier. We joke that before he was painting war scenes, and now he is directing them, but neither of us are able to laugh at this irony.

A catastrophe has befallen our country, and I have had the misfortune to experience it at close range. I shall not tell you the appalling details of war, as they will be as upsetting for me to set down as they will be for you to read. Suffice to say, I am now moving toward mending the blows to my body and mind, although the dark turn of sadness I have been suffering is not lifting as rapidly as I would wish. The nightmares linger also.

My Berthe, I miss you beyond measure, and I will not be complete until we are reunited.

With love and devotion,
Your Édouard

Berthe carries the letter in her corset, careful not to tear the pages with each rereading and repositioning. She wishes she could respond with the same loving words he has written to her. But she must send her return missive to his mother's address, as he has none, and therefore her own tone must be much more discreet. There are no guarantees that Antoinette, a well-known meddler, will be able to keep herself from reading its contents. Most likely she will not.

Dear Édouard,

I cannot convey how happy I am that you and our dear friends have survived this ordeal. I, too, am looking forward to a reunion, either at one of our mothers' soirees or with our bande in your studio. I pray this will happen soon. After all you have endured, I dare not compare my suffering to yours, but I also have had a "dark turn of sadness," as you so eloquently describe it, complete with nightmares. I daresay we shall have much to discuss of this and many other shared interests when we are able.

Yes, we are all safe in Saint-Germain, although the house is small, and we are close enough to Paris to hear the cannons. If the wind is right, or perhaps wrong, we can smell the smoke from their fire. After our bitter fight against the Germans, it is heartbreaking to know that these current hostilities are brought on by our own against our own, brother against brother. I am plagued by thoughts of the horrible things men are willing to do to each other in the name of country. But as April has opened its skies and all is in bloom, I try to believe in the promise of rebirth and the possibility of the reemergence of our life of one year ago. A life we so foolishly took for granted.

In this vein, I have begun painting again, plein air, which allows me to be in the sunshine and out of our tight accommodations. I fear I am very unpracticed after so many fallow months. My attempts are those of a novice schoolgirl, but it is better to be failing than not painting at all. I am working in watercolor and striving to capture the spontaneity of the moment with both my composition and brushstrokes. Thus far, I have not achieved this.

That is all the news from here for now. Please write soon and tell me all of yours. My best to your mother.

Berthe

WHEN THE FRENCH government defeats the Commune and is back in uncontested control of the country, the Morisots pack up and stagger home. But Paris is a ghost of itself: stores and restaurants shuttered, streets full of holes, mounds of rubble from fallen buildings in every quarter. Much of the city's heart is destroyed: the Palais des Tuileries, the Hôtel de Ville, the Préfecture de Police, too many other structures and monuments to count. The Morisots' home and Berthe's studio have been ransacked, but both still stand.

It is as if her parents have aged ten years. They're suddenly old, barely able to think or take any action beyond sitting in the few remaining chairs, with their heads bowed. Even her father cries. Berthe does her best to help them put things right, but she's as devastated as they are, and all she wants is to crawl into her bed and stay there. Again, the role of dutiful daughter falls to her, and with help from Marie and Rémy, they make the house livable, although she knows its past grandeur will take years to regain. Even Tiburce's homecoming does little to cheer them.

Berthe hasn't seen any of the other artists, as they come to Paris for short trips, rushing to pick up the pieces of their lives sundered by the war, and then quickly escaping. She heard Degas was in town, but then he left for London. Monet goes between Holland and England, Renoir is in America, and Sisley is in Rome. Édouard is still in the Basse-Pyrénées with Suzanne and Léon, so it's his mother and his brother Gène, who, along with their servants, aid in the restoration of the Morisot household, as Tiburce, Maman, and Rémy help the Manets.

Now that Édouard is reunited with his wife, he has less freedom to write, and Berthe is equally hobbled by the fear Suzanne might intercept their correspondence. They haven't seen each other in a year, since that long-ago day when he begged her to leave Paris. So many months have passed, and they have both been through such difficult times, that she worries the love he declared in her studio has been quashed. For if it has not, why is he with Suzanne rather than with her?

Gène and Antoinette are often in the Morisot house, but helpful as they have been, Gène's mere presence irritates Berthe. He's a pale shadow of his brother in both face and spirit, his wispy blond hair a rebuke of Édouard's luxurious red locks, his timidity a reproach to his brother's exuberance. Yet his features do remind her of Édouard, who should be here instead. She tries to be polite, but Maman still chastises her, after they leave, for her coldness.

"He's the Manet you should be setting your cap for," Cornélie snaps. "He may not be as extravagant as his brother, but he is the one who doesn't already have a wife."

"You don't want me to marry such a man," Berthe counters. "Aren't you the one who's always complaining that Gène is lazy and has no interest in any type of work? How his mother pretends this isn't the case and dotes on him?"

"That's neither here nor there, Berthe. He's from a fine family of means and high social standing. As a woman past thirty, you must make compromises if you are to have a successful life."

"Painting is my life, and this is how I will achieve success. It may not be your definition of success, Maman, but it's mine."

"I don't know how a daughter of mine can be such a fool."

"If I'm a fool, then it is you who made me this way. You who encouraged my art. The tutors. The studio. What did you expect to happen?" Berthe is abashed at the bitterness of her words but does not take them back.

Cornélie looks off into the distance, thinking about the question. "I considered it a good skill for a young lady to have, but never a life's work. That is for men. And frankly, I find it disrespectful for you to believe that you are as good an artist as the men you are associating with."

"That is a terrible thing to say to me!" Berthe explodes. "To whom am I being disrespectful? Degas and Édouard and the others all think I'm as good as they are. Some have told me I am better!"

"They are full of compliments because you are a woman. Talking like this just to flirt, to be sociable, no more and no less. I'm your mother, and it's upon me to tell you the truth: You are a gifted amateur, but you don't have the talent to compete in a man's arena."

Berthe glares defiantly and marches to her studio. She can be an unmarried woman and an artist, like the novelist George Sand or the sculptor Marcello. And she will be.

She doesn't speak to Cornélie for days. Unfortunately, it appears that her mother, who has been silent and passive since their return, is reverting to her judgmental self.

PAUL DURAND-RUEL OWNS an art gallery on New Bond Street in London, and he has begun purchasing and showing French artists, particularly those in Manet's bande. In contrast to how their work has been received in their home country, the paintings are popular in England. This is why Monet, Pissarro, and Degas are there, and Berthe wishes she could be also. But she must stay in Paris with her mother and her ailing grandfather, who was recently diagnosed with angina and grows weaker by the day.

Degas writes that he has told Durand-Ruel about her work, and the gallerist promised to review it when he's next in Paris. This, as well as her desire to prove her mother wrong, spurs her into her studio with renewed vigor. The 1872 Salon will soon be accepting submissions, and after her absence last year, she plans to have at least a few quality pieces to offer. Yet she progresses slowly, unsatisfied with most of what she creates, much of which she destroys. She must become more of her own artist, crystallize her unique style, but everything she paints still trumpets the influence of Camille Corot.

Berthe finds a new model, a girl of ten, and finally is working on a painting that she's almost pleased with. The child is seated with a parrot perched on the outside of a cage to her left, and Berthe is gratified by the way her various treatments of light capture the nuances of the shifting colors, which, while bright and contrasting, seem to work in harmony with each other. The green of the parrot, the red of the girl's hair, and the glittering gold of the cage's bars should be jarring, yet they are not.

She is also feeling better about her brushstrokes. The looseness she's been striving for is coming more readily. In the parrot painting, they increase the liveliness and spontaneity of the scene. But, as always, she worries it's not substantial enough for the critics, and she longs for her fellow artists to return, needing their company, their compliments and critiques.

In the fall, as the city cleans itself up and starts to reopen, they begin to trickle in. Degas, Renoir, Sisley, Pissarro, Monet, and, at last, Édouard. His studio has been damaged, but he has let it be known that he expects the bande to be able to meet there in a few weeks. Berthe hasn't seen him yet, but his mother is having her first soiree of the season on Thursday, and everyone has been invited. Even Édouard would not miss this momentous event. Or so Berthe hopes.

ALTHOUGH IT'S LATE September, Thursday is as brutally hot as any day in August, and the Manet house is bursting beyond its capacity. But it isn't just the heat and close quarters that are a drag on the party. There's a listlessness among the guests who are still burdened by the horrific events of the past year. The men talk of their war experiences and lost comrades, the women try to be cheerful, but there's a falseness to their merriment and chatter. No one shows off their new fashionable outfits, as befits the opening of the season, because there are no new fashions to be had. Nor are there any operas or symphonies or stage productions in the offing. Even Suzanne's piano playing is somber.

Cornélie is almost gleeful about the amount of weight Suzanne has gained. "When Édouard returned from the war, he must have experienced a great shock at the sight of this bucolic blooming," she whispers to Berthe.

"Suzanne is even fatter than she was before. How could she have done this to herself? Has she no pride?"

"Must you, Maman?" Berthe responds, and slips away in search of Édouard. Cornélie has indeed reverted to her old self, or perhaps she's become even more officious and critical of those around her than she was before the war.

Berthe looks toward the terrace. The French doors where she posed for *The Balcony* are thrown open as wide as they can be, and she finds Édouard in front of them, holding court. A dozen laughing people are clustered around him as he flings out witty bits of conversation. How he finds things to make light of is a marvel to Berthe, yet clearly a release to those devouring his every word. She watches him from a distance, allowing the sight and the sound of him to fill her.

A half-deaf colleague of her father's begins to pontificate about politics, drowning Édouard out, and the group around him disperses. She closes the gap between them. "Hello, Édouard," she says, trying to still the smile in her words and on her lips. "It's lovely to see you again."

He does not bother to hide his delight. "The beautiful Berthe Morisot," he declares, with a grin so wide it seems to split his face. "I couldn't be happier to see anyone." Then he takes her arm and leads her through the open doors.

The balcony, which easily held the four models when they were sitting for Édouard, feels as cramped and airless as the rooms inside. They find a spot along the railing, which due to the throng, forces them close together. Berthe presses herself as tight to him as she can. He does the same, and they look at each other.

"You're here," he says.

"We're here." Berthe has been living this moment in her dreams, and now that it's arrived, it's even more breathtaking than she imagined. To feel him against her, to see the love in his eyes, to know they are meant to be. Will be.

"But we must go somewhere else, away from all these people," he whispers.

"I should be able to come to your studio either tomorrow or the next day, in the afternoon," Berthe whispers back, well aware of the danger here. She hears Edma's voice in her head: *You are unfamiliar with the ways of men, and Édouard is all too familiar with the ways of women.* But she doesn't care.

Before Édouard can respond, Degas arrives at his elbow. He frowns at Berthe and says pointedly to Édouard, "You must go to your wife and soothe her. Her music has become so melancholy it's making everyone feel worse than they already do." When Édouard doesn't move, he adds, "Go. Tell her to play something cheerful. A polka maybe? I cannot abide all this suffocating narcissistic misery. It's too damn hot." He bows to Berthe, shaking his head to indicate his disapproval. "Excuse my language, but it is too damn hot."

RÉMY DRIVES BERTHE to Édouard's studio the next day. Maman believes he's taking her to walk with her friend Thomasine and her two children. Knowing Édouard's preference for her in black and white, Berthe dons a full-skirted white dress with a flutter of black lace at the edge of its scooped neckline and a black sash cinching her waist. She also allows more of her ringlets than usual to fall onto her forehead and around her face. Édouard likes the contrast between her light skin and dark hair.

As soon as the door closes behind her, they are kissing deeply, frantically. It's as if no time has passed. They are as they were, completely lost in each other. He is hers. She is his. When his kisses descend from her lips to the skin at the neckline of her dress, her head falls back. He lifts her as a husband would carry his bride, pushes aside the curtain, and places her down on the red sofa. He gently touches her cheek and says, "Is this all right?"

She doesn't answer, just pulls his face to hers. She's overtaken by a wave of love and warmth and wet and everything that is Édouard. She hears a soft moan and realizes it's coming from her. But she isn't embarrassed. She only wants more. More of whatever he has to give her. He aligns his body with hers, and this time when he is against her, all she wants is to be closer. She raises her hips to him.

He lowers himself and presses his mouth to the spot on her dress where it covers her undergarments, and the warmth of his breath sends a ripple through her, both pleasurable and greedy.

His hands are under her dress, on her thighs, then higher. The ripple explodes into a sensation so remarkable and giddy and overpowering that she convulses under it. Whatever this is, she needs to experience it again and again. There's a pressure between her legs, and suddenly, she's not sure how, he's inside her. For a moment, she freezes, shocked and terrified at what he's doing, what she's doing. But as he moves, her fear recedes and she wants to keep him there, move with him, their bodies linked just as are their souls.

PART FIVE

Tamara, the present

FOURTEEN

I hurry from the living room to my bedroom and close the door behind me. On my phone, *Party on the Seine* shines in all her glory, just as she's portrayed in the art books and on the internet. As she always was. As she still is. No pointing finger. But if that's the case, did I just have a break with reality? See something that wasn't there? The change seemed so authentic, so substantial, as if Édouard Manet had painted it that way.

Clambering through my memories, I search for signs of psychosis in my kite tail of a family. My excessively thin mom probably had undiagnosed anorexia, what with her anti-fat fetish and constant dieting. And then there were her "blue phases," when she'd stay in her bedroom with the drapes closed for days at a time—not eating, of course. But she always popped back, seemingly no worse for the episodes. Or so it appeared to me, a child not particularly focused on anyone aside from myself.

There's little doubt my dad was eccentric, even a touch manic. In constant motion like the finely detailed model train set he built that took up the entire basement floor. He claimed it was for me—but only he played with it, hour after hour, clack after clack. Clearly some OCD there, an obsession with order, always centering and straightening things if my mother or I left them even slightly askew. A math whiz.

But as far as I know, neither of them had hallucinations, nothing psychotic, and if you discount my ocular migraines, I never have either. Nothing like what I just saw *Party* do anyway. What I imagined I just saw *Party* do. What no painting could have done. Lack of sleep. Overwork. Poor vision. Ocular migraine. Bad lighting. LSD flashback. Any of the above. All of the above. Not to mention the possibility of a serious mental illness. None of these rings quite true, but at least one of them has to be. Right?

I suppose I could consider a supernatural explanation, but that's even more far-fetched than any of the others. Sure, the painting could be haunted, perhaps by the ghost of Berthe Morisot, who's hanging around in the brushstrokes and sending me messages. But as I said before, I'm a STEM girl, and there isn't a spiritual bone in my body. I inherited my overly rational thinking—some might say rigid, others close-minded—from my father, along with my belief in numbers and science and the need for solid substantiation in all matters. Ergo, no ghost.

I FIND MYSELF avoiding *Party*. The truth is that the painting scares me. But what am I afraid of? There's nothing to be afraid of. And yet here I am, staying out of both the living room and the study, sitting in the kitchen with my back toward that side of the apartment. I get to work early and stay late, go out with Holly, and head directly to my bedroom when I come home. Idiotic. Unwarranted. But there it is.

Jonathan Stein calls and tells me he was contacted by the Columbia Museum, the one outside Philadelphia that has a gallery focusing on Nazi loot. "Randi Wiley, the curator there, said she'd heard we'd found *Party on the Seine* and wanted to know it was available for sale."

"I thought it was all a big secret?"

"So did I," he says dryly.

"Even if I wanted to, I couldn't do it anyway, could I? The lawsuit and all."

"I told her that, and she suggested a loan until the legal issues are worked out."

"A bit pushy, isn't she?"

He laughs. "Yeah, she's formidable, but she's committed to keeping the Holocaust alive. Some fabulous art there, but it's hard to see it without getting rip-roaring furious. The audacity of those assholes."

I'm starting to warm to Jonathan now that he's loosened up and is acting like a real person. "If I did that," I say, flashing on Berthe's forefinger stretched down toward the river, "loaned it to them, would it be safe? I mean safe from Damien and his foundation. He couldn't swoop in, tell the museum it was his, and seize it, could he?"

"You can talk to Randi about that, but as long as the case remains unresolved—which, as a lawyer, I figure it will be for quite a while—I'm guessing the painting will be perfectly safe there."

I hesitate. Maybe this would be best. But am I just going to succumb to a fear with no basis? Abandon my newly resurrected family for no good reason? Yet, as Jonathan pointed out, the conditions and security here may not be the best. So I'll get a humidifier or a dehumidifier or whatever I need. I'll hire a guard. "I guess I'll pass," I say with less certainty than I hoped.

A long pause. "You sure?"

Of course I'm not. What if my grandmother times four *is* trying to communicate with me?

This last thought is proof positive that keeping the painting in my apartment isn't good for my mental health, plus it would be nice to walk into my living room without trepidation. I'm torn, but I say, "I'm sure."

"I'm not going to tell you what to do, but maybe you should take a day and think on it."

"That sounds like you are telling me what to do."

"Touché. But will you do it anyway? The thinking part I mean."

"Fair enough," I tell him. Now I have an out if I change my mind. "So, so if I did decide to loan it to the museum, how would we go about such a thing?"

He laughs. "Who's we?"

"I didn't mean it like—"

"It's cool. I'll text you Randi's contact info when we hang up. Don't know what their procedures are, but I'll bet if that's how you want to go, you'll be able to work something out."

Three days later, *Party* is on a truck heading for Pennsylvania. I move the multimedia triptych back to the space between the windows in the living room and tell myself I'm feeling much better, that it's good to have her gone. Better for me. Better for her. But I miss *Party*. I miss Grandma Berthe. And I miss the connection to my family.

FOR A FAIRLY young attorney—I'm guessing I've got five or six years on him—Wyatt Butler's office is impressive, even for a partner, which apparently he just became. And Holly wasn't wrong about his looks. If anything, her description was an understatement. The cleft in his chin, the strong jawline, the cheekbones, the broad shoulders. Need I go on? The guy is a knockout, and it's hard to respond to him as if he were a regular person. Because he isn't.

It's like the time I was in an elevator with the actor Brendan Fraser, who I didn't recognize right off but who I immediately sensed wasn't just your ordinary elevator rider—he was just too damn good-looking for everyday life. With apologies to F. Scott, let me tell you about the very beautiful. They are different from you and me.

I hand Wyatt Butler a file of papers pertaining to the foundation's suit. He listens carefully to my explanation, jotting down notes while watching me just as carefully. This is disconcerting, as his eyes are a shade of light green I've never seen before on a human face, in arresting contrast to the dark hair falling over his forehead. I'm not the type who's easily flustered, but I find I don't know where to look. Which is bullshit. I look directly at him.

"I don't mean to diminish the legal issues here, Ms. Rubin," he says when I finish, flipping through the papers I brought. "Or your concerns. But this is an extraordinary story. Much more interesting than my usual fare."

"Tamara, please. And I've got to agree with you there. Not my usual fare either."

"Wyatt." He smiles, which makes him more attractive, if that's possible. "Who inherits an Impressionist masterpiece out of nowhere?"

"Apparently me."

"And it's secure at this museum? Philly, you said. No chance the foundation can grab it?"

"I don't trust my dear cousin, so I spoke with the museum curator about it, and she said he wouldn't be able to. I need to make sure Damien Manet keeps his slippery fingers off my *Party*."

"My *Party*, huh?" An appraising look.

"Is this going to cost a fortune?" I ask, wanting to shift the conversation away from my excessive attachment to a painting.

"I'm not going to lie to you—it won't be cheap. But I'll see what I can do to keep it down."

"I'd appreciate that," I tell him, but who's going to believe a promise like that from a lawyer? Especially one flanked by floor-to-ceiling bookcases and an expansive view of Boston Harbor.

"I'll take a look into this Manet Foundation—as quickly as I can." This time it's a grin that hits me in the gut. "And talk to the woman who does our investigating. Get an estimate on how many hours she thinks she'll need. Then I'll get back to you, and you can decide how to proceed. Sound good?"

I stand and hold out my hand. "You have my contact information."

He shakes it, holds it for a nanosecond longer than I expect, and gazes at me with a flirtatious flash of perfect white teeth. "That I do."

I WALK OVER the bridge from the Seaport to South Station, then take the Red Line to the Orange Line, get off at Copley, and head down the Southwest Corridor to Calliope. If I'm going to hire Wyatt Butler, which I'm pretty sure I am, I've got to watch my pennies. No Uber for me. A text comes in as I enter the building. It's from my friend Samir, a colleague from EVTX, who left the company a few months after I did: *Check out Bioengineer.org.* Bioengineer.org is an online magazine that reports on the latest biotech news.

As soon as I get to my office, I do just that. And there, at the top of the feed, is a photo of my old boyfriend, Nick Winspear, ringing the bell on Wall Street. They took the damn company public, which is surely going to jack up the stock's value. Stock Samir and I had to sell when we left EVTX. Shares that will now be worth double or triple what we were paid for them, maybe more. Tens of thousands of dollars. Definitely enough for Wyatt Butler's fee.

So here's the deal. Nick and I were both senior vice presidents at EVTX. I was senior VP of regulatory affairs, and he was senior VP of quality assurance, both of us reporting to the chief regulatory officer. I'd been in my position for over four years, and he in his for less than three. We became a couple pretty soon after he started, something everyone in the company was aware of, including the higher-ups, and no one had an issue with.

We got on well but kept it light. Although we were exclusive, we each had our own life. Nights out with other people, separate residences and vacations, that type of thing. No long-term commitment, which both of us were happy with—especially me, still gun-shy after my ugly divorce. But when Jeffrey, the chief regulatory officer, announced his early retirement, things got sticky.

I was the most likely candidate to replace Jeffrey, which meant I'd be Nick's boss, and I couldn't be in a romantic relationship with a direct report. Nick and I discussed it, and as neither of us wanted to break up, we devised a solution. Another C-suite position was opening within a few months—chief commercial officer, in charge of commercial strategy and development—so the plan was that when they offered me CRO, I'd ask for CCO instead. In that case, Nick wouldn't be working for me, and we could continue on as we were. A perfect solution.

Except they didn't offer me the regulatory position. They offered it to Nick. The board was over three-quarters male, and the C-suite was all men. Did I have more experience in regulatory matters than Nick did? Did I have more years on the job? Was I the most qualified? The answer to all these questions was yes, but for some reason I can't fathom—ha—none of this mattered to the good ol' boys. Nick never did ask for the CCO job, which in his defense—a tiny, tiny, tiny, almost infinitesimal defense—wasn't as good a fit for his skill set as it was for mine. So he grabbed the bird in the hand and broke up with me before he signed the contract. I was ambushed and hadn't seen it coming. Nick was not who I thought he was.

I stomped out of EVTX, enraged by his duplicity and the company's misogyny. This smacked of the same overwrought male ego—not to mention my own bad choices—as the night Simon, my ex-husband, slapped me across the face during an argument about money. Sure, Simon and I had our problems, but I thought our marriage was decent, that he was a decent guy, and then, with that slap, it was over. Not who I thought he was.

Which is why there aren't going to be any more serious relationships for me. Sex and fun are cool, but nothing more than that. I don't trust men to reveal who they really are until it's too late. And, worse, I don't trust myself to be able to distinguish the good ones from the bad.

FIFTEEN

I wish I hadn't bought that multimedia triptych. When I first moved into Tremont245, I was overwhelmed by the empty rooms and blank walls. Not being much of a shopper, and even less of the decorator type, I headed over to a contemporary furniture store in the neighborhood. When Maxine, the stylishly dressed and perfectly coifed salesperson, said she was free for an hour and asked if I'd be willing to show her the apartment, I was more than happy to do so. As we walked the half dozen blocks, she cross-examined me about my tastes—clean lines, lots of color, unexpected juxtapositions—and then sold me an apartmentful of furniture, which five years in, I'm still happy with. The art gallery she recommended was another thing altogether.

Maxine called ahead to schedule an appointment. When I arrived, the owner was waiting for me. He didn't ask about my tastes, just assumed he knew from the furniture I'd ordered. Granted, there are a few pieces I bought from him that I like, but the triptych isn't one of them. I'm usually strong in my opinions, have no problem saying no, but I was bored with the whole interior design thing—as I learned to call it because apparently "decorator" is considered a derogatory term—and needed something between the living room windows.

Now, as I look at it through the open French doors, I like it even less than I did then. A mishmash of paint, sand, aluminum foil, and odd-shaped pieces of plastic stuck randomly on the three canvases—or at least that's the way it appears to me. It's no *Party*—that's for sure. I think about putting it back in the guest room, but staring at a blank wall would probably be worse.

How could I have sent her away? What had I been so afraid of? My overtired and nearsighted eyes playing tricks after a long day? It was foolish and unnecessary. Randi Wiley, the curator at the Columbia, told me they would need at least three weeks' notice before *Party* could be sent back to me—on my own dime, of course. Fair enough.

It's Saturday, and normally I'd be in the office catching up on all the things I never got to during the week. But a frigid rain is pounding outside, and the dark clouds are so low they seem to touch the rooftops across the street. As intrepid as I am, a born-and-raised New Englander, I'm not going out in that shit. My father, who grew up in northern Maine, would affectionally call me a wimp, and although this does niggle a bit, I'm still not going out in that shit.

I'm slogging through the edits to a pharmacovigilance report on an adverse drug reaction we just discovered when an email comes in from my cousin.

From: Damien Manet, Director of the Édouard Manet Foundation
To: Tamara Rubin
Cc: Jonathan Stein, Counsel to the Conference on Jewish Claims Against Germany
Re: Party on the Seine
Date: 15 November

You have not sent your attorney's contact information, as I requested, and this is unacceptable. *Party on the Seine* is fragile and must be maintained in a controlled environment, which your home is not. In an unsecured place such as yours, there are also the additional threats of theft, an act of God, or an act of man, such as arson or a burst pipe. Therefore, the painting is in grave danger, and I am offering, once again, to relieve you of this burden. Again, we will be happy to transport *Party on the Seine* to Paris at our expense.

I am sure you are aware that an Édouard Manet retrospective is to be held at the Louvre this coming summer. It will be a career-spanning show, never before accomplished. The Foundation and the museum have spent three years amassing 87 works of art for the exhibition.

Party on the Seine will be the 88th and, more than likely, the centerpiece of the show. As it was believed that the painting was destroyed during World War II, the recovery of this lost masterpiece is a world-shaking event, and the retrospective will command a wide audience of art lovers from around the globe, who deserve to enjoy its return. Especially as this is the first time it will be displayed in almost a hundred years.

In order to authenticate, ascertain damage, clean, and restore *Party on the Seine* to its original state, it must be delivered to the Louvre no later than 1 January. If you or your attorney has not contacted me by 17 November, further legal actions will be taken to ensure its safety and secure transport.

I have to admit that Damien has a point about the controlled environment and that *Party* does deserve to be seen by art lovers, but his arrogance is so off-putting that it makes it difficult to see through it. I refuse to be intimidated by his blustering, and I have to chuckle at his concern with all the dangers that could befall her in my apartment when she's actually safe at the Columbia Museum.

I think about phoning Wyatt Butler, who I officially hired a couple of days ago. He did give me his cell number and told me not to hesitate to get in touch with him at any time, but as annoying as the email is, it doesn't warrant a weekend call. So I return to my pharmacovigilance report, which is almost as annoying as Damien Manet.

WYATT CALLS ME at the office Monday afternoon. "Just spoke with your famous cousin Damien."

"He's famous?"

Wyatt laughs. "In his own mind."

"As much of a pompous jerk on the phone as he is in his emails?"

"Even more so."

"Sorry about putting you through that."

"The vast majority of my job is dealing with pompous jerks, so no need to apologize."

"Some days, I feel the same way."

"Want to run away to Bimini with me? Heard there aren't any jerks there."

"Wish I could." Who wouldn't want to run off to Bimini with a guy who looks like Wyatt Butler? A much younger guy, to boot.

A long dramatic sigh. "Me too."

"I'm guessing you didn't call to invite me to the Bahamas," I say. "What else did he tell you?"

"Not all that much. After a rather lengthy speech about how busy he is and how important his foundation is, he handed me off to a lawyer. The foundation's lawyer, he informed me, as if I would be impressed that the foundation has an in-house attorney."

"And what did the in-house attorney have to say?"

"That the Nazis stole many of Édouard Manet's works, and that the foundation has been 'extremely successful' at getting them back."

"Back to the owners?"

"Mostly to the foundation, I take it. She—Delphine Some-Unpronounceable-French-Last-Name—proudly rattled off a number of paintings they'd 'recovered.' None I'd heard of, but art history doesn't figure prominently in law school curriculum."

"Not much in business school either."

"Her point was to make sure I understood they were planning to use the same strategy in their suit for *Party on the Seine*."

"Was this extremely successful strategy used against people the Claims Conference had determined were the rightful heirs?"

"I asked that same question, and she equivocated, saying that this is a unique situation because it's Damien Manet who's claiming ownership."

"So she won't be using the same strategy."

"Which I pointed out to her. Her response was that because of Édouard's will, this will be far easier to litigate than the others."

"Do you think that's true?"

Wyatt hesitates. "Our case rests on proving the painting belonged to the Bernheims, which hopefully we'll be able to do."

"Did Damien or the lawyer say anything about an email he sent on Saturday?"

"Manet sent you another email?"

I text it over. "Is this just posturing, or do you think there's anything here?"

A long pause as he reads it. "I'm guessing if there was any meat, the lawyer would have mentioned it to me. So for now, let's assume this is Damien's style, and that there will probably be more of this type of nonsense coming at us."

"He can't make me enter *Party* into the retrospective, can he?"

"No, he can't. The painting is yours unless proven otherwise. We can't get distracted by these frivolous claims, which may be part of his tactics. Although that's probably giving him too much credit."

"Did you talk to your investigator?"

"Yes, and she, unlike us, knows a lot about art and is excited about doing the digging. Name's Nova Shepard, and she's raring to go."

"That's encouraging at least."

"I don't think you should be as pessimistic as you sound. The Claims Conference does good work, so that part is pretty unassailable. And Nova does good work too. If there's proof to be found, she'll find it."

"That's a big if."

"Is there something you haven't told me that's fueling this negativity? Is there more here than I know about?"

"No," I say quickly. "I guess I'm just worried."

"Sure you are. There's a hell of a lot of money at stake here."

"It's not just about the money . . ."

"Look, Tamara, I can see that *Party on the Seine* means a lot to you. That you have a connection to the painting that goes beyond what it's worth. It's the work of a famous ancestor of yours, handed down through generations. Then stolen from your family by the worst people of the twentieth century. I get it."

"Thanks." It's a nice speech, except it sounds a bit pat, and he's far from appreciating the true depth of my attachment. But what is the true depth of my attachment? Beats the hell out of me.

"I'd like to have Nova look into a few of those foundation cases Delphine was bragging about," Wyatt says. "See what they might tell us about their attack plan. Also to start digging up information on how the Bernheims came to own the painting. Is it okay if I put her in for ten hours? Might be all she needs. Could even be less."

I know I should ask her hourly rate, but I don't. If Nova is psyched to tackle the case, I'd be nuts to restrict her. And if she finds something, well, it could be the key to a gold mine. "Sure. I'd like to wrap this up as soon as possible."

"Got it. But I have one more question."

"Shoot."

"Would you be interested in having dinner with me Friday night?"

"Is that kosher?"

"It's not not-kosher. No superior versus inferior relationship. Nothing adversarial either. What do you say?"

I reflect on Simon's temper and Nick's deceit, on how I've sworn off serious relationships. But given Wyatt Butler's looks and the age difference between us, there's no chance of anything serious developing. "I say let's do it."

WHEN WYATT TELLS me he also lives in the South End, I suggest one of my faves, Metropolis, a small and homey place on Tremont, with excellent food and a laid-back atmosphere. It's also not so loud that you can't hear the person across the table from you—excessive noise being an unfortunate attribute of a growing number of Boston's restaurants. He admits he's never been there, and I suspect it's because he likes the pricier and noisier spots. I figure he'll just have to adapt.

He's ten minutes late, which, as far as I'm concerned is a bad move on a first date. But as soon as he walks in—his movie-star self—I'm inclined to forgive him. Everyone in the room turns to watch him cross to my table, both the men and the women, wondering, I presume, if he's a real movie star. I have an embarrassing flash of pride that he's my date.

I check myself. I'm not a sixteen-year-old with a crush, I'm a thirty-nine-year-old veteran of too many relationships to count, most of which had bad endings. And I like to be the one who calls the shots. "Beauty is as beauty does" was one of my mother's well-worn clichés. Unfortunately, in this situation it looks like beauty does whatever it wants.

"Sorry I'm late," he says as he sits down. "Rotten behavior for a first date. Got a call I had to deal with as I was walking out of the office." He leans toward me and touches my hand. "Will you forgive me and consider a second date despite my rude tardiness?"

"I think we should see how this one works out before I commit." I give him a stern look.

"Tough lady."

"Always."

He looks at me askance. "Always?"

"Most of the time."

We both laugh. I've never dated a man this much younger than I am, and although this should give me pause, it excites me instead. Exactly the kind of thinking that got me into trouble with men in the past.

A waiter comes over to take our drink order. "Dirty martini," Wyatt says. "Grey Goose. Up, with a few cheese-stuffed olives."

"Sorry, sir, only wine and beer."

A flash of a frown, then he turns to me and smiles. "Red or white?"

"How about a nice cab?"

"Now tell me," he says after he's ordered and handed the list back to the waiter. "Who are you?"

"Does that opening always work?"

"Pretty much." He pulls a sheepish face. "But I really do want to know."

"Tell me who you are first."

"I'm Wyatt Abbott Davenport Butler, a moniker that sounds more prestigious than it is. My lineage does go way back—not to any Manets, though—but disaster after disaster, brought on mostly by my ancestors' stupidity, destroyed our part of the family's fortune generations ago. The names are all that's left, and they've been passed down in lieu of status and money. Grew up dirt-poor in northern New Hampshire. No one gave a shit if my middle names were Davenport and Abbott."

"Did you?"

He looks puzzled for a moment. "Give a shit about my name?"

I nod.

"You *are* a tough lady." His eyes sparkle in amusement. "Sorry I questioned it. And now that I think about it, maybe I did. At least a little."

"Is that what motivated you to leave all that dirt behind?"

He bursts out laughing. Then he takes my hand and presses his lips against my pulse spot.

I think about ditching the bottle of wine, ditching dinner, taking him back to my place, and ripping his clothes off. But I control myself. "That doesn't answer my question," I say as calmly as I can.

We make it through the meal without offending any of the other diners, I think. But we can't keep our hands off each other. A shoulder, an arm, a cheek. When he presses his warm hand on my thigh, I almost orgasm then and there. "Let's get the check," I say, my voice husky.

We rush out into the cold air, which does nothing to cool us down, and just about run to my building. Then I do rip his clothes off. And he rips off mine. We make love two times before we finally fall into exhausted sleep. Maybe I should consider switching to younger men on a permanent basis.

SIXTEEN

Wyatt owns a town house I walk by every day on my way to and from work. It's a handsome brick building facing the Southwest Corridor Park that I've already described, the one with all the flora and fauna at the corner of West Canton Street. About half a mile from my apartment. Who knew?

In the three weeks since our dinner at Metropolis, he stayed with me that once, and I've slept at his place four times. Wyatt claims it's more convenient and comfortable at his house. It's definitely roomier and far more charming than my box of square white rooms, what with its carved woodwork and the skylight-topped staircase running four floors through the center of the house, if a bit too professionally decorated for my taste. And then there's his bedroom suite, which takes up the entire top floor, along with a bathroom the size of my living room. It's difficult for me to argue with him, as his claims are true. Along with the fact that it's a much shorter walk to Calliope.

But I don't like that we're on his territory all the time. Which is ridiculous, as he welcomed me with the mi-casa-es-su-casa thing—and four nights out of twenty-one is hardly a constant. My OCD father would have calculated that this is only 19 percent—actually, he would have said 19.047619. And then he would have also figured it the other way: It's 80 percent of all the nights we've spent together. Which is a big chunk.

It's the imbalance that makes me uncomfortable, even though my rational mind recognizes there are no dominance issues here, and I'm sure Wyatt isn't even aware of the disparity. Still, it's his preferred milk in the fridge—4 percent versus my skim—his Spotify playlist, his streaming services. Maybe my unease comes from living alone for so long, the mi-casa-es-*mi*-casa thing, or that five nights in three weeks doesn't feel as casual as I'd like.

Chill out, Tamara. Fun and excellent sex are worth a few accommodations. I don't even drink that much milk.

I've been thinking I might be ready to bring *Party* home—I confess it's partly to spite Damien, but mostly because I miss her. And when she's back, I'll want to spend more time with her, which will give me an excuse to stay at my own place. Wyatt is all for reclaiming her, as he believes having the painting in my possession will strengthen our case.

But I don't contact the Columbia. Even though I believe that what I thought I saw didn't happen, a piece of me still wonders if I could be wrong. What if Berthe does something worse than wink or point a finger? Something dangerous? Admittedly, I'm really going off the rails here. Because what would the danger be? Is she going to jump out of the frame and strangle me? Burn the house down? Yeah, right, that's exactly what a woman painted on a piece of canvas almost 150 years ago is about to do. Or maybe I'm just worried that if I see something again, it won't be Berthe's doing; it's my mind coming unhinged.

WYATT PHONES ME at the office, which we've agreed not to do, as we're both far too busy to chitchat during work hours. So this must be about *Party*.

"I should be home around seven tonight," he says instead. "Want to meet me there? We could get takeout."

Slightly annoyed, I say, "Would love to, but I'll pass." I wouldn't mind making love to that amazing specimen of a man—but I was planning on an early night. Which it won't be if I go. I need some alone time, some quiet, and I want to send a message that this is a casual thing. "Completely exhausted. How about you come to me on Friday?"

"You're way too hot to wait three days for—especially when I know you're only a few blocks away."

"It'll build up your anticipation—make it all that much better." Then I add, to forestall any more debate, "Anything new from my infamous cousin?"

"Delphine called with an offer to buy the painting from you—and settle the suit."

"If they believe I don't own it, how can they buy it? And why would I want to sell it?"

"Ten million dollars."

Although this is a fraction of what the painting has to be worth, I hesitate. Ten million dollars. I could finally pay off my business school loans, my credit card balances, and crank my retirement account back up after all the money I had to withdraw when the divorce forced the sale of our house for less than we owed on the mortgage. I'd be set for life. "Not gonna happen."

"I figured that's what you'd say. But Delphine claims if you turn them down, they're not going to stop until they get *Party on the Seine* to its 'rightful owner.' Said 'rightful owner' whom, I'm guessing, has agreed to leave it to the foundation—maybe even bequeath it now. According to her, no matter what it takes. No matter how much time or how much money."

"Did she say anything about the show at the Louvre?"

"Interestingly, she didn't mention it."

"Do you think she's bluffing about the legal stuff?"

"Could be. But I checked into the foundation's finances, and they do have almost unlimited funds."

"Has Nova come up with anything?"

"She's still waiting on Delphine to send her an English version of Édouard Manet's will, which hopefully isn't as airtight as Damien claims. But she did discover that it was common in the day for those artists to give each other paintings. Particularly early on, when no one was interested in buying their work."

"So what I was saying about Édouard giving *Party* to his brother or to Berthe might be true?"

"Let me pull up Nova's text." The clicking of keys. "Yeah, or she speculated Édouard could have given it to their daughter, Aimée Manet, his niece. Aimée was Colette Bernheim's mother. Seems like there are a number of plausible through lines here."

Just hearing these names fills me with a heady burst of optimism. "There's a connection. There's got to be."

"Unfortunately, there's no official paper trail on those kinds of gifts—or on the many swaps between painters—as they mostly went unrecorded. But people wrote lots of letters then, kept diaries, so Nova is going to search some of the archives. See what she can find."

"And because those belonged to famous people, there should be lots of information, right?"

"Presumably."

"This is fantastic. Thanks. I've got a good feeling about this."

"It's still a haystack. Going through volumes of information, searching for a tiny reference that might not even be there."

"Now it's you who's being pessimistic," I say, stung by his lack of enthusiasm.

"I'm your lawyer—along with whatever else we are—and it's my job to make sure your expectations are realistic. That your decisions are based on facts, not false hopes."

"Are you saying I should take the ten million dollars?"

"No, not at all. We can get them to go higher. Much higher after we get a formal appraisal of the painting's value. I can set that up if you'd like."

"Why should I pay for an appraisal when I'm not going to sell it to them?"

"Just informing you of possible alternatives."

"For me, there aren't any alternatives," I say, even as I'd just been considering what I might do with the money from a sale.

"One is that you could lose. The foundation is a formidable adversary. Extremely formidable. What if Nova can't find the proof you need? What if there's not enough evidence to impeach the will? They win, and then you end up with nothing. It's not all that far-fetched. Being right is no guarantee of success."

IT'S JONATHAN STEIN who calls my office the next day. Alexander tells him I'll get back to him later, but he insists on talking to me now. My first reaction is annoyance—and my second is fear.

"Is this about *Party*?" I bark into the phone.

"And hello to you too."

"Sorry. Hello. Is everything all right? Is there a glitch about my ownership?"

"No glitch with anything like that."

"Well, that's good." I relax in my chair. "So what's up?"

"I think we need to talk about this in person."

Exactly what he said when he wanted to tell me I'd inherited *Party*. "It's that serious? Did anything happen to her?"

"Your painting is fine. There have just been some, well, some odd incidents."

"But you're sure *Party* is fine?"

"Yes, I'm completely sure."

I don't like the sound of this. "Should I come to you? Or do you want to come here?"

"I'll be there in half an hour."

Odd incidents. I pace around the office while I wait, circle after circle, stare out at my little bit of river as I pass by the window, seeing nothing. Despite Jonathan's claims to the contrary, something is wrong with *Party*. Very wrong. Or he wouldn't be on his way over here to talk about what he couldn't discuss over the phone. A paperwork issue? A legal one? Something about the Bernheims? Manet? *Party*'s provenance? Something that might help Damien's claim? Or maybe, just maybe, something that will help mine against him.

When Jonathan arrives, I close the door behind him and scour his face, then wave him into one of the chairs facing my desk, take the one next to his. "What? Tell me."

"It's going to be all right, Tamara."

"Why do I get the feeling it's not going to be?"

"There was a fire at the Columbia Museum, and although—"

I press my hand over my heart, like some nineteenth-century belle on the verge of fainting. "She got burned up?" I squeeze my eyes shut against the vision of my beloved painting completely charred, lifeless. "Is she, is she gone?"

"No," he reassures me. "I know you're freaked-out, but I promise you that your painting is fine. Completely unharmed."

"Then what's wrong?"

"Pretty much every other piece of art in the Holocaust wing was destroyed."

I blink. "Was it white supremacists?"

"They don't know yet, but obviously that's one of the main leads they're following."

"What the hell is wrong with people these days?"

"It's not just these days."

"So, so wait," I say, my brain trying to catch up with all that he's telling me. "*Party* was the only thing that didn't get burned? Was it in a different place?"

"Apparently, the Manet was in the gallery along with all the other artworks the Nazis stole. That's why I wanted to talk to you about this in person."

"How many other pieces were damaged?"

"Close to a hundred."

"Can they be restored?"

"A few." His eyes are bright with unshed tears.

"Oh." How sad for the museum, for the art lovers, for the artists who struggled to create them. "Are you sure this is right? I don't understand how it's even possible she's still intact."

"No one else does either."

"It's so strange . . ."

"They're sending it back to you."

My decision made for me.

Jonathan sits up a bit straighter. "There's something else."

I'm not sure I can take in much more, especially if it's as serious as Jonathan's expression implies.

"This isn't the first time this has happened," he says.

"A fire at the Columbia?"

"No, it's not the first time *Party on the Seine* has been the sole survivor of a disaster."

"What does that even mean?"

"I'm sorry to dump this on you all at once." He leans toward me. "But you own the painting, and now that it's the same thing again, you deserve to know the history. Two incidents are unusual, could be a coincidence, but three . . ."

"What were the other two?"

"Remember the salt mine? The one in Austria where *Party* was hidden? Well, the mine was flooded right before the stash was found, and all the artworks were ruined—except one."

"*Party*?"

"It was the only painting stored in an airtight container. The thought at the time was that some high-up Nazi wanted it for his own. Maybe even Hitler."

I, of all people, can surely understand this obsession. "And the other was that earthquake in Brazil?" I ask, remembering what he told me about how the Claims Conference came to find out about *Party*. "And after the earthquake the same thing happened? *Party* was the only artwork that wasn't destroyed?"

"Yes. But it was in storage—had never been shown, no one even knew it was there—so for those two, there are possible explanations. Not so much the Columbia," he says.

When I just gawk at him, he continues. "I didn't mention anything to the museum. Although I will if it becomes relevant to their investigation, which I doubt. Only a couple of us at the Conference are aware of the painting's history—if it's even germane. It's always possible that three is a coincidence too."

"Do you believe that?"

"What else is there to believe?"

Clearly, neither of us is completely convinced, yet we're both hard-pressed to come up with another explanation. As ridiculous as it is, the idea that *Party* might have somehow been able to save herself scares the shit out of me. And she's on her way back.

WYATT IS WITH me the second time *Party* is delivered to my apartment. He's even more excited than I am, but he doesn't have foreboding crawling through his veins. Three miraculous episodes of virtually rising from the dead. That's probably the wrong analogy, but I feel like it fits. Obviously, I haven't said anything to Wyatt—or to Jonathan—about what I thought I saw in the painting, and Wyatt isn't privy to *Party*'s alleged sole-survivorship episodes. Why would I mention any of this if an overactive imagination is the explanation for the first and coincidence for the second?

Party arrives in what appears to be the same lime-green giant's coffin as the first time, although the guys unpacking it are different. I moved the triptych to the guest room a few days ago, thrilled to get it out of my line of sight, although uneasy about its replacement hanging there.

Once *Party* is returned to her spot between the windows, Wyatt and I sit on the couch gaping at it.

"Fucking A," he says. "No wonder everyone wants this. Even I want it, and I don't care that much about art."

I can barely breathe.

He points to Berthe, who's leaning against the railing, looking across the river to the unseen bank beyond, looking directly at us. Just as she was when she first arrived here. "So that's your great-great, so many greats, grandmother? She's a real beauty." He puts his hand on my thigh. "Almost as beautiful as you."

I'm dropping into the painting, like I've done so many times before. I itch for my sketchbook and pencils, to commune with my painting, with my family, but I don't want to do it while Wyatt is here. Later. When he's gone. When *Party* and I are alone. A waft of calmness sweeps over me, of wonder. Back together again. As we should be.

PART SIX

Berthe, 1872–1874

SEVENTEEN

1872

In January, the well-known London gallerist Paul Durand-Ruel buys two dozen of Manet's paintings and quickly sells a sizable number to collectors. Édouard's success invigorates him, and his high spirits warm everyone around him, especially Berthe. Although she's genuinely pleased that he's receiving the attention he deserves, she can't help feeling devalued, in his shadow, less than.

One afternoon when they're painting together, Renoir tells Berthe, a little apologetically, that Durand-Ruel is in Paris and has acquired five of his oil paintings, including *Dance at Le Moulin de la Galette*, one of Berthe's favorites. Durand-Ruel plans to take them, along with Monet's *Impression, Sunrise*, Degas's *The Absinthe Drinker*, and others by Manet, Sisley, and Pissarro, back to his London gallery. Not one of her friends, including Édouard, has mentioned any of this to her.

Berthe attempts to appear happy at Renoir's news, but her stomach churns with disappointment. Durand-Ruel apparently forgot that Degas had asked him to consider her work, or, even worse, the gallerist had decided to ignore the suggestion because he has already seen some of her attempts and found them wanting. It isn't appropriate for her, as an unmarried woman, to approach Durand-Ruel on her own. Nor is she willing to beg Degas to repeat his request or to ask Édouard for assistance. She still has some pride, diminished as it may be. For two days, she wanders dejectedly around the house, unwilling to eat or leave the premises.

"I will not allow you to descend into a full bout of neurasthenia just because you are not selling as well as the men," her mother announces. "If you do not begin to eat immediately, I'll be forced to send you to Tante Désirée's farm to fatten you up."

"I won't go." Berthe cannot imagine anything worse than being with the perpetually disgruntled Désirée, her mother's sister, who unfortunately is of similar temperament but without Cornélie's flickers of humor and compassion. And then there's her horrid uncle, Gérard, who still wants her to sit on his lap. Remaining here with Maman is also unappealing, but she's not leaving Paris while Édouard is in the city.

"You are a grown woman, Berthe," Cornélie continues. "You cannot act as if you're a child whenever something occurs that isn't to your liking. It is unbecoming."

"Unbecoming? Unbecoming to whom?" Berthe marches up the stairs to her bedroom and closes the door behind her. She throws herself on the bed and presses her face into her pillow, just like the child she isn't.

She often feels as if she is handcuffed by what others say she must be, how she must behave, what is proper. Yet she is also a woman as she has never been before. Loved and loving, experiencing an awakening she never would have believed possible.

It's difficult for them to find time alone, but when they do, Édouard is magical, teaching her about her own body and about his, the pleasure excruciating. She worries that even with the pennyroyal tea, Queen Anne's lace, and cotton-root bark he told her to use, she might become with child. But even this fear cannot curb her passion.

They speak of marrying, of being together for the rest of their lives. But this is no closer to fruition than it was when they began. The judgments of society weigh heavily on Édouard, and despite his willingness to push some of the boundaries with his art, his need to stay within them is equally powerful. The disapproval of their social circle and the possibility that this will endanger his career hovers, ghostlike, over their discussions, for Berthe understands Édouard fears that a divorce and the following scandal will forever put the coveted Legion of Honor medal beyond his reach.

He loves her, of this she has no doubt, and she believes he wishes to marry her as much as she wishes to marry him, that his desire to have a child with her is heartfelt. But his disinclination to declare their love publicly is troubling. And now with Durand-Ruel's dismissal of her work, Berthe feels even more defenseless against the tide of men's choices that shape her future, her success, and her happiness.

The next morning, a note from Édouard arrives, and her mother brings it up to her room, throwing it down on the bed. Cornélie stands with her arms crossed over her substantial bosom, glaring down at Berthe. "So this is why you have been making yourself miserable? Making your father and me miserable? Waiting for a summons from a married man? And a wastrel of one, at that."

As Berthe and Édouard have discussed the dangers of any messages between them being intercepted, she's certain there's nothing untoward inside the envelope. It's strange that her mother hasn't read it already, but Cornélie remains close by her bed as she opens it, which serves the same purpose.

Dear Berthe,

Paul Durand-Ruel came by my studio yesterday, and I showed him the two pieces you are working on. He was most impressed and is excited to see more. He would like to come to your studio and examine your other paintings. I promised I would aid in finding a time that is acceptable to both of you. He is leaving the city in three days and very much hopes you will be able to accommodate him. As you know, Paul has purchased many works by those in our bande, and I hope this will be true of yours also.

Édouard

Berthe jumps out of bed and waves the letter at her mother. "This is wonderful news, and now I must get ready for his visit." She throws off her nightclothes and puts on her painting outfit. "Which ones, which ones?" she mutters to herself as she slips on shoes.

Cornélie takes the note and reads it. "This is indeed good news," she says, her relief palpable. "Much better than I expected."

Berthe hurries down the stairs, unsure whether her mother is referring to the fact that it's an innocuous note, rather than the love letter she feared, or if Cornélie never expected someone of Durand-Ruel's stature to be interested in her work. Most likely both.

NOW BERTHE IS a whirlwind of activity, even eating the meals Marie leaves in her studio, hoping this will give her the clarity of mind she needs to choose her best work. Oils? Watercolors? Pastels? All three? The ones that are most like the others Durand-Ruel has purchased or those more uniquely hers? She places all her finished canvases against the walls, some leaning on top of each other.

Young Woman by a Window. The Mother and Sister of the Artist. Two Sisters on a Couch. Old Way to Auvers. Young Girl with a Parrot. The Harbor at Lorient. Or perhaps the new one she painted during Edma's last visit, *The Cradle,* in which Edma is gazing at her newborn daughter, Blanche, through white gauze hanging over the crib.

If she shows Durand-Ruel too many, he'll be overwhelmed. But if she shows him too few, he'll miss her breadth, both in content and style. She frets, as always, that they are all too feminine, too uninspired, and make no statement whatsoever. Still, she borrows easels from her friends, scatters them around the studio, circles for hours, switching and swapping the canvases, returning them to their previous positions. Her paintings cannot be compared to those of Édouard or Renoir or Degas or Monet, which is exactly what the gallerist will be doing. Perhaps she should tell him not to come.

But she doesn't, and Paul Durand-Ruel, a small but sprightly and well-dressed man, arrives the afternoon before he's to board a ship for London. Cornélie escorts him to Berthe's studio and introduces them, then quickly returns to the house. She leaves the doors between the two structures ajar despite the February wind blowing in at them.

Berthe is unsure how to act as he slowly moves from one painting to another, his hands clasped behind his back. Should she follow along in case he has questions? Ask him about himself and his gallery? Or remain in the background, pretending indifference? She knows not to apologize for her lack of talent, which is what she would like to do, so she stands by the window, gazing out at the withered winter garden, while remaining aware of his every move, his every intake of breath. Even though the studio is cold, she's uncomfortably warm in her velvet gown.

Finally, he turns to her. "I have no interest in works that replicate the attributes of the past."

Is he saying her paintings are too much like the past or that they are moving beyond it? She manages an innocuous nod.

He steps closer to *The Cradle.* "I see what you are doing here." He points to the translucent gauze, which, while covering the cradle, also reveals the sweet face of baby Blanche within it.

She strains to grasp what he's referring to. What has she done?

"And here." Now he's referring to the window beyond Edma, also covered by gossamer curtains. "How you've captured the play of sunlight, brighter close to the window and then radiating outward, changing as it touches the mother and changing even more as it touches the child."

This is what she was trying to do, so it must be a compliment. "Thank you," she says, hoping it's the correct interpretation.

"And the loose brushwork, the quick strokes, your light touch with the broken colors." He bows. "Magnificent, Mademoiselle Morisot. Magnificent."

Berthe is dumbfounded. Even though Édouard and the others have praised the painting, no one ever called it magnificent. And this from Paul Durand-Ruel.

"I'm searching for artists who are willing to break from the traditional and move beyond the constraints of academic painting." He once again circles the easels. "Your work does this, particularly the domestic scenes, capturing the everyday with spontaneity and intimacy. Bringing us into your subjects' world."

He gestures toward *Two Sisters on a Couch*. "And your use of these soft edges here, allowing the forms to blend into the surrounding environment, it's, well, it's exceptionally atmospheric, transient, and we are with the two young women while their moment lasts."

She regains her composure and asks him to sit. They discuss her pictures, the portraits and the landscapes, those of the others in Manet's bande. Durand-Ruel tells her that he's most drawn to artists who share a group affinity. Then he buys four of her paintings and asks her to send more to him in London. "Manet, Monet, Renoir, Degas, and Pissarro have been selling briskly there," he adds. "And I am certain you will do the same."

"I MUST GO right now to thank Manet," Berthe tells her mother after Durand-Ruel leaves, and then she immediately regrets it. She should have said she was visiting a friend and had Rémy take her to Édouard's. She's spinning from the purchase, thrilled with the five hundred francs he paid her. It seems her work does have value. She doesn't say any of this to her mother, who will surely point out the higher prices other artists have received, and add that the male gallerist is most likely only trying to flatter her.

"It is too late in the day for such nonsense," Cornélie says. "We planned to go in the morning for your sitting for the new painting, and that will be speedily enough." Then she takes both of Berthe's hands in hers. "I cannot wait for your father to come home and hear of your success. He will be so gratified. As am I."

Berthe watches Cornélie disappear into the kitchen to give Marie new orders for a more festive dinner, and she has to admit that sometimes she's too critical of her mother, just as her mother is sometimes too critical of her. She walks back into her studio and grins at the empty easels. Then she composes a subdued note to Édouard.

Dear Édouard,

Paul Durand-Ruel purchased four of my paintings and took them to London with him. I am, as you would expect, extremely pleased. I am also forever in your debt for recommending me to him. My mother and I plan to visit your studio tomorrow morning so I can express my gratitude in person. I will wear the black dress with white lace you proposed for the new portrait.

With many thanks,
Berthe

She has Rémy deliver the note to Manet, and when Rémy returns he has a response in hand. Édouard, in an equally restrained manner, writes of how happy he is for her and asks if she could also wear her deep-crowned black hat for the sitting. He adds that he is looking forward to seeing her, a euphemism they use to signal their passion.

THE FOLLOWING MORNING, Berthe takes care getting ready. The dress Édouard suggested isn't one of her favorites, as she believes it doesn't flatter her figure. Her mother has put it much more plainly, commenting that the layers of cashmere flow too freely and make her look fat, the worst criticism Cornélie can level against anyone. But Édouard has said he finds the cinch at the waist particularly provocative and that the thought of this makes him yearn for her. Which is far more important than Maman's disparagement.

She does like the hat. It's tall and sits regally on her head. She plays with the silk ends of the bow at the back, allowing a piece to hang loosely along one side of her neck. Then she pulls out tendrils of curls from the brim so they, too, hang loosely, but around her face. She adds a pair of slightly naughty pink shoes. She feels quite elegant, even a touch sassy.

On the way to the studio, she asks Rémy to stop at the florist so she can buy some violets, one of Édouard's favorite hues. She hopes he'll ask her to hold them or pin them to her dress to add a dash of color to the portrait. Cornélie, who's in a better mood than usual, agrees to this. "For all his faults, Manet did you a service, and a gift such as this is appropriate. Let us go and find a pretty bouquet."

When they arrive, Édouard greets them cordially, telling Cornélie how lovely she looks and then adding, as if an afterthought, that Berthe does also. When Berthe hands him the violets and voices her thanks, they dare not allow their eyes to meet. Édouard settles Cornélie in her usual place and promises that the maid will be by soon with tea and pastries. Antoinette isn't joining them, so Maman has brought a book, which she will hopefully tire of and return home before Édouard is finished.

Édouard finds the most comfortable chair in the studio and seats Berthe in front of a pale white wall. He steps back and scrutinizes her intensely. Berthe stares back at him, trying not to smile at her handsome, brilliant man. But she must be failing, as he shakes his head slightly, glances over at Cornélie, and grabs the bouquet of violets. "Hold these up high or pin them to your dress," he says. "Throw a splash of color into the composition."

Now she can't help but smile. "I was thinking the very thing."

"This is because we are both artists." His voice is indifferent, and he busies himself with his palette and brushes. "Sit tall, please." Then he begins painting in his feverish Édouard way, slashing colors across the canvas, flinging brushes to the ground, crying out in frustration or elation, one exclamation directly following the other. So unlike the careful way she works.

Berthe looks at him straight on, which is what he requested. As she watches him paint, she shifts between pleasure at being in his company, sorrow that they are unable to express their true feelings, and annoyance at his fear of Cornélie finding them out. Would this be such a terrible circumstance? Perhaps if her parents knew about their love for each other, they might force Édouard to marry her, to save her social standing along with their own. But as soon as the thought comes, she banishes it.

That is not the way. She will not play the role of the wronged maiden. He will announce his love for her to the world, his desire to marry her, for her to have his child, and his intention to divorce the barren Suzanne to achieve this. Despite the gossip and rumors, she will hold her head high. But he has only given vague promises about when this will occur, and she worries how much time might pass before he's ready to make his declaration.

Édouard takes a brush out of his mouth. "Your face is sad, which is not the way I want this painting to be." Then he adds in a whisper. "Or you to be."

Berthe glances over at her mother. Cornélie's book is resting open in her lap, and she's snoring softly. "Perhaps a touch of the tragic might add nuance to it? A nod to the forces that thwart our wishes."

His eyes soften, but all he says is, "Perhaps."

Cornélie wakes an hour later and announces it is time to leave. Berthe stands, not unhappy to be released from the difficult position she's been holding. She wants to raise her arms high and twist her hips to relieve the ache that posing has caused, but she cannot. If Cornélie were not here, she would do these very things, and Édouard would take her into his arms, kissing her until she's dizzy and they fall onto their humpbacked red sofa.

Instead, she walks to Édouard, who's adding touches of purple to her hat and the background. "May I?" she asks, not wanting to intrude if he's not ready for her to see it yet.

He looks at her with such longing that Berthe wonders if he's read her last thoughts. "Of course," he says with a slight bow.

Berthe is awed by what he has accomplished in a few short hours. A study in cool tones, black against white, the many shades of purple bursting in unexpected places, startling yet perfect. But it's her own expression that dominates, the verisimilitude of her unwavering and intent look, eyes that reveal so much. Too much. She turns her body to block it from Cornélie.

There is no doubt that Édouard, once again, has made love to her with his brush, but this time there's no subtlety, no doubt of his feelings. He has made her far more beautiful than she actually is, stronger and more confident than she actually is, which must be how he sees her through the mists of his enchantment. There's also no doubt she's looking out at the object of her love, not only with adoration, but with an unveiled yearning tarnished by melancholy.

He has indeed captured her shifting emotions as she sat before him. And she believes that anyone who stands in front of this painting, especially those who know them well, will immediately see what they are trying to hide.

EIGHTEEN

1873

The 1873 Salon snubs the artists in Manet's bande, with the exception of Édouard himself. Almost all the paintings submitted by Berthe, Monet, Degas, Renoir, Sisley, and Pissarro are rejected. Their work is considered too unfinished and sloppy, disrespectful to the canons of French art, and by extension, to the Salon itself. A small pastel of Berthe's, *Little Girl with Hyacinths*, is accepted but is placed poorly, clustered on the lowest row of paintings with many other trifling genre pieces, noticed by few. Berthe is deeply disappointed over the rebuke after her success with Durand-Ruel. Her friends are equally distressed.

Édouard's portrait of her, *Berthe Morisot with a Bouquet of Violets*, is not only positioned by itself on a wall but attracts much attention, most of it negative. A few critics praise his tight brushwork, but more deride his novel approach to portraiture, which delves too deeply into the inner life of his subject. And there are many complaints that his depiction of her is too modern, her straightforward confrontation with the viewer a challenge to the traditional ideals of femininity France holds so dear.

As Berthe feared, this bleeds into aspersions on her character, accusations that she's shameless and unseemly, fomenting speculation about possible impropriety between model and artist. As Édouard is well-known for taking his models as mistresses, the same is assumed of Berthe.

To further verify that she is indeed Manet's paramour, the reviewers point to the fact that no woman of her class would dare stare that unswervingly at a man if she were not. There are crude caricatures in the newspapers, mocking Édouard as a Lothario and Berthe as a fallen woman. After the Salon's opening day, Berthe doesn't return, humiliated by her own artistic failure and the insults to her honor.

Cornélie is furious at the derision, and she declares to their circle that

Bouquet of Violets is a masterpiece that is being cruelly misjudged by those who only look backward rather than forward. And, as she was present during all the sittings, she can attest that Berthe did nothing indecorous, proclaiming the shame should fall on those who speak ill of an innocent girl who posed as a favor to a family friend.

Antoinette Manet expresses the same sentiments, and the influence of the two women quiets the rumors but does not silence them. Hurt and humiliated, Berthe is grateful for these vocal protestations in her defense but fears that, as Maman has always said, Degas too, Édouard will be responsible for destroying her. And perhaps he already has. When she thanks her mother for standing by her, she also apologizes for not aways appreciating Cornélie, and promises she will do better to value her kindnesses in the future. Maman is delighted to hear this, and the two begin to argue less frequently.

Antoinette's next soiree is more crowded than ever, now that the war is two years past and Paris is reigniting its social life with vigor. Berthe is in a fit, as Édouard, unlike their mothers, has said nothing to counter the attacks on her. She finds him in lively conversation in the parlor, more vibrant than ever, intoxicated by the notice he's garnering. When he sees her, he flashes an enormous smile, seemingly unaware of her mortification and distress. Or perhaps he's just unaware, as she believes most men are, of anything beyond himself. She catches his eye and sternly nods toward an empty corner of the room.

He joins her there after a few more minutes of regaling his admirers, maintaining a respectful distance between them. Under cover of the raucous noise of the crowd, he says, "Suzanne is in Switzerland with Léon, visiting her family. If only you and I were able to spend the long night together."

She glares at him, not about to allow his flirtatiousness to dissuade her. Her standing in society is at stake, as is their happiness. "Are you aware of what is being said about me? About us?"

He laughs. "You cannot listen to the chattering hordes. They know not of what they speak."

"Unfortunately, they know exactly of what they speak," she snaps. "And although you may think this aggrandizes your reputation, it is destroying mine."

Édouard looks as if he's been slapped. "It's all idle speculation, my darling, I promise you. No one takes these rumblings seriously."

"I take them seriously."

"I wish there was something I could do, but I am sure that in a week there will be a far greater scandal that will surely eclipse this nonsense. And then it will all be forgotten."

"There *is* something you can do," she retorts, maddened by his flippancy.

He glances around. "Anything," he whispers. "You know I will do anything for you."

"If that's true, then you must do what you have promised. You must tell our families, our friends, and our colleagues that we are in love and plan to marry."

He nods slowly, looking off into the distance. "Suzanne will return by the end of the month. I will speak to her then."

Berthe is suffused with happiness, amazed that something so hurtful has been transformed into something so splendid. He will declare their love, and their future together will be assured. But before she can respond to Édouard, Degas hooks his arm through hers. "Come," he says. "There is someone you must meet." He drags her into the dining room, where there is no one for her to meet.

She turns to him with a smile that's more telling than she knows it should be, but she cannot contain her exhilaration. "Soon your silly tricks will be quite unnecessary, Edgar."

"I fear, my dearest Berthe, that this will not be so."

THE SALON'S RESPONSE to their group's work is in stark contrast to the sales the Durand-Ruel Gallery in London is generating for their "sloppy" paintings. Claude Monet, in particular, is doing quite well, and Berthe and Degas are pleased with how many of their pictures have been purchased by collectors, and how many others the gallerist has bought or consigned.

Not only is Durand-Ruel optimistic about the future of what he refers to as "your movement," but the English reviewers hold more approval than derogation, although some of their criticisms mirror what is being said in Paris. This praise, however muted, makes the Salon's rebuff all that much more difficult to abide. To be spurned in their home country, misunderstood and belittled by their own.

Monet is the first one to bluntly voice their dilemma. The Salon's rejections were stinging, but he's further enraged by the appointment of the Salon's new director, a man who has just coordinated a show at the École des Beaux-Arts exhibiting only works by the old masters. "There is no future for us at the Salon," he tells Berthe, Renoir, and Pissarro at the Morisots' soiree the week after the director's selection. "If we are to go anywhere, we must get there by ourselves."

"At least we have Durand-Ruel," Berthe points out.

Renoir nods. "Why can't we continue to pursue both?"

"In case you haven't noticed, Auguste, we cannot continue with both," Monet says, "as the Salon will not have us. And the new director will make this even more so." He purses his lips. "Berthe is correct that we have Durand-Ruel, and now is the time to take advantage of the success he has brought us."

"So you're back to reviving the idea that we put on our own exhibition?" Pissarro asks, his voice betraying neither encouragement nor derision.

Édouard steps up to them. "Not that failed plan again, Claude. If you ever did manage to put such a rash enterprise together and actually exhibited, the Salon would take it as an affront and never again consider anything you submit."

"Perhaps we don't care," Monet retorts.

"Of course you care. You might have been rejected this year, but this doesn't mitigate the Salon's power. Nor the possibility that next year the jury's decisions will be different."

Although Berthe doesn't wish to disagree with Édouard, his view is restricted by his own achievements at the Salon and his desire for the trappings of traditional success. "I don't believe the decisions will change," she tells him. "Everything they do is based on the premise of upholding French traditions and sustaining the past. How will this ever include us?"

"Where else do the critics go to see art?" Édouard demands. "The dealers and collectors? To alienate the Salon with an alternative exhibition is suicide."

"Don't you understand, Édouard?" Berthe asks him. "As far as the Salon is concerned, we're already dead."

SUZANNE RETURNED FROM Switzerland over a month ago, and as far as Berthe is aware, Édouard has said nothing to his wife about their situation. Ever since the insulting reaction to *Berthe Morisot with a Bouquet of Violets*, her mother has kept an even closer eye on Berthe and Édouard.

No more sniffles or luncheons to interfere with her scrutiny of the painting sessions, whether they are alone or with the bande. No more walks with Antoinette or naps over a closed book. Cornélie has even taken to interrogating Rémy about where he brings Berthe and when he will be retrieving her. Although Rémy is more than willing to help her thwart her mother, his employer's close surveillance makes this difficult.

Berthe hasn't been alone with Édouard in weeks. Between Cornélie's scrutiny and the end of the spring season's events and parties, there have been no opportunities. As the Manets are planning to join the Morisots for a portion of their summer holiday in Biarritz, on the southwest coast, Berthe anticipates this will finally allow them time on their own. And it will offer the opportunity to tell the families their news.

But when the Manets arrive at the coast, it is only Antoinette, Gène, Suzanne, and Léon who disembark from the carriage. Berthe does her best to hide her disappointment, although devastation would be the more apt description. From Cornélie's sour expression, she assumes she is doing a poor job, and she concentrates on the possibility that Édouard will be coming later. During dinner, she discovers that he's in Argenteuil, painting with Monet, and will remain there for the coming weeks. In fact, it turns out the mothers have arranged this visit with the express purpose of encouraging Berthe to accept Gène.

She doesn't know what's more infuriating, Édouard's absence, Cornélie's scheming, or the fact that Gène appears content with the maneuvering. Berthe decides that he looks less like Édouard than he did when he was younger. He's nervous and fidgety, not particularly talkative, prone to migraines and other illnesses, she's been told. She always thought him a sallow shadow of his brother, but now she sees he isn't even that. He has none of Édouard's exuberance, sense of humor, brilliance, or swagger, and she wants nothing to do with him.

But Cornélie and Antoinette will not be deterred. They arrange picnics and hikes, painting and swimming outings. Both families are present at the start of these contrived activities, but soon each person expresses a reason why he or she must depart early.

If Gène weren't so dull, they might share a laugh over their mothers' lack of subtlety, but he seems incapable of appreciating such absurdity. Admittedly, he's a nice man, kind to his mother and Léon, respectful of her and Maman. He even dabbles a little in painting, although his efforts are only a smudged version of his brother's. As is he.

Cornélie takes Berthe aside when she returns to the house with a full picnic basket hours before she and Gène were due back. "The bloom is off the rose," she tells her daughter. "Beauty fades quickly when you are beyond thirty."

"I thought you always claimed I never was a beauty." Berthe's tone is sardonic and, even to her own ears, disrespectful. So be it. Their newfound compatibility has evaporated under Cornélie's latest meddling.

"'Fades' is the foremost word here."

"If you believe your cruel disparagements are going to entice me to marry him, you're much mistaken. They do the opposite. I don't need to be a wife, and I surely will not be his."

Her mother's face softens, although Berthe is suspicious of this. "Bijou, Gène is of good family, with a private income and property."

"So you've said before. And as I said before, I'd rather spend the rest of my life as a poor spinster than be chained to a dull man."

"You can't mean this," Cornélie pleads. "Tell me you will at least consider him."

"You don't even like him. All your railing about how much of a laggard he is. No job. No ambition."

"That's irrelevant. All that's important to me is your future. Please, Berthe. Please think about it."

"If you actually care about me and my future, you'll give up this outlandish fantasy."

Cornélie's eyes fill with tears. "Oh, my baby girl, don't you see that it is you who must give up your outlandish fantasy?"

NINETEEN

1873

When Berthe returns to Paris in the fall, she finds a parcel waiting for her. There's no doubt it's a painting and that the address is written in Édouard's hand. She quickly covers it with the many notes and letters she received while they were on holiday and hurries toward her bedroom.

The ever-vigilant Cornélie stops her before she can reach the stairs. "What is it you have there?"

Berthe presses the bundle to her chest. "I have no idea. As you can see, I haven't opened any of them yet." She tries to squeeze by her mother, but Cornélie blocks her way.

"I meant the package."

"I haven't opened that either."

"Marie!" Cornélie calls out. "Could you please bring us a pair of scissors?"

"It's for me, not for you."

"I'm only trying to help you open it." Maman takes the scissors from Marie. "Let's see what it is." She quickly snips the twine and rips the paper to reveal a small painting. A bouquet of violets, reminiscent of the one Berthe brought to Édouard, or perhaps the same. Alongside the flowers is her red fan from *The Balcony* and a scrolled letter, which is difficult to read but clearly contains both Édouard's and her names. A note on the back says: *For Berthe, Guerlain's Violette de Paine.* A reference to her perfume and the first time he told her he loved her.

"If this is a gift," Cornélie snaps, "you may not accept it."

"You had no objection to Degas's gift last summer. Or the one before that."

"Degas is not a married man."

"But Monet and Renoir are, and you didn't say a word about the pictures they gave me." Berthe gazes down at Édouard's painting, which is exquisite, and she marvels at how he captured the essence of the flowers. She doesn't tell Cornélie about the afternoon he showed her Madame de la Tour's *The*

Language of Flowers, in which the author suggests that violets refer to a secret love. Nor does she mention that this is more than a gift; it's an apology. Or more precisely, an attempt at one.

Tomorrow is a bande painting day, and she will make clear to him that a present, no matter how dazzling, will not atone for his cowardly absence over the summer. She will accept no excuses, which are sure to be extended, and will inform him, in no uncertain terms, that the only way to redeem himself is to proclaim their love and their plans to be together, as he has promised so many times.

That evening, her father is suddenly stricken with crushing chest pains and shortness of breath. Dr. Aguillard is called. After an examination, he informs them that Papa's lungs and heart have been weakened by an attack of cardiac asthma, and that he is very ill. He is to remain in bed, taking no exercise, and no one in the household is to upset him in any way. The doctor gives Cornélie a packet of dried foxglove, which he instructs her to grind into a fine powder and brew as tea. Papa must drink as much as he can, as this is the only remedy for his condition.

Berthe is terrified by the diagnosis, and she and Cornélie rush to make the tea. Then they sit by his bed, begging him to drink it. He manages a few sips, and his breathing does seem to come a bit easier. When he finally falls asleep, the women drag themselves to their own beds.

As Berthe tries to settle herself, to calm her jangling nerves, she realizes that her mother will have to stay by Papa's side in order to nurse him, and therefore Cornélie won't be able to accompany her to Édouard's tomorrow. She wishes the state of affairs could have come about for another reason, but at least there is this.

WHEN SHE ARRIVES at the studio, Monet, Degas, Renoir, Sisley, and Pissarro are quarreling over the possibility of an independent show, something they have all been talking about more seriously of late. Édouard isn't there, apparently having just stalked off after belittling the idea as pure folly.

Degas, an exceptional mimic, places one hand out as if resting it on a walking stick, an Édouard-like gesture, and cries in a voice that sounds exactly like his friend's, "Why don't you all stay with me at the Salon? Can't you see I'm on a winning streak?"

The men break into hearty laughter, and Berthe smiles uncertainly.

"He's obviously wrong," she says. "But don't you think Édouard believes this is what would be best for us? That he's trying to help us, however misguided his methods may be."

Degas frowns at her. "He believes this because he can't think of anything or anyone beyond himself. He does not understand that his winning streak isn't ours."

"Was Édouard's behavior what prompted all that noise when I came in?" she asks.

Monet waves his hand dismissively. "Before we go into that, let me tell you about something incredible that has happened. Do you know the cartoonist and photographer Nadar?"

When Berthe indicates she does not, he continues. "No matter. He told me he's giving up his big studio on Boulevard des Capucines, and to my astonishment, he offered the space to us for our exhibition at no cost!"

"He feels sorry for us," Sisley gripes. "We aren't charity cases."

"What does that matter?" Degas retorts. "It's Boulevard des Capucines! A busy spot, with enough room to hold many dozens of paintings. And it's filled with light! Must you find fault with everything, Alfred?"

"That's wonderful, Claude," Berthe interjects in the hope of cooling the antagonisms. Consensus is going to be difficult to come by in this group of iron-willed men, but as she believes this show will be in all their best interests, it's going to be upon her to help find it. "Excellent. Do we have a date?"

This leads to a more conciliatory discussion, during which it's agreed that their exhibition will be held the following spring. Then there's a lengthy argument about the exact day: before the Salon's, to overshadow it, or afterward, to make the point that they are having the final word? This is followed by an even more raucous row over whether they should become a cooperative business, paying dues, sharing profits, and holding an exhibition every year until they achieve the acceptance and sales they deserve.

Monet and Degas are in favor of this, but the others have concerns. How much will the dues be? Who will decide who is to be included? How will the paintings be chosen? How will the profits be shared? What if there are no profits? How will the best display space be allocated? Will there be prizes?

When Monet suggests that one of the rules for inclusion be a written denunciation of the Salon and the promise not to submit there while a member of the cooperative, the shouting becomes loud enough that Berthe is sure it can be heard from the street. In the midst of this, Édouard returns.

He walks up to Berthe. "You must not ally yourself with this group of madmen! Theirs is a radical endeavor, which will end in disgrace. You cannot draw attention to yourself in this way."

Berthe stands and pulls herself to her full height. "You have no right to address me in this manner. Or to tell me what I may and may not do. I will choose with whom I associate and with whom I ally myself."

The studio falls silent.

"I'm only interested in what's best for you," Édouard says, clearly taken aback by her forceful response.

Berthe doesn't understand why he's so shocked. It's not as if he were unaware of her plans to join with the others. Or that she doesn't take well to commands. Then she realizes he's acting this way because he thinks of her as *his* and as such believes it's not only his right but his obligation to protect her. For a moment, she softens, but then she reminds herself that he has no claim to her, and her anger flares. Until they are engaged or married, she has no allegiance to him nor any need of his protection.

SHE'S FURIOUS AT Édouard's presumptions and lack of consideration, his desire to have everything while giving up nothing, yet none of this quells her longing for him. She's glad she stood up to him today, although frustrated she didn't have the opportunity to reproach him for his spinelessness in Biarritz. Nonetheless, she finds herself reliving their most intimate moments together, feels his body against hers, and then these recollections are shattered by the fact that he turned his back on the opportunity to be with her this summer. How can she love him this much when he's been so thoughtless and unkind?

My dearest Edma,

I work hard without respite or rest, and still I do not succeed. Monet, Degas, Renoir, Sisley, Pissarro, and I have agreed on a charter for our new enterprise, but the arguments have been fierce, and I have no certainty that any of this will ever come to pass. Édouard has refused to join us, and sometimes I believe he has made the right choice.

He is such a difficult man, such a brilliant man, a man so certain of himself and his destiny, and yet sometimes so faint of heart. I am sad, sad as one can be, and I wonder if there will ever be an end to this. What I see most clearly is that my situation is impossible from every point of view.

Once she sends the letter to Edma, she decides she must go to Édouard, that she needs an answer, no matter how painful it might be. It takes her days to gather her courage, and when she finally does, she stands before her wardrobe and searches for a demure outfit with a high neckline, possibly something too big for her. It's important to convey that she's serious, that she is not coming to him for love, but for resolution.

Instead, she chooses her new low-cut black gown and wraps a velvet band around her neck, a nod to Édouard's appreciation of the contrast between her pale skin and a dark fabric. Again, she wears the pink shoes, annoyed with her weakness and invigorated by her daring.

When she steps through Édouard's door, he's alone, as she suspected he might be at this hour. He rushes toward her, arms outstretched. "My darling," he cries. "It has been too long."

She keeps her own arms pressed to her side and shakes her head vigorously. "I am not here for that, Édouard."

It's as if he doesn't hear her. He grabs her by the waist and twirls her around, as he did at the Salon when she praised *The Balcony*. "My Berthe, my Berthe. I've missed you so."

"Put me down!"

"Never, never ever," he sings as he dances across the room, swinging her in step with his own, her shoes flying above the floor. "Never, never ever."

Berthe tries to pry his fingers open. "I mean it, Édouard! Put me down this instant or I'm going to tell Suzanne what you have done."

This catches his attention, and he stops abruptly, releasing her.

She stumbles backward, dizzy and wobbly on her feet. "This cannot go on any longer."

He takes her arm to steady her, and she shakes him off. "Come sit," he says, trying to lead her to the sofa. "Tell me what's troubling you."

"We can stay right here." Berthe is not about to sit with him. She's not strong enough to withstand being that close. "Why didn't you come to the coast with your family?"

"I was with Claude. You know that. I was riding a wave of prodigious painting that was so remarkable I was unable to stop. Couldn't stop. It would have been unfair to me, to my art."

"How about what's fair to me?"

"It had nothing to do with you."

"And that is exactly my point," she cries. "It never has to do with me. It always has to do with you. Just as Edgar says."

"What does Degas have to do with this?" Édouard's eyes slip away, and she can see he understands everything she wants from him. But as she anticipated, he's going to do whatever he can to sidestep.

"Are we ever to marry?" she demands.

"Of course we are." He reaches out for her, but she retreats. "You know how much I love you. How much I want to be with you."

"No. As a matter of fact, I know nothing of the sort. You say these things, but I haven't seen anything that convinces me you actually mean them."

Those incredible blue eyes lock on to hers. "After all we've been to each other," he says softly. "How can you believe anything else?"

She looks away so he won't see the longing on her face or the tears gathering in her eyes. "You must tell Suzanne, everyone. If you do not do this without delay, we will be nothing to each other."

"You don't mean that."

"How dare you assume you know what I mean and what I don't mean," Berthe explodes. "Until I'm your wife, you will not touch me!" Her voice catches on the words, and she rushes toward the door.

"Don't go," he pleads. "Stay, please. We'll talk, figure how, how to, what's the best way to ensure we are together."

She turns to him. "Talking is easy, Édouard. We've done that before. You've made promises before. All empty. It's been almost two years since I committed myself to you, and you're still married to Suzanne."

His expression is both sad and sheepish. "I'm sorry, Berthe. I'm a selfish man, a thoughtless one who tends to avoid facing thorny problems. But I promise you, this is going to change. We will find a way."

Berthe is astonished that Édouard admitted to a failing, one that is indeed true, and she's moved by his confession. But recognition of weakness doesn't extinguish it. "It's not 'we' who must find a way," she tells him, trying to keep her voice from trembling, to stay true to her conviction. "It is you who must do this."

"I will." He has the look of a small boy who has been caught in mischief and desperately wants to avoid punishment. "This time I promise I will."

She shakes her head but can't stop her tears. After the Salon's rejection, if she gives Édouard up, she will have nothing.

He pulls her to him, and she doesn't resist. She's drained, the fight gone out of her. Her arms encircle him, and her tears fall on his shirt. "Hush, hush, my sweet," he murmurs. "Please don't cry. I want to make you happy, never to make you cry."

Then he kisses her tears, her mouth, and there is nothing to do but slip into the wonder of loving him. He carries her to their sofa, and she does what she promised herself she would not. She gives in to him, gives into herself.

As they lie together, wrapped in each other's arms, legs entangled amidst the folds of her dress, Berthe runs a finger languidly through the curls of red hair on his chest. "I love you," she whispers, sliding toward a contented doze.

"And I you." Édouard tightens his arms around her, and she can feel his heart pounding when it should be slowing down. "There, there might," he stammers, then clears his throat. "I feel, I mean, I think I have an idea for a path that would keep us together. One that will be much easier . . ."

Berthe is now fully awake, alert and distrustful of the hesitation in his voice. "What path?"

"It will better for everyone," he continues in the same halting manner.

"Who's everyone?" she demands.

"You, me, our families." He swallows hard. "I think you should marry my brother Gène."

TWENTY

1873–1874

Berthe wants to take to her bed, hide beneath the covers, lie there until there's no life left in her body. But Papa is too ill, and she must help her mother tend to him. Edma and Yves can't come because they must care for their own children, and although Tante Désirée was to stay with them in Paris for a week, her bad temper made everyone, including Papa, feel worse. Much to everyone's relief, after two days Maman sent her sister home.

Many of Cornélie's friends offer their assistance, but they do little more than send their maids with food, and Marie is completely overwhelmed by the extra work a sick man creates. Berthe doesn't have a free moment to think, let alone paint, and, as she has neither the time nor the desire to go to Édouard's studio, there's no opportunity to discuss the fine points of the upcoming exhibition with her fellow artists or to smooth over their disagreements. She despairs over her father's fate, her ability to produce anything worthy in time for the exhibition, and Édouard's betrayal.

Papa's death is shocking, although expected. But there's also a sense of peace, as his last weeks had been dreadfully painful for him as well as the rest of the household. Out-of-town family descends, and there's tumult and tears for the week before the funeral. Berthe is grateful to have her sisters and brother with her to share the burden of their mother's grief.

The funeral is dignified and well attended, with mourners including her father's many political colleagues: the mayor of Paris, the president of Île-de-France, and the entire regional council. These high-ranking officials, Berthe's extended family, and the Morisots' wide social circle spill beyond the church's main sanctuary.

Even Cornélie is heartened by the size of the gathering, gratified by the respect the large company conveys. All of Berthe's painter friends are there, each noting their sorrow at her loss and then informing her of the many impediments the others are creating for the exhibition.

After the service, Antoinette, Édouard, and Gène approach. Berthe refuses to acknowledge Édouard, although the lure of him is no less powerful than always, and she greets the other Manets as civilly as she is able. She's grown suspicious that the meddling she initially attributed solely to Cornélie and Antoinette stretches beyond the mothers, that both Gène and Édouard were also involved in the machinations last summer, perhaps the real reason for Édouard's absence. When the others turn their backs in chorus and begin speaking to one another, leaving Berthe alone with Gène, her suspicions solidify, deepening the pain of Édouard's deception.

Gène smiles at her tentatively and says, "I hope you are bearing up under your loss."

"I am doing as well as can be expected." She searches for someone, anyone, who might want to express their condolences. How could Édouard scheme for her to marry Gène while promising it was he whom she would wed? She presses a handkerchief to one eye and then the other, grateful her tears will be interpreted as a daughter's sadness.

Gène touches her sleeve, his expression earnest. "I am so sorry, Berthe. I, too, had difficulty after my own father passed. It seemed so premature. So unfair."

Berthe is relieved when Edma joins them. As Gène turns to greet her sister, Berthe tries to slip away, but Edma grabs her hand. "I was just about to ask Gène to join us at the house this afternoon for a small repast," Edma says. "I was wondering if you are available to escort him there."

Aghast, Berthe stares at her. Edma too? "This luncheon is only for family."

Edma doesn't meet her eye and instead smiles at Gène. "And a few close friends."

FINALLY, THE MOURNERS disperse and quiet descends on the house. Berthe and Cornélie sleep for two days. When Berthe crawls out of bed, she discovers that the strain of the last months has caused her to lose so much weight her clothes no longer fit. And now that Cornélie doesn't have her husband to fret over, she turns to her daughter.

Berthe allows her mother to believe she's only mourning her dear papa, but her grief is more sweeping, beyond even Édouard's latest act of duplicity, encompassing the demise of the future she foolishly believed would be hers. One that has now been replaced by a yawning barrenness stretching before her.

Condolence letters and notes arrive daily, tied together by the postmaster into large packets. Cornélie claims that responding to them makes her too sad, so this task falls to Berthe. One day, a note arrives from Gène, asking Berthe to accompany him to dinner at Maison Dorée, one of the most elegant restaurants in Paris. She answers quickly, claiming she's too busy with her newly widowed mother and the upcoming exhibition to consider such an outing.

She hopes her response will put an end to Gène's efforts but fears it will not. A deep and dark dread consumes her, merging panic over what may come to pass with sorrow over what will not. The malaise is so heavy she can feel its weight pressing down on her shoulders, squeezing her stomach.

But she must not give in to self-pity, nor allow the desires of others to determine her fate. She has always claimed her wish was to live her life as a painter, not as a wife, and that is exactly what she will do. The exhibition is in three months, and this is her way forward. She has a few pictures she hopes may be good enough to be shown when completed, but she needs more. She dons her overly large painting outfit and returns to her studio.

WHILE BERTHE WAS nursing her father, Degas brought her a copy of the agreement that formally established their new communal enterprise. She signed it and paid her sixty francs dues without giving the details much notice. Reading it now, she sees she's become a member of the Anonymous Cooperative Society of Artists, Painters, Sculptors, and Engravers. A true collective, in which all the artists share both the costs and the profits, although one with a dreadful name that never would have been adopted had she been involved in the decision.

There are eleven founding members, but she, Degas, Monet, Renoir, Sisley, and Pissarro form the governing council. The first thing she suggests is that, as their purpose is to promote independent art, they refer to themselves as "the Independents," rather than the title on the charter. This is immediately agreed to, followed by a much less pleasant discussion of which other artists to include in their show.

Berthe is consumed by painting, which has the dual effect of producing a number of pictures that are suitable for the exhibition and suppressing her thoughts of Édouard. She offers three watercolors, two pastels, and four oils. The oils are the ones she has the greatest hope of selling, or at least of receiving some acclaim: *Hide and Seek*, *The Harbor at Lorient*, *The Mother and Sister of the Artist*, and *The Cradle*.

When she goes to look over the suite Nadar has loaned them, she's impressed by the many large rooms, all with tall windows facing the fashionable avenue. There will be more than enough space to hang single rows of paintings, in contrast to the suffocatingly overstuffed walls of the Salon. In their exhibition, each piece of art will have the opportunity to be seen and valued without being squeezed out by others. And, as all of the city's high society will be strolling by, they will inevitably be drawn to the colorful spectacle on full view from the street.

Thirty artists are represented, many of whom have been rejected by the Salon and some completely unknown to the Parisian art world. The council selected each work with care, choosing those they believed to best represent the independence of spirit they're promoting, as well as being of the highest quality. The founding members draw straws for the favored locations, and, under Renoir's direction, hanging the show is completed in a week.

The exhibition is set to run from April 15 to May 15, starting two weeks before the Salon and overlapping it for another two weeks. Each of the artists is assigned a date when he, or in the unique case of Berthe, she, will be responsible for selling tickets at the front table. Although the expectation is that the group will earn money from the sales, the entrance fee should at least cover their costs if things don't go as hoped.

The day before the exhibition, Berthe and Degas review the suite of rooms. "There will certainly be derision from all the well-known sources," Degas says. "But I believe there will also be many others who will appreciate that the staid art of the Salon is just that, and recognize we are the future."

Berthe would like to agree with him, but she's afraid to be too optimistic. Even works that have been accepted by the Salon are routinely derided if they lean too far beyond the traditional, which all of these do. And although

Durand-Ruel has been selling their paintings in London, the same is not true here. As it's Parisian gallerists and collectors who will be their audience, along with the Parisian critics who have been the most disparaging, this does not bode well. She doesn't voice any of this, just links her arm through Degas's and says, "From the lips of a child to the ear of God."

As they wander, Berthe begins to feel better. There is no doubt the works are magnificent, and seen together like this, the riotous colors, the thick brushstrokes, the light and the light and the light . . . so exciting, so awe-inspiring. They walk past Degas's *The Dance Class* and *After the Bath*, Renoir's *La Loge*, Cézanne's *A Modern Olympia*, Monet's *Impression, Sunrise*, and her own *The Cradle*. The future indeed.

The artists and their supporters have been heralding the upcoming show to the press and the public for months, and when it opens, it immediately attracts a crowd. Some are just curious, and a few appear to be attentive, perhaps inclined toward open-mindedness, but the majority are horrified. From lowly workers to women in the finest fashions to erudite reviewers, the response is virtually unanimous, summed up by a reporter for *La Presse*: "The debaucheries of this new school are nauseating and disgusting."

Berthe is stunned by the viciousness of these attacks. Yes, she was concerned about the response, but she never imagined this measure of derision, almost malice. She scours the papers for a positive comment. There are a small number, but even these are qualified. "The work is neither tiresome nor banal," *Le Siècle* reports. A column called Art News acknowledges that there are a few paintings the Salon might have accepted, and then goes on to criticize all the rest. *La Patrie*, while acknowledging that artists have the right to hold a renegade exhibition, wonders if perhaps it's all a joke, if a single prankster has been "dipping his brushes into paint, smearing it onto yards of canvas and signing it with different names."

Day after day, the public fills Nadar's rooms with ridicule, laughter, and hoots, all pointing to the perceived deficits in the artworks. Sloppy. Incomplete. Unfinished. Trees that are blue instead of green. Unacceptable. Lazy. Deplorable. Some visitors are so irate they demand their admission fee be refunded. Except for the hours when she is responsible for selling tickets, Berthe does not return after the opening.

But she cannot hide from the condemnation. Her mother is incensed, telling Berthe that her disgrace is akin to another death in the family. "It must be obvious, even to you, that your entire group is mad. After all that work, you didn't sell a single painting, and therefore there was no need to expose yourself to such mockery." Cornélie's eyes fill with tears, as they are wont to do at any moment since her husband died. "I beg you, Berthe, if you do not give up this nonsense even Gène Manet will not want to marry you."

Cornélie points to the review in *Le Charivari* by Louis Leroy. "Singling you out," she says, "Leroy claims your painting is shoddy, that you have no interest in spending the time needed to produce a work of art. And I quote him when he says Morisot 'makes exactly as many brushstrokes lengthwise as there are fingers, and the business is done.'"

Nor does Leroy limit himself to criticizing her. He spreads his judgments across all the artists, particularly Monet. He takes an unnatural hatred to his *Impression, Sunrise*, a magnificent painting of Le Havre harbor with a rising red sun reflected in the water that captures the fleeting quality of the light. But to Leroy, it's an abomination, and he scorns it as all impression and no sunrise, and derisively calls the entire exhibition "the work of untalented impressionists."

"Bijou, there is no hope for you in this," Cornélie tells her. "Promise me you will stop this useless pursuit and find the true meaning of a woman's life, as a wife and mother. I don't know how much more sorrow I can withstand."

Berthe is too disheartened to defend herself. Without love and without art, there is no point, and she cannot replace either of these with her mother's idea of the true meaning of a woman's life. She places her hands in her lap and looks over Cornélie's shoulder.

To make matters worse, Durand-Ruel is experiencing business difficulties and has stopped purchasing paintings while he attempts to return to solvency. Although this is crushing for Berthe, it's much more dire for some of the others who depended on his financial support to feed their families. Monet, Pissarro, and Sisley are stricken.

When the exhibition ends and they count up the receipts, it becomes even clearer how badly they fared. Sisley, Pissarro, and Monet sold a few paintings, but for meager sums, together totaling less than 1,500 francs. Berthe and Degas sold nothing, as did most of the other artists. They have a debt of 3,000 francs, and each member is assessed 190 francs in order to pay the bills. Which many of them do not have. Their charter is dissolved, and the Independents are no more.

MAMAN ENLISTS EDMA and Yves to convince Berthe to marry. Her sisters write letters describing all the advantages of being a wife, none of which Berthe believes, as she has been the recipient of their tales of marital woe. They also tell her what a suitable husband Gène Manet will make, how unassuming and mild he is, presumably a comfortable companion, and from such a good family. But "unassuming," "mild," and "comfortable" do nothing to tempt her. In fact, heralding these qualities does the opposite.

Her mother invites Gène to dinner frequently, sometimes with Antoinette and sometimes without. Gène earnestly takes up the role of courting Berthe, bringing flowers, complimenting her beauty, requesting her company on walks and painting outings. He's very polite, although he does fidget so, and seems to be constantly suffering from headaches. Berthe goes through the motions to avoid her mother's cutting comments, numb to his bland charms.

Finally, Cornélie is so desperate she asks Édouard to speak with Berthe, going as far as sending her daughter to his studio without accompanying her. In earlier days, Berthe would have been ecstatic, but she is numb to this also.

Édouard is cautious and deferential when she arrives, leading her to a chair rather than to the sofa, pouring her tea, and offering a tart. Berthe ignores the pastry and accepts the tea, but she doesn't drink it. She has no wish to hear him extol Gène's virtues, but as with so many things lately, she hasn't the strength to resist.

"I'm sorry about the exhibition," he says self-consciously. "If it makes you feel any better, I've also been the recipient of the scorn so wrongfully heaped on all of you."

"It does not," she says. Although he's sitting a respectable distance away, she can feel the power of him, of his presence. He has destroyed her, and yet her anger is as deadened as her spirits. If only her desire for him was equally so.

He forces a chuckle. "It seems that the fact that I wasn't participating did nothing to stop the chattering hordes from attacking me too."

She shrugs, although she does find it curious that everyone appears to assume he's their leader, however loudly he protests that his tight brushstrokes and realism differentiate his work from theirs. And perhaps he is, Manet's bande and all. But he is gone to her, she to him.

He's silent for a moment, then says, "He's not a bad man, my brother. In truth, quite a good one."

"A far better one than you, of that I am certain."

Édouard hangs his head. "I love you and—"

Berthe stands. "That is a lie, and I have no interest in listening to your fabrications."

"Please, Berthe, please sit." His eyes are full of pleading, and if she didn't know better, she'd think they were also full of love. "I don't deserve it, but can you please hear me out?"

She sits. After all this, how can he still bring her to her knees?

"I'm, I'm not as strong as I believed I was, and I'm as distraught over this failing as you must be."

She doubts this but says nothing.

"There isn't anything I want more than for us to be together," he continues. "But I can't bring the shame of divorce on my family. At the same time, I cannot live a life without you in it."

"I see," she says, amazed that her voice remains firm while every other part of her is curdling into pulpy mush.

"And this is why marrying Gène could work for us."

"I do not see it that way."

"Think about it, Berthe. If we become family, we can kiss each other's cheeks on meeting, spend holidays and vacations together, find opportunities to go off on our own."

She's horrified, speechless. Has he actually convinced himself this will "work" for them? Does he not understand that if she agrees to marry Gène they will never be lovers again?

"My love, my darling, don't you see?" He kneels next to her chair. "So sadly wondrous, our love. A miracle and a catastrophe entangled together. But this way, we will be linked forever, even if it's not the way we long for it to be."

She stands, and he does too. When she slaps him, he presses his hand to his face with a look of complete bewilderment. Further indication, if she needed any, that he has no comprehension of what he is asking. Or what the consequences will be.

As Berthe climbs into the carriage, she keeps her face averted from Rémy. She will not marry Gène. She will never be alone with Édouard again. She will submit no more paintings to exhibitions. She stares out the window at the newly constructed avenues branching outward, bursting with people and conveyances. No new avenues for her. Her days stretch before her, empty and hollow, filled with loneliness.

WHEN SHE RETURNS home, Cornélie takes one look at her and begins to cry. From her mother's red and swollen eyes, it's obvious that these are not the first tears of the day. Berthe sits and places her arms around her mother. "Papa wouldn't want you to be so sad all the time," she says.

Cornélie presses a handkerchief to her nose and shakes her head.

"I know how much you miss him, but—"

"I do miss him, but my tears are not for him."

Berthe pulls away. "What's wrong?" she demands, thinking of her sisters, their children, Tiburce. "Was there an accident? Is someone ill?" Please, she prays, not another loss. Her mother will not be able to bear it. Nor will she.

Cornélie shakes her head again. Her lips quiver, and her crumpled face makes her appear twice her age. "I'm, I'm not a young woman . . ."

Berthe gasps. "Are you sick? Has the doctor been here?"

"No," Maman says quickly, clutching Berthe's hands. "No, no, it is not I. It, it is you."

Berthe drops her head to the back of the couch and closes her eyes. She doesn't have the strength to hear any more of Gène Manet.

"Bijou, please, please consent to this marriage. The other Manet will never marry you, and after the catastrophe at your show, what else is there for you?"

"No," Berthe says without moving.

Cornélie is not to be dissuaded. "Gène is very much in love. He will be a good husband and take care of you."

When Berthe doesn't respond, she adds, "If you can't do this for yourself, do it for me. I may not be around much longer, and I do not want to spend my last days fearing for your future. I cannot bear for you to be alone after I'm gone."

Berthe wants to call her mother out on the heartlessness of her words, on the immorality of using Berthe's fear of her death to prod her daughter to comply with her wishes. But she has no fight left in her. And how much does it matter? How much does anything matter, given the bleakness ahead? At least if she does as Cornélie asks, as Edma and Yves and Édouard ask too, she will become a Manet, sister-in-law to Édouard, taking the scraps, holidays with him and Suzanne, a kiss on the cheek.

IN DECEMBER, BERTHE puts on a long-sleeved, unembellished black dress to marry Gène. It's an ensemble more suited to a walk through the city than to a bride, but as this is to be a civil ceremony, there will be no elaborate service and few guests. Not the wedding their mothers would have chosen, but Berthe refuses to participate in a spectacle for a marriage she has been practically forced into by those she trusted most. She uses the excuse of her father's recent death for the simplicity, but she doubts anyone is fooled.

Edma and Yves have traveled to Paris for the event, but as she holds her sisters partially responsible for this debacle, their attendance does nothing to cheer her. She knows Gène would also prefer a church and a well-attended celebratory dinner, but he's so astounded she's agreed to be his wife that he's amenable to whatever will make this so.

Edma points out that this type of adoration and acquiescence are valuable attributes in a husband. "It's always better to be the one who loves less," she says as she tries to fluff Berthe's skirt in a futile attempt to make it appear more festive. "You will always hold the most sway, and you will be shielded from the pain of the deception all men eventually commit against their wives."

Berthe turns and looks at her sister in disbelief. Edma, of all people, is aware of the excruciating pain she, Berthe, is suffering at this very moment. To be marrying Gène with Édouard standing beside his brother in support of the nuptials. To become Madame Manet with the wrong Manet as her husband. How can Edma think there is anything about this situation that will shield her from this deepest of wounds?

Edma touches her cheek. "I'm just trying to find the brighter side."

"Don't bother. There is none."

It's snowing as Rémy drives them to the municipal building, and those inside the carriage are silent during the ride. The edifice is decidedly grand, neoclassical, with pediments and ornate friezes, massive columns framing a wide stairway. Just as quietly they ascend the steps. It's all Berthe can do to stop herself from rushing back to the street and begging Rémy to take her home.

Instead, she walks through the door. The interior is far less impressive than the exterior, as nothing here has been repaired since the war. Cracks fork along the walls and floors, boulders litter the edges of the hallways. Berthe can't help but note that this destruction and lack of resurrection are an apt metaphor for what is to come.

Gène, Antoinette, Léon, Suzanne, and Édouard are already in the room when they arrive. Gène rushes to her, takes her hands. "You are so fetching, my love. My very own beautiful bride."

Berthe lowers her eyes but doesn't remove her hands from his. She's sorry she will not be the wife he hopes for, and it occurs to her that he's just as much a casualty of these maneuverings as she is.

Antoinette hugs her and calls her "daughter." Suzanne does the same and calls her "sister." Édouard and Léon bow. Cornélie, Yves, and Edma come forward to hug Antoinette and Suzanne, then nod to Gène, Léon, and Édouard. Berthe looks at her feet, and no one says anything. One big happy family.

They all appear thankful when the magistrate enters, but Berthe is filled with dismay. This is going to happen. This is going to happen now. There is no way out for her. She dares a glance at Édouard, but he's engrossed in straightening Gène's already straight bow tie. Or pretending to be.

The magistrate clears his throat, places Berthe and Gène in front of him, while the rest fan out behind them. It is mercifully quick, only a few words, the exchange of rings, a perfunctory kiss. A luncheon follows, and then she and Gène leave for his large house at 40 Rue de Villejust, where they will live. That night, Berthe experiences the act in the way Edma had described it. No sweetness, no love, no pleasure, and, yes, humiliating.

PART SEVEN

Tamara, the present

TWENTY-ONE

Jonathan calls a couple of days after *Party* arrives. "Did the delivery go okay? How does the painting look? Any damage?"

"So many questions," I tease.

"Are there any answers?"

"No damage that I can see—and, let me tell you, I've checked. Pretty sure it's the same as when it left." But I've got to confess I do feel a little differently about the painting. I haven't forgotten my imaginings about Berthe's gestures. Or about the three sole survivals. The latter like God saving the firstborn Jewish sons. Could have been a miracle. Could have been a bizarre coincidence. Could have been total fantasy.

I'm betting on the fantasy explanation for both the pass-over and the gestures, but it's not as easy to dismiss the whole emerging-unscathed-from-a-flood-and-an-earthquake-and-a-fire thing. Put this way, it sounds almost biblical itself. I checked into the incidents after Jonathan told me about them, and all three actually occurred. No fantasy there.

"I have a favor to ask," Jonathan says tentatively.

"Seeing as how I owe you about a zillion, whatever it is will be difficult to refuse."

"I've, uh, I've never seen the painting, and I was—"

"Anytime," I tell him, happy to be able to return even a splinter of his kindnesses. "I'm usually at the office until seven or eight, but you name the day and I'll meet you here whenever it's good for you."

"Tomorrow's Christmas Eve, so that won't work. But any of the next few nights after that are open."

"Do you get Christmas Day off?"

"Even we conscientious Jews at the Conference don't have to work on Christmas."

"How about you come here late afternoon. We'll hang with *Party* for a while and then get some Chinese. Good place not far from me." It's a long-standing secular tradition among Jews to go out to Chinese restaurants on Christmas, which used to be the only places open on the holiday.

Jonathan chuckles. "Excellent," he says. "See you around five."

THE CALLIOPE OFFICE is closed for four days, and although I have more than enough work to fill eight, I'm distracted by the prodigal returned. Not too much of a shocker there. How can I concentrate on the boring stuff scrolling down my computer screen when I can just raise my eyes and see her in all her glory? And how can her presence not spark guilt? A multimillion-dollar painting in my humble abode? I have to get her somewhere safer.

Wyatt left on a ski trip out west with his sister and her kids so I've had time to resume copying *Party*. When I drop into her, into the arms of my family, I'm overcome by the thrill of being together again. Even after I come out of my fog and see what a horrible facsimile I've produced, I'm still comforted. How can I let her go?

I'm looking forward to Jonathan's visit tomorrow, to having another person in the apartment. I've got to be honest here—being alone with her frightens me. Well, maybe "frightens" is too strong a word, but it definitely makes me uneasy. If I hallucinate that Berthe moves again, I'm going to have to see a shrink, an event that could reveal a problem that will overshadow everything else I believe is a problem now.

When Jonathan knocks, I'm so happy to see him that I give him a hug. He hugs me for a quick second, then extends a bottle of wine. "Hope you like cabernet," he says self-consciously, probably taken aback by the hug. We've never had any physical contact beyond a handshake.

I think about apologizing, but that would make it even more uncomfortable, so I take the bottle. "Cabernet is my favorite. Perfect choice." Much more to my taste then Wyatt's fancy martinis.

He looks around the apartment, which is essentially one open space, with my study off the living room and a short hallway leading to two bedrooms. He sees *Party* on the wall and turns to me expectantly.

I bow with a broad sweep of my arm toward the living room. "Come. Look."

He stops about six feet from *Party* and stares at it, as I suppose he'd gawk at the Grand Canyon when seeing it for the first time. I stand next to him, equally enraptured, and neither of us moves for many minutes.

"Want to sit?" I ask. He nods, and without taking our eyes from the painting, we move to the couch. I put on my glasses, and more minutes pass. I wait for him to speak, not wanting to disturb his moment.

"Now I understand why you didn't want to give it up," he finally says. "I don't remember the last time I saw a piece of art this powerful—and I've been to many of the great museums."

About five minutes pass, and I go to the kitchen, fill two wineglasses, and return to the couch. Wordlessly, we raise our glasses in a toast to *Party*, then we sit there and revel in her.

"Whoa," Jonathan says, and then begins to laugh at himself. "Now how's that for a sophisticated response to a masterwork?" He stands and steps close to the painting, steps back, then comes closer again. "I've seen a lot of Manet's work, but this is beyond his usual. Maybe even his best."

"My great-great-great-great-great-uncle was clearly a genius."

He points at Berthe. "And your great-great-great-great-grandmother was no slouch either."

"Good genes, I guess. But unfortunately, they've been watered down through the generations, as my lack of artistic genius attests."

"Have you tried?"

I shrug. "Not really."

"Not really?"

I'm embarrassed to confess to my childish colored pencils, and then I do. "I sketch it, *Party*, sometimes. Always very badly. In an effort, I suppose, to get to know it better. To get closer to it."

Jonathan nods at me thoughtfully, respectfully. "I can see how you'd want to do that." And, to his everlasting credit, he doesn't ask to see the sketches.

We have a nice dinner in a Chinese restaurant, noisy with families—mostly Jewish, we suppose. We talk about our childhoods, Jonathan's much more noteworthy than mine, with his Jewish father and his Haitian mother, who converted and became far more engaged than her husband in her adopted religion. He asks if he can come by to see *Party* again, and I tell him he's welcome anytime. All in all, a very nice Christmas. Even if I didn't receive any presents or get to go on an extravagant adventure with my cousins and aunts and uncles and grandparents.

I have two more days of my so-called vacation and try to get some work done with *Party* across from me. I go as far as taking my computer to Starbucks to avoid the lure, like an addict who can't be anywhere near her drug of choice. But I'm guessing abstinence is going to be tough when I'm addicted to a painting that's hanging on my living room wall. A painting I need to find a secure home for. Maybe I could hire a guard?

Wyatt returns with a tan that accentuates his eyes, and we have a hot-sex reunion at his place. I tried to get him to mine, but he claimed that, as we were both so behind because of the holiday, it made more sense for us to be closer to our offices. I, horny girl that I am, succumbed. Fun and casual, just the way I like it.

The next morning, as we're sipping coffee in his kitchen and watching the winter-clad wildlife making their way down the snow-covered Southwest Corridor, he gets a text. He shows me that it's from Nova Shepard, the investigator he hired. Or, more correctly, I hired. He texts her back with a blaze of thumbs and says, "Nova found an inventory of the Bernheims' art collection from before the war."

"And *Party* is on it?"

"Damn straight it is."

I lean closer. "Do you think this will do it?"

He hesitates. "If Damien Manet wasn't so vindictive, I'd say it probably would. But my bet is he's going to claim that until we have hard proof that the Bernheims' ownership is legitimate, it belongs to him. I'd put money on it."

"And that's where we're screwed by the no records of transaction," I say glumly.

"There were other paintings by your great-greats on the list, which, based on what you told me about the flooded salt mine, were probably all destroyed there. Do you want me to have Nova look into that? See if any of them survived?"

While it would certainly be fantastic to inherit more masterpieces, especially if there's one by Berthe, I can't afford it. Actually, I can't afford what I'm already spending on this suit. Maybe, if all goes well, I can have Nova do it later. "Let's stick with the one for now," I say. "But this is more proof, right? The fact that the Bernheims had a large collection? More Manets?"

"It helps, sure. But as far as the legal ownership of a single work is concerned, the fact that they owned other paintings by the same artist doesn't say all that much. Most collectors do."

WYATT IS AWARE that *Party* was found in a salt mine, but he knows nothing about the other two disasters or the triple-sole-survivor weirdness. I haven't felt the need to tell him, as he's working backward in time from the Bernheims, not forward. And, to be honest, he's never asked me about its life between the salt mines and me. For such a smart guy, he's startlingly uncurious.

Between Christmas and the first week in January, the weather is bitterly cold, with a battery of snowstorms, the likes of which the city hasn't seen in over a decade, which gives Wyatt even more ammunition to argue that we should stay at his house. On the worst nights, I do just that, having no desire to forge through sidewalks narrowed by banks of snow that have nowhere else to go. It's so bad in places that only one person can get through at a time, and you have to wait at the end of the block for them to traverse the shoulder-wide passageway before you can do the same. Wyatt keeps talking about Bimini.

I hate to think of *Party* all alone and unprotected, so when it's passable I sleep at my apartment, and Wyatt either does or doesn't join me. Mostly he does, which is making me nervous, as we're spending more nights together than I'm comfortable with. I was sure his young, beautiful self would be long gone by now.

"Nova is going to come up with what we need," he says one night at my apartment. "She always does. So you should contact some auction houses. Start to put out feelers. Can that guy from the Conference give you some leads?"

"He doesn't have anything to do with *Party* anymore."

"I could get someone at the office to check into it. It isn't good for that painting to be here."

"I know this isn't the safest place—and I'm going to start in on finding one—but I've got to admit that I do love having her here."

"See, even the way you talk about the painting is weird. It's a piece of artwork, not a person. No gender. Not a 'her.'"

"*Party* was painted by my uncle times five, and the central figure is my grandmother times four. It's more than a piece of artwork to me—it's family."

This doesn't seem to appease him, but he does back off.

Later that night, I have a dream about Berthe and *Party*, a scary one. Berthe is standing on the boat's railing instead of behind it, her fists punching out of the painting. There's this shadowy thing—an animal, a person, a ghost?—slithering around the outside of the frame, gripping the gilded edges with its formless tentacles, seemingly intent on engulfing the picture whole, sucking it into itself, destroying it.

Berthe is fighting, trying to loosen its grasp, but she can't dislodge the creature. She's losing the battle, and I rush into the painting to help her. Together, we wrestle with the being, but as we tussle, it grows, expanding in every direction. It's surrounding not only *Party* but me. A thick goo fills my nostrils, my mouth. A putrid stench of decay overwhelms me. I can't breathe. Then the creature rips Berthe's fingers from the frame. She flails her arms madly, trying to maintain her balance. But it's not working. She's losing her footing. "No!" I scream and wake myself up.

My shout wakes Wyatt too, and he takes me in his arms, murmurs comforting words about it only being a dream, only a dream, to go back to sleep. But I'm not soothed. It's absurd, but I need to make sure *Party* is okay, still hanging in the living room. That we saved it.

When Wyatt's breathing slows, I quietly climb out of bed and go to the living room. Of course it's there, and Berthe is leaning on the railing, back to her resting state. "We did it," I say out loud. "We beat it back."

Her eyes seem to shift from the far bank of the river to me, as if she's heard me and wants to respond. Then—and again I'm far from certain—it appears as if she's shaking her head at me. I moan and cover my face.

Wyatt comes in, glances from me to the painting. "You have to get rid of that thing. It's turning you into a crazy person."

And he doesn't know the half of it.

TWENTY-TWO

The dream was just a dream, a reflection of what I'd been fussing over during the day. In retrospect, it was nothing more than one big cliché, and, to tell the truth, I'm kind of embarrassed my subconscious couldn't come up with something more imaginative. And thinking Berthe answered my claim of success by shaking her head at me . . . I mean, really? It was the middle of the night, and I was, more likely than not, still dreaming. Not to mention I wasn't wearing my glasses. Still, yet another reason to get her out of my apartment.

I find myself obsessing about the whole sole-survivorship bit. I know the events were real, and that *Party* was present when all three occurred. But this says nothing about how she was able to avoid destruction—at least in the case of the fire—and how she managed to get out safely when nothing else did. Right, she didn't do anything; she's a painting, not a person. Still, I can't leave it be. Which, unless I'm willing to shell out more money for Nova to investigate, means if I want answers, the onus is on me.

I start with the most recent, the Columbia Museum, figuring that as the fire happened less than a month ago and is currently being investigated as a crime scene, the details will be easier to uncover than those farther back. I go online and read everything I can about the fire, most of which focuses on the possibility of an anti-Semitic attack. The investigators talked to the witnesses—of which there were few—studied the burn patterns, and sent samples to a lab to search for accelerants, but there's still no definitive conclusion.

I try to contact Randi, the curator who helped me with the *Party* transactions. But when I do, I'm told she's no longer with the museum. I hope she wasn't fired, as she was devoted to a job she believed was a moral necessity—although, frankly, she was kind of a pain in the ass. I ask if there's anyone still on staff who worked with her in the Holocaust wing. The person on the other end of the phone puts me on hold, where I listen to elevator music for at least five minutes before I'm transferred to some guy named Steve, who's in charge of security.

"This is an ongoing investigation, so I'm not at liberty to give out any information," he informs me.

"I'm not looking for information on the fire. I'm looking for information on the painting that wasn't destroyed, *Party on the Seine*. It belongs to me."

"Everything in the wing was destroyed. Nothing's there anymore."

"You must have an inventory of the museum's holdings. Could you please look it up for me?"

"That's part of the investigation too. And there's no point anyways. Your painting isn't here."

"Okay, but what I'm wondering about is where she—the painting, I mean, *Party on the Seine* by Édouard Manet—was hung in the wing. I was told it escaped damage when no other paintings did."

"Look, I told you before that I can't give out any information, and I don't know anything about your painting. So, like I also said before, there's nothing I can do to help you."

So much for any clarity on SOLE SURVIVOR, EPISODE THREE.

From: Damien Manet, Director of the Édouard Manet Foundation
To: Tamara Rubin
Cc: Wyatt Butler, Beacon, Exeter & Associates
Re: Party on the Seine
Date: 11 January

I have been informed that *Party on the Seine* came extraordinarily close to being consumed by fire and destroyed. This is further proof of your poor stewardship, and I once again demand that the painting be immediately sent to Paris, where the Manet Foundation will be able to protect it. We have offered to purchase it from you for $10 million in US currency, and given the danger you pose to this masterpiece, we are willing to offer $12 million in order to ensure it is properly cared for.

Now that *Party on the Seine* has been returned to your environmentally unsafe and unsecure apartment, swift action is even more crucial. As such, we have arranged for transport, and a truck will be arriving at Tremont245 between nine and ten tomorrow morning. This transfer will still allow the Louvre the time necessary to prepare the painting for the Édouard Manet retrospective and void the lawsuit against you. Please send wiring instructions for $12 million to be deposited in your bank of choice.

He has some points, but if Mr. Manet thinks I'm going to wax all apologetic and jump at his two million additional dollars, another think is in order. Wyatt offers to respond to him, and although Damien would most likely be more impressed with a lawyer's words than mine, this is personal, and a personal rejoinder is called for. Wyatt doesn't agree but eventually gives in, with the stipulation that he has veto power over the content. I tell him he will, but I don't mean it. Luckily, he has no objections.

From: Tamara Rubin
To: Damien Manet, Director of the Edouard Manet Foundation
Cc: Wyatt Butler, Beacon, Exeter & Associates
Re: Party on the Seine
Date: 1/11

It is an unfathomable tragedy that the fire at the Columbia Museum destroyed so many priceless works of art, particularly given their origin, and I mourn their loss along with you. On the other hand, it is indeed fortunate that my painting, *Party on the Seine*, was spared. I am looking at it right now, and it's with great pleasure that I tell you it is undamaged.

Unfortunately, that is all the good news I have to share. *Party on the Seine* will not be available to participate in the retrospective, a decision which, as you are well aware, is always at the owner's discretion. Your offer of $12 million for a painting worth more than ten times that amount is summarily rejected. And as before, your transporters will not be allowed access to Tremont245 tomorrow or on any other day. It is also important for you to understand you are not in a position to demand anything of me. A cease-and-desist letter will be forthcoming from my attorney if this behavior continues.

THERE'S NO IMMEDIATE response from my darling cousin, and although Wyatt and I are grateful for the pause, we doubt this will be Damien's last communication. Given the reprieve, I should be attacking the piles on my desk or finding another museum for *Party*, but I return to my survivor search the next day. This time, I take up the Manaus Museum in the capital of the Amazonas state in Brazil. Home to SOLE SURVIVOR, EPISODE TWO. The earthquake happened two years ago, and although earthquakes are rare there, this one was a biggie: People died. People got hurt. Buildings collapsed. The Manaus Museum was one of them.

I know *Party* was never shown, that it went straight into basement storage from the salt mine, and that no one even knew it was there, hence the lost-masterpiece theory. There are a large number of photos and articles online about the quake, but most of the written information is in Portuguese. Which isn't a problem, as I don't need to understand the language to figure out that the museum was completely leveled and the rubble has been razed. That whole picture-worth-a-thousand-words thing.

This is getting way too frustrating, and I kind of wish Wyatt were around to distract me. But he's on a big trial in Oklahoma City, and it's taking more than the five days he predicted. I'm glad for the alone time, as his omnipresence is starting to wear on me—a tad overzealous for a passing fling—but I could use a diversion. My friend Holly, who was the one who recommended Wyatt, has grown disgruntled by all the time I'm spending with him, which is cutting into our gal-pal fun. Fortunately, she's still happy to have dinner with me. I don't mention that Wyatt is out of town.

Our usually lively repartee lags, as Holly has zero interest in my explorations into the sole survivorships, and I'm not about to say anything else about Berthe or *Party*, my two current preoccupations. I explain that I'm exhausted from work, which isn't a lie, but stay with her in the restaurant for the after-dinner drinks she likes so much. When Wyatt calls, I can see she's pissed that I take it.

I don't react with my usual *When Harry Met Sally* fake moans when he suggests some phone sex and explain I'm at dinner with Holly so I can't talk. He ignores this and tells me Nova received the translation of Édouard's will and that, as expected, it's pretty much incontestable. The twist is that Manet didn't leave anything directly to Léon. He left his estate to his wife, Suzanne, with the stipulation that she pass it on to Léon. At first this seems auspicious, but I quickly realize it doesn't change anything.

"It's going to be okay, Tam," Wyatt tries to reassure me. "We knew everything was left to Léon. It's always been about how Colette got the painting, and Nova's on the job."

"Sure," I say. "Right. We can discuss everything later."

"Everything?" he asks with a deep NPR-host voice.

"Bye." I try to suppress my smile and focus on carefully putting my phone back in my purse.

"Somebody's besotted," Holly says, practically rolling her eyes.

"He's a child," I tell her dismissively. "The perfect definition of a boy toy."

I GRAB A few hours the next day to check out SOLE SURVIVOR, EPISODE ONE. After coming up empty on both two and three, I don't have a whole lot of confidence that this effort will go any better. But if there's one thing that's helped me get where I am, it's perseverance. Along with my father's repeated advice—ad nauseam, actually—to always finish what I start.

Episode One took place at the Altaussee Salt Mine in the Styria region of Austria. Apparently, the Nazis knew what they were doing, as salt mines have stable temperatures and low humidity, perfect for preserving works of art. Hitler's plan was to steal all the great works of art in Jewish hands and create his grand museum in Linz after he won the war. So sorry that didn't work out for you, Adolf.

I read that the Altaussee Salt Mine held one of the largest caches of Nazi loot, including pieces owned by the Rothschilds—and the much less notable Bernheims. The Monuments Men discovered the mine and the hidden artworks. I remember there was a film with that title a while back, but I never saw it and don't know anything about them. I call Jonathan to see if either he or the conference has more information.

"The Monuments Men were amazing," he tells me. "A bunch of dedicated risk-takers whose mission was to protect and recover art stolen by the Nazis. There's a movie about them and lots of books. If you want to check them out, I can give you some titles."

"Maybe I'll be able to do that in some other lifetime, but as I'm on this sole-survivor quest, that's the part of the story I'm focused on. What else do you know about the mine?"

"Is this worth your time?" he asks. "What do you expect to get out of it?"

I glance over at *Party*. "Probably nothing, but it's all so strange . . ."

"I know the Conference was involved in getting compensation for other pieces in the flood, but that's about it. Way before my time."

"Nothing else?"

"Let's see . . ." he says. "If I remember correctly, the Monuments Men discovered the mine sometime in 1945 based on tips from locals. Something about Austrian miners who got suspicious."

"That's somewhat heartening."

"I suppose. That whole better-late-than-never crap." He sighs. "The mine was apparently a labyrinth of underground rooms connected by tunnels, all of which flooded in some kind of freak hurricane. That's about all I've got—and of course, that *Party on the Seine* was in the waterproof container."

"Do you think the Conference's databases might offer me a lead?"

"I doubt we have anything beyond what you've already found out. The disaster piece was never a focus for us."

"But you're the one who told me about the whole sole-survivor thing."

"I was told about it, in confidence, by a woman who used to volunteer here."

"Can I talk to her?"

"She died about a year and a half ago. Right after we first learned about *Party* and the earthquake. A Holocaust survivor. Ninety-two, and still sharp till the end."

"How did she know?"

"Something about an uncle or a cousin who was in the Monuments Men, or who worked with them. She blurted it out when we first discovered that *Party* was the only painting to come through the earthquake. Then she made me promise I'd never mention it to anyone."

"But you told me."

"Because I was as freaked at the third occurrence as she was at the second."

"Why the secrecy?"

"No idea. I actually forgot all about it until the Columbia fire."

"It's like *Party* can save herself, or maybe even make things happen," I say. When I hear how phantasmic this sounds, I wish I could take it back.

"It's weird all right, but not *that* weird. Are you seriously thinking *Party* has supernatural powers?"

"Of course not. I'm just spinning possibilities."

"And that's possible?"

"No," I declare with conviction. "Absolutely not. It's just some kind of wild outlier."

ON MY WAY home from work the next day, I stop at the neighborhood Korean restaurant and order a poke bowl to go. Wyatt is working late, and I'm relishing the idea of a quiet night alone with *Party*. Even the crowd in the small foyer pressing in on me from all sides doesn't dampen my mood.

A woman about my age in a puffer coat complains, "You'd think with all the takeout business they do, they'd try to make the experience more pleasant—for us and their staff."

"True."

The harried man behind the front stand lifts a bag and calls out, "Fred!"

A teenage boy grabs it from him and lopes out the door.

The woman lets out a powerful poof of breath. "He came in after me. Fucking annoying."

I glance at her, thinking that she's clearly not looking forward to her evening. "Long day?" I ask.

"Got that right. You?"

"Not as bad as some," I tell her.

"Tamara!"

I squeeze my way to the stand and take the proffered bag, glad to be leaving, even if it's freezing cold out there.

"Damn," the woman says, and follows me. "You came in after me too. This is bullshit. I'm out of here." Which is curious, as you have to pay when you place your order. She falls in next to me. "Why can't anyone do their job anymore?"

I nod, sorry for having engaged her in conversation, and pick up speed.

"I'm Emily," she says, increasing her pace to keep up with me. "Nice to meet you, Tamara."

For a moment, I'm alarmed that she knows my name. But of course she heard it in the restaurant. I don't respond. Maybe she'll go away.

"I heard there's someone in this neighborhood who's got a multimillion-dollar Impressionist painting stashed in her apartment," Emily says conversationally. "Know anything about it?"

I continue walking, although I'm not sure how I'm able to. *Party*. She knows about *Party*. Shit, shit, shit. Blood roars in my ears. This wasn't some random meeting. Good ol' Emily followed me into the restaurant. Which is why her order hadn't been called. She wasn't there for food. She was there for me.

"Also heard the person lives at Tremont245. Familiar with that building?"

I stop. "I have no idea what you're talking about, so please leave me alone."

"I hate to report on a story without getting comments from all the major players. Balance is my primary objective, and it's much fairer to everyone involved."

A reporter. A goddamned reporter. I just about sprint around the corner onto Tremont and burst through the door of my building, certain Emily is going to follow me into the lobby. I rush up to the concierge desk and call out, "Pease don't let her come in, Chris. I don't know who she is."

Chris looks at me, around the empty lobby, back at me.

I lean against the wall, try to catch my breath. "Sorry," I mutter. "It's nothing. I made a mistake."

He hesitates. "Are you sure you're all right, Tamara? Is there anything I can do for you?"

"No. Thanks. I'm fine. Really, I am." I stumble to the elevator. Just fine.

TWENTY-THREE

The next morning, there are two local news vans, WBZ and WCVB, parked in front of my building. A few reporters and a couple of photographers mill around the sidewalk. I snap the kitchen shades shut, then lift a corner and peer out. Obviously, there are all kinds of newsworthy stories in a city the size of Boston. But how many are there at Tremont245?

I make a cup of coffee, hoping it will calm me, but it does the opposite. Terrific idea, Tamara. I try to eat a piece of toast to soak up the caffeine, but the bread catches in my throat. How could I have been so stupid? Spending my time on sole survivorships when I should have been concentrating on getting her the hell out of here.

I go to my computer and do a search linking Édouard Manet's name with mine. A half dozen stories pop up, all from random online sources rather than reputable newspapers. At least there's that.

MANET MASTERPIECE HANGING ON HER LIVING ROOM WALL?

ART WORLD ATWITTER.

REAL OR HOAX?

RUBIN OWNERSHIP REJECTED BY MANET FOUNDATION.

Each article has at least one mistake in it, some more than that. But even though it's often misspelled, they all get my name correct. Along with the painting's. And, worse, my address.

I raise my head from the computer. "What are we going to do?" I ask *Party*, and then worry that she might actually answer. She doesn't—probably out of kindness for my agitated state. I don't bother to check myself for thinking of a painting as a living person. I turned my phone off last night, and when I text my boss to tell him I'll be working from home, I see there's a voluminous number of incoming messages. Almost all from phones I don't recognize. My emails reach into the hundreds. I open a few, then wish I hadn't.

Collectors offering money. Fake relatives asking for money. Media requests. Art advisors and dealers and brokers offering services. Insurance agents offering services. Limited-edition printmakers offering services. Private banks soliciting me as a customer. Real estate agents soliciting. The Private Jet Shared Proprietary Program soliciting. Claims of ownership, and threats about what will happen to me if I don't immediately return the painting. If only I could call Wyatt, but he's still in Oklahoma City, and it's five in the morning there. It's all I can do to wait until seven to phone Jonathan.

"What's up?" he asks groggily.

"Sorry to bother you so early," I say, and then fill him in on what's up.

"Shit."

"Exactly."

"I was afraid this might happen." At least he doesn't say he told me so. Which he had.

"How do you think it got out?" I ask.

"Probably the Columbia fire."

"But when I called there, no one knew anything about *Party.*"

"Or that's what they told you."

"An unusually cynical observation for you."

"Maybe you're rubbing off on me."

"Jonathan . . ."

"Well, who else knew it was in your apartment?"

I think about this. "The shipping companies that transported her, I guess. People at your Conference. Damien and others at the Manet Foundation. My lawyer, his assistant, his investigator. Maybe, like you said, people at the Columbia. Alyce, the manager at my building, and probably some of the workers on the loading dock. Jesus, a lot more than I would have thought."

"And undoubtedly, more than just those."

"But why would any of them want to go to the press about this? Especially employees who might lose their jobs if they were discovered leaking private information. What do they have to gain? It's not as if—" Then I see it. Don't know why I didn't straight off. "Damien."

"What's his gain?" Jonathan asks. "Whether people know you have the painting or not doesn't make his argument any stronger."

I bark a grim laugh. "It's not about that. It's about putting pressure on me. Making things difficult so I'll sell it to him."

"I thought he was claiming it was his."

"He is, but he also offered to buy it to 'help' me avoid the time and expense of litigation. Even to pay for the transport. Said the foundation had to take it because of my 'poor stewardship.'"

"How much?"

"Twelve million."

A pause. "That's a lot of money, but it's nowhere near what it's worth."

"My lawyer says he can get him to pay a lot more."

"If you wanted to, you could always loan it to another museum while the case plays out. Then Damien couldn't claim poor stewardship—and you'd get the press off your butt."

"The poor-stewardship remark was in reference to the Columbia fire."

"Listen, Tamara, I've got to get to work, but if you want to talk more, I should be home by six."

I call Wyatt at nine. After explaining what's happened, I say, "It's Damien."

"Slimewad," Wyatt says. "But for right now, the important thing is that you don't respond. Not until I get back and we figure out the best way to handle this. Work from home and don't answer any unknown calls or texts or emails."

"But—"

"It's good you're in a doorman building," he continues. "Call down and tell them not to let anyone in and not to confirm that you live there—although they probably wouldn't do that anyway. If you need food or anything else, order online and ask the concierge to leave it outside your door."

Although I hate being told what to do, especially by a man I'm dating—actually any man, actually anybody—I'm relieved to have a plan. "When do you think you'll be back?"

"If all goes well, the trial could be over tomorrow, maybe even today. I'll get the first plane out I can. But you need to promise me you'll do what I said. I am your lawyer, after all."

"Okay, Wyatt Abbott Davenport Butler, Esquire. I'll follow your orders."

"Probably for the first and last time," he mutters.

"Probably," I agree.

WYATT COMES DIRECTLY to my place from the airport late the next night. We usually go straight to the bedroom after even a short separation, but he just gives me a quick kiss and drops his bag and briefcase on the kitchen floor. He leans against the counter. "Damien upped his offer to fifteen million."

I wave Wyatt over to the table, mix him a martini, drop in some of the cheese-stuffed olives he left in my fridge, and pour myself a glass of wine. "Not even bothering to cover his tracks," I sputter. "Can you believe the arrogance? It's out-and-out blackmail."

Wyatt sips on his drink. "This is a man you underestimate at your peril."

"I refuse to give in to his revolting tactics."

"Okay, but selling it to him would solve a shitload of problems. The case is gone—as are my fees—and those reporters disappear along with them. Not to mention that fifteen million . . ."

"I can't believe you're suggesting I cave. You said Nova will find the evidence and then *Party* will be mine, that the painting is worth way more than that."

"You can't keep it here."

"I'm going to start looking into other museums. But this time, it has to be someplace close so it'll be easy for me to visit her." The wrong thing to say to Wyatt.

"Really? Listen to yourself. I know this is upsetting, but as I've pointed out before, you're not being reasonable about this painting."

I cross my arms over my chest. "I am being reasonable. Extremely so. A museum can hold it for me until she—it—is officially mine. So why should I give in to his extortion? Why should I sell *Party* for a fraction of what I can get for her?"

"You'll only have the opportunity to sell it if we win—and your cousin isn't going to be easy to beat. Especially with the foundation bankrolling him."

"I'm not selling her to Damien. Now or ever."

"On a more positive note," he says, "news cycles are notoriously short.

And although this is a big deal to you, the story doesn't have legs. So we'll put out a statement and end all the speculation."

"Wasn't it you who said to ignore the whole thing?" I ask irritably. "Not give them anything to write about?"

"That was until I got home. If we answer them directly now, then—poof—nothing more to tell."

"You want me to talk to reporters?" I ask, horrified by the prospect.

"Not to worry. I'll write a press release on your behalf." He looks up at the ceiling. "I could say something like: The esteemed Conference on Jewish Material Claims Against Germany has determined Édouard Manet's *Party on the Seine* indisputably belongs to Tamara Rubin. The painting is in the process of being transferred to a more secure location." He grins at me. "How does that sound?"

"My lawyer in shining armor."

"Anytime, fair maiden," he says with a bow. "There may be a few gawkers and media types hanging around your loading dock for a while, but it's going to get boring pretty quickly, and, like I said, the whole thing will just fade away." He takes another hit of his drink. "There's something else."

I stiffen.

"Nova Shepard has accepted a full-time job and won't be consulting anymore."

"What about her work on *Party*?"

"She's got to start right away. Apologized profusely, but she just doesn't have the time."

"That's pretty damn unprofessional of her," I grumble.

"She's a consultant, paid by the hour. So, yeah, it's disappointing, but it happens all the time."

"You have someone else who can do the job?"

"There are a few others we use, but it may take a while to find someone who's a good fit and able to jump right in."

I refill my glass. "How can we wait? You're the one who said Damien isn't to be underestimated. Who knows what maneuvers he could concoct while we're sitting around?"

"I'll try to find another investigator as soon as I can."

"I don't want to lose *Party* while we're waiting for someone to become available. You know how much she means to me."

"Yes, I'm aware. I'm the one trying to win that damn painting back for you, remember?"

He's right. None of this is his fault. "Sorry. I'm just all caught up in . . ." I wave my hand. "In this."

"Too caught up, as far as I'm concerned."

"Are you saying you want me to get another lawyer?" I smile coquettishly.

"Tamara, Tamara, Tamara, what am I going to do with you?" he asks, as he's been asking more and more frequently of late. Then he takes my hand, pulls me up, and kisses me. "Ah," he murmurs. "I missed you."

I tell him I missed him too, and he lifts me onto the countertop and presses himself against me. I did miss him, and now I remember why. But later, I wonder why it's so difficult for him to appreciate my feelings for *Party*. It's a masterpiece many people are clearly willing to spend tens of millions of dollars on. It's not just me who's in love with her. Sometimes I think the man's capacity for empathy is limited.

THE PRESS RELEASE goes out the next morning, which causes a small flurry. Wyatt answers the media's questions, and just as he claimed, by afternoon it calms down. No news vans to be seen. Some reporters are probably still hovering, but the building has instructed the doormen to get rid of anyone loitering on the sidewalk and to only allow those with a verified purpose into the lobby, so it feels much less threatening. I'm going to hole up for today and get back to my normal life tomorrow.

In the most perfect world, I'd be able to keep her here with me, but as I don't live in that world, I call Jonathan to discuss the best spot for *Party*'s temporary placement. "How about the MFA? Or the Fogg at Harvard?" I suggest. Both museums have large Impressionist collections, and, even better, they're local.

"Going to be a problem because of your short timeline," he tells me.

"Wouldn't they jump at the chance to have a Manet?"

"They probably would, but they're huge organizations, run by bureaucracies and steeped in layers of rules and regulations, strict development policies, grant restrictions. Curatorial departments, acquisition teams, boards. And they're going to need detailed documentation before they make a decision—provenance, authenticity, expert opinions on *Party*'s significance within a larger context—which could take you months to get."

"I just want to loan it. I'm not looking for them to buy it."

"Loan or purchase, they have reputations to maintain. Can't go around accepting and hanging a random painting without knowing if it's the real deal."

"The Columbia took her right away."

"Because they're small. Much less bureaucracy. And it fit both their collection and their mission, which have nothing to do with the painting's provenance."

I'm at my desk, *Party* right across from me. I miss her already. "Is there a small one nearby?"

"I did some checking after we talked the other day, and while there are lots of them, most wouldn't be a good fit. The closest possibility is the Hamlin Museum in Waltham."

"You think they'd be willing to take her?" Waltham is a suburb a couple of rings outside Boston. A half-hour drive without traffic. Not as close as the MFA or Cambridge, but workable.

Keyboard clicks. "Curator's name is Haley McGrath. Probably too late to contact her today, but worth a try."

"Thanks, pal. I'll let you know how it goes."

That night, I have another Berthe nightmare. In a museum I've never seen before. Poorly lit. Low ceilings. Very un-museum-like. I'm in a gallery containing at least twenty gilt-framed paintings, and each is *Party on the Seine*. All but one are a quarter of the size of my *Party*, while the largest is at least twice the expanse of the original and commands an entire wall. And from there, Berthe commands the room.

Standing a few steps back from the railing, she lifts her hand imperiously and points an index finger at the closest *Party*. It goes completely black. All color, all light, all resonance sucked out. Dead. She moves on to the next. Dead. And the next. Dead. And then the next. When her painting is the only one still containing life, she spirals her arm upward, stops when it's fully extended, and stares right at me. Then she slams the arm downward. As goes her arm, so does the painting. Dead.

I bolt up in bed and, just like the last time, go into the living room, terrified that Berthe might have destroyed her own painting. And, of course, she hasn't. Because she's been dead for over 130 years. *Party* is fine, colors glowing, partyers enjoying their journey down the river.

Then I catch a whiff of a sweet, almost powdery scent—violets?—and I hear a voice in my head. Berthe's voice, I somehow know. "Do not do this," she tells me. "If I'm shown like this it will do irreparable harm. And then worse will follow."

IT'S GOOD TO be back in the office, beyond my square white walls, the confines of my own concerns. The day whirls around me, keeping me busy and distracted. My nightmare is now in the hazy past, although I can't shake the notion that Berthe was trying to send me a message.

But it was me sending the message. Another hackneyed one: that I don't want to give *Party* away. My oh-so-clever subconscious. Yet hearing voices is a whole other thing, a sign of psychosis—like hallucinations, now auditory as well as visual.

Late in the afternoon, I get a chance to call Haley McGrath at the Hamlin Museum. She's heard about my situation—who hasn't?—and is excited to talk to me about it. "Obviously, I've never seen *Party on the Seine* myself. So, tell me, is it as magnificent as they say?"

"More," I assure her, and explain why I've called.

There's a long pause. "What an incredible offer," she says, but her tone says the opposite.

"If it's good with you, I'd like to do this as soon as possible."

"I, I can see why you'd want that. Makes sense . . ."

"Is there a problem?" I ask, knowing there is.

"I'm really sorry, Ms. Rubin. I'd love nothing more than to have *Party on the Seine* in our museum, but it's impossible. We have no paintings of its stature here, and a very small endowment. It would surely bring more traffic through, but even with an increase in admission fees, we wouldn't be able to afford the additional staff this would create. Or the insurance."

I TELL WYATT I'm working late, but I leave the office early. It's freezing out, and as I trudge toward Tremont Street, I ruminate. If the Hamlin can't afford *Party*, it's likely no other small museum will be able to either. And the bigger ones will take months, maybe years, to even consider the loan. Because of the pending suit, I can't sell her to anyone but Damien—which isn't happening. And after the media mess, I can't keep her where she is.

I suppose the next logical step is a storage facility that can provide the kind of environment she needs, but the idea of her being locked up in a dark cell beyond my reach is disturbing. But first, I have to find out what those conditions are. When I get home, I check, and it turns out *Party* needs a steady temperature between 60 and 75 degrees, consistent low humidity, no direct sunlight, indirect lighting, good ventilation, regular pest control, and the absence of pollutants, including dust, smoke, and chemical vapors.

These restrictions narrow the possibilities considerably, as do the websites' warnings that anything of value needs to be properly insured, as the facilities have no coverage for the contents of individual units. Not to mention how pricey the ones that have any kind of temperature regulation are. Despite the increased cost, none of these provide humidity management or ventilation, and although they all have regular services to eradicate insects and rodents, these necessitate spraying chemicals throughout the facility.

Damn. I can provide a better environment here. The temperature would be no problem. I could buy a humidifier and an air purifier, keep the shades down, find an eco-friendly pest service, hire a guard. Except that Wyatt just released a statement declaring that *Party* was being transferred to a more secure location. An action that has to be done in order to placate the media, as well as Alyce, the building manager, who I've heard is upset by the "infamy" the painting has brought to her building. A bit hyperbolic, but she, too, needs to be appeased.

Over a sleepless night, I rehash my options and become despondent over the lack of any. At work the next day, I revisit the idea of keeping her, which I decide again is completely unworkable, silly, even. But when I get home from work, I sit on the couch and look at my marvelous painting—Berthe, Édouard, my family—and I find myself wondering if there might be a way to safely keep her with me.

I once again ask Berthe what we're going to do, but she just stands at the railing staring out at the opposite bank. So real, so unfathomable, so beautiful. Édouard must have known her well, to be able to portray her so fully, to dig into her soul like that. If I commune with her, maybe a solution will come to me—one that won't lead to Berthe's "irreparable harm."

Really, Tamara?

But suddenly, it does. I'd read about this painter, Claire Roth, who did such an impressive job forging a Degas painting that she fooled the curators and authenticators at the Isabella Stewart Gardner Museum. Although she was a talented and schooled artist, which I certainly am not, maybe I don't need to be as skilled. Or even be a forger. I just need to follow in her footsteps, swapping a fake for the real thing.

PART EIGHT

Berthe, 1875

TWENTY-FOUR

1875

Berthe has no interest in discussing meals with the cook or giving instructions to the maid or being a proper wife in any of the traditional ways. Her mother tries to entice her into decorating the house with offers of shopping sprees and gifts of furniture, but Berthe has no enthusiasm for this either. Cornélie is thrilled with the five floors and the large rooms of 40 Rue de Villejust, which is in the fashionable 16th arrondissement, across from a stately park. Berthe is unimpressed.

She rarely writes letters anymore, particularly not to Edma or Yves, both of whom she's been unable to completely forgive for their complicity with Maman. Most of the time, she stares out the window or reads, currently Charles Darwin's *On the Origin of Species,* which her mother believes is improper material for a married woman.

"Would it be equally improper if I were unmarried?" she asks during one of her mother's many visits. She had believed that the one benefit of her marriage would be that she'd no longer live in the same house as her mother, but Cornélie is here so often it sometimes feels as if she still is.

"That's not the point," Maman argues. "You're no longer young, and you should be spending your energies on having a child, rather than reading about how we are the same as monkeys."

"That's not what he says."

"Not what Gène says?" her mother asks, clearly upset by the prospect that Berthe won't produce offspring. "He doesn't want a son?"

"Not what *Darwin* says." Berthe launches into an explanation of the theory of evolution, hoping this will steer Cornélie away from the topic of children. It's not that Berthe doesn't necessarily want to be a mother. It's just that she avoids Gène's advances as much as is possible, both because the act is unpleasant and because it begs comparison to her times with Édouard. She retires to her bedroom early in the evening or remains in the parlor with her book until well after he has gone to his own room. She always closes her door, and when Gène knocks and she doesn't respond, he leaves her in peace.

Cornélie interrupts her Darwin discussion. "You must take charge of yourself and your life, Berthe. You are as thin as you have ever been, and I'm concerned about your health."

Berthe can't resist a smile. "At least you don't have to worry that I'm too thin for any man to marry."

"You are, and always have been, my difficult daughter." Maman throws her hands in the air, but the corners of her lips curve slightly upward. "I cannot believe I'm suggesting this, but maybe you should start painting again. At least you eat when you're painting."

After the independent exhibition, she pledged to stop painting, to never put herself in a position to be ridiculed like that again, but she's been feeling the itch. "Degas told me the same thing. The bande is still meeting at Édouard's studio, and he claims everyone wants me to return, that the idiots deriding the exhibition are just that, and shouldn't be taken seriously. Then he told me I'm too good a painter to give up so easily. 'Get back on the horse' were his exact words."

Surprisingly, Cornélie doesn't disagree with Degas's assertion of her talent. "I'm sure Gène would make a room for you if you asked."

Berthe does this, and Gène, always eager to please her, hires workmen to convert an unused space that opens onto the garden into a studio. Within a month, it's ready. It's spacious, with a fireplace and a tall wall of windows facing north. Rémy brings her art materials and paintings from Maman's, and even Berthe has to admit that it is quite satisfactory. She even lets Gène into her bedroom in thanks for making it possible, as an appreciative wife should.

When he asked her to marry him, Gène promised he wouldn't interfere with her desire to paint, that he believed she was serious and gifted and he wanted her to fulfill her promise. At the time, she was so disconsolate over the marriage that it wasn't a particularly compelling argument, but now she's grateful for his willingness to back her socially inappropriate desire to be a professional artist. There's no doubt he's attentive to her every comfort, and obviously it isn't his fault he's not Édouard, but even with these understandings, she's unable to warm to him.

She had always assumed, given her sisters' experiences and those of many of her other married acquaintances, that to be both a wife and an artist was impossible unless she were to marry another artist as passionate and driven as she was. And even then, she had questioned whether her work would be considered less than her husband's in the eyes of the world. With Gène, this will never be a problem. He has no profession aside from that of a tinkering painter, and he spends his days at one of his many clubs or in bed with a migraine.

When she begins to paint again, she's much out of practice and tires more easily than she did when she was working daily. But she perseveres, and by the end of the first month, the brushstrokes begin to flow more naturally. She's producing nothing of merit, to be sure, but at least it's a start. She's loath to admit it, but Cornélie was right. Her mood has lightened, and she's begun to gain weight.

Renoir and Monet stop by to see her studio, and after complimenting her new atelier and her half-finished paintings, they try to convince her to join them in a second independent show. "We think our next step should be an auction rather than an exhibition," Renoir says. "And we can't do that without you."

"We are in dire need of your diplomacy and the brilliance of your painting to make it work," Monet adds.

"What makes you believe the reaction to an auction won't be the same as it was to our exhibition?" she asks.

"It's a different setting and should draw a more serious audience," Monet explains.

"They rejected our paintings because they aren't what they're used to looking at," Renoir continues. "People don't like change, and the only way to make our work more familiar is to keep showing it. Make it less of a threat to whatever they feel threatened by."

"If you have the stomach for the scorn," Berthe says. "Which I'm not certain I do."

"What's the alternative?" Monet asks her. "If we don't stand up for ourselves, it's the same as declaring failure."

COLLECTORS WHO WANT to refresh their holdings are selling artworks to other collectors at auctions held at the Hôtel Drouot, and Renoir suggests they participate in the next one, which will take place in late March. Berthe has returned to Édouard's studio, but, afraid to be alone with him, only on bande days, and it is there that she and the five other original committee members agree to the auction. Unfortunately, many of the other artists they collaborated with at the exhibition are too dispirited to join them. But Durand-Ruel is excited by the prospect and helps develop the catalogue, writing a gushing introduction, which notes that the painters are "achieving with their palettes what poets express with their words."

Gène, as he promised, helps with the framing and the plans for transporting Berthe's paintings to the auction site. He even acquiesces, although with much consternation and fussing, to talk to his family about her choice to use Morisot instead of Manet on her work. On the designated Sunday, while dining after church at Antoinette's, he clears his throat a couple of times, flashes Berthe a slightly panicked look, and then says to the collected family, "Berthe, uh, Berthe and I . . ."

Smiling with anticipation, they all turn to him, then to her, expecting, Berthe presumes, that he's about to announce she's with child. She picks up her napkin and touches it to the corners of her mouth, places it slowly back on her lap, smooths it nervously. She hadn't foreseen this would be their assumption, although she should have. And their disappointment when this is not the case, especially Antoinette's, will make them even less likely to accept what he's actually going to tell them.

"We, uh, we've been discussing what name she should use on her paintings for the auction," Gène continues, tapping his fork on the tablecloth, a slight tremor in his fingers. "She, we, feel it would be best if, as an artist, just as an artist, she continues as Berthe Morisot."

Stunned silence greets this announcement, and Berthe doesn't look at anyone.

"But, but she's a Manet, now," Antoinette sputters. "She is no longer Berthe Morisot. She's Madame Eugène Manet. A distinction of which I know she is proud."

"That is true, Maman," Gène says. Then he takes a deep breath and adds in a rush, "Berthe believes, and, and I agree with her, that her work will be confused with Édouard's. Or worse, assumed to be his."

"I find it difficult to believe you would consent to such a thing, Gène," Antoinette declares. "She is your wife and, as such, must carry your name. In all circumstances."

"Berthe will always be a Manet," Édouard says before Gène can respond. "But she's been painting as a Morisot for over a decade. So not only would two Manets simultaneously showing artworks be problematic, but if she were to make this switch, it would confuse her many devotees, both here and in London. Perhaps even hinder recognition of her enormous talent."

For once Suzanne speaks up. "It is not your concern what name she does or does not use, Édouard. This is between your brother and *his* wife."

Berthe carefully concentrates on buttering a piece of bread. She longs to look at Édouard, to thank him with her eyes, but she's afraid if she were to do so, their connection would be revealed. Although it seems Suzanne might have already guessed.

"I'm sorry to disappoint you, Maman," Édouard continues, ignoring Suzanne. "Even as I wish Berthe would exhibit with the Salon rather than participate in this auction, I believe it is best for her to continue the use of her maiden name." Berthe can feel his gaze on her, but she doesn't return it.

Antoinette sighs dramatically. "How can a poor mother battle two grown sons?"

"Thank you for understanding my position," Berthe says to Antoinette. She gives a quick nod to both Gène and Édouard, then turns back to her mother-in-law. "As I will be offering both new and older pieces at the auction, this will simplify things tremendously. I will always be a Manet, now and forever, irrespective of how I sign my paintings. And, yes, I am proud to be one. Very proud."

She's reassured when Antoinette reaches across the table and pats her arm.

Édouard continues to champion her and her compatriots, despite his personal feelings about the auction. He contacts numerous critics, including the newly omnipresent Albert Wolff of *Le Figaro*, praising the artists and requesting the journalists' presence at the Hôtel Drouot. He tells them they will be so enthralled with the offerings that their only choice will be to extend favorable reviews. Berthe writes him a discreet note of thanks but yearns to express her gratitude in a more demonstrable way, which is now lost to her.

Still, encouraged, she works as hard as she ever has, pushing the limits of what she's done before, striving to finesse her quick brushstrokes into explosions of light. While she achieves this in a few of her domestic paintings, she longs to capture the full world, the bursting cafés, the bustling streets of Paris, the lives of those not of her gender and class.

She stands at the parlor window, gazing out on the wintry boulevard. The wide throughfare is still beautiful, even with the denuded linden branches reaching skeletal fingers to the gray sky. And the park across the way is equally so, acres of grass surrounding a wide pond ringed by beech and horse chestnut trees.

There isn't much liveliness there now, but on a summer day it is filled with men and women, those of her circle and those who are not, some young people touching more intimately than might be considered proper, some wearing less clothing than might be considered proper. Families enjoying boisterous picnics, children squealing as they touch their toes into the pond, footraces, lawn bowling, couples walking hand in hand, horses on the bridle path, an older woman sitting against a large tree reading. It would make a stupendous painting, and she longs to create it.

She wonders what would transpire if she attempted such a thing. The condemnation would most likely exceed anything voiced during the exhibition, making those critiques mild in comparison. And exceedingly personal. Her mother and mother-in-law might never forgive this transgression, and perhaps Gène wouldn't either. Despite his support of her work, which is clearly due to his promise when she agreed to marry him, he's a strong traditionalist. Yet the thought lingers.

SHE PROFFERS TWELVE paintings to be sold at the auction, including *Reading* and *Interior.* Each of the other artists offers between five and thirteen, and together they put up seventy paintings. There's a private viewing on March 22 and one for the public on March 23. The actual event is scheduled for March 24, and all the painters grow increasingly agitated as the date of the auction approaches, although each has commandeered friends and family members who have promised to bid up the prices. Some of their guests have even professed an interest in purchasing one or two of the paintings.

Berthe takes to pacing the house, climbing the five flights of stairs, reversing her steps, and walking through the grand rooms on the first floor. Gène eyes her warily but says nothing. She avoids painting and, instead, designs a mosaic on the floor of the large entryway. She orders tiles from Italy and has the coachman break them into small pieces. She fashions a picture similar to *The Harbor at Lorient*, the narrow waterway opening to the sea, a woman in a white dress and parasol perched on a rocky wall in the lower right corner. Then she hires stonemasons to put it down.

Neither she nor any of the others go to either the private or the public viewing. Berthe because she knows the sight of her own paintings, hanging like meat for sale in a butcher's shop, will further undermine her confidence. Monet, Renoir, and Degas because they believe it will bring bad luck. Pissarro and Sisley because they're both living in the countryside, where it is less expensive, and can only afford to come into Paris for one day. They will arrive the morning of the auction.

Édouard and Durand-Ruel do attend the private viewing, and although they both claim there appears to be much interest, neither is specific about what kind of interest it is. Their evasiveness drives her male counterparts to their favorite café to drink heavily. Berthe has two glasses of claret at home, more wine than she has ever consumed in a single evening.

The following day, the day of the public viewing, Berthe is dizzy and nauseated from lack of food and sleep, and although her new cook's ox-blood broth is better than Marie's, it's still repulsive. Yet she knows she needs strength to carry her through tomorrow and tries to drink as much as she can. Gène goes to his club to make himself scarce, and even Cornélie doesn't come by. It's cold and rainy, and wind whips at the eaves, so Berthe buries herself under a pile of blankets, hoping to rest, but soon she's back on her feet, walking the silent rooms.

Many of the critics who are now at the hotel for the viewing are the same men who skewered the exhibition and are likely to do so again. And what if, as happened last time, no one buys any of her paintings? A second such humiliation would be difficult to bear. Why did she ever agree to this? But, no, it's been a year since the last show, and it's possible some will change their minds.

Gène returns in the late afternoon paler and more nervous than usual. He acknowledges her with a nod but doesn't look directly at her. This isn't his usual demeanor when he arrives home for dinner. He's always so visibly pleased to see her that she feels terribly guilty she's unable to reciprocate his feelings. "Is something wrong?" she asks, standing. "Do you have another migraine?"

"No headache." His gaze bounces around the parlor. Then he places his newspaper on a table.

"Then what?" She notices the newspaper is *Le Figaro* and catches her breath. It's too early for that. No reviews will be released until tomorrow, after the auction is completed. What would be the point before the sales have taken place? She raises her eyes to Gène.

"I am sorry," he says.

"Albert Wolff?" she asks, but it's not really a question. Wolff's reviews are widely read and are almost always negative, one possible reason for their popularity. But Édouard spoke with him last month, asked him to keep his mind open and reminded him that early acceptance of a new idea often turns into prescience, a highly prized quality in an art critic.

Gène hands her the newspaper.

"How bad?" she manages to ask, but he does not answer.

Berthe takes a seat on the couch and opens to Wolff's column. It's a good thing she's sitting, because his words are even more devastating than she expected: "The impression produced by these so-called Impressionists is that of a cat walking on the keys of a piano, or of a monkey that has got hold of a box of paints." She quickly scans the rest of the page. It gets even worse.

Gène comes to sit next to her, takes her hand. "It's only one critic."

"A very prominent one," she says, staggered by the harshness of Wolff's observations. "One who most likely just decimated attendance at the auction. And of those who do come, how many will bid on paintings that have been described like this?"

THE NEXT MORNING dawns even grayer and wetter than the day before. Berthe drags herself to her wardrobe to choose a discreet outfit that will hopefully render her unremarkable. The majority of her dresses are black, but almost all of them are fitted and adorned with velvet ribbons and lace. Not exactly inconspicuous. She decides on the simplest one, two seasons out of date.

The auction is held in one of the hotel's smaller ballrooms. A substantial stage dominates, with at least a hundred chairs lined up in front of it. When she and Gène arrive, almost all the seats are taken, and she's relieved to see that the Manets and a large number of her social circle are there to champion them, although Cornélie said she could not bear to attend.

Berthe nods and tries to smile at those she knows, but her mouth doesn't want to form into anything other than a straight line. She and Gène join the other five artists in the back row, all wondering how much damage Wolff has done, but none voice their concerns. Even Degas is quiet. The sizable throng could be seen as a good omen, but it's noisy and somewhat raucous, edgy and excitable, which to Berthe seems to indicate the opposite. Gène takes one of her gloved hands in his. Degas takes the other. They each give her fingers a squeeze, but all she can do is stare straight ahead and try to breathe.

The auctioneer begins, and assistants bring a single picture forward at a time, placing it on the large easel next to his podium. Some of their paintings are set upside down, and others on their sides. It's impossible to know if this is accidental or purposeful. Berthe supposes the motive makes little difference, as the attendees laugh and jeer even when the pictures are properly placed. The response is similar to what they received at the exhibition, but because this is contained to a single room and a single moment, it is even more difficult to endure.

There is some bidding, mostly by the artists' friends and family, and some purchases, but too little of either to offer consolation to anyone. None of Berthe's paintings have been brought up yet, and when the first one, *Reading*, is announced along with her name, the heckling grows even louder. Berthe lowers her head.

"Where's the foreground? Where's the background?"

"It's all just blobs of color!"

"Who allowed that woman to wield a paintbrush? Banish her from the canvas, and from the city!"

Then a man in a fine suit and top hat, who had been leaning against the back wall, strides into the aisle and yells, "Harlot!"

Gène and all the artists jump to their feet, but Pissarro reaches the fellow first. He pulls his arm back and smashes his fist into the man's face. Blood spurts from the man's nose, and his hat falls to the floor. The crowd roars encouragement, although it's unclear for whom they are cheering. More people rise, as does the noise level. The auctioneer calls the police, and both Pissarro and his victim are escorted from the ballroom.

TWENTY-FIVE

1875

Berthe does sell a few pictures at the auction, including *The Butterfly Hunt*, *Little Girl with Hyacinths*, and *Interior*, which goes for the highest price of the day. The other artists do less well, particularly Renoir, who's compelled to take back all his paintings when the initial bids are less than the minimum price of 100 francs. A small number of additional purchases are made, although the payments are meager, and the buyers are mostly family or friends. The artists' combined compensation is 12,000 francs, much less than they invested. When the reviews come out the next day, if anything, they're worse than those for their first exhibition.

Paris-Journal: "We derived a certain amusement from the purple-colored landscapes, black streams, yellow or green women and blue children, but that is all we derived, with the exception of contempt."

Le Charivari: "Their style of painting, which is both coarse and ill-defined, seems to us to be the confirmation of ignorance and the negation of beauty and truth."

The well-respected critic M. Girard: "I've heard some call this new group The School of Impressionism, but the only impression they have made on me or the public is that of horror."

Édouard offers the bande the use of his studio as a meeting place where they can discuss the auction and its aftermath, pointedly noting that he must be elsewhere on the proposed day and time. They take him up on this and gather on a Tuesday afternoon. They voice distress at the personal slights flung at each of them, and Pissarro apologizes for his overreaction in Berthe's defense. She thanks him for his gallantry, and the men all insist if they had reached the lout in the top hat before he had, they would have done the same. Then they settle down to discuss what they should do next.

"We must commit to continue our enterprise," Degas exclaims before anyone else can speak. "We did sell some pictures, more than at the first exhibition. This is progress, and if we don't expand upon it, it will be lost."

"You aren't trying to support a family," Monet counters, clearly annoyed with Degas's certitude, his assumption that he holds all the answers. "I can't sustain this outflow of funds when the return is less than I paid out, and I may have to begin working at our family store in Le Havre. This is true of not only me. We don't all have an outside income, Edgar." Animosity has long simmered between those with family money and those without.

"If we agree to remain a group, a cooperative working for the advantage of all of us," Berthe interjects, "perhaps we can find ways to help one another when times are difficult."

Pissarro nods. "I agree with Edgar, and I'd very much like to continue to show together, to have our work seen as a new movement. Even if they continue to deride us as 'the School of Impressionism.'" He shakes his head. "But I fear I'm in the same position as Claude. I don't have the resources to take such a risk right now. I must spend my time finding portrait commissions or resort to drawing caricatures on the street."

"I didn't say that we shouldn't help each other," Degas grumbles. "I just said we should keep pressing our case. And what's wrong with being 'Impressionists'? Maybe we should adopt it as an official name. Take it from those myopic buffoons and claim it as our own."

"Now that's a suggestion I can agree to," Renoir declares. "Shall we take a vote?"

Everyone raises a hand, and then they all burst into laughter, pleased with themselves and their new moniker. The tension in the room dissipates, and Berthe lifts her teacup. "To the Impressionists!"

Then the artists decide to move forward together, and concur that it makes sense to wait a year to hold their next auction or exhibition, in order for the critical hostility to settle and, hopefully, for the financial burdens of some of the members to ease. They also agree that if the latter doesn't come to pass, those with the means will provide the necessary funds to launch their new show.

It's not a bande day, and as no one wants to take advantage of Édouard's generosity, they gather their things and bid each other goodbye. Exhilarated by their consensus and eager to get back to work, Berthe remains in the studio, lingering over an unfinished picture she left there last week. It's a portrait of a young woman looking at herself in a mirror. Her face is in profile, which is partially and waveringly reflected in the glass, as are the flowers on the table to her right.

It's coming along, especially around the woman's left shoulder and the touches of blue scattered within the dress to enhance the sensation of whiteness. She's trying to catch the model's fleeting moment of introspection with a soft color palette. Her challenge for the painting was to reveal the woman's inner life, which had excited her when she started. But now she sees it's dull in tone and constrained in subject matter, paling in contrast to the vibrant, living canvases surrounding it. Canvases created by men.

Berthe is so engrossed she doesn't hear Édouard arrive, but she's immediately attuned to his presence. They haven't been alone since the wedding, and she has no idea how he'll treat her in their new circumstances. Hopefully, as a gentleman and a brother-in-law. She's determined not to dishonor Gène or herself, and this is what she will do.

"I believe it will be one of your best." Édouard comes to stand next to her, ostensibly to more closely inspect the work. "The nuanced use of light and color here." He points to the shadows falling on the underside of the woman's cheekbone. "The way you're beginning to capture the essence of the scene. The core of her."

"It's just a picture of an insipid woman looking at herself in a mirror," Berthe says. "A simple portrait like so many others, saying nothing of import."

He grasps her shoulders, turns her so that they are face-to-face. "No painting is important just because of its subject. It gains its power from the manner in which the artist portrays that subject. And you have breathed life into what could have been a colorless and ordinary woman, revealing her soul, a glimpse into the human condition."

She breaks away from his touch. "Thank you, Édouard. I appreciate your encouragement," she says stiffly.

"It's not encouragement, woman. It's the truth!"

Berthe reaches for her drawstring bag and suspends it from her wrist strap. "I was just leaving."

"Can't you stay a little longer? I want to hear how you're doing, and how the postmortem went with your fellow renegades."

The power of him freezes her in place, but she manages to say, "I have an engagement."

"At three o'clock on a Tuesday afternoon?" he asks, his voice thick with skepticism. "How about you sit in that chair over there, and I'll sit in this one over here?" His eyes twinkle. "Would that be acceptable to you?"

God help her, she sits.

"I'm sorry about the auction, Berthe. Deeply sorry. And, of course, furious at the stupidity and cruelty of it. Especially when it's the opinions of a gaggle of small-minded morons who believe they know what art is, when all they know is what art used to be."

"Well put." She struggles to contain the smile tugging at her lips. Leave, she tells herself. Leave while you still can.

He leans forward in his chair, places his elbows on his knees. "It isn't working, what you and the rest are trying to do. Can't you see this isn't the route to recognition or success? The two failures, no matter how unwarranted, are proof of this."

"You said before that you've experienced the same negative reviews, even for the paintings exhibited by the Salon," she tells him tersely. "And yet you continue to submit your work there. Why are our shows any different?"

"Also well put." He flashes one of his intoxicating smiles.

"The Salon isn't the only way to respectability."

"I believe that it is."

"Have you ever considered that you might be wrong? Now that Paris is recovering from the war, Durand-Ruel is doing well again. He's opening a gallery here, maybe one in America. New York, he says. He believes in us, is our great champion, and he's been selling more of our pictures."

"One gallerist is not enough," Édouard insists. "I beg you not to pursue this course. Everything you've worked so hard for will come to nothing if you continue with this recklessness."

"I'm sorry you feel that way, but we are going to move forward together. They're my friends, and I respect and admire their work. We made a pact: the six of us, another show, no Salon."

He kneels at her chair, takes her hands in his. "They're my friends too, and I feel the same way about their paintings." His eyes lock on to hers, a deeper blue than usual, full of heat. "But you're the love of my life, and I can't bear for you to make such a grave mistake when you have so much to offer."

She's touched by his concern and his faith in her work. But it's his nearness, his breath falling on her breast, his intensity that are her undoing. *The love of my life.*

"You are an impossible man," she says, but the lilt in her voice conveys that she doesn't believe this is necessarily a bad trait.

"And you smell like flower petals." He kisses her, and there's nothing she can do but kiss him back. Nothing else she wants to do. They stand, and arms around each other, move to their red sofa, lie down, and press their bodies together.

BERTHE AND ÉDOUARD declare a truce. He acknowledges she's not going to submit to the Salon, and she acknowledges his disapproval of her choice. They will talk about it no more, and when she tells him the group is planning to call themselves Impressionists, he's so delighted he jokes that maybe he'll join them after all.

By tacit, rather than explicit, agreement, they also do not speak of Gène or Suzanne. When together in society, they are friends and in-laws, bonded by family and painting, nothing more. When they are alone, the story is different, delightfully and dishonorably different. They're aware what they're doing is unpardonable, completely unfair to their spouses, yet they are unable to stop. Berthe sometimes thinks of it as a disease that has invaded her body, one whose only cure is to embrace the initial source of the illness, rekindling the ailment. Ouroboros. A snake eating its own tail.

The bande works in Édouard's studio twice a week, and Berthe paints at home the rest of the time. As much as she enjoys being with the others, and with Édouard, even if they must stay at a distance from each other, she's grateful for the time alone. She's attempting something she doesn't want anyone to see, a forbidden picture. The one she envisioned while looking out the parlor window last winter.

Now that it's spring, she spends many afternoons in the park across the street with her drawing pad and pencils, pretending to sketch the lush gardens and lawns, the deeply shadowed tree-lined paths, but these are not her subjects. She especially likes to sit on a bench next to the lawn-bowling green, a meticulously manicured grass rink where teams of men, women, and sometimes children play boules.

Berthe has participated in boules on private estates, but no woman of her circle would ever consider playing in a public place. The game involves rolling wooden balls at a target in an effort to place your ball closer to the target than your opponents'. But it isn't lawn bowling she's interested in. It's the people she's not supposed to be drawing.

Boules is a comradely sport, with teams urging on their own players while cheerfully heckling the opposing ones. Families picnic alongside the rink, and spectators gather on benches to applaud their favorites. There's verve, color, enjoyment, people of every type and class. A scene embodying la Ville Lumière, the City of Light. Pure and alive, bursting with joy and laughter. She will not allow the constraints of tradition to stop her from capturing it.

Her picture takes on the form of a rough triangle, the game being played closer to one corner, a picnicking family on the grass near another, a young couple sitting improperly close at the far end. The rink is a deep velvety green, the trees darken as they climb a distant hill, and the women's bright dresses throw sparkles of color and light. The male players are a little rough-looking, wearing outfits that seem more fitting to the privacy of home, and this enhances the spontaneity. The family is jolly, although some of the women's attire is a bit risqué, and the couple is brazenly enraptured. She'll call it *Parisian Summer.*

Over the weeks, she fills two sketchbooks with drawings, enough to begin painting, but she hasn't yet put brush to canvas. It's a bold step, subjects and themes well beyond her reach, not only men to whom she is not related but those of a lower class. And what will she do with it when it's finished? Should she show it to her friends? Degas will be startled but encouraging, as he enjoys nothing more than pushing boundaries, and while the others will be more cautious, she believes they will ultimately support her efforts.

But would any of them believe the picture fitting to include in their next exhibition? The contempt and disrespect that will fall on a woman for creating a painting that includes crowds such as this will make the ridicule she received after their first two shows seem like praise. How can she ask them to consider such a thing?

And yet, just as she can't resist Édouard, knowing the involvement is madness, she can't resist *Parisian Summer*. The painting comes quickly, as if it already knows what it should be. No need for watercolors or pastels; she begins with oils. Perhaps because she doesn't believe anyone beyond her small circle of artists will view it, she doesn't fret the way she usually does. She doesn't pace in front of the canvas for hours, staring and feeling dispirited, wondering what's wrong with it, what she should do next. Instead, she allows the sweeping strokes to flow, the people to emerge from her brush, the light to dance.

She keeps her studio door locked while she's working, lest the maid or the cook, or, worse, Cornélie or Gène, enter without knocking. And when she's finished for the day, she drapes it with a drop cloth to keep it hidden. When she lifts the cloth in the morning, her heart pounds as it does when she first catches sight of Édouard. The picture is only half finished, but it already glows, each person, each conversation seemingly alive.

What is the mother saying to the little boy who just tossed his half-eaten sandwich in the picnic basket? Is that girl aware of what she's getting herself into with that handsome and lustful young man? Berthe knows the painting will be good. Better than good. And she begins spending both days and evenings with her new love, *Parisian Summer*.

Late one night, Gène comes into the studio wearing his nightclothes. "You will make yourself ill, my dear," he says. "It's after midnight, and you must—" He stares at the painting, then over at her, and then at the painting again.

Berthe doesn't move. How could she have forgotten to lock the door?

"What is this?"

She tries to gauge his frame of mind. While Gène is far from a serious artist, he does paint, and perhaps he'll understand the urge to try something novel, something daring. "It's new."

"I see that." His voice is flat. "And you believe this subject matter is proper for you to paint?"

"I, uh, I wanted to try something different," she mumbles, as if she's a naughty girl being scolded by her mother. But what exactly has she done wrong?

Gène lifts the canvas from the easel. "This is impossible," he declares in a voice more forceful than she's ever heard him use. "You cannot finish it, may not finish it. It's dangerous enough in the state it's in."

"Dangerous? An afternoon of games in the park?"

"You know the rules as well as I do. This is not for a woman to paint. And if you refuse to acknowledge the risk this poses or, worse, try to complete it, then it must be destroyed immediately. You are my wife, and I will not allow you to bring shame on yourself or on our families."

Berthe can't believe the quiet man she married is taking such an overly zealous stance. "Gène," she says, trying for a softer tone. "You don't mean that. You can't mean that. It's just a picture."

"It's not just a picture! It is a grave threat. Blasphemy, even. It's my duty to protect you from harm, and that is exactly what I plan to do."

"I do not need your protection."

"Yes, you do. This is my decision, and you will do as I tell you. Your mother has already taken to her bed in anguish over the reaction to the auction, by the aspersions cast against you, against all of us. How do you think she would respond to the dishonor and scandal a painting such as this will bring?"

He's not saying anything she hasn't thought before, but the vehemence with which he states it, this unexpectedly hard turn from a man she considered soft, throws her off balance. "Look at it, Gène. I implore you. It's good, maybe the best I've ever done. What's so wrong with a picture of people enjoying themselves in a public park? It's not as if they're naked. Why is this disgraceful? I'm an artist, and I have the right to paint what I want!"

"You know the answer to those questions." He rests *Parisian Summer* on the floor, but he still holds on to it. "Don't pretend you don't, Berthe. You're not a foolish woman."

"The rules are foolish, not me!"

"The facts are the facts, whether you like them or not." Gène lifts the canvas and carries it from the studio.

She follows him into the hallway. "What are you doing?"

He walks into the kitchen, where the cook has left a low fire burning in the open hearth. Still holding the painting with one hand, he throws a bundle of kindling and three logs on the embers, then uses the wrought-iron poker to accelerate the flames.

Berthe tries to wrestle the painting from him, but his grip on the canvas is fierce. "You say you love me," she cries. "And if you do, you won't take something so dear from me."

Gène doesn't say anything. He just prods the logs. One falls onto the kindling and bursts into flame with a loud pop. Sparks fly in all directions. Another log catches, and the blaze climbs higher.

"No," she pleads, tears streaming down her cheeks. "It's not yours to destroy!"

He drops the poker, grasps *Parisian Summer*, and throws it into the fire.

Berthe lunges for it, but he pulls her back from the flames, holds her in place. She struggles against him, but she's unable to free herself.

"Take it out!" she screams as the fire greedily eats at the canvas, abetted by the oil paint. "Please! You can still save it." But she sees this is not so, and watches as the canvas blackens, strips of it falling into the flames, leaving only a wooden rectangle to burn.

Gène finally releases her, and for the first time since he walked into her studio, his face softens. "I'm sorry, Berthe. You're right that it was a lovely painting. But I am right that no one can ever see it."

PART NINE

Tamara, the present

TWENTY-SIX

Okay, I get it, but what other choice do I have? If there's nowhere else *Party* can go while I figure out a more suitable place for her, then she has to stay here until I do—and it's incumbent on me to make the apartment as comfortable for her as possible. Humidifier. Dehumidifier. Air purifier. Closed shades. Guard. But for this to work, it must appear as if the painting is long gone, when, in reality, she hasn't left the premises.

Which is exactly what I plan to do. Thank you, Claire Roth. *Party* is four feet high and almost five feet wide, but I don't need anything that big. Which is fortunate, because it turns out that canvases are ridiculously expensive. A four-by-six primed one runs about $800, a three-by-four, just under $500. And when the cheapest frame is added in, it's upward of a thousand. I had no idea it cost so much to be an artist.

I'll just buy a smaller one, wrap it in an overabundance of paper, and it'll be good to go. I scan through online sellers and decide to skip the frame. Instead, I order more paper. And expedited delivery. Then I review temperature-controlled storage facilities to send it to. As before, I'm taken aback by the prices, but then it occurs to me that I don't need temperature control for a blank canvas. I'll arrange for the transfer to be secret, alerting only Alyce, the building manager. Afterward, she and I will make an announcement to the press that *Party* has been moved to an undisclosed location for its safety, and that will be that.

Surprise, surprise—Wyatt freaks out when I tell him. "You're going to go through all these machinations just so you can keep that damn painting in your apartment?" he demands.

"I told you before that the large museums need too much time before they'll take it, and the small ones don't have the money to insure it." We're walking down the Southwest Corridor from the T station after seeing a play in the Theater District. During the day, the massive banks of snow have started to melt, but at night they freeze into dirty icy boulders along the edges of the walkway. "And storage units don't have the right conditions."

"But your apartment does?"

"I checked it out and know what has to be done to protect it. All of which I can do."

"Tell me you're not serious."

"It's only temporary. Until I figure out a better way."

"What if there's a slipup? I'm your lawyer, and it's my job to keep you from doing anything that might negatively impact your case."

"There aren't going to be any slipups. It's simple, straightforward, and exactly what you said I'd be doing in your statement."

"My statement was about *Party on the Seine*, not some blank canvas."

"No one's going to know it's blank. It'll be wrapped and look like the real thing."

We hurry into his warm house. He drops his coat on a kitchen chair and runs his hand through his hair. "This is a bad idea. Really bad."

"I don't agree."

"Listen to me, Tam," he says, unbuttoning my coat and sliding it off my shoulders. "Someone's going to find out. It always happens, especially when there's media involved. And then all hell will break out. Thieves could come calling, and do you really want all those reporters hounding you again? Plus we have no idea what Damien's move might be if he finds out you deceived him again—but based on his past actions, it's not going to be anything good."

I look up at him and shrug.

He shakes his head and pulls me to him. "Tamara, Tamara, Tamara, what am I going to do with you?"

THE THREE-BY-FOUR-FOOT CANVAS arrives, along with enough brown paper to wrap a car. I've paid two months up front for a storage unit only a few miles away, on E Street, and hired an art carrier to bring the fake there. I've also discussed the details of the transport with Alyce, who's more than happy to make an official announcement that *Party* is no longer in the building.

Obviously, I don't need to do anything with the canvas other than packaging it to make it look bigger, but seeing it there, resting against a kitchen cabinet, all white and empty, I have the urge to fill it. If Wyatt's worst-case scenario ever did come to pass, wouldn't it be better if it were a replica of the painting? Easier to fool people if it looks like what it's supposed to be? Completely wacko, I know.

Nevertheless, I go to the art store and buy some pastels and an easel. I haven't used pastels since high school, but they're much easier to work with than oils, and no one's going to believe a pencil drawing is a masterpiece. Not that anyone is going to believe anything I paint is a masterpiece—and not that anyone is going to see it. But that's not my real intention, just an implausible excuse to do what I want to do. I slap some peanut butter on a banana, gobble it down, and set up in the living room across from *Party*.

Pastels are far superior to the pencils, the colors deep and rich, easier to nuance with the sides of the stick as well as the sharper ends, and then using a finger to push the paint in ways and directions a pencil never could. Soon, my hands and arms are streaked with blue, red, and yellow. Probably my face too. Working on a large canvas, rather than my drawing pad, and packing it with the full range of *Party* is so much more gratifying than those timid little sketches I've been making. I drop into it, am in it, driven by exuberance, one with Berthe and her world.

It's well after midnight when I return to my own world. I press my hand to my throbbing lower back, stretch my tight hamstrings, and stare at the canvas. I can't quite believe what I'm seeing. It's no Manet, that's for sure, totally rough and unfinished—but I have a sense that it isn't half bad. Well, it is bad, but still it's so much better than any of my earlier efforts that I wonder if I actually did inherit some of those artsy genes. Who knew? My high school art teachers, I guess.

TWO NIGHTS LATER, the fake is out of the building, and in the morning, Alyce calls a few reporters and tells them *Party* has been moved to another location and will not be returning to Tremont245. There's a small mention of the transport online in *The Boston Globe*, rendering the story dead. But before I can start making a protective nest for *Party*, I, of course, receive an email from Damien.

From: Damien Manet, Director of the Édouard Manet Foundation
To: Tamara Rubin

Cc: Wyatt Butler, Beacon, Exeter & Associates
Re: Party on the Seine
Date: 24 January

It has come to my attention that you have once again moved *Party on the Seine* without informing the Édouard Manet Foundation. It has been made clear to you that the Foundation is responsible for maintaining a database containing the whereabouts of the entirety of Édouard Manet's oeuvre. We are incensed that you have not given us the address where *Party on the Seine* now resides, and must have this information immediately.

As you well know, *Party on the Seine* was due to the Louvre Museum on 1 January, three weeks past. It is imperative that the painting arrive in France to be prepared for presentation at the Édouard Manet retrospective in August, and therefore a hearing on this matter is to be held on 31 January in civil court at the Tribunal de Paris.

On that date, a judge will determine if, given the overwhelming evidence that *Party on the Seine* does not belong to you, the Foundation has the authority to remove it from your custody in order to share this lost masterwork with a worldwide audience of art lovers. It is not mandatory that your attorney attend, although it is allowed. If you are unable to send a representative, you and your attorney will be informed of the outcome via email. If you find these requirements too onerous or beyond your capabilities, $20 million US is available to settle the suit.

TWENTY-SEVEN

Wyatt is still kind of pissed off at me for keeping *Party*, but I call him anyway. "You saw it?"

"I told you whenever you make a move, Damien is going to come out punching."

"That's neither here nor there. What I need to know is whether this hearing is bluster or an actual threat."

"With Damien, it's usually both."

"Can he do it?"

"I'm guessing both he and the foundation have a lot of clout in Paris, not to mention that he's already shown himself to be both nasty and persistent. He's got money, influence, and a famous name, which is a dangerous combination for you."

"Are you saying he's going to be able to take her to France?"

"I'm not going to lie to you—it could happen."

"The Conference said she's mine. They've got money, influence, and a famous name."

"Probably not going to matter to a Parisian court."

"I know you're not happy about this move, but I did what I thought was best and—"

"Which it wasn't."

I've noted before that he's never tried to understand my feelings about *Party*, but now I see it's more than that. He's just not all that interested in discovering what's driving me, in knowing me. Which I guess is the way I wanted it—enjoyable and shallow—yet it troubles me. "Look, it's over and done, no point rehashing. If you're still my lawyer, I need you to help me with this." I pause and add coquettishly, "You're still my lawyer, right?"

"I suppose," he says reluctantly.

"So what's next, Counselor?"

"I'll try to get an extension."

"What if that doesn't work?"

A pause.

"I'm not selling to him," I reiterate for at least the tenth time.

"If he succeeds in taking *Party* to Paris, he's going to try to find a way to keep it there."

"Can he do that?"

"Again, money, influence, and a famous name. Plus the French are both passionate and possessive about their art and their artists. Listen to me, Tam. Given who we're dealing with here, once he gets the painting on French soil it could take years, if ever, to get it back here."

I stare at my tiny shard of river. Obviously, there are no sailboats, just steel-colored water, which matches the small patch of gray sky above it. I hate January.

"I can probably get him to thirty."

"I don't want thirty."

"Listen to yourself. You don't want thirty million dollars?"

"I don't want to give up *Party* for thirty million dollars."

A long sigh. "I'll see what I can do about the court date, but the only way to make sure you keep this painting is to prove that Léon never inherited it."

"I'm guessing you haven't found an investigator?" I ask, although it's only been a week since Nova quit and Wyatt would have told me if he had.

"Good guess, Sherlock." Clearly, he's still holding a grudge, which my rejection of $30 million did nothing to quell.

SO NOW THAT I've honed my investigative skills by failing to discover anything about *Party*'s sole-survival adventures, I'm supposed to use this nonexistent aptitude to find evidence *Party* wasn't covered by Édouard's will? That seems to be Wyatt's implication, and although I have neither the time nor the inclination, there doesn't appear to be an alternative. Detective Rubin.

Wyatt is thrilled when I tell him I'm going to try to get some answers, and he seems to have finally forgiven me. "Terrific idea," he says. "Great stopgap measure." A stopgap fiasco is more likely.

I order a dehumidifier—which is what I need, not a humidifier—and everything else necessary to protect *Party*, except for a guard, which is prohibitively expensive. The building's security was impressive during the media onslaught, so maybe I don't need a guard at all. Between setting up *Party*'s cocoon, work, and the time Wyatt requires, I manage to buy books about Berthe, Édouard, and the other Impressionists, then fire up my computer.

I soon discover that Léon Manet changed his name from Léon Leenhoff when he was in his twenties, and there are long-standing questions about his lineage. I fall into the rabbit hole of nineteenth-century gossip.

Édouard married a woman seven years his senior, Suzanne Leenhoff, who brought her much younger brother Léon with her, and the boy lived with them until adulthood. Apparently, Léon referred to Édouard as his godfather, which is odd, because as Suzanne's brother, wouldn't he have been Édouard's brother-in-law?

It seems that everyone in their social circle found this strange also. Why the obvious ruse? And even more vexing, why the marriage? Why would Édouard, young, handsome, and outgoing, tie himself down to the older and meek Suzanne, who was apparently a quite unattractive and unsociable woman with whom he had no children? Although both Édouard and Suzanne maintained this account of Léon's birth until their deaths, this did nothing to quell the rumors.

I meet Wyatt for dinner at Aquitaine, an upscale restaurant on Tremont that's across the street from Metropolis, the site of our first date. It's pricey, but Wyatt always insists on paying—traditional male that he is—so I've given up arguing about it. I do like it here. It's narrow, snuggled into the first floor of a nineteenth-century building, with a twelve-foot ceiling clad in ornamented copper. I imagine Berthe might have visited a restaurant that looked a lot like this one. Wyatt likes it because it's trendy and has a full bar. I wish it weren't so noisy.

He's waiting with his martini and has already ordered me a cabernet. As I slide into the booth, he raises his glass. "Got the hearing moved back to the end of February, maybe even later."

"Excellent work." I raise my glass. "And I've also done some excellent work, if I do say so myself."

"Hit me."

When I finish describing some of what I learned, I add triumphantly, "So if Suzanne's claim is true, it means Léon was Édouard's brother-in-law, not his godson. And, most important for us, he definitely was not Édouard's son."

"Then why would Édouard leave everything to him?"

"There's more." I take another sip of wine, relishing the slow parsing of my discoveries. "Suzanne was Édouard's piano teacher, and there's speculation—which almost everything I've read supports—that she was also his father's mistress and gave birth to a son while she was working for the Manets. Then, in order to give the child legitimacy, she names him Léon Leenhoff and claims he's her brother."

"Couldn't get away with that now."

"She disappeared for a few months and returned with the infant. Told everyone their mother died giving birth to him, and that it was her responsibility to raise him. No internet or DNA to dispute her story. And Édouard either believed her tall tale or backed her up to uphold the Manet name. And if he did know, maybe he wanted to keep the boy in the family."

"So you're saying Édouard married his father's mistress because he wanted to hide his father's indiscretion? To maintain the honor of the family name?" Wyatt pops a cheese-stuffed olive into his mouth. "That doesn't make any sense. I don't get how that would even work—and it makes even less sense if he was as good-looking and charismatic as you say." He grins at me. "Not to mention the age difference."

"Don't see you complaining much about that." I bat my eyes flirtatiously. "And listen to this. It turns out that Antoinette Manet, Édouard's mother, disliked her daughter-in-law and wasn't particularly nice to Léon. But the best part is that the boy seemingly bore an uncanny resemblance to Édouard's father." I chuckle. "Isn't this just delicious?"

"Who knew you had such highly honed investigative talents? Maybe we won't need to hire anyone else."

I ignore him. "So this means Damien isn't a direct descendant of Édouard's. He's the descendant of Édouard's half brother, while I'm the descendant of Édouard's full brother." I raise my fists in the air. "Nah, nah, na-nah nah. I've got more of Édouard's blood in me than you do, cuz."

Wyatt laughs. "And given that you were able to discover this, Damien had to know it all along. Lying to intimidate you and further his case. What an ass."

I hold up my palm for a high five.

Wyatt high-fives me, then sobers. "You get that this has no real effect on the lawsuit, which is based on the will? Damien still would inherit *Party* through Léon, no matter his and Édouard's relationship."

"Sure, I get it. But right in his first email Damien said that as Édouard's direct descendant he was the rightful heir. That his claim was more valid because I'm only from some side branch of the family."

"If I remember correctly, he also said it was because he's Léon's direct descendant. Which is why it's all about finding solid proof that *Party* was never Léon's."

"I'm not going to be the one doing the digging."

"I hear you," he says. "My assistant contacted a few possibilities, but they all seem to be booked for the near future. And I don't like our time frame. The New York court date is the first of May. Which isn't as far away as it may seem."

THAT NIGHT, FOR the first time in a while, I dream about Berthe. She and I are dancing together. Waltzing, I think, but I don't know much about ballroom dancing. Of course, in the dream I do. She's leading, and I'm following as if I've been waltzing my entire life, classical music sweeping around us. Berthe, wearing a floor-length black velvet gown with lace along the neckline and cuffs, is slender and beautiful and extremely elegant. She beams at me, her white skin radiant and her dark eyes mischievous, as we dip and weave around a series of rooms that appear to be an oversized artist's studio. Shiny black curls fall prettily to her forehead.

There are a dozen easels holding half-finished paintings. Some I recognize as Édouard's. Others appear to be Monets or Renoirs, and the two domestic scenes have to be Berthe's. We loop through them and around overstuffed chairs that look to be some grandmother's castaways, then push through a curtain that hides a humpbacked red couch and circle that also. I'm having fun, and apparently Berthe is too. When the dance ends, we bow to each other, still holding hands.

"Excellent, child," she says in French, and I can understand her although I don't know the language. "I believe we should continue discovering each other, don't you?"

PART TEN

Berthe, 1876–1882

TWENTY-EIGHT

1876–1877

The Impressionists are planning to hold their third show at Durand-Ruel's new gallery on the Rue Le Peletier, almost exactly a year after the auction. Once again, Berthe is the only woman to exhibit. There will be over 250 works on display, of which nineteen are hers: sixteen oils and watercolors, as well as three pastels. All of her pictures depict landscapes or domestic scenes, many of women at their toilette, others of mothers and children. *Rising. Dressing. Little Girl in a Blue Dress.*

She continues to mourn the loss of *Parisian Summer*, along with the opportunity to expand her artistic horizons. She always knew these restrictions held sway, but she'd looked forward to a future when this might not be so. Now even that limited optimism is gone. She never imagined her placid husband would have the power to snuff out her hopes, to change the course of her work.

Watching *Parisian Summer* shrivel into nothingness was painful beyond measure, the image of which still stings her eyes, as the odor of burning canvas and oil paint still stings her nose. Even worse, Gène's unexpected fury and his certitude of her folly has further delineated her boundaries. As much as she had hungered to break through these barriers, she's now forced to face the reality that if she steps beyond the rigidity of the social order, she will dishonor her family. However unjustifiable that dishonor may be.

Although she recognizes it would be the Christian thing to forgive Gène, Berthe finds she cannot. While he's apologized for upsetting her and explained his reasoning many times, he remains insistent that his actions were both correct and necessary. Neither true. She could have kept *Parisian Summer* in her studio, under a drop cloth. Or if he feared she would complete it behind his back, the half-finished painting could have been stored in his bedroom or at his mother's house, waiting for the moment when she would be allowed to paint it. This last thought suggests she still clings to a shred of hope that one day things might change. A very small shred.

She tries to be magnanimous, allowing that it was her husband's conventional nature that drove his decision. Édouard's unwavering commitment to the time-honored Salon, to the powers that be, is indicative of the same inclination. But Édouard would never have done what Gène did. He would never destroy another artist's work. Then she remembers he did exactly that to Degas's painting of Suzanne. Yet another display of the Manet family's embrace of the reigning orthodoxy.

She stands in her studio, watching sunlight stream over her finished and unfinished canvases, inhaling the scent of paint and turpentine, an artist's scent, her scent. This is her world, her life, circumscribed as it may be, and she cannot stop painting any more than she can stop breathing. Her only choice is to strive to bring the domain of women to life, a corner of the world her male counterparts cannot depict. *Rising. Dressing. Little Girl in a Blue Dress*. This, too, stings.

BERTHE AND DEGAS survey the exhibition the day before the opening, just as they did prior to their first show. There are many new painters, although their bande of six remains the organizing committee, and this time the rooms are arranged by artist. The front spaces are reserved for those deemed least likely to attract criticism, like Berthe, and the more daring, like Degas, are toward the back. Monet's stunning *Japanese Girl* is nearest the entrance, while Caillebotte's *The Floor Sweepers*, a powerful painting of men in ragged clothing sweating as they arduously clean the floorboards, is hidden even farther away from the entrance than Degas's work.

"This will go better than the last," he says, then contradicts himself by adding, "Unless it doesn't."

Berthe laughs. "A definitive statement if I ever heard one."

"And apropos."

The early reviews turn out to be tentatively promising. *The New Painting*: "The artists have discovered a novel way of painting light and of depicting everyday human life. In their work, ordinary man is being celebrated in all his quirkiness and individuality." The critic Emile Belmont:

"With the innovative quality of rendering by simple, sweeping stokes, the Impressionists arouse the impression of their vision of reality."

Degas is rapturous when they gather after Durand-Ruel closes the doors on the second night. "This is proof that we are beginning to convert them to our way of thinking!" he crows to the others.

"Don't be too hasty," Sisley warns. "More reviews will be coming tomorrow."

"Oh, Alfred," Berthe says. "The first nice words we've received and you remain in despair? I agree with Edgar. We should be happy with both the heartening notices and the headway we're making."

"I'm not despairing. I'm being cautious. Many of these comments are not particularly glowing. 'A more interesting exhibition than in 1874.' 'The little canvases by Mademoiselle Morisot.' Faint praise, I'd say."

"Caution is wise," Pissarro agrees. "The more we expect, the more we will be disappointed."

"What a sad way to live your life!" Degas throws his arms wide in consternation. "If something bad is coming, that's all the more reason to take hold of the pleasure while we can."

"When did you turn into such an optimist, Edgar?" Renoir grumbles. "It doesn't become you."

Berthe stands, done with the men's back-and-forth. "I believe you are all correct, gentlemen. We should be pleased with what has been said and wary about what might be to come. But I've had a long day, and my carriage is waiting." Then she leaves them to carry on with their useless disagreements.

The next day's reviews are more mixed, but it is their old nemesis, Albert Wolff of *Le Figaro*, who is the most malicious: "Here are six lunatics, one of which is a woman, a group of unfortunates deranged by ambition. These Impressionists take some canvas, paint and brushes, throw a few colors at random, and then sign the lot. Like inmates of a madhouse who pluck up stones in the road and believe they have found diamonds."

If this were not enough, two days after his first review is published, Wolff offers another, spewing forth hot fury like a volcano that must continue to erupt until all of its molten rock is jettisoned: "Try telling M. Pissarro that trees are not purple nor the sky the color of butter, that these cannot actually be seen in nature. Try telling M. Degas about drawing, color, execution and purpose. Try to explain to M. Renoir that a woman's torso is not violet toned with green spots, indicating a corpse in the final stages of decay."

As Berthe reads his column, she's sickened by the man's vile words, by the depths of his disdain for artworks she knows to be breathtakingly bold. She reminds herself that this is what critics do, that it's their job to be provocative. But his harshness is so brazen it's difficult not to take it to heart. On the other hand, at least he appears to have spared her personally.

But he has not. As she reaches the bottom of the page, she reads: "There is also, as in all famous gangs, a woman. Her name is Berthe Morisot, and she is a curiosity. With her, feminine grace manages to preserve itself in the midst of the ravings of a frenzied mind and outbursts of delirium." This is not going to sit well with either Gène or Édouard. And it's not the reference to her mind or her delirium that will upset them.

Another trait the brothers share is a belief in the sanctity of the Manet name and the need to defend it at all costs. As Berthe feared, they both interpret Wolff's comment about her being a member of a gang as accusing her of being a mobster's gun moll, a woman of low repute. She doesn't believe this was Wolff's intent, just a part of his sensationalism.

When she explains this to Gène, he will have none of it. "I will not allow anyone to speak of you in this manner," he declares. "You are Madame Eugène Manet, a woman of unquestionable moral decency and position. This unconscionable behavior will not go unaddressed! Tomorrow, I will send Wolff a cartel challenging him to a duel."

"Gène, please. If you make more of this than it is, it will only serve to remind people of what he wrote. Best to let it be forgotten. A duel is pure folly, dangerous, and will prove nothing."

He moves from his chair to sit on the sofa next to her. "I cannot permit this disgraceful man to impugn your virtue. I know you to be an upright and respectable woman in all ways, and it is my obligation to defend you as such."

She turns from him, ashamed. Upright and respectable are far from what she is. Nor is she of unquestionable moral decency. Questionable moral decency is more apt. She is the harlot that man at the auction accused her of being, virtuous only in Gène's mind, a cuckold's fantasy. Tears fill her eyes and slide down her cheeks. If she were to confess her sin, it would surely stop the duel, but this truth would cause Gène even greater pain. His own brother. How can she be doing this? Why is she unable to stop?

"Don't cry, my Berthe." Gène puts his arm around her. "As a husband and as a Manet, I will make this wastrel suffer for both his words and his aspersions. I will let no man disparage your honor."

She allows him to kiss her and goes with him to her room, where she's fortunately able to talk him out of the duel.

A YEAR LATER, the Impressionists hold another exhibition that is relatively well-received. Although there are the usual detractors, it's as if the reviewers and the public have tired of the repeated and cutting critiques, and are now less interested in reiterating them. The crowd is much larger than it was for the previous shows, and people seem to be growing more accustomed to and are more accepting of the new style, which the unexpected number of sales confirms.

Degas claims this is proof that his push to make Impressionism commonplace is a success, and Berthe agrees with him. The rest of the bande is more grudging, not wishing to feed what they perceive as his delusions of grandiosity.

This time, Berthe's work isn't singled out for attention because she's a woman. Instead, her paintings are lauded for the nuances of her color shifts and the "symphony" of her compositions. One reviewer declares that she's the only true Impressionist in the group, who should be "praised and praised again." And a well-known journalist and art critic observes that Morisot and her fellow Impressionists are now being "talked about in cafés, clubs and drawing rooms." These are heady words.

She's overjoyed at the recognition, although Gène interprets this as verification that his insistence that she not stray beyond her limits is correct. Her interpretation is quite different. She believes that now that she's on more solid footing, her new standing might open up the prospect of growth. If Gène hadn't burned *Parisian Summer*, she would have completed it now, perhaps exhibited it. As this isn't possible, she will begin anew.

She says nothing to Gène, of course, but she needs to discuss the idea of expanding her range with another painter. Her first thought is Degas, who's always searching for a limit to break, but he can't be trusted not to gossip, even after he's promised utter secrecy. Édouard, as she well knows, is quite good at keeping secrets.

She hasn't told him anything about *Parisian Summer* or Gène's wrath, concerned the revelation might destroy his relationship with his brother, or, worse, that he might agree with Gène. But she's haunted by a powerful image of the picture she wants to paint, and Édouard has shown an indulgence for Gène's shortcomings in the past.

It's a bande day, but just she, Édouard, and Renoir are in attendance, and Renoir departs after only an hour. A month has passed since they've been alone, and, as Édouard will be going to Italy for the summer, they rush into each other's arms, laughing at their mutual desperation. He locks the door, and they quickly retire to their red sofa.

Their lovemaking, as always, devours her, separating her from anything as mundane as time or place, and when they finally collapse into each other, she's sorry for the world to return. Their breathing begins to slow, and they lie, silently and companionably, wrapped around each other. Although Berthe is still overcome by guilt over their deception, like the Impressionists' paintings, the more they continue and the more time that passes, God help her, the less awful it seems.

She throws the light blanket over them. "I need your advice."

Édouard aligns his body with hers, and she rests against his chest. "What can I help you with, my love?"

"It's a long story, and maybe you don't really want to hear it . . ."

"If it means we can stay here like this, make it as long as you want." He kisses her lightly. "Tell me."

She does, watching him closely to gauge his reaction so she can backpedal if necessary. Although his face hardens when she describes the events surrounding Gène and *Parisian Summer*, he doesn't appear as angry with his brother as she would have thought.

"Poor Gène," he says when she finishes. "You're too much for him. Every wonderful thing you are is in direct conflict with his quiet disposition. He has no idea what to do with you, so he jumps to foolish conclusions, and then feels he must see them through in order to appear strong in your eyes."

His expression clouds. "Maybe I shouldn't have pushed for the marriage. You two are as incompatible as Suzanne and I are." He barks a laugh without humor. "Gène and Suzanne make the better couple."

She's had the same thought, of course, but it's too late to change what has been done. She burrows closer and says nothing.

He wraps a curl dangling onto her forehead around his finger. "Have you been able to forgive him?"

"Some. It's been over a year, and, as you said, it's not his fault I'm a bad match for him."

"So is the advice you need related to Gène?"

"No, it's about another painting." She tells him of her newfound confidence that, given the reaction to their latest show, the Paris art world is becoming more responsive to change.

"It's been said that 'Convention is the most subtle of dictators,'" Édouard remarks. But then he counsels her to be cautious, suggesting that if she decides to pursue this course that she work on the picture in his studio when no one else is present and promises to hide it among his own paintings. He also proposes that she wait before exhibiting it, as its subject matter is certain to cause an uproar. He believes she has the right to paint what she wants, but that she should bide her time until it's clear it will be appreciated for what it is, rather than discarded for who she is.

She's pleased he's rallied behind her, yet there's a lack of enthusiasm underlying his words. As if he isn't sure this is worthwhile or viable, that he, too, believes she should stay within the lines. He's probably as worried about the family name as Gène is. She had always longed to be a Manet, but the darker side of her choice is becoming clear.

When she returns home, all these concerns disappear. Gène is waiting for her, his face pale and anxious. Her mother has taken ill and is in the hospital. They rush to her bedside, but there are doctors and nurses attending to her, and they are told to wait in the corridor.

Berthe cannot remain still, and paces past wards that reek of bedpans, dead fish, and bleach. She chokes on the combined odors and her fear. Maman has always been strong, both in body and temperament, and Berthe is certain this will continue to hold true. But why does she need so many doctors and nurses?

Gène comes to find her and says the doctor wishes to talk to them. Although Cornélie is Berthe's mother, the doctor speaks to Gène. "Madame Morisot is resting. We—"

"May I go to her?" Berthe asks.

"—have done what can be done for the moment." He continues talking to Gène, as if Berthe hadn't spoken. "Although I must inform you, Monsieur Manet, that she is not well."

Gène takes Berthe's hand. "But she will get better?"

The doctor shakes his head.

The remainder of the year is consumed by watching Maman grow frailer and trying to ease the pain that's overwhelming her from the disease no one will name. In late December, Cornélie dies at the age of fifty-six, and even with all their disagreements and her complaints about her mother, Berthe is heartbroken.

As they did after Papa died, her sisters and brother arrive. At that time, Berthe was completely focused on her mother's grief, so busy attending to Cornélie that her father's death felt almost ancillary. Now there is no such diversion, and she falls into a sadness so deep that Edma and Yves must manage both the influx of mourners and the funeral details. Gène is overly attentive, which Berthe finds maddening. She's drowning in a sorrow he cannot begin to fathom, yet he pretends he does.

Édouard is in England, but he sends Berthe an ingenious new easel he discovered in London. He includes a note expressing his condolences and explaining that this latest design is particularly useful for pastels, and that it is a New Year's present. Gène exclaims over its unique construction, yet she can tell he is not pleased his brother sent it to her. But even a gift from Édouard cannot pull Berthe from her grief, which only begins to ease with the return of the springtime sun.

TWENTY-NINE

1878–1880

In April, Berthe is astonished to discover she's pregnant. At thirty-seven, she was convinced she could not conceive. She immediately counts the time since her last monthly visitor, and is both thankful and disappointed to discover the child is Gène's, as she hasn't been with Édouard since last November. She supposes she shouldn't be surprised at her condition, as Edma, two years her elder, is also with child, and Yves, eighteen months older than Edma, had a baby just last year. She doesn't quite know how to take this turn of events. It's exciting to think she'll join the ranks of motherhood, know the sweetness of her own babe in her arms, especially at the same time Edma holds her newborn. But there are many concerns.

At her age, the physical demands of both pregnancy and giving birth will be challenging, especially because she's tended toward sickly most of her life. And although she would not admit this to anyone, now that her work has begun to be recognized, she worries a child might hinder her ability to carve out time to paint. She's also saddened that Maman didn't live to see this moment. How much joy it would have brought Cornélie to watch her most wayward child finally fulfilling all the aspirations she had for her.

When she tells Gène, he's stunned, almost disbelieving. "But, but we hardly ever," he stammers. "How, I mean, not how, but, but I thought this wasn't possible."

Berthe laughs. "I didn't either, but apparently it is. According to Dr. Aguillard, our little one should be born sometime in early November."

"Our little one . . ." His face floods with awe.

She sits on the arm of his chair, something she rarely does. "It's true. You're going to be a father."

He tentatively reaches his hand toward her belly but lets it hover just beyond her dress.

"I'm not going to break, Gène." She takes his hand and places it on her stomach. "Not much there yet, but I've been assured there will be soon."

"The greatest gift." His eyes fill with tears, and hers do too. He drops his gaze, overcome with emotion. "Thank you," he says, his voice cracking.

When they go to dinner at Antoinette's and tell the Manets the news, there's an outburst of joy and good wishes around the table, although Suzanne is subdued, either jealous over the pregnancy or fearful her husband is the father. Gène is grinning like a boy who just found hidden treasure, and Berthe, suddenly shy under all the attention, flushes with pleasure. Her child's surname will be Manet, direct kin to both Édouard and herself. Intertwining ties of love and blood.

Édouard comes in as dessert is being served, and when Gène announces her condition, Édouard appears as happy as the rest, smiling at her proudly, kissing her on both cheeks, and heartily shaking Gène's hand. "Wonderful, wonderful news," he crows. "I couldn't be happier. A niece or nephew for Oncle Édouard!"

When everyone resumes their chatter, he shoots her a questioning glance.

Berthe avoids looking at him, knowing what he's thinking, what he's hoping. And although she might prefer the child be Édouard's in her heart, her head knows it is better this way. As Édouard helps her with her coat, he whispers his question.

"Gène's," she whispers back.

When she glances up at him, she sees he's crestfallen, and she can't stop herself from touching his sleeve to show she understands.

Then he pulls himself together and smiles at her. "All for the best," he says, but she knows he doesn't mean it.

BECAUSE OF HER age and medical history, Dr. Aguillard orders Berthe to spend as much time as possible in bed. She's cut off from the bande, from Édouard, and from painting. It's a difficult confinement in many ways. Not only does she chafe under the restrictions, but she seems to suffer every malady pregnancy can bring.

She's reminded of the lonely days following Edma's marriage, but at least then she was able to paint and leave the house. Edma must remain at home awaiting her own child, and Yves has an infant and a passel of other youngsters to care for. Gène's migraines become worse and more frequent, most likely from an overabundance of fretting over her, although his absences do offer some relief from his oversolicitousness.

The summer is endless, extremely hot, and vile stenches from the street enter through her open bedroom windows, increasing her nausea tenfold. Although she's halfway through her pregnancy, she still vomits daily, which, to the doctor's consternation, causes her to lose weight rather than gain it. He upbraids her as if this is her fault.

She accepts that she will surely die before the birth, and there are many times she wishes it would happen that very day. Although the fall offers cooling weather, her discomfort grows as the final months swell her belly, along with her legs and hands. She cannot believe any woman who has experienced this wretchedness would ever consent to a second child.

In November, Isabeau Morisot Manet is born, a plump and healthy little girl. Berthe notes the irony as Édouard signs the baptismal papers and he grasps Gène's hand in congratulations. As happy as she is to give birth to a Manet, she's taken aback by Isabeau's appearance.

My dearest Edma,

It is done. I have a daughter; you, a new niece. I was planning to name her Rose, but as she is too unattractive to carry a name so evocative of beauty, I deemed to call her Isabeau. Gène is disappointed that she is not a boy, but I told him he should be happy because she looks like one. She also resembles him, nothing of the Morisot in her at all.

The child is an inflated balloon, so fat the doctor was amazed, as I had gained so little weight during my confinement. I also must tell you that her head is as flat as a paving stone. I am weak and bruised, and must agree with George Sand when she calls the marriage bed the beginning of male dominance and a wife's painful experience of birth its culmination.

Within a month, as Berthe's strength improves, so does her frame of mind. Isabeau has claimed her heart, and she's addled with love for her daughter. Everything the child does is astounding, and when Isabeau, who she calls Izzie or Izzie-belle, is napping or with the nursemaid, Berthe aches for her the way she aches for Édouard when they're apart.

Édouard comes by frequently, ostensibly to visit Isabeau, but in fact to spend time with Berthe. An advantage of their family ties, as he once promised. Gène, who seems a tad afraid of the baby, hovers nervously when his brother is in the house. Édouard is surprisingly easy with the child, considering he has none of his own, and dances through the rooms with Isabeau to make her laugh. When she beams her toothless grin, so does he.

"I can't believe you ever believed this child was homely," he says, handling the smiling little one back to Berthe. "Look at those cheeks. At that luminescent skin."

Berthe nuzzles Isabeau, who chortles with delight and grabs for her mother's curls with her chubby fingers. "Perhaps she's starting to grow out of that stage. But no matter what she looks like, she's as sweet as an angel, like a kitten, always happy." She sits the little girl on her lap and pulls her up to a stand. "Aren't you, Izzie, my little Izzie-belle? Are you just the best baby ever?"

Édouard watches her, smiling lovingly. "When do you think you'll be able to return to the studio?" His tone is suitably reserved, as the servants are about, although Gène is in his darkened bedroom with another migraine.

"I've been dying to paint my darling here," Berthe says, giving the little girl a flurry of kisses. "I suppose the nursemaid will have to hold her, but she's already starting to sit up by herself. Aren't you, you little rascal?"

"So you're planning to resume soon?" he asks politely, as if it's a casual question, when it's anything but. He's wondering how long it will be before they'll be able to be together again.

"Here, yes." She rests her chin on Isabeau's head, and locks her eyes on his. "I think it will be at least a few months before I can consider painting with the others. Although for many reasons, I wish it could be tomorrow."

"As do I," he says, holding her gaze.

"Édouard," she whispers.

He rises from his chair and sits down next to her on the sofa. He leans over to kiss the baby, pressing his body into Berthe's side, sliding a hand behind her back. She doesn't move, relishing his closeness, the warmth of him, wishing their time together could somehow be stretched. But the parlor is a dangerously open place, and she reluctantly pulls away, placing Isabeau on the cushion between them.

OVER THE COURSE of the winter, Berthe returns to painting almost daily, resuming the schedule she followed before Isabeau was born. She works in her studio and at Édouard's, maintaining her standing as a professional artist while also that of a wife and mother, much to the chagrin of many in their social circle, arbiters as they are of all that is acceptable. She's unwavering, despite the raised eyebrows and whispers, and Gène has held to his promise not to thwart her. But given his response to *Parisian Summer*, she's not at all certain this will remain the case.

The Impressionists, fully relishing their name, welcome her back into their fold. As does Édouard, his welcome both public and private. He still insists he's not an Impressionist, although the art world consistently refers to him as such. The press call him their leader, even as he continues to solely submit to the Salon and refuses to join their exhibitions. He claims less interest in light than in satire, which he used to great effect in *Luncheon on the Grass*, by placing two nude women with clothed men.

One morning, Berthe catches sight of the wet nurse feeding Isabeau on the sofa in the nursery, sunlight falling on them from a high angle. "Stay exactly as you are, Zelia," she says. "I'll be right back." She rushes into her studio for her easel and pastels, then sets them off to the right side of this exquisite tableau. Her sticks fly over the canvas as she tries to capture the fleeting light, the fleeting moment, before they disappear. Initially, Zelia stiffens and Isabeau cries out, but then the nurse resettles the baby to her breast and they both quiet.

Berthe has painted many children before, but never in such an intimate pose, never so quickly, and never without preliminary sketches. By the time Zelia shifts the baby to her other breast, Berthe has enough to use as preparation for an oil painting. She gazes at her work in wonder. Is this how Édouard does it? Without premeditation and careful study? It is not her way, but there is no denying its power.

Isabeau becomes her favorite model, and Berthe follows this first effort with paintings that depict the little girl in her cradle or in her pram or staring up in fascination at a bowl of flowers sitting on a table. One of Berthe's favorites is a portrait of the blond, blue-eyed child sitting in an oversized chair, propped up by pillows. Her smile is wide, her cheeks round and rosy, as she looks directly out of the picture, preternaturally wise and definitely no longer homely. Her features are clearly Gène's, but they have been rearranged in the most magnificent way. Berthe is ashamed she ever thought her daughter anything but radiantly beautiful, and wishes she'd never written to Edma that she believed otherwise.

Gène is horrified by *The Wet Nurse* and pleads with her not to exhibit it, but he doesn't threaten to destroy it. He's now as head over heels for Isabeau as Berthe is, and she knows he would never be able to do harm to a painting of his little girl. However, his time with the child is limited, as his headaches have grown more frequent and more intense. He's in his bedroom so often that Berthe, completely absorbed with her work and her daughter, frequently forgets he's in the house.

She tries to paint with the bande at least twice a week. The many distractions at home keep her from diving as deeply inside her work there as she's able to do when she's at the studio. And, of course, Édouard is there. They try to be discreet, but the pull between them feels so strong, so alive, that she often wonders how the others cannot notice, especially Degas. And perhaps they do.

One afternoon, Degas stands, stretches, and then ambles over to her easel. She's putting the finishing touches on a painting of Isabeau and some flowers. "I believe your work has changed for the better since you've become a mother," he says. "There's a sense of abandon, of lightness and spontaneity here. An unposed moment of childhood, so intimate and gentle."

"Too intimate and gentle?" she asks. "You know I worry about those adjectives."

"Does that matter when you're producing remarkable work?"

She doesn't answer. Despite her earlier decision to accept the restrictions of her gender and to use them to her advantage, she often imagines the painting she discussed with Édouard, sees it in its full glory, yearns to bring it to life. But then her thoughts turn to Isabeau. Now that she has a daughter, how can she take the risk of bringing scandal to her child?

Her work is coming along nicely, and even she's pleased as she prepares for their next exhibition. She didn't participate in the previous one, due to Isabeau's birth, and she's determined her return will be triumphant. She needs to display as many pieces as possible, ones that call attention to her unique style, the looseness of her strokes capturing the play of light, particularly her new insights into the color white.

Degas finds an old and rather decrepit building on Rue des Pyramides for the upcoming exhibition, and the members of the bande immediately take exception with his choice. After listening to their grousing, he says, "Do any of you have anything to offer aside from criticism? If not, I beg you to go out and find a building that better meets your specifications. If you discover a space that's large, on a street of distinction that we can afford to rent, I will be more than pleased to consider it with an open mind."

"Would be the first time," Monet mumbles to Renoir, then stands in front of Degas. "I will do exactly as you suggest, and if I'm unsuccessful, I might consider submitting to the Salon." When he walks out the door, Renoir and Sisley follow him.

Édouard turns from the painting he's been working on during the discussion. "The man has a point," he says mildly.

"Mind your own damn business," Degas snaps.

When a more suitable location isn't found, it falls to Berthe to reconcile the quarrels. This is not an easy task with these men, but after two weeks of arguments, the bande grudgingly agrees to hold the show on Rue des Pyramides. But the bickering doesn't end there. Battles erupt over lighting and noise, even how the posters are designed. Berthe is amazed when consensus is somehow achieved without anyone coming to blows.

She tenders ten oils, four watercolors, and a painted fan, one of a dozen she made during her confinement. The critical response to the exhibition is even more positive than for their last show, and her work receives much attention. Her notice exceeds most of that given to the other artists, and, to her secret delight, it's much greater than the notice given to Mary Cassatt.

Fairly or unfairly, Berthe considers Cassatt her rival, as the American is now the second woman to be labeled an Impressionist. Berthe has been involved with the group for over ten years, and Mary just waltzes in and claims an equal position. Berthe recognizes that she's being small, but she can't help a bit of gloating. Despite a sprinkling of the usual comments about her messy brushstrokes and unfinished edges, she quickly switches to basking:

"Berthe Morisot handles the palette and brush with a truly astonishing delicacy."

"A true luministe, directly rendering the sensation of color and light."

"No one ever made such a fine use of white."

"I have been seduced and charmed by Morisot's talents."

Even more amazing, Albert Wolff offers no criticism of her work. By the end of the exhibition, over sixteen thousand people have attended and, for the first time, each of the artists makes a profit. Berthe's sales are among the highest, and almost all of her paintings are purchased. To ice the cake, Durand-Ruel buys another fifteen.

THIRTY

1881–1882

The accolades spur Berthe to work even harder, and over the next year she produces dozens of oils and pastels, along with many pencil drawings and even a few prints, a new format Degas has been experimenting with. She cannot believe her good fortune. To have a beautiful, brilliant daughter and the respect of the art world, not to mention that she's actually making money, is beyond imagination. "Intoxicating" is the word that comes to mind. Her life's dream is moving forward to fruition.

The only thing that would make it even sweeter is if she were married to Édouard rather than Gène. Although in truth, Gène has become a ghost wandering in the background, overcome by headaches, often disappearing into his room for days. Because of this and the newfound fame that necessitates she produce as many paintings as possible, she and Édouard are able to steal more hours by themselves. Which is a joy that turns into potential calamity when she realizes she's pregnant again. This time, the child is not Gène's.

THE EVENING FOLLOWING her discovery, Gène is well enough to join her for dinner, and afterward they sit together in the parlor, reading. Berthe pretends to be engrossed, and although her eyes follow the words down the page, she retains nothing. She and Gène have not had relations in almost a year.

She closes her book and presses it between her hands. "I'm so pleased to see that you're feeling better. It has been a long time since a day has passed without a headache."

"One of my rare, good ones," he says from behind his paper. "For which I am grateful."

"As am I. I wish for there to be more."

"Thank you, my dear."

She fidgets with the book cover. She has always been the one to "allow" Gène into her bedroom. She has never invited him. "Do you, do you have any idea why this is so?"

He lowers the paper. "Why what is so?"

"Well, why, why it was you had such a good day?" she says inelegantly.

"There's no rhyme nor reason, as Dr. Aguillard has told us." He glances at her curiously.

"I, uh, I was just hoping that maybe, that maybe you noticed something that was different today or even yesterday. Something you did or didn't do. So then if there were, you would know what to do or not to do to keep the headaches at bay."

"I only wish it were that simple." He sighs and begins to raise his newspaper.

"Gène."

Again, a questioning look. "Are you feeling quite well tonight?"

"Yes, yes, I am quite well, thank you. It was just that I was thinking that if you felt well and I felt well, well, maybe we could, we could enjoy this together."

"Isn't that what we are doing?"

Desperate, she has no choice but to sit on the edge of his chair and take his hand. Her face flaming, she says, "I meant together in my bedroom."

Gène looks astounded, and for a moment Berthe fears he's going to refuse her. But he quickly collects himself and stands, and, hand in hand, they go to her room. After he leaves her bed for his own, she ponders the problem of timing. The child will be born in six or seven months, rather than nine, and this will be difficult to explain. But perhaps her concern is for nothing, as it's more than possible Gène will not notice. His headaches come almost daily and often keep him up all night, after which he sleeps through to the afternoon. Sometimes, he's confused about whether it's Monday or Tuesday.

This is even more important now that he's become increasingly bothered by the amount of time she spends at Édouard's. Gène has pointed out more than once that he built a studio for her so she wouldn't need to venture from the house, adding that if she remained at home she would be able to spend more time with Isabeau. It's a difficult argument to deflect.

WHEN NEXT SHE and Édouard are alone, she tells him they need to talk. He looks worried as they settle in the two chairs where Cornélie and Antoinette used to sit. "Is something troubling you? Is anything amiss?" he asks.

Berthe isn't at all certain what his reaction is going to be. He appeared disappointed when he learned Gène was Isabeau's father, but maybe she misread him. And even though the thought of his child growing within her fills her with wonder, she's terrified by the difficulties ahead. And both of these will surely be true for him too. But she has no idea which of the emotions will be stronger. She clears her throat. "I am with child."

He blinks at her, uncomprehending.

"And the baby is yours."

"With child?" His eyes widen. "Mine?"

She nods, watching his face flash from uncertainty to shock to understanding to unbridled exultation. He leaps from his chair, picks her up out of hers, and dances her around the room. "We're going to have a child! You and me, ours. Just ours. Are you sure this is really true?"

Her laughter is full-throated and her happiness vast as he waltzes her in wide circles through the studio. Then he leads her to their sofa and carefully lays her on the cushions as gently as she pictures him putting their baby down to sleep.

"It's marvelous, but also perilous," she murmurs as he takes her in his arms. "We're going to have to be very careful. I worry about Gène. Everyone else too."

"Only marvelous, my darling. Only marvelous."

After they make love, she folds herself into him, pulls his arms around her, luxuriating in the wonder of what is to come. A child they created, one who won't just share blood with the Manet family but one who will belong only to them. Then she sighs. "There will be problems. Possibly more than we can imagine."

"I've always wanted to be a father," he says, as if he hasn't heard her words, and perhaps he hasn't. "And I've regretted that I'd missed my chance. But now, now you, you wonderful, beautiful woman, you've opened up this new world to me. Given me the greatest gift there is to give."

Berthe flinches, remembering that Gène had used almost the same words. "It's not that simple."

He kisses her softly. "It is and it isn't, but now I want to savor the 'is.'"

She runs her finger along his collarbone. "We'll tell everyone the child is Gène's and hope no one will question it."

"Will Gène question it?"

"I did what I could to make him believe it's possible."

He winces. "He's not a particularly observant sort."

"Oh, Édouard, I just feel terrible for doing this to him. And he's more observant than you think. He's noticed how much time I've been spending with you, and has made it clear that he's unhappy about it."

"I'm sorry too. My poor brother doesn't deserve this." Then he brightens. "But if he never finds out, he'll be spared any pain. I've known him my entire life, and I'm certain he doesn't believe we've been together. I'd be aware if he thought I'd done such a thing. He wouldn't be able to keep it from me, as transparent as he is."

"That doesn't mean he's not suspicious."

"He told me his migraines have grown so bad that he gets confused about night and day, so this isn't going to be a problem for us." He beams. "Or for our baby."

"I hope . . ."

"This is going to be wonderful," he gushes. "I'll come by all the time, like I've been doing with Isabeau, but even more often. And I won't be just the uncle any longer. I'll be the Papa. A secret only you and I will share. Our own family, just the three of us."

WHEN SHE TELLS Gène, his initial response is similar to the first time she told him she was pregnant: confusion followed by dazed acceptance. But from there, his emotions take a different journey. No awe, no joy, no thanks. And, she fears, a touch of skepticism in his eyes. Mistrust. "I thought you were too old," is the first thing he says.

"We believed that the last time," she reminds him with as much cheer as she can muster. "And we were wrong then too."

"Are you strong enough to go through this again?"

"I'll have to be," she says, avoiding his eyes. "It will likely be taxing, but now that we have our darling Isabeau, I know a child is a reward worth suffering for."

"What about your health? With Isabeau you were so sick. And your recovery took longer than anyone expected."

Does this mean he's not suspicious of her, that he's just worried about her? She's filled with both relief and guilt at the thought. "I'll be fine. Really I will. I know what to expect, and maybe it won't be as difficult this time. Both Yves and Edma had one problematic confinement, while the others were far easier."

He nods.

"Aren't you happy about this?" she asks, hoping to stir him, convince him he's going to be a father again. "Another child, a sister or brother for Isabeau?"

"Of course I am," he says, and forces a smile.

But Berthe doesn't believe this and worries Édouard is wrong. That Gène knows far more than his brother imagines.

AS SHE'D HOPED, the second pregnancy is easier than the first. She's not the least bit nauseous and hardly ever tired. Actually, she's oddly energetic. She feels so good that she defies Dr. Aguillard's orders and continues to paint. She also defies society's orders and begins preliminary sketches for her forbidden picture.

She spends the early days of her pregnancy in the park across the street, where she worked on *Parisian Summer*, her focus once again on the people, their faces, their exchanges, their clothing. She imagines their inner life, who they really are, ignoring the trees and the benches and the bowling green. For this picture will not be set in the park. It will be in a closer space, at a soiree perhaps, raucous and exuberant, bursting with intimacy, catching life as it takes place in a single, spontaneous moment.

When she moves from drawings to a canvas far larger than her usual, the painting spills from her brush, as *Parisian Summer* did, most likely because she's exulting in the freedom to follow wherever her vision and brush want to go. To be neither a woman nor a man, solely an artist.

She works on it at Édouard's when no one else is there, and he hides it under a drop cloth when she leaves. He's extremely encouraging, admiring the wide scope of the painting, the lightness of her brushstrokes, the vibrance and depth of the facial expressions, the soft edges of the faces blending into the background.

"This is your masterpiece," he tells her. "I'm in awe of its ambition and range. How you've combined this grandness with such intimacy is miraculous. Something neither I nor any other artist we know would be able to achieve." He takes her hands in his and smiles mischievously. "If it were anyone's but yours, my jealousy would know no bounds. Who knows what I might be driven to do." Then he kisses her.

Their time in the studio is cut short by a social convention Berthe cannot ignore. When her oversized dresses are no longer able to hide her condition, she's confined to the house until the child is born. She cannot take her new painting home and has no choice but to leave it with Édouard. It's only half complete, if that, and she yearns to return to it almost as much as she yearns to hold their newborn babe.

In contrast to his constant hovering the last time, Gène mostly ignores this pregnancy, which she finds concerning. Édouard, on the other hand, visits the apartment often. And although she wishes she did not have to, she frequently shoos him away, afraid Gène's misgivings will be heightened by his brother's presence and the attention he lavishes on her.

IN DECEMBER, JUST a month after Isabeau turns three, Aimée Morisot Manet is born, a pretty baby with flaming red hair. Antoinette Manet, who the family is convinced will live forever, holds a luncheon after the baptism for her second grandchild, and everyone remarks that Aimée's hair is the same distinctive color Édouard's was when he was a child. Édouard and Berthe laugh this off as a family resemblance, but Berthe can see that Gène and Suzanne are displeased by the comments.

Her concerns grow when the baby is passed among the relatives and neither of their spouses takes an interest in holding her, appearing almost ostentatiously removed from the source of the celebration. Berthe tries to remain as far from Édouard as she can, but they're both pulled to Aimée and often find themselves close to each other, besotted with their child. This does nothing to lessen Gène and Suzanne's hard expressions or their suspicions.

Isabeau mirrors her father's and aunt's feelings, as would be expected of a child whose primacy in the family is suddenly challenged. "Leave baby Aimée here with Tante Suzanne and Oncle Édouard," she orders her mother, stomping her foot. "I do not like her, and she is not allowed to come home with us!"

Berthe recognizes that none of this bodes well for her and Édouard, for their marriages or for their baby girl. But she and Aimée are in far greater danger than he. If the truth were to be discovered, Berthe would be hailed as a harlot with a cuckolded and humiliated husband, while Édouard would just be a philanderer whose wife has long tolerated his liaisons. And poor, innocent little Aimée would be a bastard child, spurned by all.

PART ELEVEN

Aimée, 1892–1894

THIRTY-ONE

1892

14 April

It is a very, very dark day. My father passed yesterday. He has always been sickly, but I did not think he was that sickly. I keep wondering where he is if he's not here, and this makes me cry. Maman says he is in heaven, but I do not know where that is except that it is far away and he cannot get back from there.

The house feels very empty. My sister, Isabeau, is 13, three years older than I am, and she cannot stop crying. Maman cries sometimes, although not as much as Isabeau. We are a very sad household indeed.

16 April

All of the Manet and Morisot families are at our house at 40 Rue de Villejust. They have been here since the day after Father died. Many of Maman and Father's friends are here also. M. Degas and M. Monet and M. Renoir are in the parlor now, and they are very kind to me. All the Morisot aunts and uncles and cousins have been very kind to me too. It is an awful time, but I do get to stay home from school and eat all the chocolate I want.

The Manets are all very upset, especially Grand-Mère and Oncle Édouard. The only one who does not seem upset is Tante Suzanne. She is married to Oncle Édouard, but I do not know why he would ever have married such an unpleasant lady. She always has a sour expression and is not kind to anyone except her brother, Léon.

28 April

The funeral is over, and all the relatives have finally gone back to their own houses. I am relieved, and I can tell Maman is too. She has begun painting in her studio again. Even though she stands in front of the easel for many hours, she is not painting as much as she usually does. Isabeau and I are back in school. It is good not to be around all those sad people. Isabeau is still sad and doesn't want to go to school. Maman says that she must, and this makes her cry even more.

2 May

I suppose I should officially introduce myself. I am Aimée Morisot Manet, and I never thought I would like to write in a diary. But now that I have begun, I like it very much. It is nice to have someone to talk to who I can tell what I think, instead of always having to be polite and say what other people want me to say. I am often naughty and can have some bad thoughts.

I do not always do the things Maman asks me to. For example, saying my prayers every night or bringing the silver into the kitchen after breakfast, which I let Olivia, our maid, do. Although I have never admitted to these wrongdoings before, I believe that you, my dearest diary, care little about my prayers or the silver. But I worry you will think less of me if I admit to some of my thoughts.

I hesitate, but now I will say another here. I think Father never loved me as much as he loved Isabeau. He was never mean to me, but many times it seemed as if he did not see me when I was right there. It makes me feel bad even to think this, especially now that he has passed. It is also possible it is not true. So now you know me better than anyone else.

14 May

Oncle Édouard took me on an outing today. It is a Saturday, and we went in his carriage to Bois de Boulogne, a park I had never been to before that is at the end of the city. He invited Isabeau too and suggested we all paint together. Isabeau doesn't much like painting and said no, but I was happy to leave our unhappy house.

The park is very large and full of winding roads and paths and lots of different kinds of trees. There are flowers everywhere, and Oncle said May is the best time of the year to see them. Everything was so beautiful as we rode along, and I asked why we did not stop in any of these places. He told me he had a special place in mind for our painting.

He brought me to a real Swiss chalet that was built in Switzerland. He said it took months for it to get here on horse-drawn wagons that had to go over mountains. It was all in pieces and had to be put together in the park. And it is on an island in the middle of a lake! It is like a fairy tale come alive.

I did not use paint like Oncle did. I used crayons that were Isabeau's. Most of them are broken or do not have pointy tops, but they still worked. Isabeau doesn't like them anymore and said they are for babies. I am not an artist like Maman or Oncle, but I had such a good time with my crayons trying to draw the chalet. Oncle and I laughed a lot. I was sorry when we had to go home.

10 June

Maman is a very famous painter. Everyone in Paris knows who she is and thinks she is wonderful. Oncle Édouard is also very famous, and their friends like M. Monet, M. Degas, and M. Renoir are too. I have heard discussions about which of them is the best Impressionist, and it seems many people believe my mother is. I am very lucky to know so many famous artists and to be related to two of them.

15 July

It is very hot in Paris. Every other summer we go to the country, but it is not proper to take a holiday while we are in mourning.

20 July

It is a little cooler today, so Maman and I went to see an exhibit of the Duret collection. Isabeau did not join us, so I had Maman all to myself. Maman pays a lot of attention to Isabeau because she is always sad, but today she only paid attention to me.

This exhibition was especially wonderful because there were many of Maman's and Oncle Édouard's paintings. A picture of Tante Yves and Tanta Edma sitting next to each other was there, and it is one of my favorites. They are both very old now, and I cannot believe they were ever that young and pretty. But Maman paints a very good likeness, so I suppose I must believe it.

Oncle's paintings are darker than Maman's, and they look more like what you really see. I like Maman's better because they are so light and airy that they almost breathe. And even though they can look blurry, when you step back you see they are not blurry at all. They are more real than what you really see.

There were some of Oncle Édouard's paintings of Maman. In the one called "Repose," she is sitting on the red humpbacked sofa I have seen in Oncle's studio. Isabeau says this was when Maman told Oncle she was going to marry Father, but I do not believe this, because Maman does not look happy. She is sad, of this there is no doubt, but her expression also makes me think there is something that would make her happy if she could only find it. Can a person be sad and happy at the same time?

Maman came to stand behind me while I was looking at it, and I took a deep breath of her perfume, Violette de Paine, which smells light and airy, just like her paintings. It is a scent that always makes me happy, because it means I am near my dear mother. I asked her if she was both sad and happy when Oncle was painting it.

She looked at the picture for a long time before she answered. Finally, she took my hand and pressed it between both of hers. "It was a long time ago, my darling," she said. "And I was so very young." Then her eyes turned all sparkly. Sometimes grown-ups do not make any sense at all.

THIRTY-TWO

1893

25 May

I am now 11 years old, and as a special treat Maman took me with her to Giverny to visit M. Monet. I love to ride the train, so I was very excited. I was also excited because Maman told me Oncle Édouard was going to meet us there. Isabeau said it would be boring, so she did not come with us.

M. Monet's house was different from the last time we were here. It is much bigger, because he built more rooms. The best one is a big room with a very high ceiling and big windows, and many of his paintings are hanging on the walls. They are very pretty and very colorful.

He and Maman talked about one of the paintings for a long time. I was hoping Oncle would come soon so I would have someone to talk to. I looked out the window to see if his carriage had arrived, but we were at the back of the house and I could not see anything. I think Isabeau was right to stay home.

M. Monet took us to his studio so Maman could help him with the cathedral paintings he was working on. The studio is a floor lower than the big room, so there was still no view of the front drive. I stood there for a long time while Maman gave him suggestions. Finally, I walked over to see the paintings. I counted, and there were 26 of them, and they were all of the same building. Why would he want to paint the same thing 26 times?

Then I looked closer and saw that even though they were all of the same fancy church, each one was a little different. Some from close up and others from far away. Some from different sides. Others of the church in the morning or in the afternoon or at night. And there were so many different colors. Maman told him he was a master at capturing the ephemeral. I do not know what "ephemeral" means, but M. Monet was very pleased when Maman said it.

Finally, finally, Oncle arrived. I ran to him and gave him a big hug. He gave me a big hug too. He greeted M. Monet and kissed Maman on both cheeks but came right back to me. He rested his hand on my shoulder, and I pressed into his side. Then he asked me what I thought of the cathedrals. One of the things I like the most about Oncle is that he does not treat me like a little girl who does not understand anything. And that makes me think I can understand things.

I walked back and forth along the rows of paintings and looked harder to understand better. I told him what I liked was that it was like a person who has different moods. That the church was one thing but also lots of other things. That it depends on how you are looking at it and whether it is sunny or cloudy. Just like people.

His whole face became very sunny. He picked me up and danced me around the studio, but my feet didn't touch the floor. It was much more fun than listening to Maman and M. Monet talking.

I have to go to dinner now, dear diary. I will tell you more tomorrow.

26 May

The best part of yesterday was when I walked in M. Monet's garden with Maman and Oncle. M. Monet was so excited by the suggestions Maman gave him that he said he had to paint right away. So it was just the three of us. The garden is very beautiful and looks like some of M. Monet's paintings. There are so many colors here too.

In the garden there is a pond that has a pretty curved bridge over it. There are also weeping willow trees that are so big their branches go right into the water. Maman and Oncle stared at them for a long time. I dashed over the bridge to make them stop staring and play with me. Oncle linked his arm through Maman's, and they ran to where I was standing on the other side. They each took one of my hands and the three of us skipped on the curvy path with all kinds of flowers. So many flowers.

They kneeled down and hugged me. Both at the same time. And

then they hugged each other with me in the middle. It was like I was inside a sandwich of them.

7 June

Oncle brought me a present today. A new box of colored crayons! Now I do not have to use Isabeau's old broken ones. He brought Isabeau a little pink purse that is very pretty. He also gave me a sketchbook like the ones he and Maman use. Then he said we should go across the street to the park so I could try them. Maman came too. They both carried their sketchbooks and pastels. I was very glad to be the three of us again.

There were many fluffy clouds floating in the sky. Maman told me that clouds are not just white but have other colors in them too. She opened her book and drew one to show me how it had purple and blue and even some yellow. It looked very real.

I tried but did a bad job. Oncle told me to try again, that making mistakes is the best way to learn. This is very different from what my teachers at school say, but I did it anyway. The next time was better but still bad. Maman made another cloud to show me another way to paint it, like M. Monet's cathedrals. This one did not have any yellow in it, but it looked very real too.

I looked very hard at a cloud over the trees. It had some green in it, so I colored it that way. It also had purple around what looked like four cat's feet at the bottom, so I colored that too.

"Will you look at that, Berthe," Oncle said. "Our girl may have some real talent."

Maman looked at my cloud and then at Oncle Édouard. "How could she not?"

10 September

Maman and I have been going to Oncle Édouard's studio to paint. Oncle gave me my own easel that he built himself. It is smaller than his, so I can stand in front of it and my hand is in the right place. It makes me feel like a real artist.

I am still not very good, but I am getting a little better because

Maman is always teaching me things. Like how you do not need to copy something exactly. That catching the light is more important. Catching the moment. I understand about how the clouds have other colors in them. But I am not sure I understand about the light or the moment.

Now that everyone has returned to Paris from summer holiday, the other Impressionists are at Oncle's studio too. We all paint together, and they say I am my mother's daughter and my uncle's niece. M. Degas always smiles at me funny when they say this. Oncle is always telling me how good my paintings are. He has even taken some of them home with him because he likes them so much.

15 October

It is Oncle Gustave's birthday tomorrow. He is Father and Oncle Édouard's youngest brother and is visiting Paris. We were included in a dinner party at Grand-Mère Antoinette's house to celebrate. Maman did not want to go, because it would make us all sad that Father wasn't there, but Oncle Édouard said we must come so all the Manets could be together. I was surprised when she agreed. Now that Grand-Mère is ailing and does not often leave her rooms, Tante Suzanne is the hostess of all Manet family events, and I think Maman does not like Tante Suzanne. I do not either.

16 October

It rained all day today and was still raining when we arrived at Grand-Mère's. Isabeau ran out of the carriage and up the stairs without waiting for the driver and his umbrella. Maman and I took our time. Oncle Édouard greeted us at the door and led us into the parlor to visit with Oncle Gustave. I do not know him well because he lives far away, but he seems nice and looks a lot like Father.

A few Manet cousins were also present, and there were ten people around the table. Tante put place cards at every setting to show us where to sit. Oncle Édouard was at the head and she was at the foot, with Oncle Gustave at her right. Maman and I were in the middle, with the cousins.

At the last minute, Oncle Édouard changed the cards and put Maman and me on either side of him. Tante's face turned bright red, but Oncle did not seem to notice. I am now almost twelve years old, and I am beginning to think there are secrets here that everyone knows but me. But maybe he just wanted to be nice so we wouldn't be so sad without Father.

During the meal, hardly anyone talked, and most of the sounds were of people eating, which is not a nice sound, especially during the soup. I could not wait for it to be over and ate very fast. But then the maid brought in the birthday cake, and we all had to sit there while it was served with coffee and tea.

Oncle Gustave complimented Oncle Édouard on his many paintings hanging on the walls, also praising those by M. Monet and M. Degas, which Oncle explained were gifts. Oncle Édouard said he had been working very hard and was pleased their bande's style was finally starting to be appreciated. Then he smiled at Maman. "Berthe has been producing many unique and marvelous paintings, and there are many who believe she is the best of all of us."

I was very happy to hear him say this, but Maman just looked down at her hands. I wondered why none of her paintings were there.

Then Oncle Édouard told his brother there was someone else in the family who had been producing marvelous works of art. "Wait until you see," he said. Then he jumped up and left the room.

Everyone at the table looked at each other, but, as before, no one said anything. When Oncle came back into the dining room, he was holding some of my drawings. Maman pressed her hand to my leg under the table and whispered that she was sorry. I did not understand what she was sorry about because I was happy Oncle wanted to show everyone my pictures.

"The next generation of Manet talent!" Oncle cried, passing the half dozen pieces of paper around the table. He bowed to Maman. "And the next generation of Morisot talent." He had had a number of drinks and beamed at everyone. "A noble combination!"

Tante Suzanne stood and glared at Oncle. Her face was even

redder and splotchier than it was before. Then she turned from Oncle to Maman. "You," she hissed. "You are not welcome here!" Her finger shook when she pointed at me. "And you are not either."

Maman stood up, and then Isabeau and I did too. Isabeau and I were crying, and Oncle begged us all not to leave, but we did anyway.

THIRTY-THREE

1894

5 October

My dearest diary, please forgive me for neglecting you for so long. It has been almost a year since I last wrote. I have been very busy with school and traveling. I was accepted at the Legion of Honor School, and it is much more demanding than my school last year. We have been to London, Brussels, Monaco, and to Santorini, the most beautiful island in all of Greece. I have been painting in all of those places, and in Paris too.

Maman and I often paint together, and because of her lessons and patience with me I have been getting a very little bit better. Oncle tells me not to be discouraged, that it takes much time and effort to become an artist and I am still very young.

I did not realize that every artist works in a different way. Or that this does not matter as long as they create a painting they are proud of. This is what Maman says. Her style is to look at what she is going to paint for a long time and make many sketches before she even picks up a brush. When she does begin, she usually starts with a pencil drawing on the canvas. Then she builds on that with watercolors or pastels or oils. Sometimes on top of each other. She stares at the canvas she is working on and then paces back and forth before it, still staring. It can take a long time for her to finish, but she does not care.

Oncle Édouard is completely different. He hardly ever makes sketches but dives at the empty canvas with his oil paints. Sometimes he gets all sweaty and his eyes look very strange. But he does not stop painting. He seems like he is angry, but he says he is not. This is his "process," and he doesn't want to paint any other way.

Maman is teaching me how to use pastels and I think my "process" is in the middle of the two. I like to do sketches but not as many as she does. I am impatient to paint and like diving in like Oncle does.

2 November

Winter has descended on the city without any fall. Because I am getting taller, Maman asked Oncle to make me another easel, which he did. It is even nicer than the first one. We have set it up in Maman's studio so we do not have to go out in the weather to paint at Oncle's. It is lovely when the two of us are painting and the logs crackle in the fireplace.

5 November

Maman is working on a painting called "Jeanne Pontillon Wearing a Hat." And that is what it is, a portrait of my cousin Jeanne with a big floppy hat. Maman made many sketches for this when we were on holiday in Greece with Tante Edma and her family this summer. Jeanne is very pretty and makes a good model.

The picture is already very beautiful. Maman is using colors that are not on Jeanne's face but are somehow right. Maybe even better than how she actually looks. There are also many pigments in Jeanne's hat, which in actuality was mostly colorless and made of pale straw. On Maman's canvas, the hat is fashioned with quick strokes of orange and green and blue, with even some black. Some of these colors also wrap around Jeanne's neck and swirl at the back of her head. This makes it look like Jeanne is moving even though she is not. It also makes it very cheerful.

Maman is using pastels for the painting, and that is why she thought I should paint with her today. As I have told you, we do this often, but today was different. She put an empty canvas on my easel and said she wanted me to copy her painting while she was painting it. She said this would be a good way to teach me more about pastels. For me to watch and learn and try out what I was learning all at the same time.

Usually, there is nothing I like better than painting with Maman. Especially because she never does this with Isabeau. But today I did not want to try her idea because her painting is so good and mine will not be. She reminded me of what Oncle said about how helpful mistakes can be. Then she showed me her sketches and explained that although she had drawings of Jeanne from many different sides, she had decided on a three-quarter face. She said this was the best angle to show who Jeanne really is. I thought all of the sketches looked like Jeanne.

I took the sketchbook to study them more closely and found something very startling. There were a number of pages toward the back that had drawings of men. Men I did not know, and I suppose Maman did not either. They were not of our circle, and their clothes were not very nice. Also drawings of women wearing dresses the likes of which I have never seen. The only word to describe the dresses is "naughty," but I am not sure that is the correct term.

And there were sketches of men and women who were touching each other, some close together and laughing. "Scandalous," is what I thought. And I believe that is the correct word. I did not think it was proper for Maman to paint pictures like this, although I am not sure why not. All of Maman's paintings are of landscapes or women and children, and these look more like the work of M. Renoir or Oncle.

There were also many drawings of Maman, and she must have used a mirror because she is staring right out at me. A long time ago, she showed me a painting called "Self-Portrait." In that one, she did not look pretty, as she is in real life, and I did not like it. She is very beautiful in all of the drawings in the sketchbook, and there were some similarities to Oncle's "Repose." But her expression in every one of these was much more complicated, almost haunting. It was as if she had a storm of wild emotions inside her that she was trying not to show but could not keep from showing because they were too strong to stay inside.

I glanced up and saw she was watching me. I did not know what to say. Should I not have turned to the pages at the end? Was she angry with me? She came over and gently touched a few of the sketches with her finger. She had a faraway look in her eyes and a slight smile on her face. I guessed she was not angry with me.

I asked if these were hers, although I had no doubt she had drawn them. She told me they were and said she had a favorite spot on the shore of the Seine where she liked to sketch what passed by on the river. I wanted to ask her if she had made a painting from these, but I was a little scared. Again, I am not sure why. It somehow felt dangerous, so I said nothing.

She must have seen the question on my face, because she kissed the top of my head. "Do not fret, my darling. I have not painted it yet. But I am hoping that someday I will be able to."

PART TWELVE

Tamara, the present

THIRTY-FOUR

Jonathan calls about a week after *Party* was "moved" to see how I'm doing without her. I know I shouldn't disclose the actual situation, but the concern in his voice and our deepening friendship undermine my caution. "There's something I have to tell you . . ."

A pause. A sharp intake of breath. "No." The man is quick.

"Yes."

"No."

"Yes." I struggle to suppress a giggle, as I'm well aware he doesn't think this is funny, but it escapes anyway.

Another pause. "How the hell did you pull this off?" he asks with less annoyance than I would have expected. When I explain, he whistles and says, "We need to talk."

He comes over on Saturday, and when he sees *Party* still hanging on the living room wall, he crosses his arms over his chest. I show him the dehumidifier set at 45 percent, the air purifier running full force, the closed shades, the dimmed bulbs, then tell him about the eco-friendly pest control service that will be coming monthly. "And you saw how great the building security was dealing with the press, keeping all those reporters and photographers away, protecting my privacy."

He shakes his head but says nothing, eyes fixed on *Party*.

"I'm also thinking about looking into hiring a guard."

"Un-fucking-believable." He sits on the couch and throws me an appraising glance. "You certainly know how to get what you want, don't you? No line too red to cross."

I stare down at my hands, embarrassed by his all-too-accurate assessment. When I look up, I see that although his words are disapproving, there's a small smile playing around his lips. "So do you forgive me?"

"No," he says, then turns to focus on *Party*. After a few minutes, he adds, "Every time I look at this painting, I see something new." He points at Berthe. "Like the expression in her eyes. It's so lifelike, but also complicated. Is she looking out over the river because it's a beautiful sight? Or is she turning her back to the party because she doesn't want to be there? Or maybe it's a statement about how she feels about her place in the world? You can clearly see all those emotions, and maybe even a spark of mischievousness there . . . How the hell did he do something like that?"

I begin to relax. "Beats me. I told you before that sometimes I sketch it, and the harder I try to copy what's he's done, the more mystified I am about how he managed to pull it off." Then we sit in a slightly uneasy silence.

Finally, he stands. "I understand, Tamara. I really do. Even though your attempts at temperature control are notable, is it fair to the painting to be in these unstable conditions? Or that no one else gets to see it?"

"I know, I know, you're right. But it's only temporary. I'm going to start setting up meetings with museums next week to get the process started. And it's not as if she hasn't been in unstable conditions before. Plus hardly anyone saw her in Philadelphia, and in Brazil she was in storage the whole time." I give him a perky smile. "Not to mention that there weren't a whole lot of art lovers hanging out in that salt mine."

He raises his eyebrows and looks at me with a touch of amusement. "That's the best you can do?"

"Having her with me reminds me I'm not as alone as I always thought I was," I tell him, and he says no more.

After he leaves, I pass *Party* on the way to my study and sense something off. I look at her closely, and she's as she always is. Then I catch a whiff of that old-fashioned flowery aroma, and my stomach cramps. Berthe's focus shifts from the far riverbank to me. Her brow is furrowed, and she shakes her head. Inside my own head, I hear her say, "Don't."

Don't what? Don't put *Party* in storage? Don't lend her to a museum? Don't go into my study? I defiantly walk into the study but find myself closing the doors to separate myself from *Party*. Then I open them to prove there's nothing scary out there. But I'm still afraid. And it's not what's out there I'm afraid of. It's what's inside my head. Normal people don't hallucinate sights and smells or hear dead people talking to them. I must be having some kind of breakdown.

My parents told me little about our family—my father was the silent type, and my mother's mother had some kind of catastrophic rupture with her own mother—so, as I've said before, I have no idea if I have a genetic predisposition toward mental illness. But now that I know I have all these artists in my bloodline, I suppose it's possible. Lots of famous painters have their unhinged sides. Think van Gogh or Munch or O'Keeffe or Rothko.

Does this mean I should go to a shrink? I went to one once when I had a bout of anorexia in high school, but it turned out I was more into the idea of being anorexic—which was rampant in the popular cliques—than suffering from an actual eating disorder. Yet this isn't teenager me wanting to fit in. This is me as an adult perceiving the world in a way that it isn't.

"WOULD YOU LIKE me to call you Ms. Rubin or Tamara?"

"Tamara is good."

"And you can call me Dr. Hawthorn or Ruth. Whichever you're more comfortable with."

"Ruth is good," I say with a nervous laugh.

Yup, I'm in a therapist's office. I mentioned that I was feeling off to Holly—who's seen more therapists in her thirty-seven years than most people have seen a doctor in their lifetimes—and she suggested Ruth Hawthorn. I like Ruth already. Or I like how she looks, how her office looks. Both are well-worn but attractive and homey. I almost canceled a couple of times, but I guess my need to know is stronger than my fear of knowing. Maybe.

Ruth is in an oversized chair, and I'm on the couch across from her, almost as if we're just hanging out in her living room. She even offered me something to drink, and there's a bowl of candy on the coffee table between us. "Why don't you tell me what brought you in today?" she asks. "Start wherever you want, or if you'd rather, just talk a little about who you are."

I tell her who I am, where I grew up, where I went to school, what I do, that my parents are dead, no sibs, no cousins. Then I tell her about *Party*. How the painting came to me, how wonderful it is, how it was almost destroyed in a fire, and about Damien's lawsuit. Obviously, I leave out a lot.

"That sounds remarkable—and stressful."

"Yes, both. In equal measure." I realize my syntax sounds strained, which it is. As am I. "I've never been an art person, but the more time I spend with her and learn about the Impressionists, that whole world is opening up to me. Or maybe more like I'm being sucked into it," I say. "In a good way," I add quickly. Not much better, but I'm anxious. I came here to tell her I'm afraid I'm losing my mind, wanting her help, but I worry she'll agree with me. And, frankly, I'm embarrassed.

"It's wonderful to be open to new experiences," Ruth says. "And the experience of learning to appreciate art can be an especially gratifying one. But I noticed you used the word 'her' in reference to your painting."

Another awkward laugh. "Oh, you know. After being with, with the painting for all these months, it's just gotten so familiar that I guess, I guess I've personified her—it."

She smiles at me encouragingly but doesn't say anything.

Right. The therapist silence bit. So we're just going to sit here? Is she going to wait me out until I spill the beans? And which beans would those be? "I, uh, I, well, sometimes the painting is so real to me I dream about it. About Berthe."

"Can you tell me more about this?"

"And sometimes when I'm hanging out with it, it almost seems to come alive."

"I'm familiar with some of Manet's work. His paintings can be so compelling, his models so realistic and psychologically complex, that it can feel as if they're jumping off the canvas."

"Yes, yes, that's just the way *Party* is," I say, thrilled to have her confirmation. "Particularly Berthe, whose expression seems to change. Even her position."

"How does that feel? When you sense she's shifting."

So this is how it works: Shrinks make you say things you don't want to say. If that's true, Holly was right—Ruth is damn good at her job. I start to fidget, stop myself, and shrug. "Maybe just wishful thinking."

Another smile, another silence.

I remind myself that I came here to discover, not to obfuscate. What I saw, what I smelled, what I heard in my head, is more than just a wish. "Sometimes, sometimes it seems as if I hear her voice. Like, like she's communicating with me," I blurt.

Ruth doesn't appear to be at all perturbed. "What does she say?"

"I mean, well, it's not like she actually talks to me. It's more like I have a thought that's, that's somehow spoken in her voice—not that I know what her voice sounds like. And, and I don't hear it with my ears. It's in my brain, not in real life."

"Is that part of the reason you came here today?"

What the hell. "Yes. But that's not all of it." I'm amazed that as I tell her all the gory details, she's still looking at me as if I'm a normal person. When I finish, I add, "I know paintings don't change and someone who's been dead for over a hundred years can't talk to me—and there's no way I can smell her perfume. But that's what I've been experiencing, and I'm starting to worry that maybe, maybe I'm hallucinating. That I'm losing it. Or have a brain tumor or something."

"Have you had similar experiences before? Now or at any other time?"

"I'm pretty sure I haven't."

"Does this happen just when you're around the painting? Or do you have these types of incidents in other situations?"

I consider this, having never thought about it before. "Just with the painting. And it's only the painting that it happens to. Actually, it's only Berthe who ever moves, no one else, and, and I only smell the perfume when I hear her voice. In my head, I mean. Not out loud." I'm beginning to really scare myself.

"And has any of this, everything you just explained to me, affected other parts of your life? Your job, relationships?"

"My job is fine, no problems there. But my boyfriend—I mean the guy I'm seeing—well, he thinks I'm too obsessed with *Party*. He wants me to get rid of her, sell her to Damien. But I suppose our relationship is going fine. For what it is."

"There's much to explore here, and that gives us plenty to discuss during your next session, if you'd like to continue. If you don't, I'll be happy to refer you to someone else. But either way, I'd recommend psychological testing before your next therapy visit. Again, I can give you a referral."

I sit up straight. "What kind of testing?"

"There are standardized tests that can provide an additional lens to understand what you're experiencing. To help figure out what exactly is afoot here—and what isn't, which is equally important. This, along with more sessions, will hopefully pinpoint the best treatment options."

"You think I need treatment?"

Her smile is warm and reassuring, the opposite of her words. "I've known you less than an hour, Tamara, and frankly, I have no idea if you do or you don't. But I do know that whatever is going on is upsetting you, and that my goal as a therapist is to try to alleviate this. And for that, more information is necessary."

I WALK BACK to work from Ruth's. It's about two miles, but the sun is out and I need time to sort this through. I went to a therapist, and although she didn't act as if what I was telling her was any big deal while I was telling it, she recommended not only more sessions, but psychological testing. And even more upsetting, she never mentioned a neurologist. Ergo, she doesn't believe I have a brain tumor—she believes I'm mentally ill.

Would I really prefer a brain tumor? I suppose not, but if I did, it might be operable or maybe there's some medication that would make it go away. Yes, yes, I know there are medications to treat mental illnesses, but I'm pretty sure they just deal with symptoms and don't eliminate the underlying disease. So I'd still be a crazy lady.

When I reach my office, there are three minor disasters that have to be dealt with and demand my full attention until early evening. As I head home, I remind myself that this is only one woman's opinion, not even close to a definitive finding. How could I have just solved all those work problems if my brain isn't operating correctly? Maybe I should make an appointment with a neurologist on my own. Get my ears checked. Perhaps a new pair of glasses.

After dinner, I play around with the pastels. I found some cheaper canvases online, and although I haven't managed anything nearly as good as the fake I put into storage—or at least as good as I remember it was, which I'm probably overhyping—the sticks are fun, much more rewarding and forgiving than the pencils.

As often happens, I paint too long, and it's almost two when I finally climb into bed. The building is quiet, even the street sounds are muted, but

I can't fall asleep. I switch from my side to my stomach to my back, punch my pillow, curl into a fetal position. No luck. The Paris hearing is only two weeks away, and Wyatt hasn't been able to postpone it a second time. I can't afford to send him or anyone else from his firm to France to represent me, and I have a bad feeling about the outcome. He tries to be optimistic to keep me from stewing, but it's obvious he's concerned too.

THIRTY-FIVE

Wyatt remains annoyed that *Party* is still in my apartment, and he's said he doesn't want to spend the night there until she's gone. Presumably, he sees this as a way to spur me into getting rid of her, but as he's always pushed for staying at his house, I'm thinking it's just another thumb on the scale. When he offers to sleep here tonight, I worry that this is an indication he's interested in a more serious relationship than I am. Along with the increasing number of his texts, emails, and calls. But he's fun, so I push the concern away.

Unfortunately, he's beside me when I have another Berthe nightmare. In this one, she doesn't look at all like she does in *Party* or in any of the other paintings I've seen of her. She's old—which she never was—her hair completely white and wrapped in a bun at the nape of her neck. She's tenderly holding a little girl, possibly a granddaughter, and she's staring out at me with a warm smile. Soon, I realize she isn't really there, that I'm looking at a painting.

Then I'm in the painting. I'm the child, which is lovely, and I sink into my grandmother's soft bosom and snuggle there, peaceful and safe. "Grand-Mère," I say softly.

"My girl," she coos. "My sweet baby girl."

I reach up, pat her wrinkled cheek, and begin to drift off.

"You cannot sleep," she tells me. "You must find the truth."

I shake my head drowsily.

"Listen to me." She takes hold of my shoulders, pulls me away from her warm body.

I'm a little girl, and I'm scared because I don't understand what my grandmother wants me to do. And because it seems like she's mad at me.

"You must keep moving forward. It's your destiny."

I don't know what "destiny" means, so I shake my head again.

Her fingers press into my arms. Then they squeeze. It hurts, and I try to yank free. But I can't move. I'm frozen. I startle awake in a full-body sweat, the sheets wet and cold around me. I throw myself toward the middle of the bed, where it's dry, bump into Wyatt.

He grumbles and opens his eyes. When he catches sight of my face, he comes completely awake. "Another nightmare about that damn painting? Really, Tamara? You're covered with sweat, and you look like you've seen a ghost."

"It wasn't about *Party*. It, it was about, uh, a rollercoaster. I was on the top, and it was crashing down all around me. And, and it felt so real." I look down at my arms to make sure there are no bruises. There aren't.

He doesn't touch me or try to comfort me the way he usually does. "Go to sleep," is all he says.

AT BREAKFAST THE next morning, he says nothing about my dream, which is a relief, although it still looms large to me. What am I trying to tell myself? What truth do I need to find? What destiny? What am I supposed to move forward with? Is this in reference to Berthe or to Damien? To silence my own questions, I ask another one, "If the judge rules I have to send *Party* to the Louvre, can I keep it here while you appeal and I contact the museums?"

"Yeah, shouldn't be a problem. Except we never know what kinds of tricks your cousin might pull."

"Wouldn't put anything past him." I pause as another thought hits me. "If I died, who'd get *Party*?"

"Do you seriously believe Damien would kill you to get the painting? He may be a major pain in the ass, but I'm thinking murder is out of his league."

"I guess," I admit.

"Don't worry, Tam." Wyatt covers my hand with his. "We'll get him in court."

I stare into my coffee cup. Both of us know that, as of now, we don't have enough evidence linking the Bernheims to *Party* to make this happen. There appears to be a dearth of credible and available detectives in the Boston area, but Wyatt did find a qualified investigator willing to take the case.

Unfortunately, his hourly rate is four times Nova's—$300 versus $75—and in all good conscience I can't hire him while the majority of Wyatt's invoices remain unpaid.

The search for evidence has stalled because I haven't had the time or bandwidth to do any searching. Which I have many good reasons for: work, the hearing, the Berthe dreams, a psychologist's concern I might be mentally ill. My own concern I might be mentally ill. But the trial is in just a little over two months, meaning I'm going to have to find both the time and bandwidth if we're going to win. "I'll start checking into the whole gift thing."

"I'm sorry this is falling on you," Wyatt says. "But that would be great."

If we can confirm that Édouard and Berthe exchanged paintings, then we can maintain that nothing would have been officially recorded because they were gifts. Also if Édouard gave his brother paintings. Or swaps between the other Impressionists. If I could find something on *Party*, that would be the best, but even without straightforward proof, if this was common practice, as Nova said, it's a rebuttal to the questions about provenance and lack of paperwork.

You must find the truth.

I SCOUR THE INTERNET, then take another plunge into books about Berthe, Édouard, and the Impressionists. I'm coming to appreciate how difficult it was to be a female artist back then, how truly exceptional it was for Berthe to be considered an equal by the greatest painters of her day. And how devastating it would be for her to know that after her death, the acclaim she received vanished from view, that she was essentially forgotten. Today everyone knows Manet, Degas, Monet, and Renoir, all of whom she exhibited with. But outside of art historians and Impressionist aficionados, how many know Berthe Morisot?

I spend more time than I should reading about her, and have to keep reminding myself that I'm supposed to be searching for evidence for the trial. But it's difficult to find something when you don't know what you're seeking, and Berthe's ambition and perseverance are compelling. I look over at *Party*. "How did you pull it off?" I ask Berthe. "How did you keep going when everyone and everything was trying to stop you?"

Berthe leans against the railing and stares across the water at the unseen riverbank. No answers there. But I do finally find something that just might help. It turns out that, at the least, Berthe gave Édouard *Young Girl with a Parrot*, *The Artist's Sister at a Window*, *The Harbor at Lorient*, and *The Butterfly Hunt*. Édouard gave her, also at the least, *Berthe Morisot with a Bouquet of Violets*, *Young Woman in a Round Hat*, and *Mademoiselle Isabelle Lemonnier*. He gave Gène *Portrait of Eugène Manet* and *Music in the Tuileries Gardens*. There were also many swapped paintings between Berthe, Édouard, and Degas, along with Monet, Renoir, Pissarro, and Sisley, including references to how common these kinds of gifts were, and how they often went unrecorded.

The next day, work is horrendously busy, and I'm late to Wyatt's for dinner. I rush into the house and see he's already eating a taco and the guacamole is half gone. "Sorry," I say. "Hell of a day."

"I can relate," he says, and reaches for another taco. "Sit. Eat."

I sit, but I don't eat. Instead, I tell him what I discovered. "How cool is that?"

"Very cool," he says. "Maybe you should consider a career change."

I pull a face. "Wouldn't get too carried away. I didn't find anything on *Party*."

"The pervasiveness of the practice is what's important here. Kind of like—in the states where it's legal—when the prosecutor introduces testimony in a rape trial from other women the guy raped."

"So you can use it?"

"Damn straight I can. It's really helpful. Just wish we had another piece or two to add to what I'm putting together in answer to Delphine's discovery interrogatories." Wyatt has explained that, as part of the pretrial process, the opposing attorneys submit the evidence they plan to introduce in court to each other.

"Like what?"

"The provenance papers, proof Manet gave *Party* to Gène or Berthe before he died, maybe something in the memoirs or letters of the major players, biographies . . ."

So I guess what he's saying is that I need to keep looting the haystack for a needle we can't identify—and may not even exist. An assignment I can't refuse.

When my alarm goes off at six o'clock on February 27, there are emails from Damien, Wyatt, and the Manet Foundation's lawyer. The hearing was held at nine Paris time, and it's been over for hours. The judge decreed that *Party on the Seine* must be received by the Louvre no later than March 10 for cleaning in preparation for inclusion in the Édouard Manet retrospective.

THIRTY-SIX

Wyatt appeals the judge's decision, but he figures it will only buy us a few weeks, a month at the most. I'm a complete wreck, not sleeping, barely eating, trying not to succumb to grief over the impending separation. I can't lose her, not this soon—my family, my solace. And Wyatt said it will be near impossible to get her back once she's in France. I can't. I won't. Beating Damien is now my second job.

But I'm overwhelmed with job #1—the one that pays the rent—and I struggle to find the time for job #2. Three of Calliope's usual investors anted up major league for the initial trial for the clostridial myonecrosis drug, and the regulatory requirements to set up the lab are staggering. The marketing plan for Zymidline, our new release, has finally been approved, and I'm working with production on labeling. We lost months waiting for the advertising firm to come up with an acceptable strategy, and now we're under the gun to meet the rules so packaging can begin. It's slated for a September release, which is a lot less time than it might sound.

When I'm finally able to pull my head out of the office avalanche, I call Wyatt and ask if it would be more difficult for the foundation to bring *Party* to France if she were in a museum instead of in storage.

He pauses. "Storage?"

"Theoretically."

"I don't know. Maybe. There'd be more paperwork—that's for sure—so it would definitely take longer."

"I'll get on it right now."

"If you've got time to do that, there's something else that would be an even bigger help . . ."

So instead of contacting museums, I switch to job #2.

A FEW DAYS LATER, Wyatt and I are hanging out in my apartment after Sunday brunch at Aquitaine. He's working at the kitchen table, and

I'm fruitlessly researching in my study. Although it's March, Mother Nature has decided it's the middle of winter, and the snow is coming down hard, making it all the more pleasant to stay inside. For dinner, we order delivery from an Ethiopian restaurant in Back Bay, and when we finish eating, there's more than a foot of snow on the ground, and it's still coming down.

Wyatt eyes the drifts blowing across the sidewalks. "Fine," he says, as if I've badgered him into doing something he'd refused to do. "I'll stay here tonight."

"Sure." It's far too nasty out to send him home.

He's clearly not happy to be in the same apartment as *Party*, and, as if making a point, when we go to bed, he turns his back to me and falls asleep. I need to finish the art history book I'm reading anyway, an academic tome that includes thousands of footnotes—well, at least many hundreds. It's pretty dry stuff, but following my father's dictum, I persevere. And Dad turns out to be right, for I stumble across what might be that elusive needle.

According to a PhD with a dozen books under her belt, after Édouard died, Antoinette Manet, his mother, contested his will, demanding the return of the dower she'd provided at his marriage and challenging the provision that upon Suzanne's death all of Édouard's personal artworks be passed down to Léon. She said Suzanne wasn't eligible for the dower because she'd treated Antoinette with disrespect throughout her marriage and failed to give Édouard a son, a wife's most important duty. She claimed that as Léon was Suzanne's brother and not a Manet—which presumably she knew wasn't true—he wasn't a legitimate heir to Édouard's paintings, which belonged to his real family.

Mme Manet won on the dower and lost on the legitimacy of Léon's inheritance. I ponder whether this might be of help. It does offer further verification that Léon wasn't Édouard's son, doubling the evidence that Damien isn't Édouard's direct descendant—even if it's not exactly relevant to the case. But maybe it's an additional piece for Wyatt to add? I'm jacked up and can't fall asleep. I give up, and end up on the couch in the living room, hanging out with Berthe.

Wyatt finds me there in the morning, wrapped in the coverlet and sleeping. "What are you doing in here?" he demands.

I climb from the couch and press myself into him, throwing the blanket over his shoulders and pulling him closer. He wraps his arms around me, rests his chin on the top of my head. "Tamara, Tamara, Tamara, what am I going to do with you?"

We go into the kitchen, where I make coffee and he makes us smoothies. When we sit down, I tell him about the contested will. "I couldn't sleep because I thought this might be something."

"Harrumph," he says. "Let me see how I can use it."

He drafts a response to Delphine's interrogatives that combines Nova's proof that *Party* was in the Bernheims' collection, my list of documented swaps, the facts of Léon's birth, along with Antoinette's claim against Édouard's will. Wyatt sends it off, and within forty-eight hours Delphine offers us $25 million, which we reject. She counters a day later with $27 million. I interpret this as an indication our evidence is convincing, but Wyatt sees it differently.

"Take it," he recommends. "It's a huge wad of cash for a painting you never heard of a few months ago. We could both quit our jobs, travel the world," he adds, staring dreamily at the piles of snow the plows have pushed onto the sidewalks. "Live anywhere. Buy a house in Paris, another on Santorini, a condo overlooking Central Park."

This "we" freaks me out, and I say quickly, "I like my job, and I like where I live." I raise my chin. "I'm not selling to him."

"It was tough enough with just the foundation's lawsuit, but if the Louvre appeal is rejected, you're going to be out of luck. And once *Party* is on French soil, you're fucked."

"You said there might be a way to get a stay. French versus US laws."

"'Might' is the operative word here."

"I'll take my chances."

"Like I warned you before, you could easily end up with nothing—no cash and no painting."

"Tell her I won't sell *Party* to them at any price, and that I'm ready to go to court."

PARTY HASN'T MOVED in weeks, nor have I heard any voices or had a Berthe dream, all of which means I don't need any psychological testing. Even when the dreams start up again, this doesn't change my mind. Dreams are a whole different thing from the visual and auditory hallucinations that I'm sure are what Ruth Hawthorn is concerned about.

The dreams almost always take place in the studio where Berthe and I waltzed so gaily, but now the mood is more somber. Her brow is often wrinkled, and she frequently shakes her head at me while I sit in one of those overstuffed grandmother chairs and watch her paint. I wouldn't call these nightmares exactly, not the wake-up-screaming kind, but I'm concerned they might start to slither in that direction.

Ghostlike male figures often hover at the other easels, but no one except Berthe paints, and she seems as annoyed with her canvas as she is at me. I wonder if her anger is directed at the misogynous world she was forced to live in. I wish she could see me, her great-great-great-great, able to do whatever a man can do—and doing it. Then the photograph of my ex-boyfriend/ex-colleague, Nick, ringing the bell on Wall Street flashes through my mind. Well, almost anything a man can do.

Jonathan calls and asks if he can visit *Party*, offering to bring lunch. When he arrives early Saturday afternoon, we eat our wraps while sitting on the couch and gazing at the painting, chatting about her, our jobs, this and that. We haven't seen each other in a while, and it's nice to catch up. I find his presence reassuring.

When I tell him the judge ruled against us, he says, "That's a problem, but maybe not that big of one. Extraditing artwork from one country to another is difficult—both legally and practically—especially when the ruling is made in one and the art is in another. I've seen this kind of tussle lots of times. Could take months. Years, even. If it drags on and you miss the date of the retrospective or win at trial, it'll be moot."

"Really?" I cry, clapping my hands together. "Really? That's great. Are you sure?"

"Yes, Tamara." He shoots me a goofy grin. "There is a Santa Claus."

"My lawyer said it would be a long shot to keep her here." This is odd. Wyatt is usually on top of all the legal ins and outs. Unless he didn't want to be on top of them because he wants her out of my apartment.

Jonathan shrugs. "Probably focused on the actual trial."

"Will that work the same way? Will I be able keep her here even if the verdict goes wrong?"

"Well, there's the whole appeal process, which can add time. But the difference is that the foundation's lawsuit was filed in New York City, not Paris."

"She's still being sent to another country."

"True, but the legal aspects will be less complicated than they are in the Louvre appeal because both the painting and the suit are in the US. So you won't be able to push it out as far as you might be able to in the other situation."

I stare at the ceiling. "Damien upped his offer."

"How much?"

"Twenty-seven."

Jonathan whistles. "Hell of a lot of money." He looks at *Party*, and a clouded expression crosses his face. "Do you think he'd loan it to the foundation or the Louvre if you sold it to him?"

I don't want to answer this question, so I say, "I've been working on gathering evidence for the trial, but as soon as I have a second I'll start in on moving her to a museum around here."

"Excellent news. Like I said, there'll be difficulties, slow bureaucracies and paperwork, so you should start right away. But getting the painting to an environment that's more—"

Before he can finish his sentence, the front door opens and Wyatt walks in. Yes, I tanked and gave him a key after he insisted I have one to his house because my office is so close and I might need to let myself in if he isn't there. But I made my stand and refused to leave any toiletries there. Big stand.

I don't know which of the men is more startled. I've never mentioned anything about Wyatt to Jonathan, except in vague references to my lawyer on the foundation suit. And the same goes for Jonathan to Wyatt, who's just the guy from the Claims Conference.

Jonathan and I jump up from the couch, and I'm sure we look guilty. "Hey," I say cheerfully—and, in truth, I'm glad he interrupted our conversation, although I'm pissed that he hadn't contacted me before coming over, as he'd promised he would. "Good. I've wanted you two to meet." I introduce them and they shake hands, but both are wary.

Wyatt kisses me on the lips proprietarily. "I thought you were stuck home working all day."

"I am. Jonathan just came by for a quick visit with *Party*."

Wyatt eyes our discarded lunch and the two indentations in the couch where we were sitting next to each other. "A visit with *Party*?"

"It's one of my favorite paintings," Jonathan explains. "Tamara is kind enough to let me come by once in a while to see it."

Wyatt throws an arm around my shoulders, lets it casually hang there. "I'm not much of an art connoisseur, but, yeah, I really like it too."

There's a strained silence, and then Jonathan says, "I've got to get going." He nods to me. "Thanks. Very much appreciated." He starts to pick up the plates.

"Leave them," Wyatt orders. "We'll get it."

"Sure. Thanks." Jonathan takes his coat from the back of a chair and puts it on. "Nice to meet you, man," he says, and quickly makes his exit.

"What kind of a guy visits a painting?" Wyatt asks.

"One who's into art."

"Or one who's into you." His mouth is a straight line. "Did you tell him you have a boyfriend?"

"It didn't come up." Given Wyatt's mood, I don't want to get into an argument about the key thing, so instead I pick up the lunch dishes. "I have to get back to work."

"You could take time for your buddy Jonathan, but not for me?"

"This isn't a competition, Wyatt. He's a friend. Nothing more, nothing less."

"Ha." He crosses his arms over his chest. "Well, if you're so goddamned busy, I guess I'll go."

I don't stop him.

I put the dishes in the dishwasher, make myself a cup of coffee, and try to brush off Wyatt's possessiveness. Mug in hand, I head for my study. I pause to look at *Party*, as I always do. I've had her for just a little over five months—even less if you count the short sojourn in Philadelphia—yet my attachment is as deep as if she's been with me forever. Which, considering the family connection, I could argue she has been. But I recognize that she can't stay here, and I do want her to be seen and admired. "I don't know what I'm going to do without you," I tell her.

As soon as the words are out of my mouth, *Party* grows murky, the sunny sky obliterated by dark clouds. The calm river rises into towering waves that crash over the boat. A hurricane, a tornado, rips the awning from its mounts, throws the partyers into the roiling sea. As Berthe is lifted over the railing by the wind, she looks directly at me, and I catch the scent of violets. "Get back what is mine," I hear in my head.

The cup drops from my hand, spewing coffee all over the rug. I rush from the living room into my bedroom. Close the door behind me. Try to take deep breaths. No breath. My lungs ache. Can't take in any air. Did I just see what I saw? Hear what I heard? I'm coming undone. Losing my sanity.

Go. Go. Get out of here. Wyatt's? No, he'll freak. I think of Jonathan. Ridiculous. Holly.

Always game for a sleepover, she says to come on over. I stuff a change of underwear into my purse, throw a bunch of towels on the rug to sop up the coffee. Keep my eyes averted. Flee the apartment.

When I arrive, Holly takes one look at me and asks if I had a fight with Wyatt. I tell her I did, which is true, but obviously not what's bothering me. After dinner and a rom-com, I head to her guest room. She watches me go with concern. I never told her I went to see Ruth—nor have I told anyone else—and I assume she's wondering if whatever is troubling me is related to my request for the name of a therapist.

I curl into a fetal position on the unfamiliar bed and try to relax. But all I can see is Berthe catapulting off the deck. All I can hear is her begging me to get back what is hers. I swallow the Ambien Holly gave me, and within fifteen minutes there are no sights and no sounds. I sleep through the night, drugged and, thankfully, dreamless.

HOLLY HAS TO rush out in the morning, so after a hurried breakfast, I hug her goodbye and leave. She'd have let me stay if I'd asked, but, foolishly, I didn't. So now I'm standing on the street, afraid to go home.

It's drizzly and cold. I don't have a coat, as I was too frantic yesterday to think to take one. Again, I could go to Wyatt's, but how do I explain why I'm soaking wet and have no jacket? I stop in a Starbucks and order a second coffee. I don't have my laptop, and my phone has no charge, so I sit and watch rivulets of rain stream down the foggy windows. Then I order another cup.

When I finally drag myself to my building, the concierge shoots me a worried look but greets me as usual. I go up the elevator, walk down the heavily carpeted hallway, and stop in front of my door. I pull out the key and hold it in front of me, but I don't move. I'm terrified to enter my own apartment. This is absurd. This is bullshit. I turn the key in the lock. Everything is as I left it, including the wet towels on the rug. I force myself to stand in front of *Party*, and, sweet relief, she's back to her resting state.

I go into the bathroom to dry my hair. In the mirror, I see a woman who appears much older than the one I usually see there. Her eyes are bloodshot, and her shoulders are hunched. She looks dazed, miserable, defeated. All I can do is shake my head at her. The rug beckons.

I grab a brush and a bottle of cleaner, kneel in front of it. The towels I put down yesterday seem to have absorbed most of the moisture, and given how long the coffee has had to embed into the weave, I suppose it could be much worse. But even after sustained scrubbing, it's clear a professional is going to be necessary. I bundle the wet towels and stand.

I avoid looking at *Party*, but I sense the painting has dimmed again and, as if pulled by a magnet, I twist toward her. This time, there isn't any wind or waves. Just day turning into night, a full moon illuminating the partyers. Everyone is fixed in place, including Berthe.

But instead of appearing natural and lifelike as they usually do, each figure is caught in stop-action. Their bodies and faces remind me of the Tin Man from *The Wizard of Oz*. Frozen in time by some invisible hand. I'm frozen too, eyes fixed on the canvas.

Nothing happens. Nothing changes. I take a deep breath, look out the window at Tremont Street to ground myself, then slowly move my eyes back. It's the familiar cast of characters, holding their familiar poses, wearing their familiar clothes. Except they're fossilized, not quite human, muted tin images of themselves. And it's the dead of night.

Dread snakes itself into every part of me. I'm in a horror movie, aware that at any minute these ossified people are going to transform into the evil vampires they actually are. Suck my blood until I'm one of them.

Then I understand, or think I do. "Do you want to stay here?" I ask her. "To stay with me?"

The moon in the painting goes from full to a crescent sliver. As the shadows fall, the creatures begin to mumble and shift, morphing into unearthly shapes. I drop to my knees, grab my glasses from the coffee table, hoping it's my bad vision. Or an ocular migraine. An LSD flashback. "Then what?" I cry. "Tell me what you want me to do."

Berthe removes her hand from the railing and points to Manet's signature. I watch as the words "Édouard Manet" dissolve and are then overwritten by "Berthe Morisot."

I cower before her, clutching the damp towels to my stomach. *Get back what is mine.* "Are, are you trying to tell me you painted *Party*? That I should prove it's yours?"

Daylight returns to the painting, and *Party* is again as it always was. Nothing ominous, nothing hostile. I stagger to my feet. Fall into the couch. Try to catch my breath. And then I see that although the painting is in its resting state, Berthe's signature still replaces Manet's.

I raise my phone and take a picture. Once again, my screen shows *Party on the Seine* as I see her in front of me, except in the photograph the signature reads "Édouard Manet."

PART THIRTEEN

Berthe & Aimée, 1894–1895

THIRTY-SEVEN

Berthe, 1894

It is now the depths of winter, but Berthe has the sketches she made over the summer, both from the park and along the Seine, to aid her return to that time. Her clandestine painting has evolved into a crowded and merry gathering floating down the river in a brightly colored boat. She can almost hear the laughter and smell the honeysuckle as she brings it to life. She's thrilled to be creating an animated scene of ordinary Parisians enjoying themselves as well as by her audacity in doing so.

She's placed herself at the boat's railing, alone and turned away from the revelers. An enigmatic figure, lost in her own joys and sorrows, a touch off-center in the composition, no larger than any of the other occupants on the boat, yet clearly primary. This solitary woman looks out at the far bank, unseen on the canvas, directly at the viewer, the river rushing by at her feet. Berthe labors for days to create an expression that reflects her own turmoil of conflicting emotions.

And although she recognizes the arrogance of it, she also wants to illustrate a more universal truth: that as much as we may desire to stand alone, we are part of a community whose strictures shape us even when our backs are turned against it. The way she must keep this painting secret so no shame will fall on her daughters. How her freedom is manacled by the reigning dictates of decorum. And then there's Édouard, whose fear of social excommunication renders him unable to grant her greatest desire, to be his wife.

She's making small steps toward her ambitions for the painting, and while it's almost complete, much remains to be done. One afternoon, when she's painting alone in Édouard's studio, he arrives in one of his states. The Salon's decision on submissions for the 1895 exhibition will be announced within weeks, and, as always, he has worked himself into a frenzy. "It will all be for naught if I'm rejected!" he declares as he strides across the large room. "It will be the end for me."

As much as she loves him, these tirades have grown tiresome, especially since his imagined rejections rarely take place. She cannot understand why he carries on like this year after year. It's pointless and, she's beginning to believe, self-indulgent. Even so, she appreciates that he's in real despair, and she wants to soothe him. "Don't worry, my darling, your work is extraordinary, and the Salon will have no choice but to recognize it, as they always have."

"Last year was last year, and this year is this year! One has nothing to do with the other."

Berthe puts down her brush and reaches over to hug him. He allows this, but his feverish body is too agitated to remain still. He turns from her and mops his face with a paint-covered towel, leaving a streak of blue across his forehead that accentuates the crazed blue of his eyes.

"Édouard, you must take yourself in hand. You are going to make yourself ill," she says, surprised to hear her mother's words coming from her own mouth. Ah, Cornélie.

"I am ill." He circles her easel half a dozen times, flings his arms in the air. "Ill with trepidation. Ill with a foreboding of disaster!"

This turmoil is only going to escalate, and she has to contain it before he does himself actual harm. "I'm so relieved you've come at this very time," she says. Hearing the false ring in her voice, Berthe tries to sound more sincere. "I've been struggling and need your help. Can you please take a look at this? I can't seem to get the folds of the skirt of her dress right. Or the flapping of the awning. Tell me what I'm doing wrong," she says, although she has no problem with either the skirt or the awning.

Édouard enjoys nothing more than to be the expert, to come to the aid of a poor damsel in distress, and he's oblivious to the disingenuousness of her words. He moves closer to the painting. "Your masterwork," he says, taking it in. He has often called it this, proclaiming it to be her greatest achievement, far better than anything he could ever accomplish, that he wishes it were his own work. But this time, there is a bite to his words, as if it's no compliment at all.

"Thank you," she replies, hoping she's misinterpreted his tone. "You know how much your encouragement means to me."

He looks at her, his eyes focused and intense, yet almost unseeing, then he snatches the palette from her hand and seizes a brush from her easel. Before she can stop him, he lunges at the canvas. "I will show you what needs to be done!"

Berthe grabs his arm, but he shrugs her off. "Stop it!" she cries.

He seems unable to control himself, frantically attacking the painting. First, he goes after the short staccato strokes she used to create the vibrations in the skirt of the dress, enlarging them. He adds yellow to one of the shades of blue she used in the boat's awning. He laughs maniacally, and Berthe is almost afraid of him.

Even more than that, she is afraid for her painting. She lost one to fire, and she will not lose another to hubris. Fury fuels her, and with a strength she didn't know she possessed, she wrests the palette from his hand and throws it to the floor. She pushes the canvas off the easel and howls as if she's been stabbed.

Édouard stands completely still, deflated, stares at her in confusion. "But, but you asked me to help."

"I asked you to *tell* me what was wrong, not to fix it!" She drops to her knees, takes in his strokes obliterating her own, and is further enraged. "You're an artist, Édouard. How dare you ruin another artist's work? You are an arrogant and insufferable man."

"I, uh, I'm sorry, Berthe. I didn't mean—"

"I don't care if you're sorry or if you didn't mean it." She stands, holding the painting away from him, stymied over what to do next. She can't leave it here, as she doesn't trust that he won't continue to deface it, nor can she bring it home, where the girls or the staff might see it. Aimée was quite upset when she found the preliminary sketches last month, even if the child appeared confused as to why. How upset would she be to discover her mother had lied to her and that the painting was almost complete?

"Please forgive me, my love. You know how I get in these moods and don't—"

"You defiled my picture, and thus defiled me. For this there is no forgiveness." She returns the canvas to the easel and puts a drop cloth over it. "I cannot take this with me now, but I will arrange for it to be removed as soon as I can." She narrows her eyes. "I trust you will not inflict any more damage, although after your behavior, I fear this may be a foolish assumption on my part."

"I won't touch it. I promise you. But you can't leave until we've talked this through. Until—"

"I can, and I will." Berthe picks up her coat and puts it on. "As I've told you before, talk means nothing. It's actions that have meaning. And yours have spoken loudly."

THIRTY-EIGHT

Aimée, 1894–1895

15 December 1894

Oncle has not come to visit for many days. I miss him and asked Maman whether he was in Paris. Her face turned hard, and she told me he was in the city but had been very busy. I did not believe her. He would never let this much time pass without coming to see me if he were close by.

I was afraid he was ill, but Maman said he was not. Her face was still hard, and I suddenly understood that they had had a quarrel. I am ashamed to tell you, dear diary, that I stomped my foot and yelled at her. "He is not just yours. He is mine too. You cannot take him away from me because you are angry with him!" Then I went to my room. She did not come after me.

10 January 1895

Isabeau has not been feeling well, and the doctor recommended she stay in Paris with Oncle Édouard and Tante Suzanne for the holidays. Maman and I went to Tante Edma's and celebrated with the Pontillons. It was nice except I was jealous that Isabeau was with Oncle when I was not. But when we returned, he came to visit the very next day, and I was not jealous any longer. He even brought his own canvas to Maman's studio to paint with us, and I believe their quarrel has ended.

Oncle decided he would make his own rendition of Maman's "Jeanne Pontillon Wearing a Hat." He never glanced at Maman's sketches and just started brushing oil paint directly on the empty canvas. It was fascinating to watch him work, his arms gesturing wildly, his blue eyes icy with intent. I can tell that his painting is going to be much darker than Maman's and more realistic. It will be very good, but I know that I will prefer hers.

He left his easel and came to mine, his brush and palette in hand. He pointed the back of the brush at the place where I was struggling to get Jeanne's chin to look like a chin. "Would you like a little help with this?" he asked, turning the brush around and moving it closer to my canvas.

"Édouard!" Maman cried out in an angry voice. "Do not touch her work."

Oncle took a step back and looked at her with a guilty expression. "Of course. Sorry."

I was worried that they were once again going to quarrel, but he walked over to her and whispered something I could not hear. She told him to go back to his own painting, but she smiled when she said it. I was greatly relieved.

17 January 1895

Isabeau has become quite ill. Dr. Vallier fears it is tuberculosis, and Maman has banned me from the side of the house where Isabeau sleeps. Maman is with her almost all the time, and she said until Isabeau is better I must stay far away from both of them.

30 January 1895

Isabeau has taken a turn for the worse. I have been attending the Legion of Honor School as a day student for over a year, but now Maman insists I board to ensure I do not also get sick. I do not like living here at all. Aside from my concern for Isabeau and homesickness, the boarders have their habits and friendships that are different from those of the day students, and I am not included in many things.

The school is known for its academics, and no art classes are offered. There is nowhere I can paint, and I have no supplies. Oncle has come to visit twice and has promised to come again in a few days. He offered to bring me my easel and pastels, but there is no room in the dormitory for them.

2 February 1895

I am happy to report that Isabeau is on the mend, but now Maman is ill. She has pulmonary congestion, and therefore I must stay on as a boarder. I am in despair. This is not just because it is lonely here, but because I am now worried every moment about Maman.

Oncle has begun to visit more frequently and brings me news. But I fear his news is more cheerful than the actual situation. He looks very sad, and his cheeks have become hollow. Isabeau visited one day when her classes were over, and she did not look healthy either. I hope this is because she has been ill and not because Maman is not getting better.

15 February 1895

Oncle Édouard came today to fetch me home. At first, I was ecstatic, but as soon as we arrived I could tell that something was terribly wrong. Oncle explained that I was allowed to leave school because Dr. Vallier now believes Maman is not contagious. I fear that although this may be true, it is not the actual reason. But I will not write that reason down.

Tante Edma is at the house to nurse Maman, as is my cousin Jeanne. Tante Yves was here the week before, but she had to return to her husband and children. I went directly to Maman's room and could not believe what I saw. She was so small and all curled up on her bed. It was almost like she was not my beautiful mother anymore. It is as if she is a ghost of herself.

Maman motioned me to her bedside so she could hug me. She felt like a tiny bird in my arms. I did not want to cry, but I could not help it. Her voice was raggedy, barely a whisper, and I could see it was difficult for her to speak. I leaned in close, and she told me there was no need for tears, as she was getting better every day. Tante Edma said that Maman's fever was much reduced and this was a good sign. But Tante does not look well either. No one here does.

22 February 1895

Maman is now only drinking a tiny bit of milk and seems to be shrinking right before my eyes. Dr. Vallier comes almost every day, sometimes twice a day. There is a lot of whispering among the adults. I also hear crying when no one believes I am nearby. Tante Edma and Oncle Édouard keep assuring me that Maman will recover, and as much as I wish to believe this, in the deepest parts of my heart I know it is not true. Maman is now a ghost of a ghost of herself. I go to school and learn nothing. I go to Oncle's studio and paint nothing.

24 February 1895

Maman struggles to breathe, and it's hard to watch this, but I want to be with her as much as I can. Once in a while, she seems to feel better for a few minutes, and I need to be there when she does. I must tell her how much I love her and that she is the best mother there ever was. I believe this will give her strength and make her well.

26 February 1895

I am now eating as little as Maman, as putting anything into my stomach is impossible. Isabeau and I sit by Maman, one on each side of the bed, holding her hands. They are very cold and bony, blue in tone. They look like the hands of a woman of eighty. Maman is only fifty-four.

27 February 1895

Oncle Édouard took me for a carriage ride today, even though the weather was nasty. He looks almost as poorly as Maman does. His eyes are bloodshot, and his beard is in need of a trim. Even his red hair seems to have faded.

He tried to talk to me about the future, but I said there is no need. I am overjoyed to tell you, dear diary, that Maman sat up this morning and took half a glass of milk. Her cheeks were flushed, and she smiled at me. All of this must mean she is finally beginning to feel better! Thank you, dear Lord. Thank you a million times over. The recovery will most likely be long, but then she will be herself again and all will be well. When I told Oncle this, he turned away from me and looked out the window.

2 March 1895

There were so many people coming and going today. Some wanted news of Maman, and some wanted to see her. Oncle Édouard and Tante Edma decide who can and who cannot visit with her. Few were admitted. M. Degas was allowed in, and when he came out he swung his cape around his shoulders and rushed from the house. Dr. Vallier has been here most of the day, but now he has gone back to the hospital.

Tante insisted that Isabeau and I sit down to dinner with her. None of us ate anything. When Oncle joined us, he ate nothing either. We did not talk. What was there to say?

I went up to sit with Maman. I cannot bear it. I cannot. She looked so well yesterday, but today there is no denying that she is losing her struggle for breath. She is so weak and so very tired. Please Lord, please let her live.

It was too painful to watch her in such distress, and I was not able to stay with her for long. Maman, oh, my dear, dear Maman. Do not leave me. Please do not leave me. If you must go, I will go with you. Tante saw how distressed I was and brought me to my bedroom. She helped me into my nightgown and told me to sleep. How could I sleep?

Oncle came in and stayed with me until he heard Dr. Vallier's voice and went to speak with him. I climbed out of bed and sat at the top of the stairs so I could listen to what the doctor was saying. I could hear him talking, but I could not understand his words. I stayed there anyway.

I think I must have fallen asleep, because the next thing I knew, Oncle was picking me up from the floor and carrying me to my bed. He held me tight, and I could feel that his face was wet. He was also shaking and breathing hard.

I screamed, and he held me even tighter. Then I screamed again and began hitting him with my fists. I yelled that I wanted my mother, and he told me he would always take care of me. But I did not want him to take care of me. I wanted Maman. Oncle kissed my forehead like Maman always does. He told me he understood and that he wanted her too.

But now neither of us will ever be able to have her again. This is the very worst day of my life.

PART FOURTEEN

Tamara, the present

THIRTY-NINE

I look from my phone to *Party* and back to the screen. The signature on the painting still says "Berthe Morisot," and the one in the photograph still says "Édouard Manet." I stare at the ceiling, try to take deep breaths and slow my racing heart. Visual and auditory and olfactory hallucinations? Transmuting paintings and dead people talking to me? How can this be? I stretch to grasp this new version of myself. But I can't reach it. It makes no sense. How can I hold a job and live on my own if I'm demonstrably psychotic?

I text Wyatt to ask if he's home and if it's okay if I stop by. He says he is, and that I'm welcome anytime.

When I step into the foyer, he says, "You look like you need a hug." Then he wraps me in a welcoming embrace and rests his chin on my head. "Sorry I stormed out yesterday. Miss me last night?"

I nod into his chest, and the tears I've been holding off all afternoon break through. I never cry. I'm crying.

"Hey, hey." He pulls back, looks at my streaming face, and tenderly rewraps me. "I realize it's tough to be away from me, but this seems a bit excessive."

I start to laugh, which stops the tears, but then the laugh takes off in a slightly hysterical direction.

"Let's go sit. You can tell me what this is about." He leads me to the couch, and my pseudohilarity ebbs. He takes both my hands in his. "Are you okay, Tam? Did you get bad news? You haven't been to the doctor or anything, have you?"

I swipe at my eyes with my sleeve. "No, no. Nothing like that. Nothing serious like that."

"Then serious like what?"

I sigh. "I've, I've just been a little off lately. Not my usual self. I'm sure it's just stress from work, the appeal, the lawsuit . . . But I'm, I don't know, I'm feeling kind of lopsided, for lack of a better word. But not physically, more mentally."

"What does that mean?"

"I haven't been sleeping well, so that's probably the reason."

"The reason for what?"

"This, this . . ." I raise my arm, then drop it to my lap. "This discombobulation."

He brushes hair off my forehead. "You've got to be more specific."

"Well, the nightmares, for one."

He drops my hands. "*Party on the Seine*?"

"No. Not really, but there is something about the painting I wanted to talk to you about. While I've been researching, well, I'm starting to wonder if Manet actually painted it."

"There's never been any doubt he painted it, right? Are these the kinds of thoughts that are making you feel whatever you're feeling? Lopsided?"

I get up and stand at the front window, my face hidden from him. I'm backing myself into a dangerous corner here. Then I have a thought that might extricate me, and I turn around. "But if he didn't, then Damian would have no claim to her—to it."

Wyatt's expression is both bewildered and exasperated. "Obviously, there'd be no lawsuit if he didn't paint it. But the Claims Conference, the official listing of Manet's works that Damien's foundation keeps, that museum in Philadelphia, they all believe it's his."

It's tough to argue with a lawyer, especially when your case is weak.

"You told me it was on display from the late 1800s until it was stolen before the war," he continues. "So if it wasn't his, wouldn't someone have figured that out by now?"

I grasp for those straws. "It wasn't shown all that much, a lot less than most of his others. And, and because it stayed in the family, no one probably ever checked. But, either way, couldn't we try to use it against Damien? It's not as if he's been perfectly honest with us."

"That would only work if it were true."

"Maybe I should look into it more thoroughly."

His eyes narrow. "If Édouard Manet didn't paint it, who do you think did?"

I shrug as nonchalantly as I can. "Lots of people, I suppose. It does look like a lot of Renoir's work. Or it could even be an outright forgery."

"You're thinking it was Berthe, aren't you?"

"No, no, it—"

"Did you get this idea from one of your dreams? Did she tell you it was hers?"

I sit down next to him, clasp my hands on my lap, and look at the carpet. "That's a low blow." But the real blow is that his incredulity—and how outlandish what he's asking sounds even to my ears—is yet another indication I'm losing my mind.

THE NEXT DAY, I call Jonathan, but I'm better prepared for this conversation. "Did the Conference ever authenticate *Party*?" I ask, as if it were just a passing thought.

"Not that I know of, but I doubt it. Like I told you before, our investigations focus on the artworks *after* the Nazis stole them. It's not our role to authenticate anything, just to find out who a particular piece was stolen from and get it back to the family. Whether it's a great work of art or a piece of junk doesn't matter."

"Do you have any idea if anyone else might have authenticated it?"

"Why are you asking?"

"It's nuts, I know, but I've started thinking that maybe Manet didn't paint it."

"For real, or as a way to get Damien off your back?"

I'm embarrassed he saw this connection right away, while I didn't make it for a full day. But as this is the excuse I'd planned to explain my inquisitiveness, it works. "Yeah, then he'd have no case."

"Only if it were true." Just what Wyatt said. Damn lawyers.

"So how would I find out whether it's ever been authenticated?"

"You're not going to like this, but the Manet Foundation is the place that would have the most thorough and up-to-date info. They're the ones who have all the detailed provenance records. His catalogue raisonné."

"There has to be some other way."

"Well, a lot of these catalogues are public, or at least parts of them. I'd check online. Often there are physical books. Usually very fancy and expensive ones, but a larger library might have copies—Copley Square or maybe Harvard. But you've got to hope Manet's isn't private, which isn't unusual. Depends on the artist or their estate."

"Why do I have the feeling Damien would keep it private?" I say, and I can hear the bitterness in my voice. "Or at least any part I might be interested in."

A long pause. "Are you serious about this?"

"No, not really. Maybe."

"What makes you think it's not Manet's work?"

"Just, uh, just from some of the research I've been doing. You know, to find out how Colette ended up with it."

"For example?"

"Oh, I guess the less defined strokes, the soft edges, things like that. And Berthe looks very different in *Party* than she does in Édouard's other paintings of her. Even you said it was a break from his usual style, less traditional than most of his compositions . . . I don't know, the way the light falls?"

Another long pause. "Look, this isn't any of my business, but I feel we've known each other long enough that I'd like to be honest with you. Do you want to hear my thoughts?"

I don't particularly want to hear his thoughts, but I did call him for his thoughts. "Hit me."

"Frankly, proving that Édouard Manet didn't paint one of his most highly acclaimed masterpieces is more than likely a losing venture. If I were giving you odds, it'd have to be one in a thousand. Maybe one hundred thousand. I'm sorry, but unless you've got some definitive evidence, I just don't see how this can go anywhere but nowhere."

"That's what I want to look for. Evidence."

"Is there something you're leaving out here?"

"No," I say after a moment's hesitation.

His sigh is deep and long. "I've always figured you as a rational person—if a bit cynical—except when it comes to *Party*. Want to tell me what's really going on?"

"Berthe told me she painted it."

Jonathan bursts out laughing. "Well, that's a relief. And here I thought you might be going crazy."

I GO TO a different psychologist, a Dr. Zafón. He sits me down in a sterile office, nothing like Ruth's cozy one, and explains that he's going to administer two different tests, the MMPI and the Rorschach. But he doesn't tell me what the results are going to show. I figured this would be the case, so I checked out the most common psychological tests before I came.

The MMPI is used to determine whether you have any of a bunch of different mental illnesses, while the Rorschach assesses if your thought processes are logical and you see the world as it truly is. This last test, obviously, makes me nervous. Actually, they both make me nervous. The MMPI has over five hundred statements that require a yes-or-no response, and, as everyone knows, the Rorschach is based on the interpretation of inkblots. This sounds like a bunch of gibberish to me. But I'm here, and I'm looking for answers, so I pick up the pencil and start on the MMPI.

The statements are inane: *I have a cough most of the time. My soul sometimes leaves my body. My family doesn't like the work I've chosen. A minister can cure disease by putting his hand on your head. I have never been in trouble because of my sexual behavior. At least once a week, I feel suddenly hot all over without apparent cause. Sometimes I feel like I want to smash things. My judgment is better than it ever was.* And on and on and on. Really?

I STARE THROUGH my office window at my tiny piece of the Charles—no sailboats, just cloudy, chilly March, the water steel gray. I did everything Dr. Zafón asked of me, but I have zero faith that he or anyone will get any inkling of my mental status from my responses. I may not be a psychologist, but it was pretty easy to figure which MMPI answer would make you seem sane and which would not. The same for the inkblots. And then there are the underlying algorithms used for interpretation, which, by definition, are going to be based on some faulty assumptions.

I answered everything as truthfully as I could, although some of the MMPI statements were hard to force into a simple yes or no. Is my judgment better than it ever was? Generally, I'd say yes. But as of late, I'm not so sure. I've found myself wondering if I've been thinking about this all wrong. That

I'm not seeing things that aren't there. On the contrary, I'm seeing things that are.

This is equally troubling, as accepting the possibility of the paranormal goes against everything I've believed about the nature of existence. Evidence, science, and numbers are my game. Prove it or shut up. Not particularly open-minded of me, but there it is. I've never believed there were more things in heaven and earth, but apparently, for the first time in my life, I'm going to have to consider the supernatural.

Fortunately, Holly is the opposite of my practical STEM self, open to all kinds of possibilities, from reincarnation to the power of pyramids to the effects of positive—or negative—thoughts on future events. "Mindfulness" is one of her favorite words. We've never discussed ghosts, but she's gone to some séances, so I'm thinking she knows a bit about them.

We meet for lunch, and when I ask her if she believes in ghosts, she's incredulous. "You? You want to know about ghosts?"

"Just ghostlore. Like, you know, like what people who believe in ghosts think they are."

Holly smiles mischievously. "Have you met one?"

I'd planned the answer for this question. "No, I'm reading *Turn of the Screw*, Henry James, and it got me curious."

"Hmm." It's clear she's skeptical of my motives, but she goes for it anyway. "There are lots of disagreements, but I think most people would say ghosts are people who have physically died but their souls are somehow caught in a netherworld between life and death."

"Why would that happen?"

"According to 'ghostlore,' as you put it, ghosts have unresolved issues from life that keep them here. Sometimes it's guilt over things they've done—say they killed someone—or revenge for something that was done to them. The upshot is they have to right the wrong before they're set free."

"Set free to go where?"

She pops a cherry tomato into her mouth. "To a place where they're at peace, where they can finally rest, unperturbed by whatever was perturbing them."

"So you're saying they become ghosts to fix what they couldn't when they were alive?"

"That's one way to look at it. But it can also be a response to things that happened after they died. Something bad that they have to change."

"But there's no proof this is an actual thing? It's all speculation?"

"So much in this world is based on speculation. No 'proof' of the Big Bang, but most people believe it's true." She gives me a wry smile. "Scientists, even."

Instead of getting into this, I ask, "You mostly hear about haunted houses, but can a ghost haunt something else?"

"Sure. Forests are a big one, boats, graveyards. But it's always a place or an object they have a deep connection to—usually linked to whatever they need to set right."

This is simultaneously chilling and preposterous, and I flinch before I can stop myself.

Holly eyes me suspiciously. "Does this have anything to do with what you said about wanting to talk to a shrink?"

"No," I say quickly. "I told you it's about *Turn of the Screw.*"

"So you did." She taps her fork against the side of her plate. "Just don't confuse psychiatric issues with the paranormal."

FORTY

When I get back to the office, Wyatt calls. "Good or bad?" I ask instead of saying hello.

"Depends. If you're interested in racking in twenty-nine million dollars, it's good."

"And if I'm not?"

"More good." He chuckles. "The Paris judge's original decision was overruled, so you don't have to send *Party* over there—at least not right now."

I crumple into my chair. "Wow. Thanks. You're the best." I've been so caught up with this mental health business, I almost forgot about the appeal.

"That's got to be why Damien upped his offer to twenty-nine mil," he adds.

"He must be so pissed off. Frothing at the mouth with fury." I rub my hands together gleefully. "Can't you see him huddling in the foundation's war room, licking his wounds and brainstorming with his generals on their next offensive?"

"Don't forget this is just a short reprieve. The trial's coming up fast."

"Sure, but the Louvre reversal gives me confidence that we're going to win there too."

"This decision was based on a much narrower issue in a completely different venue. The New York suit has very little in common with it."

"I just want to enjoy the moment. No bursting my bubble."

"Sure, but we have to look ahead. The trial is a little over five weeks away, and I've still got plenty of prep work to do. Which means I'm going to have to add on more hours to replace the ones the appeal gobbled up. Even with the girlfriend discount, it's going to get expensive."

"It's an investment."

"A risky one. Like those financial disclaimers always remind you: Past performance is no guarantee of future success."

IT'S BEEN ALMOST a week, and I haven't heard from Ruth about the tests, like Dr. Zafón said I would. Well, really he said it could be up to two weeks before he got the results to her, but I'm incredibly edgy. I'd initially expected that he'd be the one to give me his findings, but as Ruth referred me to him, I guess she's the one who gets that privilege. It may be inflated to claim this will be a defining moment in my life, but in some ways it will. No matter what the tests ultimately show, this kind of anxiety cannot be good for my mental health.

I'm home on a Saturday afternoon when there's a knock at the door. It's Wyatt, and when he walks in he cries, "Hey, birthday girl!"

Our plan is for a celebratory dinner at No. 9 Park, one of the best restaurants in Boston, but he's hours early for that. Plus, he's got a suitcase and an impish expression on his face.

"I've got a birthday surprise for you, but first you need to pack a bag. For two nights. Include something fancy, something comfortable, and an outrageously sexy negligee."

I'm not all that fond of surprises, nor do I like making a big deal out of my birthday, but the handsomest man I've ever known is beaming at me with boyish pleasure. "I can't go anywhere," I protest. "I've got to work this weekend."

He pulls me up from my chair and kisses me deeply. "No, you don't."

"I don't?" Boy, am I easy.

"There's a limo waiting outside to take us to the Big Apple. To the Lotte New York Palace. Champagne and culinary delights on board."

"But I—"

He gives me a playful push toward my bedroom. "Go. It's all set. We're going to celebrate your birthday like you've never celebrated it before. And you're going to love it."

I DO LOVE it, although there's no denying it's way, way over the top. The limo could easily hold a dozen people and is stocked with enough alcohol and food—including caviar and foie gras—to sate all of them. The hotel is in an elegant nineteenth-century building with wide sweeping staircases and gleaming marble floors. Our suite—of course it's a suite—is the most luxurious I've ever been in, hugging the corner of the fiftieth floor, windows everywhere bursting with the spires of brightly lit skyscrapers. Not to mention there's a living room, a dining room, and two bathrooms. It's much bigger than my apartment.

We down some gummies and make love on a bed with sheets that must be two thousand count, in the soaking tub almost as big as the bed, and, later, on the living room couch. A champagne bottle cools in its bucket, and around midnight we call down for fruit parfaits and chocolate-covered strawberries.

"This has to be the most decadent evening I've ever spent," I tell him as we lie sprawled on the bed, finally exhausted.

"Happy birthday." He nuzzles my neck. "Did you enjoy it?"

"Oh, I don't know. It was okay . . ."

"Only okay?" He grabs me in a bear hug. "Take that back, woman!"

Instead, I kiss him. Then we both fall into a heavy sleep.

In the morning, we battle our hangovers with coffee and Tylenol and head out to MoMA, where Wyatt arranged for a private guide to show us their Impressionist collection. Renee, the guide, leads us to the fifth floor, where light and color fling themselves from canvases on every wall.

I swear I recognize a few of them from my waltzing dream. The only piece by Berthe is a drawing called *A Standing Girl*. Muted, almost a sketch, it draws no attention to itself—just as Berthe currently draws little attention to herself. This is no surprise, nor is the fact that there are many paintings by her more well-known cronies: Manet, Degas, Monet, Renoir.

I don't remark on this, as Wyatt has gone out of his way to let Renee know of my interest in Manet. And there are many Manets, including *Two Roses*, *Raven Head*, and another version of *Execution of the Emperor Maximilian*, which I don't like any more than the one I disliked at the MFA. But there is one, *Argenteuil*, of a couple in colorful clothes with a blue sea behind them, that's more Impressionist-like—looser brushstrokes and more light. Still, it's no *Party*.

"None of these paintings are nearly as good as yours," Wyatt tells me.

"Just thinking the same thing."

"Yours?" Renee asks, eyebrows raised.

"Only a copy," I clarify. "*Party on the Seine*."

"Oh, absolutely. That's supposed to be one of his best. Maybe even his best, one of my professors said. So horrible the Nazis destroyed it. Criminal." Obviously, Renee doesn't read Boston news reports, but I find it odd that someone in the art world is unaware the painting has resurfaced.

I nod and feign interest in *Raven Head*, avoiding her eyes.

When she turns away, Wyatt whispers, "Can't imagine how much you're going to be able to get for it." He throws an arm around my shoulder. "Maybe we should get married so I can be as rich as you."

"I'm not planning to sell it anytime soon," I tell him, "so you should probably stick to law as your avenue to riches."

He looks hurt and pulls away.

Renee is beckoning us over to Degas's *At the Milliner's*. I hold up a finger and lean into Wyatt. "Sorry, this hangover's a bitch. Don't listen to me."

"You can't just keep it in your apartment forever," he says. "Beyond the huge risk you're taking, you know how insane it makes you."

"It doesn't make me insane. It soothes me."

"Soothes you?" His voice begins to rise. "How about those nightmares? The ones that send you running into the living room, where you cower before it?"

"They're just dreams. You're making a big deal about nothing."

"It's not healthy for you. You have to get rid of it."

"Actually, I don't have to get rid of anything. I can do whatever I want with *her*." I emphasize the 'her' because I know this annoys him.

The remainder of the weekend doesn't go nearly as well as the first part.

ON MONDAY AFTERNOON, Wyatt sends me a dozen red roses. Enclosed is a note: *Sorry I was such a jerk. Of course you can do whatever you want with your painting. Can you forgive me?*

He was a jerk, but I sense the apology is sincere and tell him all is forgiven. This isn't completely true.

It's now been two weeks and I still haven't heard from Ruth, so I text her. She tells me Dr. Zafón promised to deliver the results in a few days, and that she'll let me know so we can schedule an appointment. I'm both annoyed at the delay and pleased I have a momentary reprieve.

I haven't had any Berthe nightmares recently, although there have been a few dreams in which I'm being pushed, or pushing myself, to do something

I've been procrastinating. In one, I was standing at a podium describing to a large audience the findings of a project I haven't finished. Another was just a huge monitor with hundreds of unanswered texts streaming endlessly down the screen. And last night it was my mother yelling at me because I hadn't gone to the grocery store when I promised her I would. Gee, what could these be about?

There's no denying that I've been slacking off on job #2, as my subconscious seems to be pointing out. Even though I understand the real trial isn't the same, I have to confess that winning the appeal has lessened my frenzy. And then there's everything else, including my conversation with Holly, which came a little too close to echoing what I've experienced, as well as providing a semiplausible explanation for Berthe's motive and behavior. Strike that. Not plausible at all.

Alternately, if I did open my mind to the possibility—sorry, Dad—it would suggest Berthe did paint *Party*, and if I can prove it, despite Wyatt and Jonathan's admonitions to the contrary, Damien would have no case. A huge blow to my dear cousin, for he'd not only lose the suit but have to admit that his illustrious ancestor didn't paint the masterpiece attributed to him. Wouldn't that just be the most fitting revenge? And then there's giving Berthe her due as a celebrated artist. Letting the world know of her accomplishments, restoring her rightful place in the Impressionist canon.

When I finally have a few hours, instead of turning to the Bernheims' claim to *Party* for Wyatt, I make a preliminary stab at Berthe's authorship of *Party*. Why isn't there a word like this for a painting? "Artistship"? Jonathan mentioned Berthe and Édouard's catalogues raisonnés, but before I search for similarities between their works and my painting—and hopefully find more parallels in Berthe's than in Édouard's—I pull up each of their online catalogues to see what's in them.

Although only a portion of Édouard's is public—apparently, some foundations like to keep things close to the vest—there are hundreds of paintings listed in his, including *Party on the Seine*. According to the entry, it was painted between 1896 and 1897—after Berthe died—and was first shown at the 1898 Salon to vast acclaim, probably leading to Manet's Legion of Honor medal in 1899. This is followed by a partial account of the shows and galleries where it was exhibited prior to 1936. It ends with the fact that *Party* was stolen by the Nazis in the late 1930s and presumed destroyed.

There are fewer listings of Berthe's oeuvre. Her catalogue appears to be completely public, as there isn't a Berthe Morisot Foundation. Surprise. Surprise. From just a quick appraisal, I can see that many of her works are missing, and the particulars on individual paintings have gaping holes compared to Édouard's mostly complete entries. I have a book with photos of her paintings and drawings, of which there are over four hundred.

Ah, Berthe, no wonder you're so frustrated. So many years of struggle to be accepted and appreciated, followed by so many more of losing what you'd achieved.

THE CLOCK IS ticking ever forward toward the trial, now only three weeks away, and I'm growing more frantic by the day. The Colette investigation has hit a dead end. There isn't any information about the Bernheims beyond the confiscation of their art collection and their immigration to the United States. After all they endured, I'm figuring they just wanted to keep a low profile once they were safe. Presumably, they were pretty destroyed themselves.

So I turn to Aimée Manet, Colette's mother. According to the records, Berthe was already dead when Édouard painted *Party*, as was his brother Gène, so Aimée—Berthe and Gène's daughter—was the most likely recipient, the one who would have passed it on to her own daughter. I've been over this territory before, and I've found no paperwork or even a suggestion that Édouard gifted it to her.

But if Berthe is the artist, none of this matters, as the painting is unequivocally mine. My search for similar subjects and brushstrokes in Édouard and Berthe's work didn't yield as much as I'd hoped, but AI is known for its hallucinations, so it's hard to be certain. Although there were more hits between Berthe and *Party* than Édouard, because of the low quality of the internet photos, nothing definitive. And, most likely, more hallucinations.

The only way to settle the question of artistship—I'm going to coin the term—is to find an authenticator to verify it. I could ask Jonathan for advice, but after our last conversation about the possibility that Édouard didn't paint it, I don't dare. I discover that official authenticators have advanced degrees in art history and years of experience working in museums or galleries or auction houses, along with excellent research and forensic technical skills. Then there's usually a specialization in a particular artist or movement, and a certification process by the International Foundation for Art Research. I had no idea.

When I was first thinking about this, I figured I needed a Manet scholar, but now I realize that was wrong. What I need is a Morisot expert. I quickly discover that a Manet expert would be easier to find. As Jonathan said, the official authentication boards that determine an artwork's legitimacy are often seated within each artist's foundation, and Berthe has no foundation. Another thing I'll correct if I get the chance.

Nor are there nearly as many art professionals or academics who specialize in her work. Plus, after a spate of recent lawsuits brought by owners against authenticators who'd determined the paintings they'd purchased as masterworks—for masterwork prices—were actually forgeries, many experts, both within and outside foundations, closed shop. This list includes those who specialized in Pollock, Krasner, Warhol, and Basquiat, as well as an array of other well-known artists. Then, I see that my problems are far greater than these.

Apparently, before a Morisot authenticator would even consider analyzing *Party*, I'd need full documentation of the painting's listing in Berthe's catalogue raisonné—which, of course it isn't, as it's in Manet's—along with photos, exhibition records, awards, certificates, scholarly references, correspondence, etc., etc., etc. To make matters even more difficult, the most important piece of information is verification of *Party*'s provenance, and any breaks or discrepancies in the record of ownership can raise serious questions that might impede authentication.

Not to mention that all this documentation would affirm that Édouard is the artist who painted it.

FORTY-ONE

All these concerns are rendered marginal when Alexander comes into my office the next morning. He has a laptop in his hand, and he's scowling.

He's not much of a scowler, so I ask, "What?"

He places the computer on my desk and turns it toward me. It's a new Facebook post from my account, which I haven't used in years. I stare at a photograph of me holding a mock-up of the packaging for Zymidline in one hand and a thick packet of data reports in the other. Underneath, it reads: "This drug cannot be released in September as planned. Calliope Technologies of Boston, the company that developed Zymidline, provided the FDA with false data on its safety. I am the vice president of regulatory affairs at Calliope, and it is my duty to come forward with this information before anyone is harmed."

"You didn't do this, right?" he asks.

"Of course not. And that photo, it's not real. Has to be AI. Hackers . . ." Furious, I look up at Alexander, who's in his mid-twenties and probably knows a lot more about this kind of thing than I do. "How the hell does something like this happen?"

"Lots of mean-spirited assholes without a life. Leaky security." He rests his hand on my shoulder. "This sucks. Do you have any idea why someone would want to screw you like that?"

I shake my head and hand him back his laptop. But I do know why.

When the door closes behind him, I try to tamp down my wrath, but it fights back. I call Wyatt. "Go to Facebook and check any new posts from me."

"I thought you didn't use Facebook. And I'm in the middle—"

"It's Damien."

There's the sound of clicking, then silence, then, "Fuck."

I want to scream and pound my desk. But there's no pounding and screaming in biotech.

"Post a retraction ASAP," he says. "Report it to Facebook and show it to your boss before he sees it from someone else."

"How could Damien do such a thing?"

"Does look suspicious, but what's his motive? Intimidation? Freaking you out? Making you look bad? I don't see how any of those get him closer to the painting."

"I don't know, but it reeks of him. The leak to the press about *Party* being in my apartment, the threats, the hearing to get her to the Louvre—and now this. Who else would bother?"

"A business competitor? Someone with a grudge from the past? Your ex-husband? Nick?"

"It's him. It—"

"We can talk about this later. Now it's damage control before anything else."

I comment on the post with *FALSE, FALSE, FALSE,* in all caps, followed by an explanation that I was hacked, the photo is fake, there has been no fudged data, and Zymidline is completely safe. Then I create a new post that says the same thing. I contact Facebook and follow the directions to flag the content and describe the situation. I get a text claiming they'll get back to me as soon as possible, whatever that means. Then I go in search of Tony, but he's not in the office.

At ten o'clock, FDA regulatory officials arrive to examine our lab setup for the development of the clostridial myonecrosis drug. Despite my agitation, the inspection goes well. There are a dozen or so minor things that need tweaking, but far fewer than usual for an initial review. I'm pretty pleased with myself and go back to my office with a smile on my face.

But when Calliope's CEO walks in and closes the door behind him, the smile disappears. Anthony Lurie can be a difficult guy—headstrong and prone to take offense even when none is given—and I try to avoid him as much as possible.

"Good news, Tony. The feds pretty much green-lighted the CM lab. We're on our way."

He nods, his jaw set.

"What's up?" I ask with fake cheerfulness.

He takes a seat in one of the chairs in front of my desk. "Nothing good."

"Sorry to hear that."

"It's your Facebook post."

"You know I didn't do that. My account was hacked."

"Be that as it may, it's a major problem. For you and for Calliope."

"I can't tell you how sorry I am about all this. I've already posted a retraction and notified Facebook. Lots of wackos out there."

"And because your wackos tagged our website in the post, now someone—maybe the same people or maybe not—got into the site and our email server. Your post was sent to all the newsletter recipients and to every address on our contact list, including our funders and the governmental offices we have connections with. I don't think I need to tell you what a disaster this is for both our business and our reputation."

I stare at him. "I, I don't know what to say. This is . . . It's just so awful."

"That's one way to put it."

"What can I do? How can I help?"

"The most helpful thing you can do right now is nothing."

"But I want to. I feel responsible and—"

Tony stands. "Why don't you take a few days off? I'll let you know what's been determined after the decisions are made."

I stand too. "What kind of decisions?"

"Like how we're going to get ourselves out of this mess that you—inadvertently or not—got us into."

AFTER THREE DAYS of silence, Tony texts and asks me to come to his office at noon. Angelica Grebb, the VP of legal, Barry Shaddock, the board chair, and Melissa Caplan, the head of HR, are waiting for me along with Tony. Wyatt told me that even if they acknowledged I had nothing to do with the post, Calliope would be within its rights to take disciplinary action because of the harm it did to the business. When I asked what kind of action, he said it could be anything from a slap on the wrist to termination. He figured something in between the two. From the unsmiling faces before me, I'm thinking it's going to be closer to the negative end of the spectrum.

The four of them are sitting at the conference table, and I join them. I try not to let my nervousness show, and say, "I just want to reiterate what I told Tony the other day. I didn't post it, and I'm really sorry that someone else did. I have no idea who was behind it—and Facebook told me this kind of thing happens all the time—but I do know how harmful it's been to Calliope, and I want to apologize and take responsibility for whatever unintentional hand I had in it."

"Thank you," Angelica says. "We appreciate that, but I can't overstate the negative impact this has already had on our workplace, our reputation, and on the suffering patients waiting for Zymidline to be released, a wait that will now be prolonged. And there's the potential effect on our bottom line and the company's future. The adverse publicity alone has already been devastating."

"Again, I'm so sorry."

Barry, a veteran tech wiz, who was one of the first on the biotech train, smiles sadly at me. "Tamara, we recognize that this wasn't your post, and that bad players are responsible for its spread." He clears his throat. "But even with that, the board has no choice but to terminate your contract."

Even though I've been contemplating this possibility for days, I didn't really believe it would happen. I turn to Tony. "After my 'exemplary work,' as you described it in my last review? A review that, I might add, I have a copy of."

He doesn't meet my eye. "Sorry it's come to this." He looks pleadingly at Angelica.

"Like Barry said, we had no choice," she explains. "Whether you did it on purpose or not, the aspersions against us—and against a federal agency—cannot go unanswered. It will take months, years, if ever, to clear our name. And none of this bodes well for future grants and contracts. Not to mention our investors. Letting you go will signal to all of them that we take full responsibility and will do everything we can to keep such a thing from ever happening again."

I want to yell that I'm as much a victim as Calliope is, that I'm going to sue them for wrongful termination. Their decision is a knee-jerk reaction, and I would have expected better from all the brainpower in this room. But even through my fury, self-preservation kicks in. I understand they believe that firing me is necessary to appease both the FDA and the investors—and that I'm the scapegoat. I also understand that if I say any of those things, I'll never get another job in biotech.

I stand and hold my head high. "If the decision is made, the decision is made, no matter how unjust it may be. It's my sincere hope that this can be addressed quickly and there won't be any long-term effects on the company or the patients. And, again, my apologies."

"We'll pack up your things and send them to you," Tony calls to my retreating back. "Please leave your badge and keys with Alexander."

PART FIFTEEN

Aimée, 1898–1915

FORTY-TWO

1898–1899

7 July 1898

Ah, my dearest diary, it has been more than three years since I last wrote, and there have been so many changes. But one thing that has not changed is how much I miss Maman. Everyone is always telling me that time heals wounds, along with many other clichés that are not true. A day never goes by that I do not think of her and wish she were still with me. Only Oncle Édouard understands this. He pines for her too.

Oncle has been very kind to me, and I am certain if it were not for him, I would have died of grief and loneliness long ago. Isabeau moved into an apartment in the city with two older Manet cousins soon after Maman left us, and I assumed I would remain at Maman's, which is my home, and continue at the Legion School as a day student.

But Tante Edma, Tante Yves, and Oncle believed I was too old for a nanny, and the maid would not be a proper person to oversee a 13-year-old. Both aunts wanted me to come live in their houses, but they are far away from the city, and I wanted to stay in Paris with Oncle.

Oncle told me he would like nothing more than for me to move in with him, but that this was not possible. He did not say why, but it did not need saying: Tante Suzanne would never allow it. I understood there was no other choice and told him it was better for me to be a boarder at Legion, but that I wanted to be able to come home to 40 Rue de Villejust, and maybe live there when I was older. He promised me he would make this possible. It was the only way to stay in Paris, and I do not dislike boarding as much as I did that first year.

15 July 1898

I am spending the summer with M. and Mme Renoir in Bretagne. Maman's artist friends have been very generous, so I know how much they cared for her, which makes me happy. Last summer, I was with M. Monet and his family and the one before with M. Pissarro and his. M. Degas does not have a wife, so it is not proper for me to stay with him, but he visits me often at school and takes me on painting outings.

My aunts invite me to their houses for all the holidays, and Oncle spends as much time with me as he can. He has taken over maintenance of Maman's house and often brings me home to visit my bedroom and spend time reading in the same chair Maman did. Sometimes we paint in her studio, but often I start to cry and we have to leave. I think he may have given Isabeau money, because he told me the house is now all mine.

30 September 1898

I fear I am going to be a much less dependable journal writer. Between schoolwork and social activities, I have very little free time. Now that I have had my debutante ball, I am invited to more events than I can possibly attend. Oncle is my most frequent companion, but M. Degas often accompanies me when Oncle is not available. M. Degas has a sharp wit and is quite amusing.

Last night, I went to a cotillion at the Palais des Lumières with Oncle. It is on the Champs-Élysées, and I believe it is the most exquisite ballroom in all of Paris. Dozens of chandeliers are suspended at different heights and scatter rainbows of colors everywhere. It was like being inside a jeweled box. Oncle said I was as beautiful as Maman and joked that my red hair was his contribution to my stunning appearance. We laughed because this must be true, as Father's hair was dirty blond.

23 October 1898

I fear I have none of the family talent, a squandering of the Manet and Morisot names. I was at Oncle's studio today with M. Degas and M. Renoir. Oncle is not as interested in light as the other Impressionists, but M. Degas was once again trying to show me how to catch the light, and I was once again failing. M. Renoir showed me how he does it differently from M. Degas.

But I was unable to imitate his method either. I believe there is a connection between the eye and the hand that does not exist in me. I also believe that Maman and Oncle wanted so badly for me to be an artist like them that they convinced themselves I was and tried to convince me too.

25 October 1898

It was a beautiful fall day today, and Oncle and I went to the park across from the house to paint. I used to paint with Maman here, and it made me melancholy to be there without her. But Oncle was so determined to teach me how to create depth and texture with brushstrokes that I had no time to miss her. All I had time to do was to be frustrated.

He kept telling me to be bold and confident, but then counseled me to keep my strokes tight and deliberate. This seemed contradictory and confused me. Some of the leaves had begun to turn red and orange, and I tried to paint them and follow his instructions, but every leaf I depicted came out flat. He painted the same leaves I had, and his leaves jumped off the canvas, fully formed, with veins and a midrib, so real it looked as if I could reach out and touch them.

I tried, dear diary, I tell you I did. I did not want to disappoint him. Finally, he put his arm around me, kissed my cheek, and said I was just tired and we would try another day. I told him I would enjoy that. But as much as I love being with him, this was not the truth. I am not only failing him. I am failing Maman.

15 June 1899

Once again, it has been months since I last wrote, but I did warn you that this would most likely be the case. I have wonderful news to share. Oncle has been given the Legion of Honor medal! This is one of the most distinguished awards in all of the country, bestowed by the president, who makes the final decision. It is a national order of merit for outstanding contributions to France.

Oncle is proud, and so am I. He is especially pleased because he has now achieved what his father had many years earlier. Grand-Père Auguste was also a recipient, although Grand-Père received his for work in the national judiciary, not for art. It is even more wonderful because Grand-Mère Antoinette is still alive and was able to witness this triumph for both her husband and her son.

Although the medal is usually given for many years of contributions, which Oncle has surely accomplished, there is no doubt in anyone's mind that his latest success at the Salon is what convinced the president to make the appointment. In the spring, Oncle displayed his masterpiece, "Party on the Seine," to great acclaim, and it was awarded one of the Salon's highest prizes. I believe this painting may be his best, and apparently many others agree, including the president of France.

For me, it is especially dear because Maman is the central figure in the composition, and Oncle used a style more like hers than his own, a sign of respect and admiration, I am sure. He has had many offers to purchase it, but he will not sell. He told me the painting is his final tribute to Maman, and he will not part with it.

FORTY-THREE

1905

Morning, 2 March, 1905

It is a painful anniversary. My dear mother has been gone for ten years today. It seems so much shorter. And so much longer. I was then a 13-year-old schoolgirl, and now I am a 23-year-old woman. It breaks my heart that Maman only knew me as that child. How she would have loved to see me as a wife, and now a new mother, living happily in the home that was hers for so long. My beautiful baby, Colette, would have filled her with such joy.

I went into the nursery to take Colette from her nurse. I held my precious little one in my arms and looked into her tiny face, already ringed with black curls. Just like Maman's. I kept the baby with me until the nurse came for her feeding. Empty-handed, I stared out at the park where Maman and I used to paint, now barren and desolate, waiting for spring.

Pierre was very kind at breakfast before leaving for his office. He took my hand and told me he understood why I was unhappy, and that it was a gift to have had a mother as wonderful as mine, even for only a short time. This made my eyes fill with tears. He joked that if I was going to cry because he understood, then he did not understand why I was unhappy. I tried to smile at my thoughtful husband, but instead more tears spilled.

He offered to accompany me to the cemetery when he returns home this evening, but I thanked him and turned him down. I find no solace there, just distress. Maman lies under the ground, cold and lonely, without a paintbrush in her hand.

Afternoon, 2 March

The most amazing thing just happened. Oncle came by to visit, which I expected, as this date is almost as difficult for him as it is for me. What I did not expect was the large canvas he carried. It was covered with paper, and when he unwrapped it, I saw it was "Party on the Seine." I was confused, as I thought the painting was at Durand-Ruel's gallery as part of a monthlong exhibition of Impressionist works. He propped it up against the parlor wall and told me he had retrieved it from there just this morning.

It is magnificent, simultaneously intimate and universal. As I told you before, I believe it is his greatest work. Colors burst, light flings itself over the people, sparkling the river, accenting the tree branches, bringing it all to vibrant life. Different from many of his more representational paintings. And Maman, oh, Maman. How beautiful and young she is, leaning against the railing, looking out to the far bank, her expression complex and in some ways unknowable, yet masterfully compelling.

My eyes filled again, and Oncle's did also. I thanked him for bringing it here on this day, and told him that seeing Maman like this was both wondrous and heartrending. He agreed, and we sat together on the sofa, silently looking. I do not know for how long, as it seemed as if I slipped inside the picture. I was standing next to Maman, watching the opposite shoreline as the water rushed by under our feet, and I imagined she placed her arm around my shoulders and kissed me on my forehead, as she so often did. I almost believed I smelled Violette de Paine, her favorite perfume.

Oncle cleared his throat and brought me from my reverie. "It is a gift," he said.

"Yes, a miraculous gift you have given to us, to the world."

"You misunderstand, dearest Aimée. It is a gift for you."

I could not believe what he was saying, as it was too immense a thought. Impossible. I was rendered speechless.

"You are the child of my heart, and your mother is the woman of my heart." He took my hands in his. "It is time for *Party* to be yours. Care for her well."

7 March

I cannot tell you, dear diary, how much Oncle's gift means to me. The gift of his words as much as the gift of his painting: *You are the child of my heart, and your mother is the woman of my heart.*

To have "Party on the Seine" hanging in my own house, in Maman's studio, to be able to be with her whenever I wish, is a marvel beyond all expectations. Every time I look, I see more. And the more I see, the more astounded I become. How did he make the light dance like that? How did he give every person on the boat such individuality? How did he make me want to know all their secrets though I have no idea who they are? And, of course, Maman. What was she thinking? Wishing? He has painted her many times, and yet here she is more fully fleshed than in any of the others, as if he were able to see into her soul.

1 April

It did not take long for the news of Oncle's gift to spread throughout our circle and the Parisian art world. It was met with amazement by all, save M. Degas, who came by yesterday to see where I had hung it. When I showed him, he said it was wonderful that we live at 40 Rue de Villejust, as Maman's studio is the perfect setting for the painting. Then that familiar smirk filled his face, and he told me that many people were speculating about why Oncle had chosen to part with his most famous painting and why he had given it to me. I was not about to tell him what Oncle had said.

Even Pierre was dumbfounded, and he worried that it might be unwise to keep a painting of such value in our house. I pointed out that we already had many costly paintings, those of M. Degas, M. Monet, M. Renoir, and many others, including Maman. Still, he seemed uncomfortable with the idea. But he would never deny me this pleasure and has said no more about it.

10 April

Oncle visited today and was twirling around the rooms with Colette in his arms, doting on her. He told her he had done this with me when I was a baby, and that doing the same with my child was a true delight. Then he flashed me a proud grin. More like a grandfather than an uncle. This is a scandalous thought that would bring terrible shame on Maman and the Manet name, and I will not think it again.

15 April

I brought Colette to introduce her to Grand-Mère Antoinette. Grand-Mère is not well, but she has been unwell many times and recovered. Everyone in the family seems to be confident that she will live forever, but she appeared frail to me. Oncle had arranged this visit at a time Tante Suzanne was with family in Germany, and he nervously hovered around Grand-Mère's bedroom until she told him to go to his studio and leave us alone. She has always been a bossy woman, but now that she is in her eighties, it is a much more appealing trait. "Plucky" is a better word to describe her now.

I placed Colette in her lap, and the little girl gazed up at her great-grandmother. Grand-Mère smiled down at her, and Colette, who has just begun to smile, did so too, which delighted Grand-Mère immensely. As Isabeau has no children yet, and neither Oncle nor his brother Gustave had any, Colette is the first great-grandchild, and Grand-Mère fussed over her, eliciting more toothless grins.

Watching them together, I said, "It must be amazing to hold a child who is the grandchild of your child."

She gave me a sharp glance. Then her face softened, and she patted my hand. "It is indeed a wonder, no matter which child's line this beautiful little girl comes from."

16 April

The ramblings of an old woman or a secret the Manets have long known? It would explain many things. Tante Suzanne's animosity toward Maman and myself. The feeling I've always had that there was a skeleton in the cupboard no one would speak of. Father's distance. My red hair, an unusual color that no one on either side of the family shares except for Oncle. I have also heard whispers over the years, whispers that often stopped when I walked into a room. "Party on the Seine."

It is as if an earthquake has occurred and the ground under my feet cannot hold me anymore, my very soul equally shaken. Who am I if not who I've always believed myself to be? And if I'm not, then Maman lied to me my whole life. Oncle too. How could they? The duplicity of it, the mortification of trusting them and their falsehoods. And yet if this is true, I now have a father who I am certain loves me.

I could ask Oncle, but if he hasn't spoken of this for almost a quarter of a century, why would he speak of it now? Most likely, he would maintain his story to protect Maman and me, which is what he has done for all those years. Yet I need affirmation or disavowal from someone. Someone whom I believe knows the truth. Someone who will be willing to share it. I send M. Degas a note inviting him to luncheon tomorrow.

17 April

He arrived at noon looking dapper. Cook prepared a simple lunch, as I requested: consommé, ratatouille, and fresh baguettes. The house was quiet, as Colette and her nurse were at the park enjoying the sunny spring day. M. Degas, who has known me since I was born, immediately sensed there was something here beyond a friendly sharing of food. He did not mention this during our meal, but his eyes were bright with curiosity and mischief.

When coffee and tarte tatin were served, he stretched out his legs and smiled at me in his oh-so-knowing way. "Is there something you would like to discuss with me, my dear Aimée?"

I flushed, and when he laughed delightedly at my discomfort, I could feel the flush deepen. After a bit of prodding, I blurted out my question. He immediately sobered, took a sip of coffee, and then silently stared at the tablecloth.

Finally, he raised his eyes and asked if this was something I was sure I wanted to hear. When I told him it was, he heaved a deep sigh. I could barely breathe and pressed my damp hands to my napkin. He looked at me steadily, choosing his words carefully. "I may be the only one who knows for certain," he told me. "Although, as I am sure you are aware, there has been much speculation on the subject."

I nodded and waited, although I could see the truth in his eyes.

"I am sure your mother would have told you once you entered adulthood, and that is why I will tell you now. Yes, my dear, Édouard is your father."

FORTY-FOUR

1906–1915

2 April 1906

Today was Oncle Gustave's funeral. I did not know him well, but he is my uncle, and it was only proper I attend. Pierre is in London on business and could not accompany me, so Oncle Édouard offered to take me in his carriage. It has been almost a year since M. Degas confirmed my true paternity, but I have said nothing of this to Oncle.

M. Degas explained that he had overheard Maman and Oncle discussing it when they were unaware he had come into the studio. He never told them, or anyone else, what he knew, which is quite amazing for a man who delights in gossip, particularly if it is risqué. I take this as a sign of his deep respect for Maman.

I told him I appreciated his silence, and that I would keep mine. Although I long to discuss this with Oncle, I recognize it is better this way. I fear if he and I declared to each other we were father and daughter, even privately, we might inadvertently give ourselves away and spark even greater speculation about our relationship. Just as Maman and Oncle sparked with theirs. I understand that Maman's reputation and the Manet name must be preserved at all costs. Yet it pains me not to be able to share our bond.

When Oncle arrived, I was pleased to see he was alone. Suzanne and Léon were going separately. He was very upset about Gustave's death, both because he has now lost his two brothers and because Grand-Mère is still alive and had to hear of yet another son's death. A Manet cousin is bringing her in a special carriage that is able to hold her wheelchair. On the way to the church, Oncle was nostalgic and told tales of his boyhood and the tricks he and his brothers had played on Grand-Mère, referring to Father as my father.

The funeral was as dark and dreary as the weather, and it was disagreeable to stand in the mud and rain at the graveside. Oncle raised his umbrella over both of us and put his arm around me to keep me warm. Tante Suzanne wore her usual scowl. Poor Grand-Mère was ashen, but she held her head high and did not cry. She is, as others have noted, made of iron.

My cousin Léon, who for most of my life has ignored me, walked along with us as we were leaving the cemetery, and he was surprisingly loquacious, dare I say even funny? He is much older than I am and is not actually my cousin. He is Tante Suzanne's brother, but was raised in Oncle and Tante's house after his mother died. Oncle and he are close, and that must be why he decided to be cordial to me.

Dear diary, I do not know why I said what I did once we were inside the carriage. It was unplanned and completely unexpected, especially to me. Perhaps it was Oncle's solicitousness. He asked the driver to bring me a towel to dry my hair and then requested another to cover the seat so the sogginess of my dress would be better absorbed. He pressed me close to fend off the damp and cold. I rested my head on his shoulder and told him I knew he was my father.

He froze for a moment, then said in a wavery voice, "Oh, child, if only that were true."

I sat up. "Monsieur Degas told me it is."

"Edgar knows nothing of this."

"There are many other signs." I pointed to my hair and stared into his eyes, begging him without words to acknowledge me. To claim me.

He bowed his head, kissed both of my hands, and pressed them over his heart. When he finally looked up, his expression a mix of longing, sorrow, and happiness, not dissimilar to Maman's expression in "Party," he said, "My darling, darling daughter, your mother and I wanted so much for us to be a real family. If only she were here with us now."

I told him maybe Maman was. Then we promised each other that this would be our secret, one we would take to our graves.

15 October 1906

It is with unbearable sorrow that I tell you, dear diary, that Oncle, Papa, did indeed take our secret to his grave, for he passed yesterday. Grand-Mère has now outlived all three of her children, and I am a true orphan, as bereft as any has ever been. We had just begun to revel in being father and daughter, even if we had to do this surreptitiously.

I lost my desire for painting six years ago when I realized I did not have the talent, but this past summer Papa enticed me to start again. I returned to his studio, although it was more to be near him than to paint. M. Degas, M. Renoir, and M. Monet all still work together there, annoying and encouraging each other as they always have.

I still have little talent, but this does not bother me as much as it once did, and I was happy just to play at it rather than work at it. Papa was thrilled I was enjoying myself, and I know he was also thrilled to be with me, sharing our knowledge with no one, even, ironically, M. Degas. We often found ourselves smiling at each other, something I now remember Papa and Maman did all the time. Which I suppose is why there were so many rumors.

Pierre, as always, is wonderful, and my darling Colette has been of great help, although she is too little to understand. She toddles toward me when she sees me crying and puts her tiny chubby hand on whatever part of me she can reach. She tells me not to be sad and that she will kiss my boo-boo and make it go away. If only this were possible. The cycle of life yet again.

24 October 1906

I am not going to speak of the funeral. I will now take comfort in my husband and child, and I will never paint again. It would be far too painful.

5 April 1915

I must smile as I reread my last entry, for I am painting once again after almost ten years. And this is why I am writing to you, dear diary, after such a lengthy pause. I have now begun to sit in front of

"Party on the Seine," Colette by my side, she with her crayons, and me with my pastels, just as I did with Maman, in this very room, and it would be my greatest pleasure if someday Colette were to do the same with her own child. I am teaching her as Maman and Papa taught me. She is using the first easel Papa made for me when I was her age.

I have lent "Party" out for a few Impressionist exhibitions and a one-man show of Papa's work, although only in Paris. There have been requests from many far-flung places, which I refuse because I can't bear to part with her for the amount of time required. And now that I'm painting "Party" with Colette, I plan to turn down further entreaties, as I have turned down all offers to purchase the painting.

For I do so love to see my daughter's face fierce with concentration as she tries to draw her grandmother's black curls, which are so similar to her own. She is ten now, something I have difficulty believing. It is impossible that so many years have passed. If only Maman and Papa were here with us, the family painting together. But maybe they are not as far away as I fear. Often they feel very close. Especially Maman.

1 May 1915

Unfortunately, both M. Pissarro and M. Sisley are no longer with us, but I still see M. Degas frequently. M. Monet and M. Renoir less so, but at least a few times a season. They are now all extremely successful, their work in enormous demand, and are often in London or Brussels or New York City for exhibitions. They are fêted throughout France, as is Papa, who is renowned as the Father of Impressionism, even though he never exhibited with the bande. It is marvelous that after all those years of hard work they are finally receiving the acknowledgment they deserve.

But I am sorry to tell you, dear diary, that Maman's acclaim is nowhere near theirs. Yes, there are still sales to collectors and a few to museums, but it is Manet, Renoir, Monet, and Degas who are considered the great Impressionists. The very men who sought Maman's advice and worked with her for so many years are exalted, while she is diminished. Dare I say forgotten?

I discussed this with M. Degas, and he granted it was a problem. He talked with the other artists, and they all agreed to speak highly of Maman's work to gallerists and collectors, to encourage her inclusion in exhibitions. Their efforts have resulted in additional shows and a smattering of sales, and I can only hope this is the beginning of a change.

12 September 1915

The strangest thing happened today as Colette and I were copying "Party." Colette was drawing the girl on the boat wearing a large red bow in her hair. Papa painted this bow with a series of staccato stokes that have little definition at the edges. Loose and flecked with light, more like Maman's than his, and it is clear that her work had a strong influence on him.

I smiled at my daughter and picked up my pastels, glancing at "Party" to get my bearings. As I did, it seemed as if Maman turned her head toward me, lifted her hand from the railing and pointed at Papa's signature. I blinked, looked over at Colette, who appeared to notice nothing out of the ordinary. Then, right before my eyes, Papa's signature vanished and Maman's replaced it.

I knew this was a quirk in my eyesight, which has always been less than ideal, but nevertheless I asked Colette if she saw anything unusual about the painting. She looked up for a quick moment, glanced distractedly at "Party," shook her head, and resumed her coloring. Then I asked her whose signature was at the bottom.

Clearly exasperated and focused on her own work, she told me it was Oncle Édouard's, just as it always had been.

PART SIXTEEN

Tamara, the present

FORTY-FIVE

I walk home from Calliope, numb, disbelieving. It's impossible, and yet there it is. Fired. Terminated. Gainfully unemployed. No job. No benefits. No income. There'll be a little money from selling my stock, but I'm not fully vested, so it won't be much. They'll have to give me some kind of severance, won't they? I've never been fired before, and maybe the rules are different. No unemployment in Massachusetts if you're fired for cause, I know that, but does that mean no severance or COBRA either? Will Tony even give me a recommendation? How can you recommend a person you've sacked?

I don't want to talk to anyone. Talking will make it true. Or more true. I wander in circles around the apartment, but it's too small for this to last long. I'm too nauseous to eat. No escaping into work. Can't focus on a book, and I hate watching television during the day. I could go to bed and pull the covers over my head, hide in sleep. But I won't be able to sleep. Too revved. Too angry. Too broke.

If I took Damien's millions, all my financial problems would disappear. I'd be able to live a life of pure hedonism, everyone's dream. But this is exactly why he got me fired—it had to be him—and I'm not about to hand him exactly what he wants, what he's been trying to destroy my life for. Ever.

I flop on my bed and close my eyes. I could always sue Calliope for wrongful termination, make them reinstate me and maybe get back pay. But that's a plan I can't afford even with the girlfriend discount. And anyway, do I really want that job back? I'll find a new one, a better one. I could start my own consulting firm. Or figure out what career #3 would look like. I'm not without options. This makes me feel a little better, and, surprisingly, I fall asleep.

When I wake, it's dark. I was supposed to meet Wyatt for dinner at seven.

It's eight. I run into the kitchen, retrieve my phone from my purse. There are three texts, three calls, three messages.

"I'm so sorry," I say as soon as he answers. Seems like I've been saying sorry a lot today.

"Where are you?"

"I'm, I'm home. I fell asleep."

"What's wrong?"

I explain, and he says he'll be right over.

"Damien wants me broke," I tell him when he arrives. "No job. No money for rent or for lawyers. No way to fight him."

Wyatt doesn't contradict me, but he doesn't agree with me either. Instead, he asks, "Have you eaten anything?"

"Breakfast."

"Let's go get some dinner—and a strong drink."

I lean my head on the back of the couch. "I'm never leaving this apartment ever again."

"How about I pick up some comfort food then? Italian? Or I could pop into Tatte and grab some decadent pastry?"

"I'm never eating ever again."

"That's what I like to hear. A positive attitude."

"Just call me Pollyanna."

"A movie, Ms. Pollyanna? A silly rom-com?"

I open my eyes and give him a dour smile. "All I want to do right now is wallow in self-pity—and for you to say 'poor baby' lots of times."

"Poor baby lots of times." He laughs. "Fair enough. If it's okay with you, I think I'll stick around for the pity party."

WHEN WYATT CHECKS his phone the next morning, he whistles. "Fucker."

I've barely slept all night, and I look up at him groggily. "Huh?"

He hands me the phone. It's an email from Delphine, the Manet Foundation's lawyer, reiterating that the twenty-nine mil is still on the table.

I jerk awake. "And when I refuse, what else is he going to do to mess up my life?"

"I don't know what else he's got, but the man is clearly on a mission. And willing to go in for the kill." He forces a smile. "Poor baby."

"Wah, wah, wah."

"I'll go into the office and see what I can find out. Whether he was behind the firing or just taking advantage of it—or maybe it was just a coincidence."

"No coincidence," I mutter.

He climbs out of bed and kisses my forehead. "Will you be all right alone, poor baby?"

"Okay, okay, enough with the 'poor baby.' I'm fine—or will be. Go." It's six thirty, the time I usually start my day. But I have no reason to start my day. I have no day. "I'll try to get some sleep. Tough night."

"I'm sure," he says, pulling on his pants. "I'll check in with you later."

As soon as he leaves, exhaustion overwhelms me and tugs me down into a fragmented sleep. I dream of an old house, lovely but tired. I'm in a shadowy room with a towering ceiling and large mullioned windows bordered by billowing old-fashioned velvet curtains. Berthe's paintings cover the walls: *Two Sisters on a Couch*, *The Mother and Sister of the Artist*, *The Cradle*, *Young Woman with a Parrot*.

Then I'm on the street, staring up at it from outside. It's ornate, four or five stories tall, with intricately carved wrought-iron balconies climbing the limestone facade across three of the floors. Window boxes filled with flowers. A grand, rounded entry door.

I'm back inside again, frantically trying to find a child, and growing more desperate, filled with fear. I call for her as I run along hallways. Up and down a wide stairway, up and down the narrow back stairs. Across a broad foyer with a mosaic floor that looks like one of Berthe's paintings. In and out of rooms streaked with sunlight. But she's not here. The house is dead, empty. Then I remember there's a basement.

I stumble down rickety stairs. A basement with a dirt floor, a ceiling so low I can barely stand. I push cobwebs from my face, from my mouth. Shout again. Barrels everywhere. A maze of barrels. Maybe she's hiding behind one. "Where are you?" I call over and over until my voice is a reedy rasp. "If I can't find you, we'll lose everything." But the basement is as dead and empty as the floors above.

When I wake, I'm covered in sweat. I roll over to the dry side of the bed and admonish myself again for my lack of creativity. Searching feverishly for something I've lost? Something I want to regain more than anything? Gee. My job. My life. My sense of self.

I take a shower, then go to the kitchen to make coffee. Just like any other morning: wash up, breakfast, off to work. After I choke down half a bagel, I go into the living room and flip open the box of pastels. As I sketch the flirty girl, I lose myself in my strokes, become only present in the moment, everything else gone. A gift.

When I resurface from my immersion, I blink. It's ten o'clock on a Wednesday morning, and I'm scratching pastel sticks on a pad of paper like a bored child home from school with a cold. I gaze at my exquisite *Party*. What if Damien succeeds? What if he takes her away from me? As I study her, it occurs to me that maybe I misinterpreted my dream. That it wasn't about me searching for myself—it was me searching for what I need to best Damien. In a house full of Berthe's paintings. Berthe's house? *If I can't find you, we'll lose everything.*

I LOOK UP Berthe Morisot's residences. Immediately, the screen is filled with a photograph of an opulent five-story house clinging tightly to a Parisian sidewalk: 40 Rue de Villejust. It has wrought-iron balconies and window boxes on three levels. Beneath the photo, it says that Berthe Morisot lived there for most of her life, passing it on to her daughter Aimée Manet Deniaus, who passed it on to her daughter, Colette Deniaus Bernheim.

I call Jonathan and tell him what I found, but not what led me to it. Dreams aren't hallucinations, so I suppose there's nothing to hide, but it's difficult to deny the supernatural undertones. Berthe's house, Aimée and Colette's too. The same house I ran through in a dream before I knew any of this. I try to keep my voice from giving away my turmoil. "We know the Nazis stole the artwork, so, so, do you think they could they have taken the house too?"

"Sure. They grabbed property, businesses, whatever had value—especially from Jews. Give me the address again. There might be some information on it in our archives."

"Thanks, pal. Appreciate it."

When I get off the phone, I look at the photograph on my screen, my heart hammering. It's all too weird. Impossible. And yet there it is. *Party* probably hung in that very house, maybe was even painted there. But, no, in order for everyone to believe it was a Manet, it would have been in his house. Berthe worked with the other Impressionists at Édouard's studio, so maybe she painted it there. But if that's the case, wouldn't the other artists have seen her working on it? So does that mean it *is* a Manet? And that I'm having a psychotic break?

"What's going on?" I ask Berthe.

No response. I'm losing it. Certifiably mad. Please help me, Berthe. Someone please help me.

The sound of my cell startles me. Jonathan.

"You working from home?" he asks. "Called your office, and your assistant said to try your cell."

I close my eyes. Another whack. Too much. I give him a quick account of yesterday's events.

"Well, that sucks," he says. "How about I come by after work and bring you a consolation dinner? I've found something that might cheer you up—but don't get too excited. Very preliminary, but at the least it'll distract you a little. What do you say?"

He arrives with a large pot and a loaf of French bread. Turns out he's made jambalaya, which he claims is the best antidote to melancholy. "Not chicken soup?" I ask.

"Didn't your mother teach you anything?" He frowns. "Chicken soup is for illness. Jambalaya is for stress."

I take the pot from him and place it on the stovetop. Then I pour us each a glass of wine, and we sit on the couch facing *Party*. "So what did you find out?" I ask, without giving him time to look at the painting.

"Not all that much. Just that 40 Rue de Villejust did belong to the Bernheims until they 'sold' it to a Heinrich Achenbach in 1940."

"No selling involved?"

"Turns out Achenbach was SS. A colonel or something like that—and although there are documents verifying the property changed hands, there are no records of money being transferred."

"Bastards."

Jonathan nods in agreement. "Achenbach disappeared right before Hitler committed suicide. Never seen again. Probably escaped to Brazil, where so many of his Nazi brethren were welcomed—and hidden."

"He just abandoned the house?"

"Probably figured his life was more important than a house he hadn't paid a penny for." Jonathan sighs. "There was a major housing shortage after the war in Paris—so many buildings had been bombed and ransacked during the fighting—and the city used anything that was still standing for people to live in. That's probably what happened to 40 Rue de Villejust, but any specifics about your house are nonexistent until the mid-'60s."

I wait as he scrolls through his phone. *Your house.*

"It was purchased from the government in 1967 and upgraded into nice flats by the Fournier family. They held on to it until the '90s, sold it, and then it was sold again a couple more times. Now it's owned by an Étienne Beaumont and has something like eight rental apartments."

"I can't believe you found all this out so fast."

He shrugs. "That's the Conference's mission. Been at it for decades, and the databases have grown quite extensive over time."

"So just another pilfered property to enter into the databases more than eighty years later."

"But it's property that might belong to you." He pauses. "And this is the part I thought would cheer you up—it's now my job to find out if it is."

"The Conference is going to investigate? You're going to investigate?"

"And if the house is yours, as I suspect, figure out how to get it back."

My mind is racing. Could I own a beautiful old building in Paris? What would I do with a beautiful old building in Paris? Sell it, undoubtably, but not before I search it. Granted, it's unlikely any family belongings would still be there after this long, but it's not impossible. And I need to follow every lead. Clutch at every crumb. The trial is less than three weeks away. "Will they send you to Paris?" I demand. Then I add, more levelly, "To check it out, I mean." Calm down, Tamara. Pull yourself together.

He throws me a questioning look. "Maybe, especially if the current owner is resistant—something that's common and makes perfect sense. This Mr. Beaumont bought a property he believed was legitimately available for sale—which it technically was—and now he's going to be told he has to give it up."

"Doesn't the German government pay for what's confiscated?"

"They do, but it can be a long negotiation. Sometimes decades. Especially when there's rental income involved."

"If you went over there," I say, straining to sound noncommittal, "would you have access to the building?"

"Probably. It's all part of the investigation process. Why?"

"Oh, I was just thinking, you know, that, that maybe I'd like to see the house where my ancestors lived." I wave my hand to show it's no big deal. "Now that I've got all this free time."

FORTY-SIX

Over jambalaya, which I struggle to eat because my stomach feels as if it's the size of a pea, I recount the sad Calliope saga: the fake whistleblower post, the hacked website, the firing, Damien's lawyer calling the next day to reiterate the offer. "My dear cousin is a real sneaky son of a bitch."

"Growing sneakier every day." Jonathan rips a piece of bread from the loaf. "Sometimes I'm almost sorry I contacted you."

"Why do you say that?"

"I know how much you love *Party*, but it seems like ever since you found out about it, there's been a kind of reign of terror. The lawsuit, the threats, the Louvre, the leaked info, this."

I nod, afraid if I look at him I might lose my tenuous grip and start to cry. "Damien's reign of terror."

"I'm sorry it's been so tough on you."

"Not like it's your fault," I say, swirling the wine in my glass, still avoiding his eyes. I'm moved by his concern, his obvious empathy. I suppose both are necessary for his job, but it also appears to be who Jonathan is. How would he react if told him about Berthe, about what's been happening with *Party*?

"I know it's not," he says. "I just wish I could do more to help you with the fallout."

I glance into the living room, hoping for a hint. *Party* is still. What a relief it would be to unburden myself. But if Dr. Zafón's tests indicate a mental illness, this confession would be horribly embarrassing. And yet if it's all in my head, why is it only *Party* that makes me hallucinate? Wouldn't I hear and see and smell imaginary things in other circumstances? This back-and-forth is crazy-making, probably both in the figurative and the literal sense. I need to get it off my chest. Hash it out. Jonathan is a thoughtful man, not one to race to fast conclusions.

"There's, there's something else, but I, I don't know . . ."

"Don't know what?"

I begin with Berthe's first wink, the dreams, the changes in the painting, the voice in my head, the violet perfume, the alternating signatures. He doesn't interrupt me, but there's a skeptical look on his face. "I know I'm probably seeing things that aren't there," I add, sidestepping. "Saying it out loud makes me realize how outlandish the whole idea is."

"Got to agree it's outlandish, but lots of things are both outlandish and true."

"Really?" I'm incredulous that he might take this seriously—relieved and horrified in equal measure. "You think this could be one of them?"

"I don't know. Do you?"

"No, no, it can't be. No." I shake my head vigorously. "But it, it feels real—and in its own weird way, almost deliberate."

"Deliberate how?"

I inspect my hands. "It's almost like Berthe is trying to tell me something. Has been from the start."

"Do you have any idea what that might be?"

"I think she painted *Party*," I blurt. "And, and she wants me to find proof of it. To tell the world."

"Which would make you the rightful owner."

"I don't think that's the point." I take a deep breath. "It's more about her rightful place in the art world. Or, or, I don't know what I'm saying, but what if she's actually haunting the painting?"

"I wouldn't go that far," he says quickly. "It's a pretty big leap of faith—especially when your vision isn't that good. But I think I told you before that my mother's side of the family is from Haiti. And lots of people on the island believe there's a strong link between the living and the dead. Sort of like ghosts, but more like the spirits of ancestors."

"Aren't those ghosts?"

"Not exactly." He gazes out the window. "They're not evil, not trying to scare you or get you to do anything. More like souls who are there to protect you. I guess."

"Berthe is my ancestor."

Jonathan holds up his hands. "My parents aren't into any of that stuff.

Mom really hates it all and converted to Judaism as soon as they got engaged—so my knowledge is pretty sketchy. Just visits to my grandmother every few years when I was growing up."

"Do you believe any of it?"

"No, but I suppose I'm more open to the possibility than a lot of other Westerners might be."

I pour us more wine, play with the stem of my glass. "The other night, I had a dream I was in an old house, frantically searching for something—for a little girl."

"And?"

"Again, it also sounds outlandish, but this was before I found out about Berthe and 40 Rue de Villejust. Before I saw pictures of it . . ."

"And?"

"The house in my dream looked a lot like the photograph I found on the internet."

THE NEXT MORNING, there's an email from Ruth. She received the test results from Dr. Zafón and wants to Zoom with me at noon. Even though I've been waiting for this for what feels like forever, now that the moment's here, I don't know if I can take any more bad news. I want to tell her I'm busy—and will be for the foreseeable future. But I don't.

"As I'm sure you discussed with Dr. Zafón, neither the MMPI nor the Rorschach diagnose a particular disease," she says when we connect. "They're used as backup, providing additional evidence to help a clinician do that."

I nod.

"Let's begin with the MMPI. Your profile is largely within normal limits, and that, along with the overall life history you reported, points to generally good psychological adjustment."

"Well, that's a relief," I say, although I don't like the qualifying words: "largely," "generally."

"Yes. There was one somewhat elevated score that reflects unusual psychological occurrences. In your case, this might be the hallucinations you reported."

"Are you saying I'm psychotic?"

"What I'm saying is that your score on that particular scale—which, remember, is only a single marker—could raise the question of an emerging psychotic process. But—and this is important to understand—it can also be interpreted as a reaction to stress. And from what you told me, you've been under a lot of that lately."

"So the results don't really tell you anything?"

Ruth laughs. "I wouldn't say that, because the scores suggest we can rule out a variety of psychological disorders. But you'll want to continue to track, in therapy, any additional experiences you might have."

"What about the Rorschach?"

"Again, like the MMPI, the results aren't definitive, but in my opinion, the interpretations need further consideration. First off, your cognitive functioning is very high, but some of your responses might be considered idiosyncratic and indicative of possible perceptual distortions."

"Which signifies what?"

"Again, it doesn't *signify* anything. It, along with the MMPI scores, point out possible avenues to explore in order to understand what's going on and how to manage it. For example, treatment options will differ depending on whether your experience appears to reflect a break from reality or is a reaction to stress."

Which basically means I'm no closer to knowing if I have a mental illness or a haunted painting.

AS JONATHAN PREDICTED, Étienne Beaumont refuses to consider selling the building. Despite discussions with the federal government, the Parisian authorities, and the German office of the Claims Conference, the man will not budge. Hence, Jonathan is scheduled to leave for Paris in a few days to try to change Beaumont's mind.

I ask if I can tag along, and I can hear the frown in his voice when he says, "I can't tell you not to, but I can tell you I believe the chances of finding anything in the house are close to nil."

There's not much to argue with here. "It's the 'close to' part I'm counting on," I offer weakly.

"It's not just the ghost piece that's weak—to say the least—but no one in your family has lived there in almost a century, and countless others have.

And then there are all the renovations the house has gone through. Again, it's your choice, but, the paranormal notwithstanding, the reality is that it's highly unlikely anything that belonged to them is still there."

Of course they haven't lived there for generations. Of course the fact I dreamed about a house that looks somewhat like Berthe's house means nothing. Of course the whole idea is madness. I try to talk myself out of it but fail, and I make a reservation for a nonrefundable flight to Paris, economy with no extras.

It leaves in the middle of the night, with a stopover in Iceland, and takes over ten hours. But it still costs a small fortune, as does the bare-bones hotel I choose in the 13th arrondissement. Jonathan warns me that everything in the city, especially food, is expensive, yet, once again, I tell myself that this is an investment in my future. Still, the doubts are there. And I'm afraid, even as I'm not sure whether I'm afraid of finding nothing or finding something. Bottom line: I'm a wreck.

"THIS IS PURE insanity," Wyatt says over dinner the night before I'm due to leave. That word—or variations of it—keeps popping up. And I don't like this at all.

"I know you think it's a bad idea," I say, as evenly as I can. "And maybe you're right, but I want to give it a try." I'd played with concocting a story about a visit to a college roommate somewhere out west, but I couldn't pull it off. So I told him the truth, but said nothing about meeting Jonathan over there.

"Waste of money," he mutters. "Waste of time."

"Seems I've got plenty of the latter these days." I'm immediately sorry I said this, because now he's going to tell me I may have the time but I don't have the money.

"You know I'm going to have to charge you at my regular rate when I'm in New York for the trial," he says. "So far I've been fudging my hours to charge you less, but the firm's rules about travel are unbendable. Full-time for at least two days, plus expenses, billed to your account. It's going to be costly."

"I'll pay whatever I owe," I say. Although I have no idea how I'm going to be able to do this.

"When you were bringing in a salary, you were always complaining about your student loans pulling you down. Credit cards."

I place my fork on the table. "Can we drop this, please?"

"I'm pretty sure we've got what we need to win," he says. "So it's not necessary."

"The trial is in less than two weeks. Is 'pretty sure' good enough? You're the one who's always urging me to investigate, to come up with more information. If I don't find anything, we're no worse off than we are now. But how huge would it be if I did?"

"Can you honestly tell me you believe you're going to discover something from the nineteenth century in some random old house? And that something is going to help our current case? What are you basing this on?"

"My research, books about Berthe living at 40 Rue de Villejust. About her daughter Aimée living there even after Berthe died, raising her daughter where she grew up. About that daughter, Colette Bernheim, doing the same until the Nazis stole it from her. Maybe there are clues there." As I'm speaking, I can see all the holes he's going to shoot into this.

"Clues? What kind of clues?"

"What if Berthe did paint *Party*? And what if I can find proof of it there? Then Damien's suit evaporates."

He blinks, stares at me. "It's like you're bewitched."

"Just because you don't believe there are other ways to get at the truth, that doesn't mean I can't."

"What other ways?"

"Like the photograph of the house. That it was Berthe's, Colette's too—and it could be mine."

"Whether the house belongs to you or not doesn't have anything to do with proving Berthe painted *Party*. Or with getting more evidence for the trial."

"I've just got a gut feeling about it," I say.

I'm beyond losing it. I'm lost.

PART SEVENTEEN

Colette, 1928–1941

FORTY-SEVEN

1928–1929

Since Colette was a little girl, she and her mother have whiled away many an afternoon sketching Grand-Oncle Édouard's painting, *Party on the Seine*. Now, years later, they sit at easels as they did then, beneath a wall of windows in what was originally Grand-Mère Berthe's studio at 40 Rue de Villejust, the house where Colette grew up and where Maman still lives.

When she was young, she used crayons, but now they both paint with pastels. Maman has told her about doing the same when she was a girl, but Grand-Mère died young, and after that, Maman painted by herself. It makes Colette melancholy to think of Aimée as a child, orphaned at thirteen, all alone in this room where her mother was, and still is, such a strong presence.

Colette would have thought she'd become bored copying the same scene so many times over, but that isn't the case. It's a brilliant work, full of life and light, a flat canvas that pulls you into a complex three-dimensional world. A boat gliding down the river, holding dozens of Parisians enjoying a sunny day, and yet it's so much more. Some are talking, some are eating, some are flirting. Men in high fashion and men in shirts without sleeves. Children, lovers, and among the crinolines and stylish hats of the wealthy are a few women wearing quite indecorous dresses that plunge deep at the neckline. So many stories to wonder about, so many lives to imagine.

A lone woman, with curling dark hair and burning dark eyes, leans against the railing and gazes out over the water, boldly staring at the viewer with an impenetrable expression. There is no story to wonder about here, as this is Grand-Mère Berthe, who was married to Édouard Manet's brother Gène, Colette's grandfather. All long dead before Colette was born. She wishes she could have known them, been a part of the expanding world her grandmother and great-uncle partially created. She glances over at Aimée, grateful to have this.

It's a soothing ritual, painting with Maman, which brings them closer to each other and to Grand-Mère Berthe, and these compatible moments have often led to their deepest conversations. Now that Colette is a married woman with a newborn daughter of her own, she foresees a future in which they will someday do the same with Genevieve. Three generations painting together. How lovely that will be.

Maman puts down her brush and wipes her hands on the towel hanging from her easel. "I hope you are planning to leave *Party* where she is when this house becomes yours."

Colette is not fond of what she considers her mother's morbid sensibilities. "That isn't happening for a very long time, so, no, I haven't given it much thought."

Until they find a suitable residence for their own family, Colette and Samuel are temporarily at his parents' grand home. The Bernheims have already bequeathed most of their extensive art collection to Samuel, and Maman has promised Colette almost all of hers when they find the right place. Which is why Colette has been having difficulty finding a house large enough to hold both of their collections.

The Bernheims are Jewish, although this is a small part of the family's life, and Colette is now also Jewish. As far back as she knows, the Manets, Morisots, and Deniauses have been Catholic, similarly unobservant, and Colette's conversion has changed little.

Despite their religion, the Bernheims' art tends toward the Renaissance, a good portion of it Christian in nature, while Colette's collection will be almost completely composed of works by the Impressionists, including many painted by Grand-Mère Berthe. There are others, mostly gifted to Grand-Mère by artists with whom she was friends: two Degases, four Monets, a Renoir, and, of course, a number of Manets. *Party* is the only painting Maman wishes to keep with her until she dies.

Colette prefers the verve and high color of the more current pieces to the dark tones and depressing subjects of the fifteenth and sixteenth centuries, which the Bernheims favor. Yet there is no doubt that her husband's collection is larger and more distinguished than her own. His two van Eycks alone are more valuable than all of her Impressionist paintings will ever be. Not to mention the small Rembrandt. Samuel comes from a long line of successful and philanthropic businessmen, all of whom had a tradition of supporting the arts.

"This is where *Party* belongs," Maman is saying. "She's been hanging on this wall ever since Oncle Édouard gave her to me almost twenty-five years ago, and she's been watching over us ever since. Such a comforting presence. Sometimes, seeing her up there, I imagine I catch a whiff of her perfume and almost feel as if your grandmother is still alive."

"Certainly, then, she'll stay right where she is," Colette assures her mother. Samuel has agreed that after Aimée's death, they will move their family to 40 Rue de Villejust, an event neither anticipates will happen anytime soon.

"I can hardly bear to think of any of Samuel's gloomy paintings in this house." Aimée gives an exaggerated shiver. "Promise me you'll hide them in dark corners and put none of them in this room. Especially not Federico Barocci's horrid *Madonna*."

"It's an important piece," Colette counters halfheartedly.

Her mother shoots her an amused look. "You dislike it as much as I do."

Mother and daughter smile fondly at each other and return to their painting.

A FEW MONTHS later, much sooner than Colette had imagined, the question of where *Party* will hang becomes more imminent. She holds Maman's frigid and blue-veined hand, tears running down her cheeks as she listens to the shallow breaths rattling her mother's chest. It will not be long, and Colette feels as if her insides are being wrenched out. What they'd assumed was only a head cold turned into pneumonia, and now it appears to have become lethal. It was the pneumonia that took Grand-Mère Berthe.

It is beyond sad that Genevieve will grow up without the kindness and love Maman would have showered on her. There will be no three generations painting together, and the little girl will remember nothing of her grandmother. Colette vows to do everything she can to keep Aimée alive for the child. And for herself.

Maman's eyes suddenly fly open, all vestiges of passing vanquished in her direct stare. "You must never sell *Party*." Her words are distinct and brook no argument.

"Never," Colette assures her, hope rising that despite the doctor's certitude her mother is taking a turn for the better. "But it won't be my decision for a long time. It's your painting, and you're going to recover and enjoy it for many more years to come."

"It must remain in the family," Aimée continues in the same strident tone. "It's your legacy. Genevieve's too."

Colette sits on the edge of the bed and grips both her mother's hands in hers. "I know, Oncle's work and Grand-Mère's likeness. I promise I'll protect it, along with the others, when it's my turn to do so."

Maman shakes her head furiously, and Colette is both startled and encouraged by the energy behind the gesture. "You misunderstand. It's your legacy in more ways than you know." Her voice becomes labored, clearly exhausted by her efforts. "More, more than any of the others, because . . ." She struggles for breath and then adds in a whisper, "Because it, it holds your grandmother's spirit along with a secret that can never be revealed." Aimée's eyelids drop as abruptly as they opened. Her face is ghostly pale, and her hands seem even colder than they were before. The rattling resumes.

"What secret?" Colette begs, although all she wants is to keep her mother with her. "What can't be revealed?"

But there is no more to be said.

IT IS CHRISTMAS Eve, and Colette sits with Genevieve in her lap, Samuel in the armchair next to her. They have moved into 40 Rue de Villejust, and as her mother asked, Colette has done her best to distribute the Bernheim paintings to lesser locations in the house. The family is now in the parlor, where almost all the artwork is by the Impressionists, although *Party* hangs downstairs in Grand-Mère's studio, as it had when Aimée was alive.

Colette and Samuel have been looking forward to Genevieve's first Christmas, to the gleam in their child's eyes as she gazes up at the sparkling tree. The fire roars and, as they hoped, the baby is completely entranced. Except it's the fire that fascinates Genevieve, rather than the tree. She hasn't even noticed it or the many colorful ornaments clinging to its wide branches. This amuses both of them.

They touch their small Pontarlier goblets together. The absinthe in the reservoir of her glass is a milky white, while his retains its green tone. The more water added, the cloudier absinthe becomes. She isn't particularly fond of the drink, but it's Samuel's favorite.

Samuel chuckles at Genevieve's lack of interest in the tree they spent such care trimming. "The first of many times our girl will surprise us," Samuel says with an affectionate smile for both his wife and his daughter. He is smitten with Genevieve, and it's clear to anyone who sees them together that he is equally smitten with Colette.

Colette blows a kiss at her husband. She's so fortunate in both of them. And she looks forward to their many years together in this magnificent house, now home to the third generation of Morisot women, enjoying their magnificent art collection and many more magnificent children. "I believe you are correct, my dear," she tells him. "It shall be a grand adventure."

FORTY-EIGHT

1934–1937

Now it's Colette's turn to copy *Party on the Seine* with her daughter in Grand-Mère's studio. She even dug up the small easel she used when she was a girl from the maze of Aimée's barrels still stored in the cellar. They sit together in front of *Party*, she with her pastels and the little girl with her crayons. The child is only six, but it's already obvious she has some of the family's artistic aptitude.

Genevieve grabs fistfuls of crayons, and sometimes using three of them at once, dashes off her version of the painting. "Arrière-Grand-Mère!" she shouts as she draws a flurry of curls with black and brown crayons clutched in her hand. Then she drops the two brown ones and focuses more closely on Berthe's eyes. With a few ill-defined dark strokes that leave tiny flashes of white, she manages to capture the puzzling expression in them.

"You're so good at this," Colette tells her. "Maybe you'll be a famous painter like your great-grandmother Berthe one day."

"I'm good at this!" she cries, and then closely considers *Party*. "Just like Arrière-Grand-Mère Berthe, who made it."

"She didn't paint it, darling. The artist was your great-uncle Édouard Manet."

"It was not!" Genevieve stamps her foot. "Arrière-Grand-Mère did it."

Colette pulls Genevieve into her lap, although the child is almost too big to fit. She wraps her arms around her precocious daughter, imaginative and creative in so many ways. If only she were able to have another child, but it has been six years, and she fears it may never happen. At least the one she has is a gem. She twirls one of Genevieve's curls around her finger. "And what makes you think your great-grandmother painted it?"

"She told me."

Colette laughs. "I didn't know you two spoke."

"She talks to me inside my head."

THE FAMILY HAS always been committed to sharing its art collection, loaning pieces to museums across Europe for shows and exhibitions. But Colette misses *Party* when it's gone, and tells Samuel she wants to stop lending it out.

"But that's what we do, my dear. The Bernheims have always been dedicated to supporting the community of the arts. Particularly museums."

"I wasn't suggesting that we stop our support. I'd just like to keep *Party on the Seine* with me. And Genevieve loves the painting so."

"I understand how much this painting means to you, but it's such a glorious work that it doesn't seem right to keep it to ourselves when it's possible for so many others to enjoy it."

"You're a much better person than I am, and I admit I may not be acting in the most charitable way. But it makes me so happy to be with her, and so unhappy when she's gone. Especially when the trips are long, like the last one to Munich."

"I'm not fond of what's going on in Germany anyway." He frowns. "That Hitler is more of a threat than anyone seems to want to acknowledge."

"But not to us here in France."

"We thought we were safe before the Great War." Then he clears his throat. "So what if we compromise and only lend it to Paris museums and just for important shows? The Louvre or l'Orangerie?"

His words about Germany give Colette pause, but she cannot believe there is any real danger to her family and agrees to his suggestion, hoping these requests will be few. But within a few weeks the Louvre approaches her about a special exhibition of Degas's and Manet's work to be called "The Impressionist Duo." It will be a four-week show, and they promise to transport *Party* to the museum two days prior to the opening and return it one day after closing. Colette consoles herself that the exhibition isn't until November, almost nine months away.

She and Genevieve still sit in the studio and copy *Party*, but Colette has found an art tutor for her daughter, and the girl has begun working on her own creations, some of which are astonishingly good. They are painting together quietly one Saturday afternoon when Genevieve points at *Party* and says, "Arrière-Grand-Mère doesn't want to go to the Louvre."

Colette stares at her daughter. "She told you this inside your head?"

Genevieve nods and turns back to her canvas.

THE SÉANCE WITH Mademoiselle Beauséjour is at Colette's house this month. She and eight other women of her circle meet every four weeks with the respected spiritualist, and much has been revealed over time. Jeanne learned that her departed mother was no longer angry with her for marrying beneath her station. Mademoiselle told Yvonne that she would be with child within a year, which she was. Through Mademoiselle's fingers on a Ouija board, Lya's little son reported that he was happy in heaven, so she shouldn't be sad. And then there was the time at Rachelle's home when the table under their fingers began to move on its own. Or so it seemed.

Colette is the most skeptical of the group, although Rachelle and Lena have also voiced doubts. Everyone else is a true believer, convinced whatever occurs at the séance is indisputable. While Colette would not claim this impossible, for no one can know all the answers, she thinks of these engagements as entertainment, akin to watching a magician or a theatrical performance. Samuel refers to the séances as her "frivolous afternoons," which is exactly what they are.

Today they are in Berthe's studio, as the upstairs rooms are being redecorated. Everyone is seated at a large table with ten chairs that the servants brought down earlier, and, as Mademoiselle had instructed, it's covered with a white tablecloth that hangs to the floor. Three lit candles sit in its center, and the drapes have been drawn.

Mademoiselle is dressed in a sinuous robe, twinkling with blue stars representing the constellations. She has placed two enameled pots at either end of the table, from which curls of incense swirl upward, filling the air with the musky smell of patchouli. The women hold hands, uniting the circle, and close their eyes as Mademoiselle begins her whispered chant.

"It is now time to rid our minds of earthly cares and open ourselves to what is beyond," she says. "Let the spirits know we wish to communicate with them. That we seek their guidance."

As always, the women do as she asks, for this is the ritual's preamble. Then they wait silently for Mademoiselle to fall into her trance. This happens quickly, her eyes focused somewhere far beyond the room, her breathing even. "Join us, oh worthy and wise ones," she says in a much deeper voice than her usual timbre, closer to a man's, which is how she speaks when she's in a trance. "We welcome you into our séance, ready to receive your messages and insights."

Suddenly, she wrenches her hands from the others' and jerks to a stand, something she's never done before. She clutches the clasp at the top of her robe. "No!" she shouts in her normal voice, also highly uncommon. "Do not come here. Leave us this very moment!"

The women look at one another, both anxious and excited. Colette wonders if this is a response to an actual spirit or a new act the medium has mastered. But as she watches Mademoiselle's face drain of color and her eyes bolt to every corner of the room, she can't help but think it might be real. Mademoiselle is usually more tempered, speaking in a measured way. She never shouts, never appears disturbed.

Then Mademoiselle turns abruptly, as if pushed, and stumbles toward *Party.* She raises her hands to her ears, her expression akin to the man in Edvard Munch's *The Scream.* She backs away from the painting until her shoulders hit the far wall. "She, she says she will not go to the Louvre," Mademoiselle croaks, then looks at Colette, her eyes full of terror. "Do you know what this means?"

"No, not at all," Colette says. It is as if the floor has dropped out from under her, as if all that is solid in her world is disintegrating.

Mademoiselle Beauséjour is shaking visibly. "She, she says she cannot be considered a Manet. And can never be. That if this happens, she will not be accountable for the consequences." The medium steadies herself against the table. "I must take my leave, ladies. I, I am not well."

That same afternoon, Colette informs the museum that she is very sorry, but *Party on the Seine* will not be available for the exhibition.

FORTY-NINE

1940–1941

Samuel comes home from work early, his face pasty white. Colette rushes to him. "What's wrong? Are you ill?"

He collapses into his armchair and drops his head into his hands.

"Should I call Dr. Auclair?"

"No," he mumbles. "Nothing like that."

She kneels by his chair. "Then what?"

"You and Genevieve must leave Paris immediately. I've arranged for papers and transportation. Colleagues in London—"

"We're not going to London or anywhere else without you."

"It's all been planned. Once you arrive, some of my business associates will meet you and help you get settled. I'll join you as soon as I've put our affairs in order here."

Germany now occupies France and is pushing its way across Europe in an attempt to conquer the continent, an effort that is succeeding at a frightening pace. The Bernheims' quiet life, as well as the lives of everyone in the country, has been upended by the occupation and the fear of what might be to come. Rumors abound about the implementation of anti-Jewish laws similar to those passed in Germany, but as far as Colette knows, none have been enacted. Now she sees she has been a fool to dismiss Samuel's earlier concerns.

"The Germans?" she whispers.

He raises his head and nods.

She reels back on her heels. "But, but the French government will never allow those thugs to do the things here that they've done in their own country," she says, grasping at the possibility. "That can't happen."

His eyes are red-rimmed and bloodshot. "There is no French government any longer. At least not as we knew it. It's the Germans who make the rules now. All the laws. And they're in charge of enforcing them, along with that damn Vichy regime in the south, which is in lockstep with the Nazis."

Colette has never heard Samuel swear before, and she's astounded as much by this as by what he's saying. *Lockstep with the Nazis. No French government.* She clutches at the locket around her neck and takes the chair next to his, her legs unsteady.

"There's been talk that a Commissariat Général for Jewish Affairs is being created," he continues. "To write laws restricting our rights, including property and citizenship. I was skeptical about this, but now I know it's true."

"But these laws can't be aimed at us," she protests. "The Bernheims are an esteemed Parisian family, and have been for generations. As is my side, the Manets, Morisots, and Deniauses, none of whom are even Jewish."

Samuel pulls an envelope from his jacket pocket and hands it to her. "My associate, Lucien Desrosiers, a Christian, was recruited against his will to the Commissariat Général. He passed this to me in secret this morning. He said it's only a draft, but assured me it will soon be finalized. And executed."

Colette pulls four pages from the envelope. The first is a document entitled "Seizure Decree," the words surrounded by a circle of swastikas. It's an order for the confiscation of the art collection of Samuel Bernheim. The other three pages list all the individual works they own, along with a startlingly complete and detailed description of each piece and its estimated value.

"How, how do they know all of this?"

He stares out the window and says in a voice void of emotion, "Records, informants, intimidation, violence."

"But they can't just come into our house and take what's ours. What isn't theirs. It's against the law." As soon as she says this, she realizes how infantile she sounds.

Samuel runs his fingers through his hair.

"They're, they're going to make theft legal?" she stammers.

"If they're stealing from Jews, it's not illegal. It's been happening in Germany and Austria, and there are stories of much worse." Samuel looks as if he's aged a decade since breakfast this morning, and it's clear he believes everything he's saying. Her husband is not a fatalistic man, and his words terrify her.

She scans the walls of the parlor, at the priceless pieces in this single room. And there are so many more throughout the house, including *Party*. "We must hide them then. We have Christian friends who will help us. Our vault at the bank. My aunt's summer house in Arles."

"There isn't time. It's more important to save ourselves than it is to save paintings."

She's shaken that he would consider leaving their art collection unprotected. "The Germans are awful people, but they aren't going to hurt us. We're civilians. We're nothing to them."

"Ah, my innocent shiksa." He smiles at her forlornly. "I wanted to marry you because I loved you so much, but given the times, it's clear that because I loved you I should not have done so."

Now Colette is truly afraid. "Is Genevieve in danger?"

"That is why you both must go to London."

"If we don't have time to save them all, I'll at least take *Party* with me."

Samuel starts to shake his head, thinks better of it. "We must begin packing immediately. The travel documents will be delivered tomorrow night, and the car will arrive before dawn the following morning."

THEY KEEP GENEVIEVE home from school the next day. She's thirteen and full of questions. Samuel is at his office, and it falls to Colette to try to answer these in a way that won't frighten the child. Which is difficult.

Colette is trying to decide which winter clothes to leave behind because Samuel said they could each bring only one suitcase, when Genevieve stomps into her bedroom. "Why can't we stay here?" she demands.

"It's only for a short time, darling, and we'll be back home before you know it," Colette says. "Think of this as a surprise holiday. An adventure."

But Genevieve is not having it. "Is this because of the Germans?"

"Partially," Colette says, not wanting to lie. "They're doing terrible things in France, and Papa and I think we'll all be better off in England, where the Germans can't reach."

"Why can't they? They have boats and planes."

"But they aren't there now." She opens her arms to offer the girl a hug, but Genevieve steps away.

"Why isn't Papa coming with us?"

"You know how busy he is, how much work he has to do. It's not as easy for him to leave as it is for us. He'll join us in London as soon as he can. It shouldn't be very long."

"If it's not long, why don't we just wait for him and go together?"

Colette grabs Genevieve by the shoulders. "I know you don't want to leave school and your friends, but this is what we're going to do. And it will be much easier on all of us if you accept this and finish sorting your things. Nelly will be there to help you soon."

Genevieve wrenches herself from her mother's grip and trudges off to her room, where she proceeds to slam drawers. Colette is relieved that at least she's packing.

By the time Samuel arrives home, their suitcases are waiting in the foyer, and the butler has wrapped *Party* for travel. No one eats much dinner, and there's little conversation at the table. When their dinner plates are removed and dessert served, Samuel clears his throat.

"There is no reason to worry," he tells them. "Everything is finalized for your trip, and I've leased us a lovely apartment in Mayfair, not far from Hyde Park. It's already furnished, and I'll meet you there within the week." His smile is strained. "So our separation will be short."

Genevieve starts to cry and climbs into her father's lap, more six-year-old than thirteen. It amazes Colette how she can shift from a young woman to a child and then back within minutes. "It will be as if I'm on a business trip, Pumpkin," Samuel reassures her, and Genevieve's sobs grow louder at her father's use of his nickname for her. "Not even enough time to miss me."

Colette wishes she could cry and crawl into Samuel's lap too, but of course she can do neither. "Think about how much fun we'll have in London, Genny. Plays, museums—" She's interrupted by a loud crashing at the front door, followed by the sound of breaking glass.

They all jump to their feet, and Samuel turns Genevieve toward the kitchen door. "Tell Cook I said to hide you," he whispers. "Someplace no one will find." Then he gives her a little push.

To Colette's great relief, the girl goes without argument. Then Colette snatches up the third place setting and throws it into a breakfront drawer.

"Good thinking," Samuel says. "Now you go too."

Another bang, even louder than the first, reverberates under their feet. Shrieking wood. Angry male voices. Boots.

"Run," Samuel orders. But before she can, half a dozen armed men wearing Nazi uniforms, covered with swastikas and medals, swarm into the dining room. Samuel stands in front of her, squares his shoulders, and says, "I am a French citizen, and this is my home. Therefore I must ask you to leave."

"Not anymore you're not." A large man with at least six rows of medals across his chest chuckles. "Jews are no longer citizens of France. You have no more status than a dog." He looks around at his men and grins. "Even less. A dog has some value to his master, companionship, hunting, but you and your brethren have less than none."

His comrades howl in appreciation, and the officer pauses in feigned contemplation. "Although I must admit that some of your women are quite juicy."

Colette cringes behind Samuel, clutching his waist. How can this be happening? Such vileness. Such hatred. Spewed against her kindhearted husband, her little daughter. Herself. Is she going to be raped? Killed? Genevieve.

"I still must ask you to leave," Samuel says, his voice strong, unruffled. "You are on my property, and you are not welcome."

"Not your property either." The man waves a sheet of paper at Samuel. It's printed on parchment and is the official version of the seizure decree his friend Lucien gave him. When Samuel makes no move toward it, the men raise their guns and point them at him. Then the man pushes the decree into Samuel's chest. "Take it!"

It drops to the floor, but Samuel doesn't move.

"Do what he says," Colette begs.

The men form a circle around them, press in closer. One of them, a boy, actually, his eyes hard and pale as a white marble, rams his gun into Samuel's temple. "Pick it up, Jew!" he orders.

Samuel bends gracefully, picks up the paper, and then stands tall again. He doesn't look at it.

"Read it!" the officer roars. "Out loud, so we can all hear how far you've fallen!"

Samuel calmly does. When he finishes, he and Colette are tied onto chairs facing in opposite directions, unable to see each other and too far apart to communicate. Then the Germans proceed to ransack the house. They pull paintings off the walls, sculptures from their niches, then take each one to their leader, Lieutenant Colonel Heinrich Achenbach, so he can check it against his list.

They bring Colette's jewelry box down from the bedroom and dump it out at her feet, grinning wildly as they scoop up the pieces and stuff them into their pockets. Necklaces, bracelets, earrings, pins, gemstones, silver and gold, family heirlooms, and presents from Samuel. But all Colette can think of is Genevieve, hiding, terrified and alone. Don't find her. Don't find her. Pease don't find her.

Achenbach yells to his charges not to forget the wrapped painting in the foyer.

Colette has been able to maintain her composure, to follow Samuel's example and remain stoic and silent, but the thought of her beloved *Party*, the one thing her mother begged her to never part with, being carried away by their grimy hands is too much, and she moans.

An older German, the buttons of his uniform stretching to contain his girth, places a gun on her collarbone and moves it with a gentle, tickling motion. "One of your special paintings? Please do not fear, my dear, as I promise we will take very good care of it." Then he jerks the gun hard up against the bottom of her chin.

She whimpers, closes her eyes. But instead of shooting her, he bursts out laughing and pulls the gun away. "Got ya!" he cries, and laughs even harder.

Colette slumps into the chair, furious and humiliated. If they're going to kill her, just do it. But their evil is too deep for that. For in their depraved minds, it's more fun to terrify and belittle their victims than to kill them. Or to terrify and belittle them before they kill them. She bows her head. Her poor baby girl.

After what seems like hours, Achenbach comes back as the last of their art collection is being carried out the door. He stands with his legs wide and scrutinizes the two of them. "Today is my wife's birthday, and we're having a little celebration with our children this evening."

Colette gawks at him. What now? He pulls a knife from his boot, and it crosses her mind that being shot would be much better than being stabbed to death. What a bizarre thought. Probably her last. Again, she closes her eyes. Then, to her immense surprise, he slices through the ropes holding them to their chairs. She and Samuel run into each other's arms.

"My wife is a very charitable woman," Achenbach muses. "So in her honor, I've decided not to kill you." He eyes their grand, if denuded, home. "And now that I think about it, this house will make a perfect birthday present for her," he adds, and strides out the broken front door.

As soon as they're certain he's gone, they rush into the kitchen, searching for Genevieve. They call her name. Call again. Call for Cook.

Silence. The servants have fled.

Frantic, they rush up and down both the front and back stairs, through every room, every floor, their voices raw with fear. Then Samuel grabs her arm. "The cellar."

The cellar is dark and dank, with a dirt floor and a low ceiling. It's cluttered with many generations of Morisot and Bernheim castoffs, barrel after barrel of them. As Colette gropes her way down the wobbly steps, she yells her daughter's name. "Genevieve!" she yells again when she reaches the bottom.

"Maman!" a small voice cries, and Colette falls to her knees. Samuel runs past her, following the sound, and scoops the child up in his arms. Tears stream down both their faces as he carries Genevieve to her mother.

THE TRAVEL DOCUMENTS arrive later that evening, and at dawn the three of them climb into the car Samuel ordered for two and hold on to each other in the back seat. Three suitcases are in the trunk, but no *Party*. They arrive in London the following afternoon, but stay for only a few months, bombing raids driving them from the city. The United States is still accepting a few Jewish immigrants and, with the last of their money, they secure passage on a ship to New York City.

After a rough crossing, which renders them all horribly seasick, Colette and her little family travel by train to Norwich, Connecticut, where they are met by Samuel's cousin, Clara. Clara is horrified by how emaciated they are, and she proclaims that she will spend the next month fattening them up. She settles them into a room in her boardinghouse and proceeds to cook and feed them day and night. Her husband, Harry, offers Samuel a job in his jewelry store.

Their wealth, property, and art collection may be gone, but Colette is so grateful they are alive and together that this matters little. It's not a bad life, but she recognizes that neither she nor Samuel will ever completely recover from the trauma, although she hopes Genevieve will. Colette also knows that, for her, the loss of *Party* will be a gaping wound that will never heal.

PART EIGHTEEN

Tamara, the present

FIFTY

The next evening, I pack a carry-on and arrive at the eerily quiet airport at eleven. I'm the last group to board—as the cheap seats always are—and find myself two rows from the back of the plane. I congratulate myself on somehow managing to snag an aisle, but my pleasure fades when it becomes clear a near-constant queue waiting for the bathroom will be hovering over me for much of the flight.

Can you honestly tell me you believe you're going to discover something from the nineteenth century in some random old house? And that something is going to help our current case? Wyatt.

An emerging psychotic process. Ruth.

Lots of things are both outlandish and true. Jonathan.

It's noon when I clear customs at Charles de Gaulle, and then I have to wait an hour for a taxi. The ride to the hotel takes forever and gobbles a sizable bite of my newly acquired euros. When I arrive, grimy and exhausted, they inform me my room won't be available for at least another three hours. The lobby is cramped and poorly lit, and even though I'm in Paris, the wondrous City of Light, I don't have the energy to go anywhere else. I sit down in a lumpy chair and immediately fall asleep.

A small woman with stunning black hair shakes me and hands me a key. I stumble up two flights of stairs, traverse a dark hallway, and manage to find my room. It's better appointed than I expect, although certainly not luxurious. But I don't really care, as all I want to do is climb into the bed.

When I wake it's three in the morning, dark and quiet, and I can't fall back asleep. I take a shower and hang up a couple of shirts. Then there's nothing else to do. I can't call Jonathan until at least seven, as he's been here for a while and is presumably beyond jet lag. I'm simultaneously wired and wiped out, so I lie back down and stare out the single window, which I hadn't closed the drapes over yesterday. Not much to see except the darkened panes of a building about fifteen feet beyond my own. Despite knowing better, I have a deluded sense of optimism about this. "Deluded" being an apt descriptor.

My sliver of hope dissipates when I talk to Jonathan. "The Parisian office of the Claims Conference has been helpful," he says, "but Beaumont refuses to allow us into the property."

"Can he do that?"

"Not indefinitely, but it seems he's going to try everything he can to drag it out."

"More than a couple of days?"

A pause. "Could be."

"Damn," I say, and my voice catches. I have only two days here. Eleven until the trial.

"Look, I have a breakfast meeting with the director of a historical commission that's been documenting looted assets forever. Worked with her before, and she's had a lot of success at returning confiscated property."

"Can she help you get into the house?" Meaning can she help *me* get into the house?

"They have a good relationship with the city authorities."

"And the city will force him?"

"It's possible. I've got to run, but how about we meet in the entry hall of the National Library at noon? It's right around the corner from your hotel. Can't miss it—a bunch of glass towers, considered a modern marvel. And there's a good café."

I BARELY HAVE any memory of arriving yesterday, and now I look around. Despite my edginess, I'm charmed by both the hotel and the bohemian neighborhood surrounding it. Cobblestone streets cluttered with narrow buildings pressing into one another. Residences, hotels, boutiques, restaurants and bars, modest local groceries, and bakeries. The hotel has a small restaurant with tables under a red awning—how French—so I sit on the sidewalk, sip an espresso, and partake in Parisian tourists' favorite ritual: people watching.

When I finish breakfast, I head to 40 Rue de Villejust. I shouldn't have had that second cup as my nerves are already in high gear. I'm on my way to Berthe's home. Where she lived and painted. Where Aimée and Colette grew up and then created their own households. Three generations of Morisot women, my grandmothers times four, three, and two. How extraordinary. My spirits rise.

Following my GPS, I spend almost two hours making my way through the avenues of Paris. Finally, I turn a corner, and there it is, right across the street from me. I gape, press my back against the fence encircling a small park. It's hard to breathe. The house looks just like the one in my dream. I stare, try to reclaim my equilibrium. Limestone-clad. Friezes under the mansard roof. Multiple sets of French doors opening onto wrought-iron balconies that stretch across three floors, large and small, all ornate. I'm gripped by a sense of being lifted above the scene—the house, me standing before it. Impossible. Impossibly so.

Then a wave of pleasure flows through me. After growing up with no extended family or heritage, here it is: my roots. If only *Party* were with me now so I could tell Berthe where I am, let her know that, despite the uncanny circumstances, I feel as if I've come home.

An elderly woman clutching an oversized purse steps from the massive, rounded main door. I swiftly cross the street, hoping to slip in before it closes or at least catch a glimpse into the entryway. But the heavy door swings back into place, and the lock clicks before I reach the sidewalk.

I move back and look up at the towering facade. Jonathan said the building had been cut up into eight apartments, some of which must have stunning classical details, although I get the sense from the peeling paint and the chips on the front stoop that most will be tired. My heart pounds. Is it possible this house could be mine? That Berthe led me to it?

One of the photographs online showed a large garden in the back. Because it's a town house with outside walls flush with its neighbors', the garden isn't visible from where I'm standing. I head around the block and find an alleyway, running between the houses on Rue de Villejust and those on the street behind it.

No one is about, and I nonchalantly saunter through it, my breathing growing easier. I stop at the rear of 40. There's a tall fence of green latticework hiding the house, but a few slats are broken and I peer through. The garden remains, ill tended and overgrown, but the brick walkways and raised flower beds are still as they must have been when Berthe lived here.

There's a wall of windows overlooking it, and I have no difficulty picturing her standing inside in front of her easel, palette and brush in hand.

An angry dog barks behind me. I back away from the lattice as a man struggles to keep his German shepherd from lunging at me. He frowns as his eyes sweep suspiciously over my jeans, T-shirt, and running shoes, an outfit that screams "Tourist." Nosy tourist, at that. I smile and nod as pleasantly as I can, then walk quickly in the opposite direction. The dog growls. I move faster.

Everything tells me this is a fool's mission, that I'll soon be staggering home, empty-handed, humiliated and even more broke than I was before. Sitting in Ruth Hawthorn's office while she tries to figure out which particular type of psychosis I suffer from. The appropriate treatment options.

I TAKE A bus to the library, which as Jonathan promised, is easy to find. Four steel-and-glass towers rise above the district, sleek and translucent. I cross a wide plaza and into the entrance hall that forms the base of all the towers. It's full of light with soaring ceilings and a jumble of activity, yet another Parisian wonder. I'm early, and I try to calm myself by wandering.

Each of the four buildings has its own atrium, with even more sun cascading through floors of bookshelves and glass-fronted reading rooms. I discover elevated walkways connecting different parts of the towers and marvel at the views into the interior spaces and outward to the city and river. Still, it all weighs heavy.

At noon, I meet Jonathan back in the entry. I throw my arms around him in a tight hug, holding on for too long, trying to blink back my inexplicable tears before he can see them. I want to clutch onto his solid self, an anchor in the buffeting sea of my raging emotions.

He holds me until I let go. "You okay?" He scans my face.

"Fine," I manage. "Just jet-lagged, I guess."

He touches my back as we're led to a table, guiding me as you might an unsteady child. When we sit, he says breezily, "Told you this was an incredible place, didn't I?" But the concern etching his mouth belies his cheerful small talk.

"Got a chance to walk around for a bit. Amazing." I focus on placing the napkin on my lap. "How did your meeting go?"

He hesitates. "Overall, it went well."

I look up. "Overall?"

"Sophie's group is more involved with art and cultural artifacts than with real estate."

"She won't be able to help?"

"Not specifically, but she set up an appointment for me with a guy who handles restitution for commercial and residential properties. It's later this afternoon, so hopefully we can get moving soon."

We're interrupted by the waiter. Jonathan orders a baguette with tuna, anchovies, olives, and a hard-boiled egg—which sounds awful to me—and I opt for a salad that I don't really want, as I have no stomach for food. The server leaves, and I say, "I went to the house."

He leans back in his chair. "Did it look like it did in your dream?"

I nod but don't meet his eye.

"And?"

I try to sort through my reactions. "I, I couldn't believe it. How could I have dreamed it before I ever saw it? Weird, scary. I was freaked, still am, but it was also kind of nice. Like being with the family I never knew I had." I laugh, if a bit hollowly. "Or, more correctly, the ghosts of that family."

He gives me a probing look, likely trying to determine whether I mean metaphorical or actual ghosts. "That all makes sense," he finally says. "It's such an odd situation, bizarre on so many levels."

I lean forward. "What if there's nothing inside?"

"You're a tough woman, Tamara. Look what you've been through these last few months, what you've come through. If there's nothing there, there's nothing there. You'll keep fighting Damien—and, hopefully, win—and now we've got your ownership of 40 to pursue. Most likely another win."

"What if there *is* something inside?"

He laughs heartily. "See? You just proved my point. Survivors survive."

"Thank you," I say, and our eyes lock. "You're a generous man."

"And here I thought you liked me because of my stunning good looks."

I feel a tingling that surprises me, although it probably shouldn't. "That too." I reposition my napkin and tell him I'm going to the Louvre after lunch to see some of Berthe's and Édouard's paintings.

He's suggesting other pieces I shouldn't miss when my phone rings. Wyatt. I start to turn the ringer off, then reconsider. "Sorry, it's my lawyer. He might have some updates, so I need to take this." Then I remember Jonathan knows my lawyer is also my boyfriend. Awkward.

"Yes, it's important to talk to your lawyer," he says with a straight face.

I accept the call. "Hey, is this important, or can I get back to you? I'm in a meeting with someone from the Claims Conference."

"Nothing urgent," Wyatt says. "Just wondered how your trip was going and if you'd found anything yet."

"In the process," I assure him. "Busy afternoon. I'll call you later."

"Also wanted to tell you I miss you."

"That's good. Sure. Talk then." As I put the phone back in my purse, heat rises into my cheeks.

Jonathan lifts an eyebrow.

I stab my fork into the salad. "No news."

I TAKE A taxi to the Louvre, and along the way I check the museum's website for its Morisot and Manet holdings. There are eleven paintings by Berthe in their collection and ninety-two by Édouard. As I skim the Manet entry, I see that portraits of Édouard by other artists are included on his list, but still the numerical imbalance is glaring. As it was at MoMA.

There are only three Morisots on display. But at least thirty Manets hang on the walls, including *Olympia*, which caused such a stir in his day; *Luncheon on the Grass*, also a painting that outraged the public; *The Absinthe Drinker*; and yet another version of *Execution of Maximilian*—this one much larger than the two I've seen before, but no more appealing. With the exception of *Maximilian*, Édouard's paintings are truly amazing, the in-your-face satire of *Olympia* and *Luncheon*, the deep shadows of tall-hatted *Drinker*. But they are all representational, created with tight strokes, and none bear more than a passing resemblance to *Party*.

I spend most of my time with Berthe. *The Cradle* is one of her most famous, a picture of her sister Edma with her newborn baby, the child covered by the partially transparent netting hanging from the top of the cradle, light streaming through it and falling on the little girl's face.

The Harbor at Lorient is equally remarkable, and I take a number of photos of it, as the play of sun on the water resembles the rendition of the river in *Party*. *Young Woman in a White Dress* is another example of her ability to capture the subtleties of fabric and sunlight. Further indication, if I needed any, that Berthe is not getting her due. Even in her own hometown.

Since *Party* arrived, my main motivation has been to retain ownership of her, lately by proving Berthe's artistship. But now my desire to resurrect Berthe's reputation as an Impressionist—equal to or better than the rest—has grown almost as pressing. It occurs to me that if all goes well, I could be the one to establish a Berthe Morisot Foundation. I go back to the hotel and wait to hear how Jonathan's meeting went.

When I get there, the concierge hands me an envelope with my name on it. It's from Damien.

> I wish to reiterate that our offer still stands. The trial is fast approaching, and as we have received no notification from your attorney that you have any proof that Party on the Seine rightfully belonged to the Bernheims, I respectfully remind you that your chances of success are negligible.

FIFTY-ONE

I text Jonathan and give him a quick summary of Damien's note, including the telling fact that it was delivered to my Paris hotel—which was obviously the point.

Il pleut de la merde, as they say here, Jonathan texts back. I don't know what that means, but then he apprises me: *It's raining shit.* He adds that he's on his way to my hotel, and suggests we meet for a drink at the café off the lobby, as he has dinner with colleagues in an hour.

When he arrives, he sits in the chair across from me and holds out his hand. I give him the piece of paper, and he reads it. Then he reads it again.

"So nice of him to inform me of what I already know," I say.

"I doubt that was his intention."

"He knows everything I do. Wherever I go." I'm aware Damien must have had someone following me in Boston, but to know he's doing the same in Paris is somehow even more unnerving. Logically, it should be the other way around—this is his city, after all—but that's not what it feels like. "It creeps me out."

Jonathan covers my hand with his. "Of course it does, especially after the other things he's done." His hand is darker and larger than mine, warm and comforting.

I don't need any additional complications in my life, but I don't pull away. "If he knows I'm here—and why—do you think he could be the one behind Beaumont's refusal to let you into the property? Bribing him to spite me?"

"Doesn't seem worth his time."

I grimace. "Many things don't seem to be worth his time."

Jonathan takes his hand away, and I miss the connection. "Well, my meeting went well with the guy from real estate restitution, Oliver Moreau. He said there are ways to get around difficult owners—backed by both international and French laws."

"What if Damien is paying the owner to resist?"

"Even if he is, it shouldn't matter. The French were complicit in the deportation and murder of tens of thousands of Jews, as well as lots of others. So after the war, the government passed heavy-duty legislation to try to assuage their guilt—and to bury their Nazi collaboration under good deeds. Including funding. Some of the laws here are almost as stringent as the ones enacted in postwar Germany."

"And this Oliver thinks he can get Beaumont to let us in?"

"He does. And the Conference authorized him to begin right away."

"How soon?"

Jonathan shakes his head, but his eyes are twinkling. "You're going to give yourself a heart attack before this is over."

Which I'm forced to acknowledge is a distinct possibility.

I ONLY HAVE tomorrow and part of the next day here, and I don't have the money to stay longer. I've no idea what the penalties might be for changing my flight, but I do know this hotel, second-rate as it may be, is far from cheap. And then there's the whole Damien mess. He has someone prying into my whereabouts, and he wants me to know it. Flexing his muscles in an attempt to scare me into submission. Sorry, cuz, I'm not the submitting type.

I call Wyatt but don't say anything about Damien's note or the owner's stubbornness. Instead, I explain to him that the Conference is arranging for a restitution expert to facilitate my ownership argument, and that I hope that I'll be able to get inside tomorrow. Then I tell him about the amazing artwork I saw at the Louvre.

He's not particularly enthusiastic about my art adventures, and he cuts me off to remind me that we should be fine even when—he quickly changes "when" to "if"—I find nothing. He still has no idea Jonathan is here. And, based on his response when they met, I'm not about to enlighten him.

I sleep better than I expect, but at five in the morning I'm wide awake with no chance of dozing off again. I search the websites of the Musée d'Orsay and the Musée de l'Orangerie, both with extensive collections of Impressionist art. Which one should I visit first? I check their collection databases and find inequities similar to the Louvre's in their holdings of Berthe versus Édouard. I'll show them—I won't go to either one. I'm sure they'll take this as a significant insult and promptly rebalance their collections.

As soon as the hotel's café opens, I go down. It's chilly this early, but at least there's elbow room and something to look at besides the back of a building. There's a booklet in the lobby for a hop-on-and-off bus that circles the city, which sounds like fun, although the price is high: fifty euros for the day. It's my third visit here, but one can never get enough of Paris. This is what credit cards are for, and I promise myself I'll begin my true frugal life when I get home.

It's a beautiful spring afternoon, Paris at its best. I once again visit the opera house, Notre-Dame—which I haven't seen since its restoration—the Arc de Triomphe, and the Eiffel Tower. I'm strolling around the Grand Palais when Jonathan texts. Oliver has pulled off a coup in record time. I'm to meet them at five at the house. Berthe's house. Maybe my house. A house that could provide answers to all of my questions.

He says we won't be able to get into any of the apartments today, as the tenants haven't been notified, but we'll have full access to the areas that aren't occupied. It's already after four thirty, and I jump off the bus when it reaches the stop closest to Rue de Villejust. I rush down the last few blocks and see that Jonathan and Oliver are already waiting for me. Oliver is younger than I expect, maybe midtwenties, or maybe just youthful-looking because of his long blond hair and slight frame.

Jonathan introduces us, and Oliver holds up a key ring, grinning at me. No doubt he's been informed of my impatience. When he turns the knob and the heavy front door creaks open, I gasp and grab Jonathan's hand. Jonathan shakes his head slightly and drops mine. Right. This may be my life, but it's his job.

When we step inside, I'm crushed. The large rooms filled with stripes of sunlight and billowing curtains I saw in my dream are gone. The spacious entry is foreshortened, closed in by walls on either side, a door embedded in one. I see that the mosaic on the floor is reminiscent of *The Harbor at Lorient*, but it's cut off by the new wall, and what's left is barely discernible. Tiles are missing, some replaced by larger ones that muddle the original design, and many of the ones that remain are cracked. The ceilings are high, but their majesty is nullified by the narrowness of the space. Berthe would not be happy. Neither would Aimée or Colette. And neither am I.

The wide stairway is the same as it was in my dream, but some of the columns in the balustrades are missing and the bare treads are scuffed, a few separating from the molding. A tiny elevator with open grates that can't hold more than two people is pressed into one side of the stairs. So much is similar, and so much is different—although the differences appear due to events that transpired long after any Morisots lived here, which doesn't bode well. I have to remind myself to keep breathing.

Oliver consults the stack of papers in his hand, finds the blueprints, flips through them. "According to this, there are eight apartments, one each on the first and second floors, two on the third and fourth, and two on the fifth, which was once the attic."

I tilt my head back and try to peer through to the top, but the stairway grows murkier and narrower as it climbs, and it's impossible to discern anything beyond the third floor. The original skylight must have been broken and replaced with plaster. The house in my dream has been demolished, destroyed by greedy landlords who stole its history, its soul. Nothing belonging to any of the Morisots can possibly still exist here. They have been silenced. Erased.

"It's a travesty what they did to these regal old buildings," Jonathan says. "Just came in and gouged out their souls."

I'm stunned that his words so closely mirror my thoughts—yet another coupling of our sensibilities, gloomy as our common thoughts may be. I'm afraid my voice will reveal the depth of my sorrow, so I say nothing. I should have known. Perhaps I had.

Jonathan asks Oliver about the particulars of the process to reclaim a building. I climb to the second floor as they talk, catching little of the conversation, caring even less. There's no point in going into any of the apartments, in searching for whatever I foolishly duped myself into thinking was here. I suddenly remember that in my dream I was looking for a child I never found. An unsuccessful search, just like this one.

The first thing I'm going to do if this godforsaken building becomes mine is to sell it. As quickly as possible. My family might have lived here once, but they're not here anymore, and I want no part of this shell of what once was. Although I'll gladly take the money, recovering at least some of what was stolen from them. It appears Wyatt's case will have to stand on its own.

I think about going up to the third floor, but the stairs narrow as they rise and the apartment walls press closer in. A waste of time, and I've wasted enough. I square my shoulders, lift my chin, and descend to the entry. As Jonathan said, I'm a survivor, and I'll weather this too. Even if right now it feels like it's going to break me.

"Oliver thinks you've got a good shot here," Jonathan calls up to me. "And if that's what you want, we can start setting up the preliminaries before I head home—and then we'll keep going until it's yours."

"Thank you both," I say. "And, yes, that's what I'd like to do."

The men are pleased with my answer, and I can tell Jonathan is pleased that I'm handling the disappointment so well. Ha. As we head to the door, it strikes me that my dream ended in the basement. Yes, in the dream I found nothing there, but I ask Oliver if the house has a basement anyway.

He opens the blueprints. "It seems that there is a cellar, but there aren't any apartments down there."

"Do you have a key?"

"I might, but access is probably through the first-floor apartment." He traces his finger over the lines, trying to find it. "Yes, here it is, but . . ." He traces again. "But it looks like there's also a way in through the garden."

FIFTY-TWO

Oliver unlocks the rear gate, and we enter the garden. Even though it's been abandoned for years—perhaps decades—sprouts of green poke between the bricks, and random flowers push their way through the leaf-strewn dirt in the beds. The tenacity of life. Hope. My heart pounds. Foolish girl.

There are two doors on the back of the house. One is stately, with wide moldings and large windows above and around it. The other is narrow and barely taller than I am. It's obvious which one leads to the basement. It takes Oliver a number of tries to find the correct key. As Oliver struggles to get the door open, I clutch Jonathan's arm, and this time he lets me hold on to him.

With an avalanche of dirt and the scream of splintering wood, it finally releases, swinging outward. A fetid odor rises from its depths, and all three of us back up. "Are you certain you want to do this?" Oliver asks me.

I begin to shake my head, but then I hear my father's voice telling me to finish what I start. "Yes," I say with more enthusiasm than I have, then I hesitate. "But I'd really like one of you to come with me."

The two exchange a glance, and it's clear that they're both eager to see what's down there. Jonathan clicks on his phone's flashlight. He draws closer and shines it on the stairs sinking into the shadows.

Oliver stands next to him and peers in. "I don't think we're going to be able to stand up down there." He suddenly appears less eager than he was before.

"A dirt floor?" I ask.

Jonathan looks at me strangely, and then nods in recognition. I told him the details of my dream. The rickety stairs. The low ceiling. The packed earthen floor. He waves his hand inside the threshold. "Cobwebs," he tells me.

"I'm ready," I say.

Oliver is clearly confused, but neither of us is about to explain. The cobwebs aren't as bad as in the dream, but I'm the third one down and still have to push them from my face and mouth, so maybe they are. The smell is horrendous, and I press my sleeve to my nose in a futile attempt to stanch it. I can stand upright, although barely, but Jonathan and Oliver are forced to hunch over.

"It looks—and smells—like no one's been down here in years," Oliver says.

Jonathan hands me his phone. I move it around the murky space. It's the way it was in my dream, but now the barrels have been replaced by a tangled mess of baffling objects covered with sheets, serpentine corridors slithering between them. Still, the same shadows, the same maze, the same claustrophobia, the same desperation gathering in my chest. *Where are you? If I can't find you, we'll lose everything.*

Berthe sent me here. No other explanation, terrifying as it is. There's something in this place. Something she and I both need. My hand is unsteady. I wave the phone, slicing the darkness with shards of light that jump from the corners to the lumpy silhouettes. And then I see it. A single barrel. Whatever I need to find is inside.

I quickly walk toward it, stumble, straighten, Jonathan and Oliver right behind me. Jonathan knows what I'm thinking, but Oliver, once again, is baffled. The barrel has a cover nailed to its top. It's warped and breaking away along the edges. "We need to open it," I say.

Oliver shakes his head. "I'm sorry, but we can't do that. I'm only authorized to let you look, not to move or touch anything."

I turn to him. "I've traveled over three thousand miles and spent money I don't have to see what's inside this barrel. Please. I can't leave until I do."

"It's not my—"

"Can we just humor her?" Jonathan interrupts. "We won't take anything, and we'll put it back exactly as it was. You yourself said no one's been down here in years."

Oliver looks from Jonathan to me. I was right about his age. He's got to be new to this job, unsure whether to follow Beaumont's instructions or a request from a much more experienced colleague.

"I promise you won't get into any trouble—this will stay between us." Jonathan takes the phone from me. "There's got to be a crowbar down here, or something else I can use as a wedge," he mutters as he swings the light around the room. It lands on a large flathead screwdriver, and he grabs it.

It takes only a few nudges to loosen the cover. It pops open with only two more, and I jump at the sharp crack. When the scent of violets floods the air, I seize Jonathan's sleeve, stifle a cry. It smells like my living room right before I hear Berthe's voice in my head. But there's no voice. All I hear is the sound of my ragged breathing.

Jonathan tips the barrel on its side, and a few items spill to the floor. Clothing—old-fashioned women's clothing. A necklace.

"Don't," Oliver says.

I drop to my knees. Jonathan empties the rest of the barrel, holds the flashlight over the contents. I scramble through them. More clothes, shoes, jewelry. Sketch pads. Berthe's? I grab one. Empty. The next too. Then I see a thick leather-bound volume embossed in gold. I open it carefully. Jonathan crouches and looks over my shoulder. It's in French, meaningless to me. But Jonathan is fluent—his mother's first language—and his eyes widen.

"That's enough," Oliver barks before I can ask Jonathan what he sees. "You need to put everything back now. Including the cover." He checks his phone. "I let you look, which I shouldn't have, and I've got to return the keys to Beaumont's office in fifteen minutes. When the house is officially yours, you'll be able to do what you like with the contents, but for now we have to go."

"All I need is a few more minutes," I mumble as I continue my search. We can't go. I haven't found it yet. Ten days. I throw a glance at Jonathan, imploring his support.

He ignores me and begins to return the items to the barrel. "Fair enough," he says. "Thanks, Oliver. Much appreciated. I owe you one."

"These belong to my family." I clutch a dress to my chest. "Maybe even to Berthe Morisot herself, or my great-great-grandmother. Or her daughter. That means none of it is Beaumont's. It all belongs to me—no matter what the Nazis stole or what Beaumont believes he bought." I'm not leaving. Not without what I came for. Not when it's only inches away.

"Legally, that's not exactly true," Oliver begins, but Jonathan cuts him off.

"It's cool, Tamara," he says as he rights the barrel and gently tries to pry the dress from my grip. "We're leaving."

I struggle against him for a moment, then notice from his stiff stance that he's slipped something into the back of his pants. I stop resisting and stand, almost hitting my head. Jonathan repositions the cover, smashes it into place with the butt of the screwdriver, returns the barrel to its original position.

We climb out of the basement, and Oliver locks both the door and the gate behind us. Then he and Jonathan make plans to meet tomorrow to start processing my claim, and everyone says goodbye.

We watch Oliver stride through the alley toward the street, and I can barely contain myself until he's turned the corner. "What?" I demand. "What did you take?"

Jonathan grins and touches his back. "It's Aimée Manet's diary. But I'm going to leave it where it is until we're somewhere more private. There's a quiet bar in my hotel. Let's go there and see what she has to say."

PART NINETEEN

Aimée, 1920–1921

FIFTY-THREE

1920–1921

15 December 1920

Ah, how lovely to find you once more, my dearest diary. It is more than five years since I last wrote, and if I had not been organizing the contents of the cellar, it would probably have been at least another five. For there you were, in a barrel of Maman's dresses. I have no idea how this could have occurred, but now that we have been reunited I shall resume our conversations.

There is no point in recapping the last years, as all is well. Colette, at fifteen, has grown into a gracious and kind young lady with many prospects for a fine marriage. Pierre and I both enjoy good health and remain residents of Maman's house on Rue de Villejust, which suits us just fine. I still miss Maman and Papa, although the years have softened, but not eradicated, the pain. It is my immense joy to sit in Maman's old studio, across from Papa's "Party on the Seine," remembering them both.

There is one distressing thing in my full and happy life. It is that while Manet, Degas, Monet, Renoir, and the others are now the toast of the town, of the world, Maman is not. I do not understand why her brilliant work has been pushed aside as if she were not as talented as her friends and fellow artists, all of whom considered her their equal. In some instances, their better. She created just as many splendid paintings as the men, but none of this seems to matter, and my efforts to alter this turn of events have met with failure, which is a grave disappointment.

18 December 1920

I have come across some of Maman's sketchbooks in a different storage barrel in the cellar, these full of drawings. She did so many preliminary sketches, viewing a single scene from a variety of angles, striving to find the very best one for her final composition. So different from Papa's method of attacking the canvas.

20 December 1920

Cousin Léon came for dinner last night, and we had a lovely evening. When I was a child, Tante Suzanne made certain that he and I remained apart, and our age difference allowed this easily. But now that she is gone, we have grown quite close. His wife, Elouise, and I do not have much in common, but I do very much fancy his son, Lambert, who is a well-respected barrister.

7 January 1921

The holidays this year were particularly merry, as Colette has a beau whom we like very much. The Bernheims are an old French family of much distinction, and Samuel appears to be a fine young man. We entertained the three of them at 40 Villejust, and we were entertained by them at their mansion close to the Champ de Mars, as prestigious an address as any in the city.

They are charming people, cultured, philanthropic, and very much involved in the arts. Their art collection, mostly old masters, is beyond measure, and we enjoyed roaming their galleries. The young couple appears quite in love, and our only reservation is that the Bernheims are Jews. While we have nothing against the Jewish people, this is an unusual match for a girl of our social circle. But Pierre and I have discussed it, and we will not object to the marriage if that is what Colette wants.

10 January 1921

The oddest thing happened today, and I do not know what to make of it. I found more of Maman's sketchbooks in another barrel. Sadly, ones from right before she passed. I was looking through them, reminiscing about how she tried so hard to teach me to paint, showing me her preliminary drawings to demonstrate how they shaped her final pieces. How patient she was with my lack of natural talent, especially now that I know who my true father is. I can only imagine what hopes she and Papa had for their only child's artistic potential. I was pained by this realization, but that is not what is odd.

It is some of her sketches. Interspersed with drawings for a number of her last pieces, "Portrait of Jeanne Pontillon," "Boating on the Lake," and "Woman with Child on a Boat," were preliminary drawings for "Party on the Seine." I suppose she and Papa could have been working together and he scribbled ideas in her book. But Papa was not one for scribbling ideas. He almost always went directly to the canvas.

I also recognize her strokes, the buoyancy of them, the colorful pastels she used for shading. Even an unaccomplished eye can see the similarities between the drawings for "Party" and those for her other works, the way the light and shadows bounce off every surface. Also the similarities between the sketches and the painting currently hanging in her studio with the signature of Édouard Manet, the one I have loaned to museums and galleries as an example of Papa's finest work.

11 January 1921

I woke up in the middle of the night and remembered a particular afternoon when Maman was teaching me to paint. She had handed me a sketchbook so I could more closely study her drawings for "Jeanne Pontillon Wearing a Hat," and I realized that it was the very book I was looking at yesterday.

Even as I child with limited experiences, I recall being shocked by drawings of men I did not know who were clearly not of our class, and women wearing what I believed at the time to be "naughty" dresses. I was astounded that some of the men and women were touching each other in an overly familiar way.

I did not fully understand then that a female painter in the 1890s was not allowed to depict men to whom she was not related, nor that for a woman to paint such an unruly scene composed of strangers would bring scandal upon her and her family. But I do remember feeling uncomfortable with the drawings, sensing that somehow they were wrong.

I did not say anything then, but Maman must have sensed my distress. She told me that she hadn't begun a painting from the sketches but hoped to be able to one day. And now these sketches prove that she did. Is this why Papa claimed it as his? To maintain Maman's reputation, and to protect me, while allowing an exceptional piece of art to be seen?

This seems the most likely explanation, but I wonder if there is another, less charitable reason. No, that cannot be. Papa and Maman were very much in love, and he would never have done anything to hurt her or to demean her talent. Yet he was nothing if not ambitious, and loath as I am to admit it, he did consider his reputation and artistic legacy above all else.

15 January 1921

I do not know what to do with my new knowledge about "Party." I have spent many hours comparing her sketches to the painting, and I am certain it is her work. If I were to disclose what I have learned, it might reinvigorate Maman's standing as an exalted Impressionist, but it would also besmirch Papa's name, marking him as a plagiarizer, if that is the correct term, and, as awful as it is to think, perhaps a thief. And what of Pierre and myself? Of Colette? Proclaiming a painting we own to be the work of one artist when it is the work of another? The former far more famous than the latter.

Pierre suggests that we leave it be. He believes there will be a terrible uproar that will, in the end, mar Maman and Papa's reputations, along with our own.

20 February 1921

When Papa died, he left Léon the paintings he had not sold or given away, and so I presumed Léon would be the best person with whom to discuss "Party on the Seine." He recently established the Édouard Manet Foundation, to which we have contributed generously, and Léon and I have had many conversations about the ongoing work on Papa's catalogue raisonné. We also have discussed the future goals of the foundation, including acquiring as many pieces of Papa's as possible to display in its gallery, and Léon plans to do this by cajoling collectors to bequest their Manet paintings to the foundation in their wills.

Neither Léon, nor anyone else, is aware of my paternity, and he was not pleased with my hesitation to commit to giving "Party" to the foundation after my death. I have no intention of doing so, as the painting will go to Colette, who loves it so. And it will be hers to pass down to her children and then to theirs. When Léon learns that my mother painted it, it should quiet his needling.

Against Pierre's advice, I brought Maman's sketchbook to Léon, anticipating a lively discussion on the best way to handle the matter. This is not what transpired. I should have known I could not depend on a man who would forswear his given surname in exchange for that of Manet. Nor one so overzealous in his adoration that he gave up a fine job in the civil service in order to create an homage to his idol, to whom he is not even directly related.

At first, Léon appeared receptive to the possibility that Maman had painted "Party." He took her sketchbook and walked to the fireplace, ostensibly to see it more clearly closer to the light. And then, before I had any inclination of what he planned, he tossed it into the fire.

I remained seated, momentarily unable to understand what he was doing. Then I leapt up and grabbed his arm. "Stop it!" I cried, snatching a poker in hope of retrieving the book from the flames.

Léon shrugged off my hand and stood wide-legged in front of the fireplace, blocking my access. "It is impossible that your mother, a woman, painted such a masterpiece. Especially when she never created anything like this before. These are frivolous studies of Édouard's work, clearly copies, and I will not have you causing difficulties for him or the foundation with your fraudulent accusations."

I tried to push him aside, but he is larger and stronger than I am. "You saw it. You saw it yourself," I told him. "'Party' is a Morisot, not a Manet!"

He stepped aside with a slight smile on his lips, and we both stared at the blackened sketchbook as it crumbled into the ashes. "Suit yourself," he said. "If you must go public with this preposterous allegation, please do not allow me to stand in your way."

PART TWENTY

Tamara, the present

FIFTY-FOUR

Jonathan and I are seated in a deserted alcove at his hotel's bar, and I struggle to remain silent while he translates the legible parts of Aimée's diary. I'm bursting with questions, dying to discuss the implications, but I'm afraid to break his concentration—even though he reads as if the words were in English, his speech unhesitating. Yet when he closes the gilt-edged cover, I find myself speechless.

He smiles at me. "It's a lot to digest."

I try to grasp what this might mean.

He opens the diary and gently tries to pry some of the pages apart. During its years in the barrel, water must have seeped in, and many of the individual sheets are stuck together or they're too waterlogged to be decipherable. Most of the earliest entries are completely soaked, only the later ones spared.

My mind buzzes as I watch his efforts. Is this what I think it is? What Berthe sent me to find? Proof she's the true creator of *Party on the Seine*? Proof she's not dead in the way I always understood "dead" to be? That my certainty, my science, my numbers can't explain everything? What would Dad think? "So Berthe did paint it . . ."

"Seems likely."

More comfortable with the pragmatic, I ask, "Will the judge consider this enough to rule *Party* is mine?"

He thinks about this. "From what you've told me about the other evidence you have, it will definitely be a positive addition."

I don't like the sound of his nuanced reply. "Only 'a positive addition'?"

"Given its contents and where it was found," he says, carefully choosing his words, "it would appear to be Aimée Manet's diary, written in the early twentieth century. And I suppose we can assume Aimée believed what she wrote was true, but unfortunately, that's about as far as it goes. There's no definitive proof of either of those things, so there's no evidence to legally support them."

I don't like this unnuanced reply any more than his nuanced one. "There may be more of her *Party* sketches down there. They could easily have been in another barrel we didn't see in the dark. Would that help?"

He shrugs. "Marginally, but either way, Oliver was annoyed with our manhandling the contents of the barrel, and it's unlikely he's going to let me in there again this visit." Jonathan doesn't voice it, but his meaning is clear: The trial will be long over by the time he returns to Paris.

"But she says right there that she found the sketches," I persist. "That Léon destroyed them. Doesn't that mean anything?"

"Think about it from a judge's point of view. Here's a diary the defendant claims she found in an ancestral home that has been bought, sold, and renovated many times since a family member lived there. The diary's age and authorship haven't been verified, and although the entries indicate that Morisot painted it, this is only one person's contention—one who might have been biased, and who can't testify or be questioned."

"If only we could get *Party* authenticated before the trial." I sigh. "I looked into it once, and apparently no expert would even consider starting the process without all the provenance paperwork up front—all of which confirms Édouard painted it."

"It's too bad it wasn't done years before, but that's not all that surprising, given that it hasn't been shown for almost a century—and it was never sold. Did you check AI authenticators?"

"Really? I had no idea. Do you think they might not need paperwork?"

"Based on the little I know about their analytical techniques, I'd guess their focus would be on the painting itself instead of its history. There's some kind of large machine involved. Maybe like an MRI they put the painting inside of?"

I'm elated by this possibility. "I'll do it as soon as I get home. We still have ten days before the trial, and if all they have to do is run *Party* through a machine, maybe that would do it."

"Again, I've got no idea how it actually works, but go for it," he says, yet I can see he's skeptical. "You should also call Wyatt. This is his area, not mine.

He may have a completely different interpretation, know a way to make the diary a more powerful piece of evidence."

I finish my glass of wine and wave down the server for another. "Aimée kept referring to Édouard as 'Papa.' Do you think that means she could be Berthe and Édouard's illegitimate child?"

"That's what's implied, although Aimée doesn't say how she knows this. But if it's true, it would make you a straight-line descendant of both Édouard and Berthe." He grins. "Pretty impressive bloodline."

I dreamily contemplate this new and intoxicating family connection. Directly descended from both Édouard Manet and Berthe Morisot? How could this have been lost through the generations? My grandmother's estrangement from her own mother is one answer. But maybe Aimée, as part of a family dedicated to upholding the Manet name, never told anyone, including Colette, about who her father really was or who really painted *Party*, believing she was saving both artists' reputations.

"Then Édouard would be my grandfather times four, not my uncle," I say, stating the obvious, but liking the sound of the words. "How cool is that?"

"Very cool for you," he says, then sobers. "But in terms of the trial, Édouard left everything to Léon, and that will supersede your relationship to Édouard, no matter how direct."

I swirl the wine in my glass, precariously riding the emotional waves that keep coming at me. And then another one hits, and I burst out laughing.

Jonathan's expression shifts to puzzlement. "What?"

"I, I," I stammer between giggles. "I can't believe you stole the diary. Right out from under Oliver's nose. A blatantly illegal act, counselor—and gutsy as hell."

"Seemed like the thing to do at the moment." He gives me a long look. "And then there's the elephant in the room. Or maybe I should say the ghost in the room."

I run my finger along the gilt on the cover. "She did lead us to this."

"And if this whole adventure is about Berthe wanting you to prove she painted *Party*, the diary supports that. A diary you found in a house—and in a barrel—you saw in a dream, before you knew they existed."

A ripple of panic rises up my back, and I take his hand in both of mine. "It was one thing to speculate about it, but now, now with this evidence—if it is evidence—well, it's scaring the shit out of me." Even though it might mean I can stop worrying about my mental health.

He gently rubs the forefinger of his other hand between two of my knuckles. "It's okay to be scared by something this inexplicable. Something that goes against everything you thought you believed in."

"I don't know what I believe in anymore."

"My take is that the only people who are sure about the nature of being are the ones who don't ask enough questions."

"You really think Berthe's spirit could be inside *Party*?"

"I consider myself a person who likes to ask questions, so I'll ask you this: Why not?"

"Because it's impossible."

His eyes fasten on to mine. "Is it?"

I drop my head into my hands.

Jonathan gets up, slips onto my side of the booth, and gathers me up in his arms. "It's also okay to be confused."

I wrap my arms around him, bury my face in his chest. "Thank you," I whisper.

He hugs me tighter. "So how serious is this thing with Wyatt?"

I CALL WYATT when I get back to my hotel, tell him about the diary, about Jonathan reading it to me in English.

"Stein's with you in Paris?"

"Yeah," I say casually. "He got in yesterday, I think. The Conference is working on my claim for 40 Villejust, and he's helping."

"Why didn't you tell me that?"

"I didn't think it was important."

His voice is hard. "I think it is."

"Wyatt, are you listening to what I'm saying? Aimée Manet's diary says she found evidence Berthe painted *Party*—this could be a real boost for us."

"It's in French?"

"Yes, but the relevant parts aren't that long. It shouldn't be hard to find someone to translate it before the trial."

"If we're going to use it as evidence, I need to get it to Delphine. Discovery. There isn't as much time as you think."

"Isn't she French?" I counter, pleased with my quick retort. "I've got the diary with me now, so I'll text you photos of the important pages, and you can send them on to Delphine. When I get home, we'll find someone to translate them before the trial for the English speakers."

A long pause. "Tell me exactly what Aimée wrote."

After I do, he says, "Legally, the sides are well-balanced, and it's going to be a tough call on the judge's part, but every little bit helps."

"Aren't you impressed I actually found something?" I demand. "That the trip turned out to be worthwhile after all?" Before I left, he'd said going to Paris wasn't necessary because he was pretty sure we'd win without any additional evidence, and now that I found some he's changing his tune? Is this because he's pissed I proved him wrong?

"I guess," he says grudgingly. "But you've got to admit it was a long shot."

Annoyed, I tell him I'll call when I get back, probably the day after. He offers to pick me up at the airport, but I decline, using the excuse that international flights with a connection are notoriously unreliable.

I'm a little surprised when he doesn't argue. The man has a serious jealous streak, although in this case it's not unfounded.

I told Jonathan that Wyatt and I had been dating casually for about six months but it looked like the relationship had run its course. He was pleased with this answer and was gentleman enough not to suggest we go up to his room. Which was probably a good thing. Given the way I was feeling, the longing he was sparking in me, I might have agreed. But I need to break up with Wyatt first.

JONATHAN CALLS BEFORE I leave in the morning. I tell him what Wyatt said, his concern about the diary being in French.

"I'll write a translation for you," he offers. "No problem. The pertinent part is, what, six, seven pages?"

"That would be great, thanks." Although I wonder how great Wyatt will think this is.

"I'm meeting with Oliver this afternoon," Jonathan says. "And I've got a bunch of paperwork to do here on your claim—and on another client's—so I'm thinking I'll be heading to Boston in a couple of days. Is it okay if I transcribe it then?"

"Should be fine. He'll just need it a day or two before the trial. I already told him what it says."

"The first of May, right?"

"Right."

There's a strained silence, and then we both start to talk at the same time. We laugh, and I say, "Got to get packing. Let me know when you're back in town."

Although I have more than enough to mull over, I spend most of the flight thinking about Jonathan, his growing pull on me, the electricity between us. And although it's definitely about sex, it's more than that. I've never experienced a friendship that turned into a love affair, but I can already recognize the power—and the depth—of such a thing. It's not just his body I want. It's him.

IT'S EARLY EVENING when I get home, and I go directly to the living room. "I found Aimée's diary," I say.

Berthe stares out over the river.

"It's going to help at the trial, but it remains to be seen how much. Even though there's a time crunch, I'm going to try to get *Party* authenticated before we go to court. If I can't, I'll do it after—and I won't stop until we prove to the world it's your work."

Again, no response.

"And it looks like 40 Villejust could be mine too. You, Aimée, Colette, and now me, owning the very same house. Four generations of Morisot women."

And then, just as when we'd only recently met, she winks at me.

FIFTY-FIVE

Last night, I set my alarm for six, well aware jet lag would try to keep me in bed. I did have to fight against the gravity of my oh-so-comfortable mattress, but the trial is in a week, and the need to get *Party* authenticated overrides all else.

I make a strong pot of coffee and look up how AI art authentication works. Apparently, while human authenticators consider connoisseurship based on the discerning eye of experts and prolific paper trails, AI is more of a forensic investigation, good at pinpointing irregularities and anachronisms. Its focus is on the composition of the painting itself, running a myriad of minuscule comparisons between the primary work and the oeuvre of the artist in question. In this case, of the two artists in question. No preliminary documentation required.

I find websites for a half dozen companies doing this type of work, and the nerd in me gets immediately sucked in. These neural networks have been trained on databases of authenticated work—as well as forgeries—and can race through hundreds of thousands of pieces of data in seconds. Comparing and contrasting brushstrokes, color palette, composition, pigments, binders, canvases, hidden layers, underdrawings—and so much more—in far less time than it would take to list them. They can also detect signs of tampering, alteration, and overpainting, all of which will be crucial to settling the question of attribution to either Berthe or Édouard.

Two of the companies are in the Boston area, and I send them photos along with my information, stressing that I'll be able to bring *Party on the Seine* to them as soon as they can take her, and that time is an issue. It's too early to call their offices, but at nine I will.

I text Wyatt to set up dinner tonight, and then pick a restaurant we haven't been to together. No history is best. Even though we never promised to be exclusive—or even discussed it—Jonathan will be back tomorrow, and I want to get this over with before he comes home. It occurs to me that this could be a stupid move, that ditching a guy who holds *Party*'s future in his hands is pure folly and I should wait until after the trial. But I don't want to wait, and I know Wyatt well enough to believe that however upset he might be, he's not going to turn his back on the case. He may not be the man for me, but I appreciate how seriously he's committed to his work.

Wyatt and I have had fun, but what I feel for Jonathan is qualitatively different. Maybe I'm getting ahead of myself, but somehow I don't think I am. Either way, I can't be with Wyatt anymore, not when I want someone else this much. I have no desire to hurt him, and dread the coming evening. He's a decent guy, but it's time. Breaking up is always harder on the breakee than it is on the breaker, but it's no picnic for either.

My looming anxiety is dispelled when I speak with Naomi Land, the lead analyst and co-owner of AuthentAI, one of the local companies I contacted earlier. They're a small start-up in Kendall Square in Cambridge, just a couple of miles away, and the price is steep. But when she tells me she can fit *Party* in sometime this week, I jump on it. Again, what credit cards are for.

I call Jonathan, but he doesn't answer, so I text him the news. I'll tell Wyatt tonight.

I GET TO the restaurant early and order a martini, an unusual drink for me, but I'm hoping the hard liquor will buttress me for what's to come. I'm not sure how Wyatt is going to respond, but given his jealous streak, he might get extremely angry—especially when he finds out it's Jonathan. On the other hand, his lawyerly training should allow him to keep his cool.

He comes in and pulls me up for a kiss, holds me close, too close for a public place, too close for me. "I missed you," he murmurs into my hair.

I step away quickly and sit. "Well, I'm back," I say self-consciously. "And I have some excellent news."

"Always up for excellent news." He waves for the waiter. "Is it champagne news, or should I go with my usual?"

"Usual is good." Then I launch into the AuthentAI story. "They may have a slot for her as soon as tomorrow. The next day at the latest. And

Naomi said the process usually takes no more than two or three days—so we should get the report back before the trial."

"Well done, very well done. Now if that diary is telling the truth, and if the authentication comes through in our favor, we might be able to close Damien down."

I frown. *If. If. Might.* "Why would Aimée lie in her own diary?"

"I'm not saying she did, but how can we know?"

"I know."

"You okay?" Wyatt cocks his head. "You seem kind of edgy, not as happy as I'd expect."

"I am happy. On cloud nine." I don't think I've ever used that phrase before, and heat rises up my neck at the falseness of it. "But, uh, there's something else we need to discuss."

Unaware of my discomfort, he grins. "You? You want to discuss something besides your painting?" He reaches under the table and runs his hand up the inside of my thigh. "Something like this?"

I shift away from him. "It's just that, that while I was away, I was thinking—"

"About me, I hope."

"No. Well, actually, yes." I take a gulp of my martini, but the straight vodka is too harsh for me, and I start to cough.

"Slow down there, girl." Wyatt leans over and gently rubs my back. "So you were thinking about me when you were in Paris . . ."

I down half a glass of water, and the coughing subsides. "Yes, but I was thinking about this before that. Now and then, I guess. Since we've been dating."

"So you're saying you've been thinking about me since we started dating?" He drops his chin to his fist in a gesture like *The Thinker*, those incredible green eyes sparkling. "Okay, now that you've come clean, I will too. I've been thinking about you."

"Wyatt, listen to me. This, this is hard enough, so please just let me say what I have to say."

He sits back in his chair, the sparkle replaced by wariness.

"I think, I think that we should take a break."

"A break?" he repeats, but it's clear he understands exactly what I'm saying.

Except what I said was wrong. "Not just a break, I think, well, I think we should stop dating."

He looks from my flushed face to the now-empty martini glass. "Jonathan Stein."

I close my eyes. "Yes."

"I fucking knew it. Knew it from the day I saw the two of you sitting so cozy on your couch and he claimed to be *visiting* that damn painting."

"It wasn't like that. We were just friends then."

He glares at me. "You didn't look like just friends."

"It doesn't really matter," I try to explain. "It's not only that. It's other things too. We, you and I—"

"Are you in love with him?"

"I don't know," I say honestly, but I also wonder if I might be in the process of falling. Something I've never thought about while I've been with Wyatt. Anytime he nudged toward anything close to love or permanence, I've backed away.

"And you know you're not in love with me."

I don't want to respond, but I have no choice. "I'm sorry Wyatt, really sorry, but I'm not."

"And you don't think that could ever change?" His voice cracks.

I look at him pleadingly.

"So this is it." He stands and throws two twenties on the table. "I'd hoped for a different ending, but if that's how you feel, I'm not going to plead with you."

"We've had a great time together, and I care about—"

"It's okay, Tamara. I'm a big boy. No need for platitudes."

"They're not—"

"I want you to know I'm still your lawyer, and that I intend to do everything I can to win your case. Send me the authentication report when you get it, and I'll take it from there."

"Thank you. I appreciate—"

He turns and walks out the door before I can say anything more.

JONATHAN'S PLANE ARRIVES late the next night, and in the morning we make plans for him to come over at dinnertime to write up the translation. He figures that, as only six pages are directly related to the case, it will take less than an hour, and offers to pick up dinner. I wonder how much translating and eating we'll actually do, and blood pumps in my ears.

The trial is five days away, and although Naomi thought she'd be able to take *Party* today, now it looks like tomorrow at the earliest. And Jonathan will be here soon. My nerves are on high alert, jangling at the least bit of noise, squeezing my stomach, messing with my head. I take a long shower, shave my legs.

He walks in with a large bag of Thai food, then glances into the living room, sees *Party* is still there, and shakes his head. While he may not have movie-star looks, he's quite a handsome guy, and being close to him drives warmth through my body. When he puts the bag on the counter, I step in for a hug.

He wraps his arms around me, and I press tight to him. He laughs and says, "Good to see you too."

We stand like that for a long time. Then he loosens his grip and asks in a teasing voice, "How hungry are you? Should I do the translation before dinner or after?"

Our eyes meet, and the kiss is inevitable. The relief of it is piercing, as is the pent-up desire. My knees buckle, and we laugh when he grabs me so I don't fall. We're still laughing as we wrap our arms around each other and go into the bedroom.

I lie down on the bed, and he takes a step back, devouring me with his gaze. I raise my arms to pull him to me, but instead he takes my forefinger and places it in his mouth. This is so surprising, so stunningly sexy, that I gasp. He smiles and bends toward me, begins to unbutton my shirt, running his tongue leisurely downward as each button pops open. When the shirt drops to the bed, he unzips my jeans and buries his face there. His breath is warm, and I strain toward it, then peel my pants off so he can get even closer. I cry out as an orgasm floods through me.

Jonathan pulls his shirt over his head, and the sight of his golden skin and his muscular body stuns me. He's so beautiful. I reach for him, delirious to touch him, to feel him against me, to merge. And when we do, he begins slowly, bringing me to another orgasm before we explode together.

He gathers me to him. "I'm glad that's over," he says. "The waiting part, I mean."

"Me too."

"But your wait wasn't nearly as long as mine."

"Meaning?"

"I've wanted this since that first day I saw you. When you were all pissed off at me because you were convinced I was scamming you. Can't resist a fiery woman."

EARLY THE NEXT morning, Naomi calls. If I can get the painting to her in the next few hours, she'll be able to start the analysis this afternoon. Jonathan and I have been up most of the night, talking for hours, making love another time before falling into exhausted sleep. But both of us are wide awake now.

Jonathan rushes to UPS for packing materials, and I reserve a U-Haul. Then I text Chris, one of the concierges, who's become a friend. As we'd worked out earlier, he contacts a guy on the loading dock, and I'm cleared to bring my box down the service elevator when it's ready and put it in the truck from there—without Alyce or anyone else knowing. I pick up the truck, Jonathan and I load *Party* inside it, and we drive to Cambridge.

Naomi meets us at the entrance to her building and directs us to the back, where two twentysomethings in jeans and T-shirts—probably analysts on her team—wait to carry *Party* inside. I touch the box before turning her over to them, reminding myself that this is a good separation, one that will hopefully keep us together.

FIFTY-SIX

The trial is scheduled to begin at nine o'clock tomorrow morning, and I still don't have the report from AuthentAI. Naomi has been very apologetic, but since I left *Party* with her their system has crashed twice and two of her staff have come down with the flu. Most of the computational analysis has been completed, but the data needs to be reviewed by actual humans, and then they might want to do more computational analysis before everything's final. The report will not be available in time.

I texted Wyatt yesterday to let him know. His assistant got back to me, saying Wyatt was disappointed but remained confident he'd be successful with the evidence and the experts he has. Which she then itemized: Nova, the detective who did the preliminary investigations on the case; the director of the New York office of the Claims Conference; a literature professor at Columbia whose expertise is in early twentieth-century diaries; and an art historian from NYU who specializes in the Impressionists. I find it hard to believe he's really confident, but I need him to be.

I'm a complete mess, and if it weren't for Jonathan I'd be an even bigger one. We've only been together together for a short time, but it feels longer, which I attribute to our months of friendship and the intensity of our connection, physical and otherwise. We can't get enough of each other. In addition to lots of lovemaking, we've been sharing our childhoods, our secrets, our successes and failures, our hopes and, of course, everything *Party*.

It's as if our relationship is evolving in all directions at once. We're discovering each other in the present and plunging into the future, while hungry for every detail of the past to make the other whole, known. He's been unfailingly supportive about the trial and has taken my concerns as his. This is clearly not a casual relationship, and despite my previous rejection of anything serious, I'm all in. Yet another mind opener.

ALTHOUGH I'D ALWAYS assumed I'd be at the trial, Wyatt told me he doesn't want me there, and I'd reluctantly acquiesced. The last thing I want to do right now is piss him off. So I spend the day roaming the city in the rain, my hand around the phone in my pocket. It's set at the highest volume, and I put it on vibrate just in case.

It's after four thirty when Wyatt calls. "I have disappointing news," he says in a professional voice. "The judge has ruled against you."

"I, I don't understand." And for a moment, I don't.

"It was the lack of provenance, as we previously discussed. With nothing to legally establish the Bernheims owned it, Édouard Manet's will took precedence."

"What about AuthentAI? Once we have verification that Berthe painted it—which could come any day now—won't that cancel this out?"

"That would have to be a separate lawsuit, in which you sue Damien Manet to claim it from him."

"Could we do that?"

"If the final report supports the claim, it will be up to you to pursue a suit."

"What about an appeal?"

"That's also possible."

"Then she'd be able to stay here. Can you do that right away?"

"There's no guarantee the judge would allow you to retain possession while an appeal is being adjudicated. As it stands, Damien Manet is now the legal owner of *Party on the Seine*, and he can take possession of it at his convenience."

"But you can still start the appeal, right? Ask the judge if I can keep her until a decision is made?"

"As I just told you, requesting a stay is possible, but given the legal basis of this decision, I don't see any substantial questions of the law or fact that would likely result in a reversal of the court's decision. Therefore, it's unlikely the judge will allow you to keep it during the appeal process."

"But it's worth a try, isn't it? Can you start it now?"

"Another lawyer can start it, yes."

"Another lawyer?"

"I think that would be best."

After he hangs up, I stare at the dark phone in my hand, barely comprehending. My brain seems to be stuck in low gear, but then a flood of despair overtakes me.

I've lost her. Wyatt isn't going to help me, and I don't have the money to hire another lawyer. I've had her for just six months, but I can't imagine life without her. She's become a part of me, my friend and companion, my helpmate and confidante. I recognize this is patently absurd, but that's how it feels. *Party* is Berthe, and Berthe is *Party*. My family. Which means I'm losing all of them.

I wrap the wool coverlet around my shoulders, then lift it over my head, curl into a fetal position, and try to bury every part of me in it. It's too small to do that, but I keep trying. It's as if I'm coated in ice. It doesn't occur to me to get a larger blanket.

From: Damien Manet, Director of the Édouard Manet Foundation
To: Tamara Rubin
Cc: Wyatt Butler, Beacon, Exeter & Associates
Re: Party on the Seine
Date: 1 May

Now that the court has ruled that I am the rightful owner of *Party on the Seine*, I have arranged transport to procure my painting at 9:00 on the morning of 6 May. I have discovered that it is at CubeSmart, located at 380 E Street, Boston, Massachusetts.

A truck, equipped with all the necessary packing materials, will arrive at that address at the abovementioned date and time. Please ensure that all paperwork has been completed to facilitate a smooth transfer from the storage facility. I thank you in advance for your compliance on this issue.

I am sure you will be pleased to learn that, despite the late date, which is months beyond the official deadline, the Louvre has accepted *Party on the Seine* for inclusion in the Édouard Manet retrospective to be held in August.

WHEN JONATHAN COMES over, he doesn't say anything, which I appreciate, just holds me as I sob. Then he leads me into the living room, grabbing some napkins off the counter as we walk by. "I'm not going to tell you I know how you feel, because I don't," he says when we sit and my tears slow. "But I'm here for whatever you need."

"Thank you." I press a napkin to my face. I hate to cry, which is useless and will get me nowhere, so I pull myself together. "I, I need to figure out how to keep her."

"You want to do that right now?"

I nod. "Wyatt said there's little chance the judge will approve a stay if I appeal, and that *Party* would most likely be sent to Damien during the process. But talking to Wyatt was like talking to a lawyer-bot, so I have no idea if this is true. Is it?"

"I don't know the reasoning behind the ruling, but he does. So I'd guess his take is on the mark."

"And that I'd need a new suit if it's authenticated as Berthe's?"

"Wyatt might sound like a bot, but he's got his information right. In almost all cases, new evidence can't be admitted on appeal, which means you'd have to file a different suit against Damien."

"I can't afford to do that. I still owe Beacon, Exeter a ton of money, and just had to get a new credit card because I maxed out my other two."

"I don't have the legal expertise to file a suit for you—especially one that involves a foreign country—but I've got a few friends who might be willing to give you a break on the price."

"My school loans are also overdue." I try to smile. "What made me think going to Harvard Business School was a good idea?"

He wraps me in his arms, and we sit like that for a long time, staring at the damn hooks hanging on the empty wall.

I CALL NAOMI and tell her I need to get the painting first thing in the morning, then beg her to finish her report before that. I want to be with *Party* for every minute I can, but I want the report almost as badly.

Naomi is still full of apologies, as the software and staff issues haven't been resolved. "It might only be another week, and—"

"I don't have another week. Can you at least run whatever tests you need the actual canvas for? I need to get her, it, tomorrow."

She hesitates, and I hear keyboard clicks, followed by a deep sigh. "You've been really patient, and I appreciate that, and I promise I'll do my damnedest to make it happen. But you understand there's no way I can get the official statement to you by tomorrow? That's going to be at least another four or five days."

"I understand." Which I guess I do, although given the ruling it's hard to contain my frustration. If she'd finished in the two to three days she originally promised—it's now five and counting—everything would be different. So different. But I know all too well about unexpected staffing and computer problems, so I add, "Thanks." Which is about all I can muster.

AT EIGHT IN the morning, Jonathan and I head to AuthentAI. "I'm not going to bother with any nonsense about faking another move to CubeSmart," I say as we cross the Longfellow Bridge into Cambridge.

"You don't think Damien will start back in about how bad it is for you to keep her in your apartment?" He now refers to *Party* as "her" too, which I find extremely endearing.

"Who cares if he does? What's he going to do, sue me? I'll just tell him to pick her up at my place. He's in full gloating mode, and I bet he won't make waves as long as he gets his grubby hands on *Party*." I wince. "Too pleased with himself to pick nits."

Chris, my concierge buddy, does his loading dock trick, and by nine, *Party* is back home. Jonathan helps me hang her up and rushes off to work. A tear rolls down my cheek as I sit with my Morisot. Although there's no movement, I sense Berthe's sympathy.

"I don't know how I'm going to bear it," I tell her melodramatically. "I don't know if I'll ever be able to get you back here or get you the recognition you deserve. But once the authentication comes in, I promise I'm going to do everything I can to make that happen. It could be years, which might not sound like that long a time to you, but it's going to be an eternity for me."

There's a waft of violet perfume. Then she turns her head toward me, a sly smile playing across her face, and I hear, "Not to worry, child. The wait will be far shorter than that."

FIFTY-SEVEN

Jonathan offers to meet the movers when they come to pack *Party* into her coffin and send her to France, sparing me the experience. I take him up on it and sit at Starbucks, waiting for the all-clear sign. They're fast, and I'm back in the apartment by ten. Jonathan has to go into his office, and when he leaves, even though I don't believe in crying, I sob like a little girl whose mother has deserted her. Or her great-great-great-great-grandmother. Then I take a nap. No dreams.

That afternoon, I once again wander around Boston, but now I'm pining for *Party* and Berthe. I keep checking for a text from Naomi. Obviously, her verdict isn't going to change anything right now, but it will give me hope. If the response is what I expect and I can land a decent job, I'll get *Party* authenticated by an old-fashioned expert and then hire a lawyer to sue my dear cousin.

I worry about the effect the Calliope disaster might have on my job search, but when I contact Tony, my old boss, he tells me he'll give me the strong references I deserve. He says they're still in damage-control mode around the fallout, but everyone has been more understanding than they expected. He apologizes again and asks me how I'm doing. "Just got back from Paris," I tell him breezily.

I send texts to friends, colleagues, and anyone else I can think of to inform them I've left Calliope and I'm looking for something better, asking if they hear of anything suitable to please let me know. I meet with two biotech headhunters and sign up with the one who promises she'll be able to find me a suitable position within the month.

Jonathan suggests we take a trip to Paris in August to see *Party* at the Louvre, but right now I can't imagine standing behind a velvet rope surrounded by casual observers who will stop for a few seconds and then move on to the next painting. I also have the sense that something bad could happen there. Berthe has to be furious that *Party* will be shown as a Manet—at a retrospective where her creation will be heralded as his masterwork. And it seems that she actually might have the power to make something happen. Flood, earthquake, fire.

Jonathan says he can make it a business trip, which would cover hotel and meals, and offered to pay my plane fare. Even though we're already using the L-word and talking about him giving up his apartment when his lease ends, I'm not comfortable with this. Which I guess makes the decision for me. But still, how I would adore seeing her, being with her, even if it has to be from behind a velvet rope.

NAOMI STILL HASN'T finished her report—although she claims it's imminent—and I'm starting to wonder if the thing will ever be completed. Or, worse, that it has been, and the result is not the one she knows I want. I busy myself with the job search to keep from ruminating over the report too much, which sometimes works and sometimes doesn't.

I'm on a phone interview for a position I'm not interested in—which I'm doing because it's good practice for one I am—when I notice Wyatt is calling. We haven't spoken since the day of the trial, and then I got the distinct impression he wanted nothing more to do with me.

When the interview is over, I hesitate before I punch his number, afraid he might want to talk about something personal. But it could be about *Party*, so I call him back. "Hey," I say tentatively.

"There's something I need to tell you."

"About the case?"

"Something very weird and awful has happened."

"Is *Party* all right?"

A long sigh. "Yes, Tamara, *Party* is fine. It's Damien who isn't."

"What's wrong with him?"

"There was a fire at his house, a nasty one, and, well, he's dead."

I freeze. "Damien was killed in a fire? Are you sure?"

"Obviously, I'm sure," he says sharply. "Why else would I be calling you?"

"That's, that is awful. What a horrible way to die."

"Delphine told me. She was very upset, but she wanted you to know that Damien's will states unequivocally that all of his artwork goes to the foundation—in case you were entertaining other ideas."

"Was *Party* at his house when it happened?"

"Really? I just told you a man has died—a relative of yours, even—and all you want to know is whether that fucking painting was there when he was killed?" Another long sigh. "But yes, *Party on the Seine* was in the house and it was unscathed, although almost everything else wasn't."

Not to worry, child. The wait will be far shorter than that.

"DO YOU THINK Berthe could have killed him?" I ask Jonathan over dinner that night at a Greek restaurant.

"Producing dreams is one thing. Murder is another."

"Or maybe it's the other way around, and she's a hero who snatched *Party* from the flames, rescuing a major work of art. Maybe that's what she did the other times too." I push the potatoes around with my fork, nibble at a piece of eggplant. Then I tell him what I heard in my head the last time I sat with *Party*.

"Look, you just found out about Damien's death. So why don't we let it sit for a while? Get some distance before attempting to process the metaphysics of the thing."

I turn his hand palm up and kiss it. "Sounds good."

An hour later, even though it's nine o'clock at night, Naomi calls. She says there's a 95 percent certainty *Party on the Seine* is primarily the work of Berthe Morisot, a percentage she explains is about as high as they ever go. The odd piece is that there's also 80 percent certainty that Édouard Manet painted over a few random places on the canvas—dabs of paint on the woman's skirt and the awning, seemingly swiftly applied, which Naomi describes as more of an edit than a collaboration.

JONATHAN SENDS THE AuthentAI report to Delphine. When he doesn't hear back, he telephones and leaves her a message—of course she doesn't take his call—informing her that we intend to initiate a lawsuit for the return of *Party on the Seine* to its rightful owner. When he doesn't hear back, he emails her the preliminary details of the lawsuit. Still no response.

Fortunately, he has to go to Paris for work—including a meeting with Oliver to review his progress on 40 Rue de Villejust—so he pays a visit to the foundation.

He calls me, jubilant. The foundation is in chaos, and Delphine was so distraught she broke down and cried when he met with her—he's guessing her relationship with Damien was more than just business. Either way, apparently no one, especially Delphine, has the stomach for a legal battle, and the foundation quickly agrees to relinquish its rights to the painting.

In less than two months—a full six weeks before the dreaded Manet retrospective—*Party* will be on her way back to me.

ON THE BIG day, Jonathan takes an hour off so we can be together when *Party* arrives. We move the triptych back to the guest room and watch out the window for the truck, even though there's a good chance we won't see it, because it will likely go through the alley to the loading dock. We laugh at our mutual nervousness, and if it weren't early afternoon, I'd have poured us both a hefty drink.

I finally get a call from the dock that she's here, and I tell them to have the guards bring her up. No need to get the overly curious Alyce—or anyone else—involved. The fewer eyes, the better. Jonathan and I wait at the elevator and lead them to the apartment. The same green coffin, the same swift extrication, the same heavy hooks, the same efficient installation. Different men, who bow out as soon as they're finished, the same way the others did.

Jonathan and I clasp hands as we stand in front of her, and I'm overcome by the sheer joy of being with my painting again. My painting. "Oh," is all I can manage.

"That's one word for it," he says, then kisses me and returns to work.

When he leaves, I sit on the couch, enraptured. I'd been too overwhelmed to notice earlier, but now I see that Berthe's signature adorns the bottom right corner, although everything else is as it was when *Party* first arrived. I lift my phone. Click. I close my eyes and then slowly open them, force myself to look at the photo. Relief floods. For there on my screen, for the first time, is *Party on the Seine* exactly as I see it before me. No sign of Manet, just Morisot.

I lean my head back and wonder if this means Berthe has been released.

That, as Holly suggested, she's righted the wrong that trapped her in the painting and has moved on to a place where she's at peace. A comforting thought, which, despite all that's happened, I can't entirely believe. Then a less heartening notion hits me. How could she be at peace if it came at the cost of a man's life? If she did actually kill Damien.

"Did you?" I ask before I realize I don't want to know.

The smell of violets fills the room, and Berthe turns to me with an enigmatic smile. In my head, I hear, "You are right, child. Some things are better left unsaid."

EPILOGUE

MORISOT RETROSPECTIVE EXTENDED SIX MONTHS

BOSTON – The Museum of Fine Arts announced yesterday that it will extend its blockbuster show of Berthe Morisot's works for an additional six months. At the end of its Boston engagement, the retrospective will embark on a yearlong tour, including stops in Paris, Tokyo and Dubai, after which *Party on the Seine* will return to the MFA as part its permanent collection.

"This extension, as well as the excitement for the worldwide tour, is validation of the brilliance of Berthe Morisot, who never before received the recognition she deserves as an Impressionist painter equal to Monet, Degas, Renoir and Manet, her friends and colleagues," said Tamara Rubin, cofounder and director of the Berthe Morisot Foundation. Rubin is a descendant of Morisot and the previous owner of *Party on the Seine*, the centerpiece of the current show.

Two years ago, Rubin was informed by the Conference on Jewish Material Claims Against Germany that she was the sole heir to a painting by Edouard Manet that had been stolen by the Nazis from her Parisian family in 1940. This painting, believed destroyed but discovered after an earthquake in Brazil, was *Party on the Seine*. It was through Rubin's tireless efforts, as well as multiple authentications, that it was determined to be the work of Morisot rather than Manet.

Once the tale of the misattributed lost masterpiece—along with allegations of a scandalous love affair and an illegitimate child—became public, interest in *Party on the Seine* drove its price to unheard of heights for a Morisot, although Rubin sold it to the MFA for far less than an anonymous buyer offered. "I wanted *Party* to be shared," she said. "And now it will be."

AUTHOR'S NOTE

The expression "historical fiction" might be considered by some to be an oxymoron, and perhaps it is. After all, by definition history is something that actually happened, while fiction is something that did not. And yet this novel is a work of historical fiction, a combination of facts and imagination that creates something altogether new. I believe it's valuable to stipulate where I've modified the facts. It isn't practical to note every deviation, but I'll point out the ones I consider the most significant.

The Lost Masterpiece takes place in three overlapping time periods of the past, seen through the eyes of three women—Berthe, 1868–1894; Aimée, 1892–1921; and Colette, 1928–1941—and one in the present day, seen through the eyes of Tamara. Berthe Morisot is the only one of these four women who actually existed. The other three are figments of my imagination, although I've tried to depict their historical moments as accurately as possible.

Berthe's sections—and to some extent Aimée's—include other bona fide persons, who, after extensive research, I hope I've faithfully rendered in terms of their achievements, circumstances, and temperaments. This list includes Édouard Manet, Edgar Degas, Pierre-Auguste Renoir, Camille Pissarro, and Alfred Sisley, along with Berthe and Édouard's families. With some exceptions, the historical events follow in the sequence and years in which they occurred.

Excluding *Party on the Seine*, the paintings referred to in the novel are authentic works of art, yet the exact time each was created and/or exhibited may have been shifted a bit. For example, Morisot's *Dahlias* was painted in 1876, which is six years later than she painted it in the novel, and there is disagreement about which year Manet's *The Balcony* was shown at the Salon. Also, some of the paintings said to be in specific museums in the narrative are not at those locations. For example, *The Cradle*, *Olympia*, and *The Harbor at Lorient* are not at the Louvre.

Some of the letters written between Berthe and her sister Edma contain direct quotes translated from their actual correspondence, as when Edma tells Berthe that she despairs of her choice of marriage: *I follow you about in the studio and wish that I could escape and breathe in the air in which we lived for many long years.* Or when Berthe confesses her feelings for Édouard Manet to Edma: *I do not know who I am. I do not know what I do. I believe I am drowning.*

There are also places in which a character's dialogue includes statements he or she actually made. Degas did say, "I had a fearful shock when I saw it like that," in reference to his painting *Monsieur et Madame Édouard Manet*, which Édouard cut up. And Édouard did tell Berthe, "You can count on my timeless devotion, but I nonetheless will not play the role of a child's nurse."

Then there are the changes made in deference to the story, a few of which are prominent departures from the truth. *Party on the Seine* is a fictional painting, created by neither Morisot nor Manet. In reality, Édouard died in 1883, twelve years earlier than Berthe, rather than outliving her as he does in the novel. Berthe and Gène's daughter's name was Julie, not Isabeau. Most sources agree that Édouard and Berthe were in love and a few claim they had an affair, but there is no verification of the latter. They certainly did not have a child together, so no kite tail of daughters descend from Aimée.

Some of the more minor deviations are half truth/half fiction. For example, the scene in which Édouard paints over *Party* obviously didn't happen as portrayed—as we're talking about an imaginary painting—but a similar episode did take place in 1870, when he overpainted Berthe's *The Mother and Sister of the Artist*, much to Berthe's fury. Berthe and Gène lived at 40 Rue de Villejust while they were married, but Berthe moved out after he died and did not stay in the house or pass it on to her daughter. The street is now known as Rue Paul Valéry, after the famous poet who lived there, who, coincidentally, was Berthe's cousin. Édouard did receive the Legion of Honor medal, but this occurred many years earlier than it does in the novel, and, of course, it was not awarded because of *Party on the Seine*.

A number of other inventions are worth noting. There is no Boston office of the Conference on Jewish Material Claims Against Germany and no Édouard Manet Foundation, in either Paris or New York. The descriptions of Boston are factual, but there is no building called Tremont245. Eugène Manet did not actually go by Gène, but the nickname was created to avoid confusion with the many other and more well-known characters whose names began with *E*. For the same reason, the name of Édouard's mother was changed from her real name, Eugénie, to Antoinette.

It is assumed that Edma had a happier marriage than is depicted, and Gène Manet was a bit livelier than portrayed. Léon Leenhoff never changed his last name to Manet, and there is no evidence that Eugénie Manet disliked him. She did dislike her daughter-in-law Suzanne, and while in reality Eugénie did contest Édouard's will in terms of Suzanne receiving the dower, she didn't dispute Léon's claim to the paintings. Édouard did write Berthe a loving note on the back of *Violets*, but the words in the novel are not what he wrote. It's unclear whether Degas and Pissarro participated in the 1875 auction, and the exhibition that followed in 1876 is typically referred to as either the second or third Impressionist show, as some don't consider the auction to be an exhibition.

As I said, there are other minor alterations, and if you have any questions about the veracity of specific items, I direct you to the following books: *Berthe Morisot: The First Lady of Impressionism* by Margaret Shennan; *Growing Up with the Impressionists: The Diary of Julie Manet*, translated and edited by Jane Roberts; *The Correspondence of Berthe Morisot with Her Family and Friends*, edited by Denis Rouart and translated by Betty W. Hubbard; *Impressionist Quartet: The Intimate Genius of Manet and Morisot, Degas and Cassatt* by Jeffrey Meyers; *Berthe Morisot: Paintings & Drawings*, from the Zedign Art Series; and *The Private Lives of the Impressionists* by Sue Roe.

ACKNOWLEDGMENTS

Many thanks to all those without whom this book would never have seen the light of day. As always, thank you to Dan Fleishman, my husband of over forty years, as well as Jan Brogan, my writing partner of over thirty years. If it weren't for their careful reading, critiquing, and brainstorming throughout the arduous process of writing a novel, I would have given up long ago. Also thanks to Scott Fleishman, Josette Rudow, and Dr. Lisa Shaw, for their expert advice. And to my agent, Miriam Altshuler, and my editor extraordinaire, Amy Gash, thank you, thank you, thank you, and thank you again.